PARCAE'S WISH

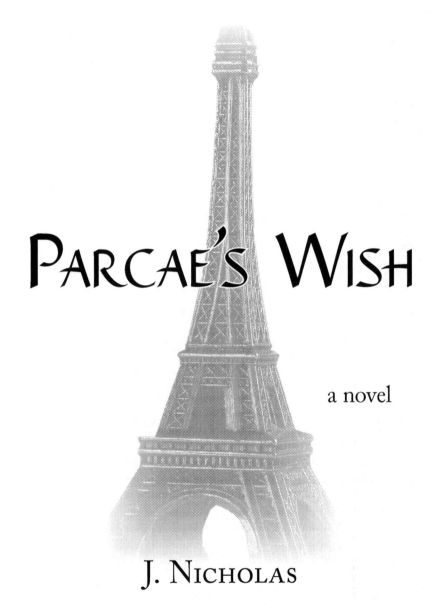

PARCAE'S WISH

a novel

J. NICHOLAS

iUniverse, Inc.
Bloomington

PARCAE'S WISH
A NOVEL

iUniverse books may be ordered through booksellers or by contacting:

iUniverse
1663 Liberty Drive
Bloomington, IN 47403
www.iuniverse.com
1-800-Authors (1-800-288-4677)

ISBN: 978-1-4759-7631-1 (sc)
ISBN: 978-1-4759-7632-8 (hc)
ISBN: 978-1-4759-7633-5 (e)

Library of Congress Control Number: 2013902859

Printed in the United States of America

iUniverse rev. date: 2/15/2013

Parcae's Wish is dedicated to my beloved wife and soul mate, Carol Ann Kotch Fedoryk, who went with God on October 15, 2003, after a courageous and inspirational battle against inflammatory breast cancer. Without her encouragement and love, this novel would never have been finished.

Acknowledgments

Many people provided support and encouragement as I worked to create this novel. Without all of you, this would not have been possible; however, several people invested a great deal of time and effort, including Vic Silvesti, who did a first read and gave honest feedback on the novel, and Lisa Wroble, who helped with editing and answered questions about the publishing process.

Prologue

I DIED YESTERDAY. IT didn't make the evening news or cause any great ripples in the world. There weren't even any people there when it happened. Oh, there was one. But that's for later.

I hadn't planned it that way. Not that I'd thought there would be some cortege leading up to the ceremony, where speaker after speaker recalled how I helped this country get through one of its most trying times. And even though that was true, I didn't expect anyone to extol my part in that episode. How could they, when most didn't know the truth of what had happened? And, if they did, they couldn't say. So what would have been said would have been a lie, just like my life.

I had expected, though, that it wouldn't end the way it did, or when. I was only fifty-five, not that old by most standards. But, then again, I hadn't lived a standard life. Funny how I can finally tell the story now that I'm dead.

Somewhere on an island …

Somewhere, some moment in time, on a desolate patch of rocky earth in the middle of some great body of water, you could hear the winds gather, their eerie howls a harbinger of what was to follow.

Heeding that forewarning, knowing all too well the fury of the forces to be unleashed, the star-backed, illuminated heavens retreated, cowering in mortal terror at the impending onslaught, until there was only darkness.

The darkness would not last. The air was too heavy, too close. The muted sounds of the sea washed against the pebbled beach, its stillness the ominous portent the universe would be charged with unendurable light. This time, unlike before, the heavens would be angry, filled with a destructive rage that those foolish enough to cross its path would either never forget or never remember.

The rains began. Their metallic clatter was made sharper by the weathered clay roof of the house.

She was asleep—if one could call it sleep. As always, it was a trance for her more than any form of renewal. "A dream state," she confided when they came to know one another. "A dream state," she told him, but one where her spirit was freed from her earthly body to roam wherever it desired.

That night, though, as she twisted and turned on the bed, her tan body coated in sweat, she sensed that something was wrong, that something terrible had happened or was about to happen. It was a feeling she had not experienced before when in this state. She was still a young woman, unlike her mother and grandmother, who she knew often felt this sensation. But those who had heard her name, or believed in her powers, knew that what she dreamed would come to be. That was why the feeling shook her very soul.

An explosion above the house lifted her from her trance. She gasped for breath; the blackness of the room turned into the most intense brilliance her eyes had ever beheld. For that instant, whatever name you desired to think her—sorceress, voodoo priestess, daughter of Satan, or even mere woman—she was blinded and unaware as to where she was.

"Jwah!" She shouted the man's name, her voice shaken, as her trembling hand groped the bed.

The flapping of an unhinged window shutter drew her attention. As she glided over the wet and slippery stone floors to close it, and as the rain beat upon her face, she heard music hauntingly drifting in her direction.

She knew then, probably had always known but wished otherwise, what he was about to do. In spite of what she had told him, that this time the gods were bored of his silly game and not to be trifled with, he had ignored her warnings and once more had decided he would play.

She raced from the primitive dwelling into the starless, rain-soaked night, her naked feet scarcely touching the coral steps as she ran toward the foaming sea. She could hear the music rising over the storm's growing ferocity. He had told her once what the music was called in his world, but she had since forgotten. She just knew that he would listen to it only when he was alone on his boat, and only when there was a storm like this one over the island.

She could now see him, his profile silhouetted against the gray and murky horizon, the lamp from below the boat's deck casting dancing shadows across the unfolding mainsail. For a moment, the island's multitude of red and white flowers shone even brighter, as if they were candles, and she saw his face.

"Jwah!" she shrieked. The clash and tin of the musical instruments, which imitated the weapons of war, echoed in her mind as she ran. "No! No! Not this time. You cannot go. You must not. You will only lose!"

He must have heard her, for although he didn't stop, he did turn his head, and as the currents pulled the boat from the wooden dock, he lifted his arm and waved. She knew it was his last farewell.

"No! No!" She ran onto the dock and sobbed into the thick, enveloping fog where the battered sailboat and fading strain of the *1812 Overture* had just disappeared.

"You don't understand! You have to understand—this time you will not return! This time you will have your wish, and they will finally let you die!"

Chapter 1

WITH ONLY OPEN PARKWAY lanes before me, I was working at keeping the Teutonic toy under its natural speed of eighty. These were the moments when I enjoyed driving the vehicle the autobahn aficionados referred to as the "whispering bomb." Inside my mobile concert hall, the Allman Brothers were shouting, "That just may be your man downstairs … I don't know … I ain't gonna find out."

It was the summer of 1987, and the July sky was perfect. It was the kind of day that my wife, Katya, said reminded her of Bermuda.

"With those puffy white clouds so delicately framed by that background of higher blue sky," she would proclaim in that clipped British accent of hers I loved. "But what makes them uniquely Bermuda clouds," she would go on, ever the impressionist, "is their faint, translucent hint of pink which peeks its way through."

It was early Friday afternoon, and I was light-years ahead of the weekend horde of sun and surf worshippers. It was a great feeling to get that jump on the shore crowd and avoid the nerve-racking, bumper-to-bumper aggravation that would follow. I pictured myself curled up on the sunporch, an ice-cold drink never more than an arm's length away, with "Judy Blue Eyes" playing on the Blaupunkt. At the speed I was moving, I would be at the summer cottage in Sea Isle, my vision realized, in less than an hour.

Katya and I talked about living year-round down the Jersey Shore. Once we came close when we almost bought a country gentleman's estate in Rumson. Well, that's how I liked to think of it. The property was less than a quarter mile from the ocean—an easy bike ride. But as

1

hard as we tried, the owner wouldn't budge from his already-inflated asking price. Sometimes it was funny how things turned out, because in retrospect, it was a blessing in disguise.

Those two-hour daily commutes from there to my office in Midtown Manhattan would have taken their toll. At least Katya didn't have a commute, as the museum allowed her to take a sabbatical each summer. Then again, as I liked to tease her, perhaps they were only too glad to reduce their bloated payroll costs.

Passing exit 123, I looked for Cubbies Marina. Whenever I got to this point in my travels, I felt I was now officially at the Shore. It reminded me of the way things would have looked in a much earlier age, with its array of timeworn wooden sailboats and rust-encrusted fishing scows—not the slightest trace of go-go eighties upscale commercialization. You knew that anyone with enough nerve to set foot on one of those vessels was not your typical weekend sailor.

There were many marinas along the Jersey coast, but Cubbies intrigued me. I could imagine those sailboats, their crews easing them from the docks at the break of dawn, staying under motor power until they cleared the reeds and marshes to reach the estuary of the Cheesequake River. Then they'd swing into action, their sails unfurling, and caught by the brisk sea winds, they'd go racing for the open Atlantic. Of course, like so many of us, those ancient and rust-bucketed fishing boats would, without the slightest fanfare, just keep chugging out into the ocean until they reached wherever it was they were headed.

"Beeeep...Beeeep"

Nothing like modern technology to bring you back to reality. I forced my eyes from Cubbies, lowered the stereo volume, and picked up the phone.

"Hello?"

"Chris, Andy here. I'm glad I reached you before I left for LA."

"Andy, what's up?" Andrew Kiner was general counsel and my most trusted associate at DFT Entertainment, the organization for which I was president and chief operating officer.

"It seems Great Air is balking at the recent WXRA revisions we submitted," he said, telling me what was down and not up. "All of a sudden they woke up and felt the revenue multiples couldn't carry the debt load for the station," he continued in his usual no-nonsense, machine-gun fashion.

"You know how they don't commingle revenue projections for their radio properties, insisting that every broadcast entity is a stand-alone unit, left to rise and fall on its own merit. If they didn't take that narrow-minded, pigheaded position and instead bundled all of their stations as a mini-network and treated this deal for what it really is—their entry into the New York market—this thing would be a no-brainer for them."

"So what else is new? We anticipated this when they started their due diligence and heard some of their preliminary reactions."

"Well, for one thing, they're maintaining that what we pay our talent is way out of line with industry norms and excessive in comparison with their own in-house talent."

"Then tell them to check the latest Arbitron book. Our guys deserve it. Theirs don't. Period and end of story." I downshifted into fourth gear and swung into the fast lane as the open-topped Jeep that had been a half mile ahead loomed less than fifty feet away. "But before I say what I feel," I said, pausing to glance into the passenger-side mirror, watching the Jeep fade from view, "what exactly is it, pray tell, that they're suggesting?"

"They didn't come out and say it … but … but I think they're hinting that we should restructure some of those contracts … or even—"

"Andy, if you don't spit it out by the time I get to Sea Isle, perhaps we should think about restructuring your contact."

"They want us to fire the Caseys. If we don't, Chris, I'm afraid this deal is history."

Few things left in my life could surprise me, but I was not yet at a place where I could always best my temper. For the moment, that ugly genie was still in the bottle.

"Andy, I know at times the Casey clan can get on one's nerves. Especially when the new book comes out and they are once again sitting smugly in the catbird's seat as the number-one morning-drive program in the metro area. And while we're on this subject, we all know that their approach when it comes to renegotiating is bizarre,

3

to say the least. What with their off-the-wall attempts at recreating some cockamamie sixties-style sit-in."

I smiled as I remembered the Caseys prone on the ground, their limbs spread-eagled as they blocked WXRA's entranceway, the last time this sticky topic had come up.

"Except in their case," I continued, "capitalistic gain is always their modus operandi. Having said all that, we also know that these same eccentricities are what make them what they are—the biggest radio personalities and draw on the entire East Coast."

"I understand that, Chris. More to the point, though, those bastards at Great Air do also." His words sounded weaker than his meaning as the transmission faded.

Right about then, I was pulling into the Long Branch toll plaza, fishing in my pockets for the correct change and thinking of those lucky sailors back at Cubbies. One thing that did serve me well in the corporate world, however, was that I was a quick study. That was doubly so when others were trying their damnedest to send me on that early retirement cruise.

"Andy, the SOBs want us to fire the Caseys, which in turn will drive the ratings through the floor, taking the sales price along with it and allowing one of the more prized radio names in the business to be gobbled up for a fraction of its worth." I was annoyed for not realizing this ploy sooner.

"You forgot one small detail," Andy said, his voice loud and clear, the quality of our communication restored.

"What's that?"

"Our friends at the FCC!"

At the mention of that den of thieves, the cork went flying out of the bottle; the genie was out.

The Federal Communication Commission, or FCC, was created in 1934 by Congress to monitor and regulate, among other matters, radio and television stations and the broadcast networks. Since then, that charter had been expanded to cover cable and wireless traffic that in many ways bore little resemblance to the industry the original FCC members were concerned with.

The one issue that remained constant, much to my ever-mounting frustrations, was the one of ownership—a misnomer if ever there was one, considering that the owner, in truth, was just a licensee, someone whom the FCC, in their magnanimity, granted a renewal privilege every fourth year.

Airing pro bono public service offerings, being a good corporate citizen, maintaining decent programming standards, and, probably most importantly of all, keeping the necessary politicians happy—a euphemism in my circles for buying them off—were all part of the renewal process. Most of the time, especially when it came to the major players—and we were definitely recognized as one—renewal was nothing but a formality. Unfortunately, sometimes the system didn't work the way it was supposed to, and other factors, such as egos or personalities, played a larger part than they should have. In our case, they constituted more than just a part; they were the whole ball of wax.

And it cost us a station.

After five years of bickering, millions in attorneys' fees, and a circle-the-wagons, us-versus-them attitude, we lost the only real asset a TV or radio station had—we lost an FCC license and, with it, the privilege to broadcast. And as if that weren't bad enough, it was WCAK we lost, one of our crown jewels.

We also lost, give or take a few million, $200 million. Without that license, we were not much different from a luxury home sitting atop a toxic dump. The physical assets could be sold, but at a fraction of their previous value.

Well, the wound hadn't healed. The FCC, like all politically motivated institutions, had a long memory. There was no way they were about to stop with that initial victory. They smelled blood, and the rest of the stations were on the menu, scheduled to be their main course. My instincts told me that whatever stumbling blocks we faced with the sale of WXRA ultimately originated with these folks.

"Chris … Christof! Are you still there?"

"Damn it. Yes, I'm still here." The edge in my voice said more than my words. "What's their interest in the Great Air negotiations beyond the existing legal proceedings they have pending against the other properties? Those proceedings that our outside counsel assures us have no bearing on the WXRA sale."

"Chris, let's not go over that again," he answered defensively.

"The legislation enacted last year clearly exempted WXRA from the rest of the lawsuits. But to answer your question, our man on the committee, Teddy Simmons, says he's hearing rumblings of Great Air trying to cut some kind of deal with Walker to influence the sale price however they can."

I knew it. My instincts were right on the money. The mention of Vince Walker, the chair of the FCC and sleazebag nonpareil, caused me to accelerate and pass one very surprised state employee.

Once we'd lost that first station, the FCC had filed against us as if we were unfit parents. If we couldn't do a good job with our firstborn, why expect anything better for the remainder of the litter? So, with debatable exception of WXRA—counselor's comments duly noted—we were now entangled in legal battles for the rest of the nineteen stations. But these lawsuits were public knowledge. They had been going on for years and, in all likelihood, would continue to do so through the next decade. There had to be something else behind this.

"Andy, we felt from the get-go that Great Air would try to pull an end run and put Walker in its pocket. What's changed now?"

"I'm not sure, but something isn't quite kosher. The obvious scenario unfolds pretty much as you stated. Let's say we don't fire the Caseys but rather, when you consider the personalities involved, attempt to renegotiate their contract. They are now the proverbial disgruntled employees. However, in their case, they have an open forum to air, pardon the pun, their grievances. Ratings fall. Revenue follows. And zap, the station's sales price plummets right behind."

He continued, "But here's the kicker. Walker mounts a public opinion campaign through his media-controlled sycophants and exerts pressure on us to drop the WXRA legal exemption and settle by having the FCC designate the new station owners. And take one guess who that might be."

I spat out the initials *GA* and then added, "There's one other, somewhat minor item you almost forgot under this wonderful scenario."

"What's that?"

"The stock price of our parent goes down the tube."

Like the majority of American companies in the eighties,

including our competition, our motto was "grow today or be history tomorrow." Today's competitor was nothing more than a future, a possible acquisition, a strategic cornerstone. Said another way, we hedged our options any way we could, grabbing a piece of everybody who was slower, less focused. After all, that was how DFT, the multinational industrial conglomerate, had acquired the group of broadcast stations we were discussing, further ensuring its status as one of Wall Street's favorites.

DFT was also led to believe that, as the new owners, they had an agreement with the FCC that the pending litigation would be dropped and they would be allowed eternal "quiet enjoyment" from further action—a sort of quid pro quo not to rattle each other's cage. Regrettably, it didn't work out the way they had planned.

Instead, about a year after the deal was approved, the FCC trumped up one charge after another in much the same manner as they had against the former owners. All of this formed the basis for the current legal contentions.

About the time WCAK was lost, my predecessor was rolled out to pasture and I was brought in as president of DFT Entertainment to restore some integrity to their business. Perhaps more appropriately stated, to help maintain market price of their broadcast empire, which was estimated to be in excess of $1 billion.

WHOOOP! WHOOOP! WHOOOP!

The state trooper's siren caused me to leap out of both my thoughts and my concert seat. He was less than a car length behind, bumper-car close, his flashing red lights signaling to me to pull over. His face had an ear-to-ear grin that reminded me of a great white shark, poised and about to sink his teeth into some unsuspecting surfer.

"Andy, I need to hang up now." I cursed myself for not paying more attention to my speed and downshifted into second gear, slowing the Bimmer onto the highway shoulder. "There's a state trooper that wants to talk with me. I'll call you back later."

"I have a three fifteen flight for LA, so figure I'll be leaving in about fifteen minutes."

"Okay, I'll call back as soon as I can. If we miss each other, I'll catch you tomorrow at the Century Towers."

"Right. Talk with you later." He tossed in "good luck," seemingly as an afterthought, before disconnecting.

I kept the irritation off my face as the trooper approached my lowered window. "License and registration, please."

Ouch. I guess license is the operative word. I noticed the trooper still grinning, his eyes examining my car as he ran his fingers over it.

His gray eyes peered over his aviator sunglasses and into my face. "Nice car you have here, sir," he said. His left hand rested on the door, fingering it. "But, in my opinion, I think it's too much engine for this part of Jersey. In my opinion, it's more of a big-city car or maybe even one of those fancy Long Islander vehicles."

'No one's asking your opinion,' I thought, glad that my mind was overloaded with more serious issues, or I might have made some kind of wisecrack guaranteed to elevate the summer temperatures. I handed him the information.

"Sir, when you passed me, I was doing sixty-five. You must have been doing at least eighty. Fortunately for you, my gun clocked you at seventy-five." The grin became a leer. "Seems this is your lucky day, Mr. Douglas. You were moving too slow to have your license suspended. I'd appreciate it, though, if you would please remain in your car while I check your driving record."

I have news for you, Shark; you can't have my license, because someone else has first dibs. This had better not drag on too long. I need to call Andy pronto..

After an interminable period during which I watched his every gesture in my mirror, he returned.

"More good news, Mr. Douglas. Your motor vehicle record doesn't reflect any outstanding violations. Nonetheless, I'm required to issue a summons for exceeding the parkway speed limit." He handed me the ticket. "Like I said, this vehicle has too much engine for these parts. I'm sure we'll be seeing each other soon." He delivered his lecture with the same frozen smile plastered across his face and then walked back to his patrol car. "Have a nice day," he added over his shoulder.

Why did I get the sense that he was probably right? I stared at him in the rearview mirror as he got in his car. He reminded me of that insane shark hunter from the movie Jaws — a sort of Robert Shaw of the parkway.

Keeping below the speed limit, I was off the parkway and his fishing grounds in less than a minute.

Damn it, Andy!

I was on the phone and connected to his office in seconds.

"Good afternoon, DFT Entertainment. Mr. Kiner's office. May I help you?" Roberta, Andy's secretary, announced.

"Roberta, it's Chris. Get me Andy."

"I'm sorry, Mr. Douglas, but Mr. Kiner left for Newark Airport. You just missed him. He did want me to tell you that he would be meeting Mr. Simmons at the Century Hotel this evening. He also said he would call you tomorrow morning around eight thirty your time."

Damn. "Okay, thanks, Roberta. Please transfer me to Cindy." A few seconds later, Cindy, my indispensable secretary, came on the phone.

"Cindy, any messages I should know about?"

"Oh? Good afternoon, Mr. Douglas. Yes … yes, there are. Mr. Paulson called and would like to switch Tuesday's luncheon engagement to a different restaurant. It recently opened and is certain to be the best in Manhattan, according to Mr. Paulson. It's called Le Bernardin. And Mr.—"

"Tell Billy that Le Bernardin is fine with me and that I can't wait to see him."

"Also, Mr. Landon called regarding your quarterly business plan critique next week at corporate. And a Miss Kelso—"

"Call Landon back and tell him I'm in a meeting with some major sponsors and can't be disturbed and will call him Monday morning."

"I'll do that immediately, Mr. Douglas. And a Miss Kelso also telephoned and wanted to speak with you. She implied that you would know who she was but didn't wish to leave a number. The rest were the usual appointment requests, which I penciled into your calendar accordingly."

"Kelso? Can't be important. Never heard of her."

"Is there anything that you might need?"

There was, but unless she had clout with the local traffic judge or the administrative judge overseeing the stations' litigation, there wasn't anything else I needed from her. "No. Thanks, Cindy. Have a nice weekend."

I had known Cindy as long as I had known Andy, and to this day, she still addressed me as Mr. Douglas—or, whenever she lightened up a tad, as sir. What could you expect? She was English right down to that stiff upper lip of hers. I had to admit, though, she was the best secretary I ever had. As for Landon, he could wait until Monday. He was the number-one flunky of Rick Carlson, chairman of DFT Inc. If it were urgent, Rick would have called me personally.

When Rick Carlson brought me on board to head Entertainment, I knew, since we were wholly owned by DFT Inc., I would face decisions that were not always in the best interest of my divisions. I could live with that. What I didn't know was the real agenda Carlson had: to divest all of Entertainment as quickly as possible. But I also knew that stock price was what really motivated him—not the product, not market shares, and not even earnings. His bottom line was Wall Street—Wall Street and share value. If some of these other measurements of success coincided with his main objective, so be it. One thing you could bet on: Rick Carlson was not going to allow his stock to be devalued by the negotiations with Great Air or by the interference of the FCC.

I realized I shouldn't be too harsh on Rick. My bonus and stock options were also precariously linked to the same share price I was so disdainfully dismissing. In a way, I should have been rooting for him.

Well, when Andy called back, we could rehash where we stood. Maybe Simmons could shed some more light on the whole thing. Although I was sure that the obvious scenario we'd come up with was the core of their strategy, it was just that—too obvious. As for Kelso, the name didn't strike a chord. She was probably some sales type who would try to convince me to forget about the competition and sign up with her outfit.

Uh oh. The bridge was going up over the Point Pleasant Inlet and Manasquan River. I couldn't remember ever passing through without stopping at that bridge. In spite of that inconvenience, I always drove this way because of the magnificent vista it offered—an unblocked view of the open Atlantic Ocean as far as the eye could see.

This was a good excuse to pull off onto the side road at that outdoor garden shop for flowers. It certainly beat waiting for some rinky-dink, twenty-foot sailboat to clear the bridge.

Fifteen minutes later, I slid back into congested but moving Point Pleasant traffic.

When I had just received my driver's license, I would make my way to this part of the Jersey Shore as often as possible. In those days, I took Routes 1 and 9 and then Route 35 to avoid the parkway tolls. Time didn't matter then—money did.

When I would pass those great ocean homes at Bay Head and Mantoloking, all twice as large as the home we looked at in Rumson, I would stare in awe. Not being able to relate to such riches and opulence, I would imagine these were the homes of powerful captains of industry or Wall Street tycoons. In my naive but fertile imagination, those were the only people who could afford such mansions. As I passed by the same places twenty-five years later, I thought that perhaps I hadn't been so naive after all.

It was about five minutes to my destination. I wished I were about to roll the Bimmer up a long driveway into one of those homes.

I don't believe I ever noticed our summer cottage as a kid. Those mansions were on the right side of the tracks; they were on the ocean side of the highway. So no matter which way we were driving, north or south, we would always face toward the ocean side and away from the cottage.

The smell of the salt air and surrounding sights invariably brought back fond memories.

The morning after my senior prom, my date and I drove here and walked the beach the way thousands of teenagers had before us and thousands have done since. We were very much in love and talked about our future together—college, good jobs, and then marriage. She was going to be a journalist and was accepted at Columbia University. I was going to work on Wall Street.

I remembered that day as though it were yesterday. We were on the beach when I asked her, "If you were granted three wishes, what would they be?" I gave the strict caveat that all had to be used outside of our own relationship.

"The first," she said, answering so quickly it was as though this were a question she had planned on being asked her entire young life, "would be to meet a Buddhist, someone from India." I never asked her why this qualification, but I assumed she meant that she didn't want to meet some nouveau Buddhist who had adopted that religion because it seemed the trendy thing to do.

"My second wish is to meet a bullfighter." This wish also had a distinctive geographic qualification. "It must be a Spanish bullfighter—one who kills the bulls afterward, and not someone who just toys with them as they do in Portugal."

"And my third wish is to visit a steel mill with chemistry in action." She then added her city of choice, "Pittsburgh."

Yeah … they were not your typical wishes. Now, mine, on the other hand …

Beeep…Beeep…Bee.

"Hello?"

"Chris, where are you? I thought you would be home by now."

"Oh? Kat? … Hi. Actually, I am. I'm pulling into the driveway right this second and can see you through the kitchen window. You look terrific."

Chapter 2

IT WAS THE FOURTH year we had rented our summer cottage, which was set back some fifty feet from the road and encircled by those ubiquitous southern Jersey black pines. This charming two-story saltbox, with its gray, weathered cedar-shake exterior, never let us forget that the ocean was nearby.

The owners were two well-tailored, middle-aged women who wanted to be far away from the oppressive summer heat and the traffic that the seasonal tourists—or bennies, as the locals called them—brought. When we saw them next, they were off for the welcoming coolness of Vermont.

Their Realtor walked us through the living and dining rooms and the newly renovated European-style kitchen. Almost hidden behind the kitchen was a cozy TV room and guest bedroom.

Running the length of the house, which had to have been forty-plus feet, and looking like an advertisement from *Homes & Gardens*, the screened-in porch made it a done deal. This is where we would share those quiet summer evenings, its due-west direction enticingly hypnotic as we would stare at the sun melting into the horizon.

Somewhere in the process, we received an implied "The ladies approve of you" from the Realtor, so Katya and I booked it for the season.

Excluding those days when I was away on business, as well as the rare weekend when Kat and I might visit some friends, this served as our summer address. Occasionally, when there were late-night business commitments, I would stay at our Manhattan apartment. As for our primary residence in Madison, the mail was forwarded, the alarm system was turned on, and, most important, we had a neighbor who was nosy enough to watch for anything unusual.

"I was beginning to worry about you. It's nearly three."

As I closed the car door and turned toward her voice, I saw Katya strolling down the driveway. She had tied her shoulder-length strawberry-blonde hair, made even blonder by the sun, behind her neck, which was the way she preferred to wear it during the hot, humid weather. She was wearing a red-checkered, ankle-length cotton dress with a sleeveless white T-shirt beneath it. Her tanned feet were bare.

"Hi, darling." She kissed me on the cheek.

"Sorry about the delay." I returned her kiss. "The bridge was up. And to boot, I was given a speeding ticket by Robert Shaw."

"Robert Shaw?"

"Just teasing. In a strange way, the officer reminded me of him. Here, I picked these. Hope you like them." I smiled and handed her the bouquet of wildflowers. As our hands touched, I gazed into her green eyes and felt the same electric shock that I always did upon being introduced to them.

She took the flowers, and we walked up the driveway.

"Anyway, what are you doing here yourself? I was under the impression you were at the local Musée d'Orsay doing research for your thesis."

"Hmmm," she purred. "These are really quite lovely. Well." She paused again and then continued. "I ran into Libby when I left the library for lunch. So we decided to eat together at the Lobster Shanty. And, well, by the time we finished, I was in no mood to return. Especially since it was Friday, the sun was shining and you were coming home early. Besides, I needed to get the house ready for the Zeitners." The expression on her face suggested she believed I had forgotten their visit.

"Remember, they're coming tomorrow afternoon and staying through Monday morning," she said.

"Certainly I remember." I feigned indignation at the thought of being reminded. There was no sense telling her it had slipped my mind. Anyway, I looked forward to having Slaus and Marcy over.

He was a psychiatrist, very Freudian and very European. Getting together gave me the opportunity to play doctor with him. I analyzed his patients as he described their symptoms and various hang-ups—all anonymously—before I proceeded to certify each, as I invariably did, by saying, "The fool's crazy."

Libby was another story. In my biased opinion, she was working extra hard on her way to her third divorce. She lived in one of those oceanfront properties I drooled over. Her husband was more than thirty years her senior and had been married more times than she. All his exes were set for life—which was the reason I believed Libby was more intrigued by the Mrs. Ex title than her current one. Those late-night singles matches with the club tennis pro would probably soon fulfill her ambition.

"What did you and Libby talk about?" I asked. "Her latest backhand lesson?"

Katya's green eyes flashed in defense of her luncheon partner. "Oh, come on, Chris," she said in protest, a little too loudly. "You sound like a bitter old man. Her husband is never home. What else would you expect?"

"I expect to get out of this monkey suit," I said, changing the subject, as I had struck a nerve, "shower, and hit the beach. Come on; let's go in."

Each year Katya did something different with the cottage interior. That way, when we looked at the old photos, we could tell one year from the other. This year she reversed the dining- and living-room furniture, explaining that it flowed better when entertaining. Since I had to move each piece back when leaving in September, I much preferred her pastels of the local environment: they were permanent and nowhere as physically challenging.

I stopped to gaze at one of her recent artistic statements. "You know, this watercolor you just did from the Bluffs' terrace, facing south toward Mantoloking Beach, is as good a work as you've done."

Partially listening to her response about why she'd chosen not to use oils and how the sunlight could have been better, I was halfway up the stairway and out of my clothes when I was alerted by a particular inflection in her voice—the one that she used when, more often than not, she knew the answer to the question.

"Christof, who is Miss Kelso?"

"Miss Kelso?" I repeated the name, halting in midflight, trying to connect a face with the name. "It doesn't ring a bell with me. Why?"

"Oh, it's probably nothing important, but Cindy called a few minutes before you came home and said that the lady in question telephoned your office a second time. This time, Cindy said she was quite rude. She claimed to be an old, personal acquaintance of yours and demanded she be given your home phone number if you weren't going to get around to taking her calls. Cindy didn't give her the number, of course, but she did take Kelso's in the event you thought it important or for some reason wished to have it." Katya's voice sounded strained when she pronounced the last few words.

"That's odd. Now that you bring it up, Cindy mentioned her name when I called in for my messages. I didn't pay much attention to it. I had the impression she was some female marketing type. You know, the sort," I shouted down the stairs, "that all the major corporations have gone out of their way to hire, trying to meet their EEO quotas."

"She's a persistent little devil," I mumbled to myself, resuming my climb up the stairs. "But I'll be damned if I let her have a crack at our account after this behavior."

The force of the water from the shower relaxed my muscles and washed away some of the week's tension. There were two thoughts that lingered, swirling relentlessly through my mind. I knew the FCC situation was going to snowball. To what extent, I wasn't sure, and that concerned me. But underneath that significant, very real problem, the sort of problem I had spent my entire business career solving, I was beginning to sense something else. Something was eating away at me about this Kelso woman. What was it about her that I should know?

*****

Rrriiinnnggg! Rrriiinnnggg!

The intrusion so close to my ear by this persistent pest woke me before I was ready.

"Hello?" I propped the phone between the pillow and my ear.

"Chris, it's me. Andy. You sound as though I woke you."

"Andy? Oh ... Yeah ... What time is it?"

"About five thirty-five, Saturday morning, Pacific Coast time. Can we talk?"

"Yeah ... Okay. Just give me a sec to shake off the cobwebs." My body, of its own accord, tumbled out of bed and lurched toward the bathroom. A minute later, and somewhat more awake, I was back on the phone. I noticed that Katya was not in the bedroom.

"Okay, tell me how the meeting with Simmons went." I recalled why Andy would be calling at such an early hour.

"Not well." His disappointment was clear. "It appears that Walker is accelerating his efforts against us. Simmons doesn't know or won't say—I'm not sure—but he intimated that something has made Walker extremely cocky about the whole situation. He told me Walker has demanded that the FCC's staff attorneys be prepared to present their case to the circuit court no later than October. No more delaying motions or out of court sidebar considerations or any other bullshit. Walker is ready to wrap this thing up. And," he continued, "Simmons thinks they've met with Rackley, the judge who would most likely be assigned to the case."

"No idea what has changed?" My mind was now fully alert after Andy's thirty-second doom-and-gloom recap. "I agree. Walker wouldn't do this unless he felt a sure thing. If he pursues this and doesn't look good in the process, he can kiss his chair good-bye. It stinks," I said suspiciously. My tongue recoiled from the unexpected memory of how much I'd drunk last night. "He's getting something else from this, and I don't think it's just from Great Air."

"And Teddy Simmons was different," Andy said. "He wasn't the Teddy I'm accustomed to dealing with. It was as if he were afraid to be seen with me. He switched dinner arrangements from the Century to some flea-bitten, out-of-the-way restaurant in West Hollywood that I'd never heard of. I'm telling you, Chris, you should have seen him. He behaved as if he didn't have the foggiest idea what it was we were asking of him."

"How about Rackley? Can we approach him and get him to see things our ...? No, check that," I said, tempering my words before my thought was completed. "Can someone from our outside counsel at Latwick and Jennings approach him? Ari, for instance?"

"That's touchy. It can tip Simmons's relations with us."

"Fine, we wait a week or so until it leaks," I said a bit too loudly, not caring a damn about Simmons's position. "We paid him what he wanted."

Andy continued as though he hadn't heard me. "Even then, you know Rackley's reputation when it comes to the private sector. He's not exactly a fan of big business."

"Thank you, Jimmy Carter," I mumbled, deciding what our next move would be.

"Okay," I said a few moments later. "The hell with Simmons. We need to do it ASAP. Have Ari see if he can get to the bottom of this. At least see if he can confirm Great Air's strategy. Or why Walker is pushing as hard as he is. Tell Ari to contact me immediately if he has any reservations after you speak with him."

"No problem, Chris. I'll call him as soon as we hang up. I have until eleven my time before meeting with Great Air to continue the WXRA negotiations. Hopefully I'll find out more about their less-than-enthusiastic response to the talent issues they were hinting at yesterday, and why this intransigent stubbornness regarding debt structure."

"Let's hope so." My free hand massaged the throb developing across my temple.

"Macpherson, Harris, and Bartlow flew out with me from our offices. I didn't think at this stage it was necessary for someone from Latwick to be present."

Macpherson was Andy's counterpart at DFT Inc. He was also DFT's eyes and ears. We used Latwick and company when addressing FCC regulatory issues, their primary area of expertise. These reviews were still part of Great Air's due diligence—they were important because they would help finalize the parameters of the ultimate contract, but they were of a somewhat exploratory nature. Latwick was more effective behind the scenes.

"I agree." The throbbing was getting worse. "How long do you expect the meeting to last?"

"With any luck, we can make some headway and break around

six or seven tonight. We'll pick it back up Monday as a group, but we'll continue with our guys for most of Sunday."

"Good luck," I offered sympathetically, recalling Andy's departing words before my rendezvous with the shark. "Call me as soon as you learn anything."

"Absolutely. Talk to you later."

I slipped into the striped blue seersucker robe Katya had bought for my last birthday and stepped down the staircase. Entering the kitchen, I found a handwritten note next to the half-filled coffeepot.

'Couldn't sleep. Got up around six. Walked on the beach for a while. Went to the market for some things for this evening. Be back by noon.'

I poured a glass of orange juice and a cup of coffee and plopped into the bentwood rocker on the sunporch.

I was jolted back to last evening.

It had been midnight when I stumbled into bed. Katya had gone up earlier. She had decided it was time right after I started, as she said, "Ranting on, making the same point over and over again." She had been sobbing. *Damn me!*

These arguments always began the same way—with friendly, intelligent, non-argumentative discussion and a bit of give and take. And they always ended the same—with me losing self-control. It wasn't that I raised my voice. But she made a remark, I imagined a slight, and something just clicked. The clear sign to her this was happening was when I became repetitive and sounded like a broken record.

"Why am I always fooled?" she would say as she stormed out of the room in tears.

In my business circles, where there existed a veneer of restrained civility, my colleagues characterized me as intense and focused—driven, some might say. But I was ever the gentleman. To be less could only be described, and rather charitably at that, as being guilty of bad form.

I wasn't stupid. I was aware that my drinking was the catalyst. What had I had last night? A couple of Finlandia vodkas. Then a glass or two of wine with dinner. After that, some twenty-year-old cognac. It was about when I'd poured the second snifter that I'd more or less lost it. Yet both Katya and I knew that the booze was only a trigger, an excuse for some deep remembrance or some scar from the past that, when combined with the wrong remark from her, rose to the surface to haunt us.

I needed another cup of coffee. When I returned to the kitchen, I saw our neighbors through the window, getting ready to take off with their three kids.

I poked my head out the window and greeted them with a much cheerier show than I'd thought possible. "Hey! Royce, Betty. Great morning, isn't it?"

Royce Ingersten stopped packing the Volvo station wagon. "And a good morning to you too, Chris. I see Katya got an early start today." He smiled.

Royce did take notice of every last detail. "Yeah ... Well, she had to do some shopping at the Central Market." I returned his smile. "Slaus and Marcy are coming for the weekend."

"Say hello for us," Betty chimed in, strapping her two boys and little baby girl into their car seats. "Royce and I are headed to a six-year-olds birthday party. There'll probably be over fifty kids there, each one wilder than the next."

"I can well imagine." My smile began to fade.

"Well, got to be rolling," Royce announced.

I returned their waves and watched them back down the driveway until they pulled onto the ocean road and disappeared. "So long," I murmured.

I walked back to the porch and settled into the rocker. We all have those one or two defining moments that we wish somehow were not tied to our lives—moments that make us less than who we were and that never again allow the sum of our particular lives to equal the whole.

For Katya and me, that moment was when our daughter, Beth, was killed. Afterward, the two of us lived for a while with a couple of psychiatrists Slaus recommended. That had been more than five years ago. One day, after a few months, I just stopped going. Katya still went, though not with same frequency as in the beginning, which had been practically every day.

I was never certain why I stopped. One reason I gave to Katya, and which I knew to be true, was my concern with my career. "Can you picture someone in my position seeing a shrink on a regular basis?" I asked her one day after she returned from a therapy session. "My career would be ruins in nothing flat."

I recognized that society's attitude toward psychotherapy was changing, becoming more accepting and understanding, although I doubted it would reach the point for a gentler and kinder one.

Certainly I wasn't about to bet the farm on that happening too soon with many of my business associates, knowing what I did about the opinions in that club. Oh, it was okay—as a matter of fact, it was rather chichi—for one's spouse to be under the care of a psychiatrist. The same could be said for the on-air personalities—or "the talent," as they were more often called.

Analysis merely confirmed their unique status as different from the rest of us.

My status was another story. As a top executive of an old, very visible, very respectable, publicly traded big-board corporation, I was required to convey the opposite perception: stability, levelheadedness, and decisiveness. I recalled my interviews with DFT, which had reinforced this notion.

"We know you have all the right degrees and the proper experience, but what we really want to know is, can we count on you? Are you a stable, reliable individual or not?"

In no uncertain terms, there wasn't room for any flaws in this suit.

I threw myself into my job, working six or seven days a week. It was the classic therapy. There were even days when I didn't come home from the office. I became even more successful and was generally recognized as one of the top executives in the broadcast industry—a guy who had a keen head for numbers and for talent promotion, a rare combination in this business.

One day, one of the boutique search firms contacted me about the top honcho's spot at DFT Entertainment. After an exhausting interview process, I landed one of the elite jobs in the broadcast world. Granted, some people believed DFT had a bit of baggage with the FCC cloud hanging over it, but as for me, I was happy.

But what of Katya? How was she coping with my success and, more importantly, my tendency to shut myself off from her and the memory of our daughter? I didn't like to think a great deal about that question. And, anyway, the morning was speeding by, and I had my assigned household duties and a few perfunctory office tasks to complete before our weekend guests arrived. I knew I would never get rid of my headache by going down that all-too-familiar, slippery slope. Perhaps later …

The office tasks took more of my attention than I had anticipated. Soon Katya was calling to me. "Chris, they're here."

I looked at my watch, surprised that it was one o'clock. "Be right there. I need a second to wrap up this paperwork."

Where had it all gone?

Shoving the papers into my attaché case, I glanced through the curtained window. I saw the Zeitners rolling up the driveway in their new XKJ; they had indeed arrived.

I had been immersed in my office materials for more than three hours, halting only for a fifteen-minute interlude when Katya returned. I'd apologized once again. Her familiar reaction had been succinct. "I understand, Christof. Let's move on," she'd said with a smile and those sad green eyes. She'd touched me as only she was able to do.

I never liked myself on those occasions.

Double-timing it down the stairs and through the sun porch, I intercepted Slaus unloading the car. "Here, let me get that," I said, and I reached for the overnight bag he was lifting from the trunk.

"Chris, you old war dog." Slaus grabbed my free hand and pumped it enthusiastically.

He tossed me the bag and lugged some miscellaneous beach ware out of the car. He seemed to be beside himself with anticipation. "It's been too, too long. Must be four, five weeks since we saw each other." Somehow he also tucked an overstuffed tennis bag under his arm.

"I think the last time we saw you guys was at Circle in the Square, early June."

"It's just great to be together. And why aren't we in the water already?"

I laughed and looked for Marcy and Katya. "Where are the ladies?" I asked.

"Katya took Marcy through the front of the house. Something about showing her how much better the furniture arrangement is this year."

We heard the animated voices of our wives in the living room as we entered. I grabbed Marcy from behind, interrupting them. "And maybe next year we can move the refrigerator or something heavy into one of the bedrooms."

She hugged me and kissed me on the side of the cheek and then playfully asked, "Why would you want to do something like that?"

"Don't tell me that Kat hasn't told you about my insatiable raving for midnight snacks? And speaking of cravings, Marcy, you look fabulous."

She smiled. "It is my favorite time of the year."

Marcy spent most of her summer swimming or playing tennis, both of which she excelled at. She was at the level where she could handily dispose of the rest of this weekend group.

"Marcy, enough already. Put on your bathing suit so we can get to the beach," Slaus yelled, as he raced up the stairs."

"Whatever you say, dear. I'll be right there." She winked, answering him in the patient tone that everyone knew meant "when I'm good and ready."

"I assume the Tucson room is ours as usual." Marcy and Slaus preferred that room because its pickled wooden floors and brightly painted artifacts, which the homeowners had collected throughout the Southwest, were in line with their own taste. The room stood in marked contrast to the remainder of the house, which was filled with English décor, including overstuffed chintz sofas and chairs and wall-to-wall sisal carpeting.

"Wherever you like is fine. But I do hear the good doctor shuffling above us, so I believe your assumption is correct." The three of us burst into laughter at the image of this normally reserved medical professional behaving like a schoolboy who couldn't wait to get to the seashore.

A few minutes later, we were all dressed in the prescribed shore uniform of a bathing suit, a T-shirt cover-up, and Docksiders; had crossed the highway; and were walking toward the small wooden ramp we had to pass over to reach the ocean. We displayed our summer resident badges to the sun-bleached and bored-looking teenage gatekeeper and stepped down the ramp onto the hot sand.

As we walked between the ten-foot-high, crested, and grassy sand dunes, which shielded the shore homes from the sunbathers, I couldn't help but think of the unrest that festered beneath this gorgeous vista. For along this part of the Jersey Shore, there was a feeling of exclusivity that bordered on hostility when it came to visitors.

For years, the state and local residents had been at war over the doctrine of riparian rights—or, in the common vernacular, whether to allow the common riffraff to use the beaches. In the state's view, the beach and immediate ocean beyond were part of nature's province and, as such, belonged to everyone. The local owners—and, more specifically, the beachfront property owners—as one might expect, took an opposite view, maintaining that they hadn't plunked down millions of their hard-earned dollars for their mansions only to be forced by some civil servant to share their paradise with whomever this so-called everyone was.

The recent situation had nonresidents confined to a block of sand a quarter mile away from the nearest access. The township also limited daily visitors by providing minimal parking—twenty spots a few blocks removed from the same entrance. The remainder of the streets were plastered with tow-away signs that were impossible to miss. The result was private beaches. There was one other minor detail, though. The beaches were a definite bargain; they were free.

It was this equal opportunity that enabled us to set our chairs and towels on the sand a few feet from the onrushing surf, with the nearest human company over a few hundred feet in the distance.

Kat sat motionless in her chair, staring at the water for several minutes before overcoming her inertia, disrobing, and applying sunscreen around the edges of her European-style bikini. Marcy shed her clothes, raced toward the ocean, and, without hesitating at the temperature, plunged into an oncoming wave. The good doctor, having attained his goal, was now the picture of motionless serenity. Seemingly oblivious to all, he had nestled himself into his recliner and, accompanied by the current *New York Times* best seller, Turow's *Presumed Innocent*, had been transported somewhere else.

I closed my eyes beneath my sunglasses, and my mind drifted in and out of a sun and salt air induced trance. After what seemed like minutes, but in reality was closer to an hour, I heard somewhere in the distance something that sounded like Katya. "Come on, Marcy. Let's go for a walk," the voice said impatiently. "We have two duds that pass for husbands. One is Sleeping Beauty. And the other ... Well, the other should have stayed at the library."

Remaining seated but mustering enough strength to remove my sunglasses, I squinted at the shadowy outline of my wife and offered my best lackluster "I don't really want to get up and go" response. Slaus, seemingly disregarding what was going on, was engrossed in his murder mystery.

Katya glared down at me, and I felt an understanding pass between us. When she spoke, I knew that she meant something different from what she said. "No, Chris. That's okay. You had your chance. And, anyway, Marcy and I need to talk some girl talk. We'll see you in a while." Katya spun around and, with a dismissive wave, scampered across the hot sands to join Marcy.

I watched them walk along the water's edge until they were tiny shapes in the distance. I was about to turn away, their fading images burned in my mind's eye, when Slaus interrupted my reverie.

"How are things, Chris?"

Stanislaus's question caught me off guard.

"Oh, you know ... I'm—we're, that is—just fine."

"Interesting. Quite intriguing, actually. You told me that you've read this novel." He smiled. "I'm at the part where the assistant district attorney has just been accused of murdering his mistress. Don't give me any clues, though; it will only spoil the suspense."

I angled my body to face him. "All you'll get out of me, Herr Doktor, is that things aren't always what they seem."

He placed his novel on his chest and peered at me over his prescription, wire-rimmed sunglasses, which had slid halfway down his nose. His voice was subdued. "Is that a clue or a rather less-than-enigmatic subliminal message that I should be analyzing? If it's the latter, I must warn you, my good friend, my fees are as high as they come."

I had to smile at his style. "Is it that obvious?"

"Which? That the ADA didn't do it? Or that you and Katya appear, as we doctors like to say, medium cool?"

"Herr Doktor, you said you preferred not to talk about the book you're reading," I said, choosing my words carefully. "Well, I don't think we should open up the other subject either. Katya and I ... Well, we love each other very much. You know that. Nothing has affected, or will affect, that aspect of our lives."

His lips pursed. His eyes continued to stare at me over his reading glasses. At length he sighed. "Okay, I hear you. But if you happen to change your mind ..."

"Yes, I know. You care for both of us, as we do for you and Marcy. We've been best friends forever." I smiled. "There's really nothing to talk about, Slaus. Everything's just as you said—it's cool."

He pulled himself upright in his chair and repositioned his glasses higher onto the bridge of his nose. "Enough then of this idle chatter," he declared. "What's Katya cooking up for our dinner?"

Five or six hours later, after showering and changing, we were all mellow and enjoying a pre-dinner cocktail. In the pleasant interlude between, an interlude in which Slaus and I decided by not talking that everything was in fact absolutely cool, the girls returned from their stroll and indentured their awaiting servants into two sets of competitive tennis at the club. Finally, all that physical activity was over and we were allowed to resume our hard-earned slothfulness on the sun porch.

"So, as I was saying, this new patient can best be described as ..." Slaus halted his characterization for a second as if to ensure that he had our undivided attention. Then he proclaimed in exaggerated bluntness, lacking any semblance of a bedside manner, "Someone insufferably and hopelessly pathetic."

"Oh, stop it, Slaus. That's cruel and certainly no way to speak about one of your patients," Marcy said. She was unable to help herself even though she knew he purposely took a controversial approach in order to invoke responses like hers.

"But she is pathetic, my darling," he went on, undeterred by his wife's rebuke. "There is no better medical term to categorize her condition. She has a great job, both in terms of dollars and career fulfillment—things most women her age would die for. Yet she thinks of herself as a total, abysmal failure. A loser, in precise medical terminology." He shook his head in affected sympathy.

"Pathetic, I say—utterly pathetic." He winked and extended his empty beer mug in my direction. "Here, my good man. Any more where this came from?"

"There's plenty more in the fridge. Everybody else okay?"

"Yup," Katya answered. I could see she was still nursing her first and last Pernod and water, its murky yellowish tint becoming jade green as the liquor began to separate from the water and settle toward the bottom of her glass.

"Just a short refill for me," Marcy said. "More ice this time and less Absolut."

When I walked into the kitchen, I was distracted by the commotion coming from the Ingerstens' driveway. Through the open window, I saw that they had just come back from their all-day birthday celebration. Royce seemed pretty heated, but I couldn't make out what he was telling Betty. She jabbed her finger at him, her face turning flusher than the day's sunburn. I could catch only fragments of what she was saying.

"How could you let them ... Why ... Why ... You know there's no truth to that rumor ... It's a lie ... She would never do such a thing."

That was all I heard, as Royce carried their youngest, who was asleep in his arms, and hurriedly shushed the rest of the brood into the house, followed closely by Betty.

"Hey, son of Shadow! Where's my beer?"

"Be right there," I yelled back, reminded of my purpose. I grabbed a Heineken from the refrigerator and wondered what the neighbors' argument was about.

The remainder of the evening passed as it normally did with the Zeitners: spirited conversation over a gourmet dinner Katya had prepared, excellent wine, and good friendship.

A phone call from Andy before we went to bed was all that marred an otherwise perfect summer evening.

"Katya? Hello, I hope I'm not disturbing you."

"Andy, it's always good to hear from you. Of course you are. How are Alice and the children?"

"They're all fine. Seriously, Katya, is this a bad time?"

"No, Andy. You know me. Just kidding," Katya said as I entered the kitchen. "Here's Chris." She handed me the phone and rejoined the Zeitners.

"Andy, what's going on?"

"Horrible news! I'm afraid Great Air is terminating the negotiations, effective a few minutes ago."

"What? What the hell happened?"

"Let me read the key points from the official statement they're planning to release to the press. It'll say it better than I could." He sounded subdued and defeated.

"Great Air Inc., after an extensive review of the radio station WXRA, has determined that DFT's inflated asking price of $85 million does not merit any further consideration." He paused and then asked, "Are you sitting, Chris?" He continued reading. "It is our further opinion that DFT has willfully misrepresented the financial values of said property and have not, in our estimation, negotiated in good faith."

It was late. I was exhausted. Whatever resources I had left when it came to evenness of temper had deserted me. Trying to restrain my anger, I raised my voice—slightly, I thought, but it was enough to bring Katya rushing into the kitchen with her finger pressed against her lips.

"Andy, what the hell are those bastards trying to pull?" I hissed the words into the telephone. "Why do they think they can get away with this bullshit? When did all this happen?" I said, forgetting that Andy had just told me that it happened only minutes ago.

"Christof, listen to me. The whole damn thing happened no more than fifteen minutes ago. We were caught completely off guard. Houseman, their point man in these negotiations, was summoned from the conference room to take a message. When he returned five minutes later, he dropped the news like a bomb on us. He didn't say anything else. Up to that time, things looked like they were moving back on track. Even the negative ratios, their guys said, were just a matter of how certain line items could be restructured and repackaged with FASB rules. Those were their exact comments. Then whammo! They walked right out of the meeting without any discussion or anything as soon as Houseman came back from his call."

"Andy, this is a goddamn setup. They knew before the meeting how it was going to end. Good faith, my ass! And I'll tell you one other thing. It's all tied together—Simmons's quirky behavior, the FFC's acceleration of the hearings, and now this, Great Air's transparently false pretense of buying this market through us."

I could imagine what Carlson's reaction to this fiasco would be. He should be told of this development without any further delay and certainly before it hit the papers. In my muddled state, I almost forgot about the existing pipeline he had but was reminded by Andy's next remark.

"Mcpherson was steaming. He said he was calling Carlson to advise him of this very disappointing turn of events. Then he left with the words that he didn't think Carlson would be happy. As if I needed reminding."

"No, he is not going to be happy. I'd better call Carlson. The breakdown in negotiations is bad enough. The BS about misrepresentation and not acting in good faith is another. It's clearly part of their strategy to discredit us in any way they can politically, vis-à-vis the FCC. Carlson will want to have a counter release prepared and ready to fly, denying any such tactic, as well as spinning some of the heat on them."

Andy seemingly anticipated my next thought. "I'll put together an updated brief indicating the status of everything and fax it to you and the corporate offices first thing tomorrow. Oh, and one other item: Ari hasn't been able to reach Rackley. He tried, but it seems His Honor is incommunicado and out of the country until sometime later in the week."

"Well, keep on trying. Tell him to call me." I was growing more frustrated by the moment. "Listen, we'll talk later. Right now I need to give Carlson a call."

"Okay, Chris. Speak to you tomorrow."

I took two minutes before telephoning Carlson to apologize to everyone for my absence. Making light of my conversation with Andy, I dismissed it as some minor nuisance that would be resolved in the course of the workweek. Not really sure anyone was convinced, I also indicated I needed a few minutes for one more call. This time, not willing to take any chances of being overheard, I made the call from the upstairs bedroom.

Richard Carlson's primary address was in Greenville, South Carolina, near the sprawling corporate offices of his baby, DFT Inc, the ever-expanding multinational conglomerate he had ruled for more than fourteen years. He also had condos in Vail and Maui.

After a few rings, a man answered. "Good evening. The Carlson residence."

"This is Mr. Douglas. I need to speak with Mr. Carlson." I recognized the voice as Carlson's butler.

"I'm sorry, sir, but Mr. Carlson is not available. Would you care to leave a message?"

"Is there any way to reach him? You know who I am, don't you? This is urgent."

"Yes, sir, Mr. Douglas. You are Mr. Christof Douglas, president of Mr. Carlson's entertainment subsidiary. I'm quite sorry, sir. Mr. Carlson left strict instructions not to be disturbed. He will be telephoning in tomorrow for his messages, as I just indicated, if you care to leave one."

Damn it! Carlson knew everything. Mcpherson had gotten to him first. "Tell him that I called regarding the WXRA situation. Make certain you advise him that Great Air will be announcing a press release tomorrow or Monday. Ask him to call 908-435-6755 as soon as he can. And make sure you tell him I said it was urgent."

"Thank you, sir," he said in the pompous manner he had used throughout. "Is there anything else?"

"No, that's it," I said, and I slammed the phone into the cradle.

Carlson knew what was going on. The word surprise was not part of his vocabulary. And Mcpherson's role was to guarantee that it remained that way. Mine too. That was rule number one. One thing I came to understand after my arrival at DFT was the rigid and formal organizational pecking stratum that it lived by.

Every company had an organizational hierarchy, thick volumes of unread procedures, and endless streams of red tape. For those corporations that lived by the acquisitional and divestiture sword as their basis for growth, it was imperative for their survival that they created a strict delineation between corporate staff and those of us such as myself in the various divisions and subsidiaries. After all, we were in essence nothing more than an asset or liability on the balance sheet, one day to be sold or discarded when we happened to appear in accounting as the latter.

What did I have in common, in the business sense, with the CEOs of my sister divisions? Divisions that made tennis racquets or armaments for the federal government? How about apparel and accessories for the fashion conscious, or cigarettes for the addicted? My sector—broadcasting—had zilch in common except to perform for the pleasure of corporate, driving it ecstatic whenever its bottom line, which was shareholder value, happened to increase.

Enough of this whining. It was late, and I had been on the phone or bellyaching too long. It was time to rejoin my guests.

I was surprised to find only Katya still up. She was in the kitchen, her back toward me as she leaned over the sink, rinsing the remaining dinner dishes. I grabbed a few dishes and placed them in the dishwasher.

I broke the silence, pushing thoughts of prior discussions from my mind. "Where did Slaus and Marcy disappear to?" Her hand touched mine as she handed me a dish.

Katya turned to me, but then she turned back to the dishes in her hand. Her response was between disappointment and annoyance. I also detected some weariness in it, but not necessarily because of the lateness of the hour.

"They were tired and retired," she said in a singsong lilt. "We weren't sure how long you were going to be on that second call. By the long look on your face, you seemed more than a bit upset when you went upstairs." She turned again to me; this time she didn't look away when she spoke. "And quite preoccupied with it."

I gazed into her eyes. Once upon a time, we'd known what these moments were for, what we felt and desired from each other. "Yeah, I guess I was ... I guess I am," I said, hoping that maybe she shared the same sense. "There's a problem with the sale of WXRA. That last call was to Carlson. He wasn't in, so I left a message."

"It must be serious for you to try and reach him at this hour." Her face was a few inches from mine.

I stared into Katya's eyes and touched her arm. "Are you tired?" My voice was as gentle as my touch. "Let's forget about the dishes and go upstairs. We both have to be exhausted."

How I wished for her answer to be yes.

She smiled. It was that pained smile that I had seen far too often, where even though I knew it was a smile, the corners of her lips always seemed to remain curved downward. One or two eternal seconds passed before it disappeared from her face.

"No, Chris," she whispered, "that's all right. You go ahead without me. I'll be up later."

Chapter 3

REGARDLESS OF WHICH YEAR it was, Sunday at the Jersey Shore was pretty much the same summer after summer.

After a leisurely and subdued breakfast, Katya attended Mass at Saint Bartholomew's Episcopalian Church, while the agnostics in the group played an hour or so of Canadian doubles. We alternated in the afternoon between baking in the sun and cooling off in the surf. We capped off our evening with dinner at the Bluffs.

It was, for the most part, the type of July day that made you feel contented with your lot in life.

Sometime amid all this contentment, I called Carlson but was met with the same stonewalling, although I was at least told that my message had been delivered. And, as expected, Andy faxed me, as well as the necessary executives on DFT's corporate staff, a recap of the aborted negotiations. Nothing had changed.

But that was yesterday.

As I drove down the sleepy streets and through the early morning mist, memories of last Friday overtook me. Not now, buddy. Not now. I shook my head, dismissing the images of the carefree, smiling teenage couple walking arm in arm along the ocean's edge. Those nostalgic trips were best kept to Friday afternoons.

There was no place for drippy sentimentality at six o'clock on Monday morning. It was the beginning of my seventy-mile commute to the city, and the start of what would be a long and grueling week.

Before I drove away, I told Kat that because of the quarterly review meetings in South Carolina and the time I needed to prepare for them, I would be staying at the apartment for the next couple of days. "I probably won't be back until Thursday, after the reviews are finished," I told her as I walked to the Bimmer.

She shrugged in a kind of passive non-response, handed me my attaché case, and kissed me on the cheek. When she stepped around the car door, allowing me to squeeze behind the steering wheel, she said in a quiet voice, "I guess this kiss will last you a long time then."

When I paid the parkway toll, I noticed off to the side of the shoulder the familiar blue-and-white markings of a state police vehicle. I slipped into the merging traffic and glanced over, wondering if I could recognize anyone. I couldn't make out the face. An imperceptible nod of the head. Yes, it could very well be who I thought it was. For the next few miles, I remained below the fifty-five-mile-per-hour speed limit, and I reached my office an hour and forty-five minutes later.

"Good morning, Cindy." No matter how early I made it in, Cindy was already at her desk and hard at work. "See if you can get Mr. Carlson. Will you, please?"

She greeted me, handed me Friday's messages, and lifted the telephone to her ear. "Your staff meeting at nine thirty is in the thirty-ninth-floor conference room," she reminded me.

"Thank you, Cindy." I nodded and moved past her to my office. Why did I always feel like the lord of the manor when I spoke to her?

In addition to the messages from Friday that Cindy had relayed to me, she had taken a call a few minutes earlier from Sean Casey of morning-drive fame. He wanted to meet with me as soon as possible, preferably after signing off his program later in the morning. Cindy had underlined the words said it was important in red.

Sean and I had developed a decent business relationship since I'd come on board. As president, I was officially his boss, although there was some dispute at times regarding that hierarchy. That, in addition to the status of the Great Air negotiations and the fact that Sean's name had surfaced as a potential stumbling block to the deal, left no doubt that I should meet with him.

"Do I have a half hour to fit Sean in this morning?" I asked Cindy over the intercom.

"The only scheduled appointment you have this morning is your staff meeting. As per your instructions, I've kept this week flexible in order to allow you the necessary preparation time for your quarterly critique. Miss Lieber, of course, has accordingly planned her week's itinerary as well."

Judy Lieber was CFO for DFT Entertainment. For the past two weeks, her accounting staff had invested hundreds of tedious hours in pulling the quarter's financial results together. We had already met with each division head to go over the results, but we still needed some time to fine-tune everything and get our stories straight.

I could see from behind my unobstructed thirty-fifth-floor perch all the way down the Hudson River, past the newly constructed American Express skyscraper on Wall Street, and out into the open Atlantic. Sometimes when I looked especially long in that direction, losing myself in it, I felt as though I were staring into life's secret abyss, that perhaps I even understood its mysteries and was not just seeing the tip of Manhattan. This Monday, I realized, would not be one of those days. This Monday, I gazed only long enough to see if one of those boats from Cubbies happened to be there.

I swiveled my chair from the window, knowing I had to call Landon, if for no other reason than to confirm the week's agenda at corporate. I buzzed Cindy. "Get me Landon. Remind him I'm returning his call. The rest of the messages can wait."

Turning my attention to my in-box, I flipped through the files requiring my sign-off. At first I found nothing unusual, just the normal rubber stamping. When a contract was placed in this folder, it had already been discussed and approved by me. I did not tolerate exceptions to this rule.

About a third of the way into the pile, I came across a blatant exception. It was an amended advertising contract with Geo Computer—one I couldn't recall reviewing. And Geo was not our average sponsor; it was our largest, representing revenues between 6 to 7 percent of our annual gross, which translated to around $30 million annually. I began reading the contract.

"Mr. Douglas, I have Mr. Landon for you."

I pressed the extension and continued reading.

"Hello, Norman. How are things in Greenville?" My voice was courteous, although perhaps a bit disdainful.

"Busy, busy, busy. Extremely hectic, almost chaotic. More so with everyone trying to finalize arrangements and agendas for the upcoming business review. Which is why I called on Friday." He was polite, although obviously annoyed.

I was too involved in searching the contract for modifications or potential revenue shortfalls to be drawn into any Mickey Mouse debate with this bozo. "Yeah, well, I'm sorry I missed you. I'm still on for Thursday afternoon, right?"

"That was one of the reasons I called," he answered smugly. "You've been moved up to the ten forty-five Thursday morning slot. Your sector will go on right after Space and Technology. You'll have the same time allotment as originally scheduled. Although, things have been known to change quite suddenly around here, as I'm sure you know." His self-importance was obvious when he added, "We need a copy of your presentation to be in my office no later than five o'clock tomorrow afternoon."

I almost said "fuck off" but considered the source and let it pass. "That's tight, but we'll make the deadline."

Landon resumed in his prissy affectation. "The main reason for my call is that Mr. Carlson will be meeting with you at three o'clock sharp on Wednesday afternoon. Please be there fifteen minutes prior."

Well he did say 'please.' "If it's Rick's wish, I'll be glad to be there. Anything specific he wanted to cover?"

"Mr. Carlson didn't discuss the meeting's purpose with me," he shot back defensively.

"Just asking. See y' all Wednesday then." I forgot the little weasel the moment I hung up and refocused on the Geo contract in my hands.

The departmental routing appeared normal; legal had reviewed it, followed by our marketing VP, Herman Weitzer. If legal ever made changes to a contract, they noted them accordingly with attached page markers. This baby had two strikes against it: no markers, and no one had told me about it!

I turned the pages to the revenue clauses. I reread the legalese for when the commercial slots were to be played, the number and length of plays, and the per-airing charge. For the life of me, I couldn't ever remember that contract being discussed with me. Why was it here for my signature? Forget about it. Quit wasting your time, my common sense finally offered. Ask Herman at the staff meeting what this is all about.

At that moment, Cindy, completely out of character and as flustered and upset as I had ever seen her, burst into my office, waving the day's newspapers wildly about in front of her.

In a voice two octaves higher than usual, she shrieked, "Mr. Douglas! Mr. Douglas! This is the lady who was trying to reach you Friday. Look!"

She placed the newspaper on my desk, and my eyes followed her finger to where it was pointing. I saw a grainy, fuzzy photograph of a woman dressed in what appeared to be camouflage field khakis. On her head, and covering most of her face, she wore a hat with the brim pressed against the crown in the fashion of an Australian bush hat. In bold print above the picture was the following headline:

JOURNALIST MURDERED IN FOUR-STAR HOTEL

I was in no mood for this melodrama. "Cindy, please. To whom or what are you referring?"

"Why, Miss Kelso, of course!" Her tone resonated with utter disbelief at the mere thought of such a question. "You remember—that rude lady who telephoned you on Friday. The one who said she was a personal friend of yours. Remember? She wanted—no," she corrected herself, "she insisted that I give her your private number. I, sir, most assuredly would never give it to her."

"Mrs. Douglas relayed your message to me, Cindy." I was becoming more frustrated by the second. "Here, let me see the paper."

She handed me the newspaper. "It's she, Mr. Douglas. I'm positive that the murdered woman is the woman—the Miss Kelso who called you." Cindy was now jabbing with her index finger where she wanted me to look.

I began to read the words aloud.

"The body of freelance journalist Sammantha Kelso was discovered in her suite at the Plaza Diana yesterday morning. Police reported that she had been murdered but would release no details."

My voice faded to something resembling a low monotone. "Ms. Kelso, age forty-two, was well known throughout Europe for her exposés of illegal corporate practices."

"I am right, am I not? Mr. Douglas? It is the lady who called, isn't it?" Cindy asked.

"Shhh!" I muttered, my voice barely a whisper. "According to an unofficial source, although she was born in the United States, Ms. Kelso had resided for the past fifteen years in Great Britain and France."

That was it. That was everything the article said about Kelso. The remainder of the story focused on the hotel, the reactions of its guests, and the usual tabloid-style reporting that highlighted the increasing crime rate, fears that tourists held about visiting the city, and so on.

"Mr. Douglas? Sir?"

A tingling sensation began to creep up my spine.

"Should we notify the authorities, Mr. Douglas?"

"Huh?" I stammered, finally realizing that I was the Mr. Douglas whom Cindy was addressing. "What ... Yes, what is it?"

I felt her staring at my motionless profile. "I was inquiring, sir," she repeated, "if we should report what we know about this Ms. Kelso to the authorities. After all, she did call us—er, you. Maybe we can be of some help in their investigation."

For some strange reason, my body began to tremble. For a second, I thought my spirit was shaking itself loose from its earthly bonds as the tingling sensation grew greater, working its way up my spine and gathering strength with its assent. It lasted but a moment, passing as suddenly as it had come.

"Mr. Douglas, are you feeling all right?" The quiver in her voice suggested she had experienced her own sense of wonder at what she had just witnessed. "May I get you some water? Or perhaps a cup of tea?"

I made eye contact with her and then turned my face toward the window, my voice returning as I did. "No ... No, thanks. It's nothing. It's nothing," I repeated.

I looked around my office. It was as though I were a stranger to it; I was so struck by its opulence. The handmade, customized rosewood furniture; the Baccarat crystal lamps atop the Italian marble tables; and the rich celadon Karastan wall-to-wall carpeting accented so gracefully by the antique Tabriz Persian rug displayed in front of my desk—I felt as if I were seeing it all for the first time.

I didn't have a clue what we should do about the police. My mind was with neither Cindy's words nor the newspaper story as I turned from the window and stepped uncertainly toward the open office door. When I reached the reception area, I halted, my back to Cindy, and answered her. "If you believe we should notify the police … the authorities … then, please … by all means, do so. As for me … I have to go … It's late … Very late."

A few minutes later, waiting for the elevator to arrive, I tried to understand what had just occurred. Who was Sammantha Kelso? Why in God's name did she want to speak with me? Was she …? Answers, if there were any to those questions, would have to come later, as the elevator doors separated and a friendly greeting shattered my absorption with those thoughts.

"Good morning, Chris." It was Gerry Souk, vice president of technology.

I shook the spell as best I could. "All set for the meeting?" I asked, attempting to make small talk.

"Yes, sir. We had an outstanding week in my department. We ran our first full-blown system test linking our PCs with all our remote locations and DFT corporate. It worked like a charm."

"Sounds like we're making progress." The images of PCs, remote locations, and the name Kelso mixed incongruously in my mind. "I'd like to use that communication link with DFT corporate this week. It'll help buy us some time."

"Super. Just let me know when, and I'll personally help."

The elevator doors opened, and we walked silently to the conference room. As soon as we entered the filled room, heads turned, acknowledging our arrival, and then everyone moved as if on cue to his or her seat. My eyes surveyed the crowd.

Damn it! Where in hell is Weitzer? I needed to discuss the Geo Computer contract with him.

"Where the hell is Herman?" I asked, bringing the meeting to order.

"Excuse me, Mr. Douglas?"

I peered down the table toward the voice. My gaze rested on Jack Hite, a member of Weitzer's marketing department. "Yes, Jack? What is it?" He appeared uncomfortable.

"Herman left me a message this morning." He halted as soon as he completed his statement, and waited, expecting me to interrupt him.

Not to disappoint him, I asked, "Yessss?"

"He told me to attend this meeting in his absence due to a death in the immediate family and to present the weekly forecasts." He slumped back into his chair.

What the hell is this character doing here? Weitzer, when we talk... "That's fine," I replied. "Before we get to the forecasts, are you familiar with any of the Geo Computer contract revisions?"

"Only that there were some." His voice wavered. "Because it is such a major account, Herman handled it personally."

Why was I not surprised by his response? "Jack, when Herman calls in, tell him I need to speak with him about this subject. Make certain he understands I consider it urgent."

Cutting off whatever he started to say, I turned to Judy Lieber and played the straight man and asked how we were doing this month. Since I had reviewed the numbers already and knew I would be spending the next two days cooped up further doing so, the question was posed more for the group's benefit than mine.

Half tuning her out as she started to talk about our Boston station yet still paying enough attention to respond or jump in, my mind drifted back to the morning's events. The drone of Judy's voice—rattling off ratings, profits, and suddenly confusing, if not meaningless, numbers and percentages—intermingled randomly with what I had read about Kelso. I had never felt anything like the weird feeling that had come over me a few minutes ago in my office. Cindy must have thought I was going crazy.

Slaus called it a healthy paranoia and not an overreaction when a person felt something that wasn't quite the way it was supposed to be and acted on it. Well, I was starting to feel that sensation. Except, in my scenario, I was perhaps a few frames earlier and uncertain what I was supposed to act on. Why did Kelso tell Cindy I would know her? She was unrecognizable in that fuzzy newspaper snapshot. And what did she want?

"Chris, all in all," Lieber concluded as I shifted gears and tuned her back in, "the first two weeks of July, I am pleased to announce, look as though they will be a continuance of this past fiscal quarter, with sales running five percent ahead of a very aggressive forecast." Judy smiled, seemingly satisfied with the way the numbers were falling into place.

I complimented everyone for a job well done and turned to Tex Follner, president of our four-station TV division.

"Yes, Chris, the numbers are lining up rather nicely," Tex said with a twang. In spite of the positive report he was about to deliver, he invoked a bored yawn from a few people around the table. Bending his head to read from the pro forma revenue statement in front of him and the spring book rating's result, Tex droned on.

After a few minutes, I interrupted him. "Tex, listen, I really do appreciate your sharing this data with us, but what I'm interested in is how hard or soft these projections are. For instance, I know you didn't handle the details, but are you familiar with any of the Geo Computer amendments I was asking Jack about?"

"Well, sure, Herman talked to me about it," Tex answered. He was visibly uncomfortable with the question. "He told me the only thing that changed was the way the termination wording was structured." He paused and looked around the table. "He told me they had some sort of right to cancel the agreement if it was determined that the station did something illegal or some such nonsense. Everything else remained the same, he told me."

Reacting as if it were an afterthought, or as though his golf game or masculinity had been challenged, he protested loudly, "Hell, Chris, if I were to worry about that sort of bullshit, we would never get a goddamn broadcast out."

I chose not to explore that remark, and I also knew there wasn't any sense pursuing the topic with Tex further. I noted that I would recheck the termination section later and then turned again to Weitzer's surrogate.

"Jack, any idea to what Tex is referring?"

He coughed as though he were trying to dislodge whatever had taken residence in his throat. "No, no, I don't, Mr. Douglas. As I said before, he never discussed any of the terms with me."

This discussion was headed nowhere fast. "All right, forget I asked. Just make sure Herman gets in touch with me when he calls." I paused to allow my annoyance to subside. There was an awkward silence in the room. "Okay, okay, everyone," I said, finally breaking the silence. "Terry, what's happening in HR?"

As Terry began explaining the nuances of the new 401(k) plan, the phone rang. Tex, seated next to it, picked it up and, for my benefit, mouthed the word 'Carlson.' I motioned for Terry to continue and moved to the other end of the conference room to take the call.

"Hello, Rick?" I said, taking the phone from Tex.

Carlson's secretary greeted me instead. "Please hold for Mr. Carlson, Mr. Douglas. He will be right with you."

Carlson came on the phone a few seconds later. Addressing me in his silky voice, he began as he always did—with a question. "Chris, my boy, how is everything?" Rick Carlson, who was approaching seventy, was cherubic in appearance, even down to the rosy, apple cheeks, and his effortlessly avuncular appearance belied his cunning. Whenever he asked a question, he usually knew the answer.

Out of years of habit, I answered automatically, "Not too bad." Then, before the next breath, shaking my head, I corrected that gross misrepresentation. "Well, actually, things have been better. We seem to have hit a major snag with the Great Air negotiations. Did you get my message—or Macpherson's?"

He answered in the same smooth tone. "Yes, Chris, I did. But what is your sense of the situation?"

There wasn't any doubt he had discussed this subject with Macpherson. But I also knew he was interested in understanding my perspective.

"Rick, I'm not sure what happened Saturday. I can tell you this much: the SOBs decided well in advance." After recapping my conversation with Andy, plus my previous meetings and discussions with Great Air's management, I sensed a degree of coolness when I got to the issue of the FCC.

"What do you mean exactly?" Carlson's voice assumed an unfamiliar strain, "When you say that Walker was about to accelerate the process?"

"We don't know why or what occurred," I said, wishing I did know. "Simmons was under the impression that Walker would be ready for the district court of appeals by October and that he was openly cocky about his chances of winning. I asked Andy to see if Ari Schwab could find out anything from Rackley."

"Did he?"

"No. It turns out that His Honor is out of the country until later in the week."

There was no longer any hint of coolness in his tone; it was as though the last few remarks had not occurred as the trademark smoothness returned. "I don't believe it would be advisable for Schwab to talk with Judge Rackley. Let me make some phone calls of my own. If afterward I still feel it's necessary to proceed with this tack, I'll so inform you."

Uh, oh, my instincts warned me. It looked as though he was giving me a push to the sidelines—a small push, but a push nevertheless. His overall reaction was rather strange. In all our dealings, he was extremely aggressive and usually the first to demand Schwab's involvement when it came to anything remotely connected with FCC matters.

"Okay, Rick. I'll call Andy and advise him to low-key it until further notice." I paused and then volunteered, "How do you want to handle the press? Shouldn't we try to exert some damage control?"

"Landon is addressing that," Carlson shot back. "For the time being, this subject should be placed on hold."

That didn't sound like a small push to the bench. He was sending me back to the minors.

Changing his tone now that his message had been delivered, his voice became almost conspiratorial. "And, anyway, Chris," he confided, "I'm quite certain there are other, equally pressing problems in that sector of yours to keep your energies challenged."

"Actually," I said, attempting to maintain a positive attitude about being relegated to the farm team, "except for this unexpected business with WXRA, things are in pretty good shape. I think you'll be pleased with my third-quarter financial projections."

"Now, that's more like it. I'm looking forward to hearing you talk at great length about this subject when you arrive in Greenville. I wish that all our divisions were in hands as able as yours, Chris. See you Wednesday afternoon."

The telephone went dead.

I returned to my seat. Mosely, who was head of our radio division, had just begun speaking. The call from Carlson had taken less than ten minutes, yet I had a sense that plans years in the making had been finalized during that short period.

My palms were bathed in sweat. What was wrong with me? First, the Kelso thing, and now this suspicion toward Rick's motivation. Big deal! So he wanted to sell the station. The fact of the matter was that he wanted to sell every station. I had been aware of that for nearly two years, soon after coming aboard. And, what's more, I bought into it—hook, line, and sinker. So what! Was it a crime that he wanted the most he could get for them?

"We're planning to switch the program format at WQUT in Chicago next month," Mosely droned, pulling my attention from Carlson's call. "The new format has an excellent shot at increasing share points, which could translate into additional annual revenues of approximately one million dollars."

If we used the same multiplier of sales price to earnings that we had used to peg the original WXRA offering, that meant we could increase the asking price for WQUT by approximately $5 million.

"Let's do it then," I blurted out, a little too loudly and before Mosely had even finished his presentation.

The remainder of the meeting stayed on track without any external disruptions. No one inquired about the status of WXRA, so I didn't have to tap-dance around that subject. I wrapped up the meeting by thanking everyone for the outstanding last quarter performance and the fine start to the new one. On my way out the door, Ross Mosely collared me.

"Chris, can I speak with you? Privately. It won't take a minute. It's about the WXRA negotiations."

Damn it! I didn't stop; I just continued down the corridor to the elevator. "Sure, Ross. But it has to be sometime later in the afternoon. Right now I'm on my way to another meeting." For a second, I thought about saying with whom—Casey did work in Mosely's division, after all. Instead I pressed the down button for the elevator. "Anything that I might do for you now?"

He shrugged his shoulders and stalled as we waited for some people to pass. He didn't surprise me with his question. "How close is the sale? I guess what I really mean ... How far behind are the rest of the stations?"

"I wish I could tell you," I answered truthfully. "In many ways, I knew more about the answer last Friday than I do today, Ross."

The elevator's arrival gave me a reprieve. We stepped between the occupants, and I stared in private contemplation at the blinking numbers and lights that all too slowly announced each floor. When the doors slid open, I walked quickly through them. Mosely kept pace, never more than a foot behind.

"Listen, Ross, it would be nice to continue this discussion, but I can't," I said over my shoulder.

We walked in awkward silence until we reached my office suite. "Look, I don't know what else to say," I said. "I'll call you later, all right? We'll set something up to talk, okay?"

He backed away, nodding in agreement. The bewildered expression on his face said volumes. "Okay, Chris. I guess I haven't any choice." After a few feet, he turned, retraced his path, and vanished down the hallway.

Cindy was alone at her desk; the empty seats in the reception area meant Casey had not arrived. I started to ask where he was, but Cindy interrupted.

"Mr. Casey just called. He's on his way up from the studio. Oh, one other item, Mr. Douglas. The police just telephoned approximately ten minutes ago regarding that woman—that Ms. Kelso."

"The police? You called them! Why?"

Cindy jumped from her chair and stepped behind it as if taking refuge. "No, no, Mr. Douglas." She quivered. "I didn't call them." Her eyes widened; her hands clutched the top of the chair as she explained. "After you said ... After you told me that I should proceed to do as I so wished," she said, reminding me of what I'd said, "I only became more confused."

She looked to be on the verge of tears, but then, apparently gathering her courage, she removed her hands from her support and clasped them together, wringing them until her knuckles were white.

"I said the police called here. They advised me that your office telephone number was found on a piece of paper in her room. Upon checking the hotel records, they said there were two calls made from her room last Friday that matched the number on the paper."

I could see tears in Cindy's eyes. "They—the police, that is— informed me that they wanted to come by and speak with you ... uh, speak with us this afternoon around three o'clock."

As I listened to her explanation, my tension eased. What was so terrible about what she'd said? What would cause me to lose my cool? This damn affair wasn't any of my concern.

I walked over to Cindy and placed one arm around her shoulders. I felt her flinch. Then I guided her from behind the imagined sanctuary of her chair. "Cindy, I'm sorry," I said in the most tranquil voice I was capable of mustering. "You were quite right in your dealings with the police. Please try to understand. It's just been a tough morning."

I forced a smile. "Here now," I said. "It's my turn to offer you something." Although our smiles became more natural in appearance, I couldn't help but think how silly the two of us must have looked. "Some water? Or perhaps some Earl Grey?"

"Oh no, Mr. Douglas," she said with a schoolgirl's giggle. "I'm all right now." She pulled herself erect and jutted her chin upward in an exaggerated manner. "That's my job. You're not supposed to do that sort of work."

As I started to scold her for her chauvinistic attitude, I was halted midsentence by a loud grunting noise from behind.

"Hrrump! Hrrump!" The noise repeated, louder the second time.

I turned to see Sean Casey standing fewer than five feet away. He was in the midst of clearing his throat a third time as if to announce his three-hundred-pound presence. On his round, familiar face, he wore a grin that matched his girth.

In that recognizable radio baritone of his, and with a bit of roguishness thrown in for the circumstances, he asked, "Would it be advisable for me to come back later? I will if you prefer, as it appears I'm interrupting something that the two of you find delightfully important!"

Chapter 4

CASEY HAD CAUGHT US by surprise. Both of our faces flushed, Cindy's twice as much as mine.

I dropped my arm from her shoulders and sheepishly reached out and gripped Casey's mammoth, ham-like right hand in both of mine. "Of course you are." Winking at Cindy, I added, "We can pick this up some time later."

As I ushered Sean into my inner office, I saw that this remark had colored her face an even darker crimson. "Cindy, some Diet Pepsi for Mr. Casey, please," I said politely, moving to re-establish our normal business relationship.

"Certainly, Mr. Douglas." The steadiness of her voice indicated that our roles had slid back into place.

Casey mumbled something about a Dewar's and water as he plopped onto the leather sofa at the far end of my office. He smirked and waved a finger at me. "Chris, me laddie, you shock me, you do." He playfully castigated me in a heavy, assumed Irish brogue. "Feeling around with your secretary like that."

I walked past him and sat behind my desk. Just as I started to reply, Cindy appeared with Casey's Pepsi, interrupting any further adolescent banter.

"Seriously, Sean," I said after Cindy had closed the door. "Didn't you want to see me about something?" Casey's eyes fixed on me as he sipped his drink, his Adam's apple bobbing as he swallowed. The smile disappeared when he set the half-drained glass on the marbled coffee table.

"Yes, I did at that, Chris. I wanted to ask you where the Great Air and WXRA negotiations stood." He made no effort to hide the distain his voice carried toward the prospective buyer. Sean Casey owed an enormous part of his broadcasting fame to his voice, and when he chose, he could play it as if it were a maestro's cherished instrument.

"Ross Mosely was just asking me the same question. Quite frankly, I don't know." I shrugged. "At this juncture, it seems they have developed cold feet and may be backing out of the deal. But, then again, as far as I know, the situation could change as fast as this most recent about-face." I shrugged again, more out of nervousness than for emphasis.

His eyes widened as they riveted on me. When he spoke, his mouth formed every syllable as though he were on stage, while his body shifted forward.

"There was some talk I heard on the street—rumors, perhaps—that you … Ah." He paused to revise his remark and cede me the benefit of doubt. "I should say, Carlson and his crew of pirates were trying to get out of my contract."

He took another long drink of his cola and then arched one bushy eyebrow while squinting with the opposite eye. "There wouldn't be any truth now to those so-called rumors, would there be, laddie?"

An image of Long John Silver from the black-and-white movie classic *Treasure Island* flashed into my mind. Half expecting the corpulent pirate sitting before me to draw a broad sword from beneath his jacket or to blurt out, "Aye, aye, matey," depending upon my response, I opted for discretion and not valor.

"Sean, I don't think that is something that DFT would ever seriously consider," I said unsteadily. Then, realizing I had no basis for that statement, I switched gears. "Certainly it's not something I would ever entertain."

Ugh! Those statements sounded a bit too much like weasel words, to use a technical business term for discussions such as these. He remained quiet, both his eyebrows stretched between his temples, waiting for a more definitive answer.

Casey earned $2 million a year. In many—if not most—ways, he was WXRA. He had been with the station for twenty years, and in the past couple of years, he had introduced his wife and son as part of the program. And, as Andy and I had discussed, his was the number-one program in the metro area. So I did the only thing I could—I lied.

Summoning whatever inner reserve and fire I still possessed, considering the morning I was having, I leaned across my desk and gave it my best shot. In a voice louder than normal and with an exaggerated twinge of outrage, I said, "Sean, are you kidding? Let's get real. You are WXRA! Everybody who is anybody knows that without you, revenues would go down the tubes in nothing flat."

Sneering at the improbability of such a thought, I stressed his original point. "Contract! Give me a break. Listen to me. I don't want to hear any more nonsense about your contract while I'm still president of this outfit."

There was not a peep from Casey. Taking heart at not seeing anything resembling a cutlass appear, I continued to stroke the massive talent sitting in front of me.

"Now, don't go and get a bigger head than you already have because of what I just said, but by the same token, I don't want to hear anything more about those damn negotiations either. No one—I repeat, no one—would ever be foolish enough to tamper with you or your program." Unfortunately, I broke one of the cardinal rules of salesmanship next by not quitting while ahead. "Unless, of course they were total, incompetent assholes."

It was amazing to see such an enormous man move as Sean did. He leaped from his seat, running right over my trailing words.
"I'm warning you, Christof Douglas; don't go jerking me around. You hear what I'm telling you? Don't jerk me around! If I find out, and I will find out, that you're bullshitting me, my attorneys will slap this company with the largest lawsuit it ever dreamed of—one that I can assure you will make the FCC litigation seem like a day in traffic court."

He took another long sip from his drink. He inhaled deeply, and I could see he was gathering another head of steam. He exhaled a moment later and, letting the full range of his voice rise to a piercing crescendo, raged on.

"You're damn right I'm this station! And don't you forget it. I know precisely what my contract does and doesn't specify. If my radio station is sold, it doesn't matter in a pig's ass who the new owners are, because they have to pick it up as is, assume it one hundred percent—lock, stock, and barrel!"

That outburst of energy appeared to be too much for him, and he fell backward into his seat. Pulling a raunchy, much-too-used handkerchief from his pocket, he blew his nose so hard I feared he would have a stroke.

Theatrics aside, he was legally on target. But I also knew him well enough to know that he hated the thought of getting himself entangled in an activity that he found personally distasteful. In this scenario, he would have to spend long, painfully boring hours with the non-talent people of our industry, such as lawyers and accountants, the people he did his utmost to avoid. And money wasn't the issue. If it so happened there was money in the end, all the better, but I knew that in Sean's case, his contract was a matter of status and honor and principle, not dollars. It helped to have been down this road before.

I rose from my chair and walked toward what was now a deflated and emotionally spent ex-pirate and eased myself onto the couch beside him. "Sean, you and I know what you've done for this station. Any potential buyer would understand as well. Listen to me. Take some advice. Just pay attention to your program; concern yourself with that, and let this other nonsense—for that's what it is—take care of itself."

I waited to see his reaction and continued to try to ease the tension. "Hell, laddie, these negotiations could go for another ten years if the past is any indicator. But who cares? As you so eloquently stated, your contract points out the obligations of any prospective buyer." I nearly blurted out, "Caveat emptor," but bit my tongue.

He stuffed his handkerchief into his bulging trouser pocket and stared at the windows that overlooked the Hudson. When he spoke, he used a voice I didn't recognize, so pedestrian and uncharacteristically flat was its tone.

"Christ," he began, mispronouncing my name, still not bothering to acknowledge that I was next to him, "we've only known each other for a few years." Casey paused and then began again, mispronouncing my name once more. "Christ, it's only been a short period but one that has been packed with more pressure than I've had in my entire career. You, for the most part, have been toler—or, shall we say, reasonable with what some other less-understanding and smaller-minded person might come to interpret"—he swiveled his large body and licked his lips—"as excessive and occasionally petulant behavior on my part."

There was a trace of melancholy to his words as he raised his hand, signaling me not to interrupt. "It's quite true, laddie, and I do sincerely and profoundly appreciate it."

He sighed and pushed forward, straining to get off the couch. It was as though the weight of the world was added to his already immense shoulders as he shuffled to the windows behind my desk, keeping his back to me. "In the past few years, this business has changed," Casey said. "It's—speaking in all candor—no longer any fun for me. It's just a business now. But what can I say? I guess it was inevitable."

I could see his head tilt so that he could observe my reaction through the corner of one eye. "Yeah, I guess it was inevitable. What else could you expect when the suits—those boys from downtown—the so-called investment types …" He turned from the window to look at me. In a tone more wary than weary, he said, "Don't take this personally, Christ, but as soon as the suits from downtown commenced sponsoring … Strike that." He laughed at the use of a term to which he owed a great deal of his fame and fortune. Shaking his head, he went on. "Ironic, isn't it? Sponsor! Let's strike that from the record, as I don't like the connotation."

I had to smile.

"Let's change it to … started to smell the easy money. Yes! Yes, that's good. I like that." I could see his nose wrinkle, head nodding in affirmation. He seemed pleased with himself. I also sensed a second wind coming on.

"Buy a radio station. Better yet, buy two. Why not a TV station also? Who gives a rat's ass if you know the first thing about running it! Tuck it into your portfolio and keep it like some big game trophy you just hunted down and slaughtered. Keep it, that is, until it no longer tickles your fancy. Then pick up the yellow pages, contact the nearest suit, add twenty-five percent to the price you've paid, and dispose of it. Oops, my error. I think the correct word is divest, not dispose."

A confused look came over him, punctuated by those bushy, arched eyebrows that made me think of a question mark. "Chris," he asked, pronouncing my name correctly, "are you a suit?"

How could I answer? At that moment, I could not be sure myself.

"You were never sure," Parcae told me every time I would try to explain.

I rose from the couch and approached Casey. When we were less than a foot apart, I stopped. We stared in silence for a second before I walked back to the leather chair behind my desk.

Speaking as much to the room as to Casey, I finally answered him. "That's a good question, Sean. Sometimes ... I guess, sometimes, Sean, that's all I am."

For what seemed like a few minutes, but in reality was only seconds, the room was still. Then Casey stepped toward the door, his shuffling feet breaking the silence. In that mellow baritone, which miraculously had now been restored, he left me with one parting comment. "I'm sorry to hear you say that, me lad. I thought—believed, even—that you had some real potential." He departed as he had entered, mumbling to himself about the scotch he should have had.

Cindy walked through the door before I had a chance to dwell on Casey's perceptions. "Ms. Lieber has been waiting." Cindy motioned for our financial manager to enter.

"Thanks, Cindy. Please get Andy on the phone." I smiled in greeting to Judy.

For the next couple of hours, we pored over the financial results of the fiscal year to date, sparing me any further thoughts of my meeting with Casey. At last I received some positive feedback, as our stations were performing extremely well. Sometime during this process, Andy called back. I relayed Carlson's message to defer Ari's contact with Rackley. Andy didn't like it either, but what was our choice? The only other interruption was when Cindy buzzed me late in the afternoon.

"Yes?"

"Mr. Douglas, I'm sorry to bother you, but there are two detectives from the New York City Homicide Department here to see you."

Her announcement caught me off guard. Having forgotten about them—maybe blocked them out—and the purpose of their visit, I stalled. "Get them some coffee or whatever. I need about two minutes to wrap up what we're doing; then bring them in."

I apologized to Judy and asked if she would mind continuing by herself in her office until I could rejoin her.

Cindy entered with the two detectives trailing behind her. "Mr. Douglas, this is Detective Hopkins and Detective White," Cindy said, nervously introducing the pair of somber, gray-suited police officers.

I shook their hands, their free hands displaying their badges. If this was meant to impress or intimidate me, it worked. Working to overcome my own nervousness, in my most senior-executive, "I know this is serious" tone, I invited each to take a seat in the chairs in front of my desk. The three of us sat, protected from the other by the polished, partner-sized rosewood desk between us.

"Would either of you care for some refreshments?" I asked.

Hopkins spoke first. "No thank you, Mr. Douglas. His tone was measured and firm but polite. "Miss Nettleton has already asked us. We're fine." His stare was harder than his voice. "Detective White and I appreciate your availability on such short notice, though."

It had been so long since I had addressed Cindy as Miss Nettleton that I almost asked him who Miss Nettleton was. I caught myself, smiled, and nodded. I noticed that she was still in the room. "Cindy, please see, see that we're not disturbed," I said.

"If you don't mind, Mr. Douglas"—Hopkins smiled and motioned for her to sit—"we'd prefer for Miss Nettleton to stay."

Before I was able to respond, Cindy had moved to the sofa and made herself at home. She smoothed some imagined wrinkles in her dress, folded her hands neatly into her lap, and looked up at Hopkins.

I shrugged. "How can I ... How can we help you?"

Both officers shifted their chairs, positioning them to allow the four of us to see each other.

"Did you know Sammantha Kelso, Mr. Douglas?" My eyes shifted from Hopkins to White, who had asked the question.

"No ... No, I don't believe I do—or did," I replied, adjusting my tenses. Seemingly from nowhere, a disturbing feeling began to drift over me. It was similar to the one I'd felt earlier that morning when I had started to read about Kelso.

White turned to Cindy. "And you, Miss Nettleton? Did you by any chance happen to know who she was?"

Although my gaze shifted to White, I was aware that Hopkins hadn't taken his eyes off me.

Stiffening her back, she perked herself up, and with a chipper ring to her voice, she threw herself into her response. "No, Detective White. I never knew her. The only time I had occasion to speak with her was last week—Friday afternoon, to be precise." Her eyes rolled in my direction and then returned to the detective as she continued her circumstantial narrative.

"Twice. She telephoned twice—that is, for Mr. Douglas. The second time she called she wanted his home number. She told me it was extremely important. Urgent, I recall, was the word she used. I, of course, knew where Mr. Douglas was but certainly was not about to reveal it to her."

A look of confusion, or perhaps frustration, came over White, which Cindy must have noticed, because she digressed from her recollections to explain. "He and his wife have a summer cottage at the New Jersey Shore, where they spend most of the weekends. Well, Mr. Douglas does, that is. Mrs. Douglas essentially lives there for the entire summer season."

She continued, "When I told her, as I told Mrs. Douglas, that I would never release the numbers to any of their residences—you see, there is also an apartment in Manhattan—that was when Miss Kelso became quite ..." Cindy hesitated. She turned to Hopkins and then back to White, her expression becoming smugger by the second as though the very solution to the case hinged on her words. "Quite snippy with me," she said at last.

"Snippy, Miss Nettleton?" Hopkins asked. "What do you mean by that?"

Looking pleased to be the center of this murder investigation,

Cindy—or Miss Nettleton, as she now seemed to go by—plunged on.

"Well, Officer Hopkins, as I just said, she—this Miss Kelso—demanded that I give her Mr. Douglas's home telephone number. She insisted that she had to have it. She said that if I told him who she was, he would know her and most definitely call back, and therefore it was all right for me to give his number."

Both detectives swiveled in my direction. My stomach began to churn. "Mr. Douglas, I believe you just stated you didn't know her," Hopkins said.

When had that notebook appeared in his hands? "Detective Hopkins, to the best of my knowledge, I had never met or spoken to this woman in my life. I didn't recognize her when I saw the picture in the paper either."

A few seconds passed before White continued. "She was a journalist, I understand. Do you have any idea why she was calling you, Mr. Douglas?" He smiled and then checked through some notes he had on his lap. "Freelance," he said, lifting his head back up toward me, "it states here, according to our records. Was she doing some writing for you, perhaps?"

"Detective White," I said, my eyes narrowing, "how could she possibly be doing any work for me if I didn't know who the hell she was?"

With an exaggerated shrug, he turned toward his partner. "I don't know. Maybe she was working for someone else in the company?" His smile got a little broader. "This is a big company, right? How many people are employed here—a couple thousand?"

"Where?" I asked, uncertain where this line of questioning was going. "In this building or the entire company?"

"Oh, let's say, for openers, at this location."

"About four hundred, give or take."

"What about the remainder of the company?"

"Another eight hundred or so"

"That's a lot of people. Could it be possible that someone else in the company hired her?" His eyes searched my face, and then he inserted his own version of a corporate disclaimer. "Mind you, without your knowledge, of course."

I barely nodded in agreement, ceding the possibility.

Hopkins went on. "Maybe someone hired her, and something didn't go as planned. Or maybe it did go as planned … Or whatever." He puckered his mouth between his words and scratched his chin.

"Anything's possible, Detective Hopkins," I said, not really in the least convinced that it was possible. "But why would she call me then? And why would she say that I would know who she was?"

Hopkins ignored my questions. "Mr. Douglas, can you think of anyone else who might have a reason to hire her? Someone like Kelso? A writer—or a reporter?"

"Well," I replied after a few seconds, "every station has a small PR staff—some larger and more sophisticated than others. And, of course, here at corporate we also have one. That's a logical place where any sort of contact with the print media would initially occur. If you wish, we can prepare a list of the names from these departments for your information."

"That would be a start, thank you," Hopkins agreed. Although his smile had returned, his voice was cool. I got the impression he didn't buy into this theory any more than I did.

White looked at Cindy. "Miss Nettleton, when did you say you found out about the deceased?" For the first time, he substituted this very impersonal and dehumanizing word.

"Uh … sometime … I think … sometime early this morning I read about it. Yes … yes, I read about it in the *Post*. Then afterward in the *Times*."

"Yet you didn't—" White halted in midsentence. He rolled his head toward me and repeated his question. "And you, Mr. Douglas. When did you find out?"

Where was all this heading? "When Cindy brought the newspaper into my office and pointed it out."

"Yet neither of you," White said, rotating his head between us, "thought it important enough to call the police about the calls last Friday."

Cindy's expression suggested that she now regretted her involvement with this whole affair.

Why the hell didn't I throw them the hell out right then and there? Tell them to call my attorney and stop wasting my time!

"To be honest, we didn't know what to do," I said. "I was late for a meeting when I read about the deceas—Miss Kelso—and, quite candidly, it completely slipped my mind afterward." I was hoping to see some display of understanding from them but wasn't counting on it. "That is until Miss … Miss Cindy informed me that you had arrived."

No sooner had I said it than I realized it was a mistake. "That's not quite right. Cindy did mention to me around eleven or thereabouts that you had called and wanted to see us this afternoon."

Neither detective spoke a word. Much to my relief, and certainly to the relief of Cindy, who squirmed in her seat, White finally announced, "I see. I guess I can understand, Mr. Douglas."

I wasn't sure who was more surprised, Cindy or me.

Probably she was, as she barely managed a weak, "No, sir," when White asked her if she had anything more to add.

The two detectives glanced at each other and rose from their seats. "Mr. Douglas, Miss Nettleton, I think we've taken enough of your time. You've both been more than helpful," Hopkins said. He smiled as he handed me his card. "If you think about anything later to add, give me a call." He gave me a hard stare. "Immediately this time. Right, Mr. Douglas?"

I got up and walked around my desk and shook their hands. I nodded to both of them. Cindy seemed only too happy to escort the pair to the elevators. Bouncing up from the sofa, she cried out, "Oh, yes, sir. He—I mean, we—most assuredly will."

I watched as the three left. My stomach was churning, and I needed desperately to use the bathroom. I waited as long as I could and then went into the hallway. There was no one in sight.

Opening the door to the men's room, I saw both detectives, their gray suits facing me as they stood in front of the urinals. Hopkins spied me over his shoulder.

"Hey, Mr. Douglas, I'm glad that you popped in." He wore a larger grin than any I had seen earlier. "Saved us a return trip to your office," he said over the flush of the water. He zipped his fly and stepped toward the wash basin. "Yeah, there was something else we forgot to ask you."

Pushing by bodily endurance to its limit, I hurried to a stall and opened it as I said, "What was that?"

Hopkins began to dig through his pockets. "Let me see. I have it here someplace." He was patting and poking into each suit-jacket and shirt pocket. "I remembered it when we were by the elevator and I reached for my car keys."

"Perhaps we should continue this in a few minutes back in my office. Sorry, don't mean to be rude, but I do need a bit of privacy." I closed the lavatory door behind me and locked it.

Hopkins was undaunted. "No problem, Mr. Douglas. No problem at all. Let me just read you what I have. Won't take a sec. Aah, okay, I found it. Does the name Ladillya—Maria Ladillya—mean anything to you?"

I was lucky I was behind a closed door. *It was Parcae ... How could I ever forget that name?* My pulse started to race. My head became lighter. I squeezed my temples as hard as I could, trying to force the blood back into my head.

Hopkins repeated his question. "Mr. Douglas, did you hear what I said? Maria Ladillya. Did you know the woman?"

I struggled to control my voice. I didn't answer him; I couldn't. Something was stopping me from doing so—I said something that sounded like "I ... I don't think so."

Why? Why her name? After all those years. It was a name from another world.

And then, like a hot piece of steel, like the bullet that once, so long ago, burned deep into my flesh, it struck me. I felt my heart about to burst through my heaving chest and heard the sound of blood pounding in my ears. I feared my heart would fail me, so strong, so sudden was the rush. I knew who Sammantha Kelso was! It was as if a veil had just been lifted from my eyes. I now understood why those sensations had been invading—even battering—my psyche so relentlessly. No! The police didn't have to tell me now. I knew why Kelso had been so adamant, so persistent about speaking with me and why she said I would know her.

Maria ... Maria ... I loved you so! Maria Ladillya was ... She was Sammantha Kelso. Maria Ladillya was the girl ... I was supposed to marry!

The room was still as it spun around me. And then, in a voice too normal, too in the here and now, I heard, "Okay, Mr. Douglas. We just needed to ask. As we said in your office, if anything else comes to mind, give us a call."

My eyes were sealed, but my ears heard their shoes clicking on the tiled floor, the clicks fading with each step toward the bathroom exit. I heard the metal door slam shut and then allowed the tears to fall from my eyes as the room filled with a deathly silence I knew all too well.

Chapter 5

"HEY, WATCH IT, WILL ya, pal!" The driver of a yellow Peugeot taxi slammed his brakes and swerved between traffic lanes to avoid the careless, self-absorbed man crossing Second Avenue.

To the hundreds of bustling people around me, I likely gave the impression of someone who affected all the appearances of style, and certainly what passed for power as defined by the haute couture and trend brokers of so-called society.

I was dressed that day not much differently from any of the thousand days that preceded it. I wore a chalky, lightweight wool three-button Gieves & Hawkes suit with navy pinstripes, the kind with a double-vented jacket and three-quarter-inch cuffed trousers. My white shirt was Charvet's best, handmade from the finest Egyptian cotton—French cuffed for monogrammed gold cufflinks, of course. The Huntsman silver tie I wore complemented my attire and added the desired touch of reserved sophistication. My wing tips were from Polo. Their burnished orange tones were my sole concession to flair. And, shunning the ubiquitous Oyster Rolex, I preferred the more understated Concord Mariner—the model with gold bezel and links. The only other jewelry was on my left hand: a simple, unadorned eighteen-carat-gold wedding ring. The date December 22, 1972, was inscribed on it.

Despite the fact that the July sun was beginning to hide behind the Midtown skyscrapers, the blacktopped streets felt spongy from another day of ninety-degree temperatures.

Approximately two hours before, I had rushed from my office, traveling first uptown on Broadway and then at Fifty-Ninth Street over to Madison Avenue until I reached Sixty-Fourth Street. I turned east off Madison for approximately one hundred yards. There, alone on the opposite side of the narrow, tree-lined street, I stood and confronted the façade of the Plaza Diana Hotel.

Why? Why did she come back? After all those years? And why did she have to die, killed the way she was—left to die in some hotel room? And why in God's name didn't she tell me who she really was? Maybe if she had, she would still be alive. Maybe things would be different.

I thought of entering the hotel, as if that action would somehow answer those questions, but quickly thought otherwise. Maybe at some other time I would feel safe with myself and be able to cross that street to enter its lobby.

Sometime later I found myself at Fifty-Third Street on a still-very-crowded Fifth Avenue. I was drawn to a young couple who were standing with their two children on the steps of Saint Thomas's Episcopal Cathedral, their happy smiles stirring some lost memory of another lifetime.

As I stood in front of the wooden doors, I realized I had never entered this hallowed structure. It was though I were under some foreign command, for as soon as the thought occurred, I found myself crossing the cathedral's threshold, passing through the tiled narthex and the interior doors to take a seat in one of the rear pews. Basking in the magnificence of the Gothic architecture, my soul absorbed its tranquility.

I was not alone in the church that afternoon. There were more than a score of kindred souls. As I sat there, staring upon the altar and stained-glass windows, I could have been mistaken for just another business type from one of the surrounding office buildings—someone taking the time for a few minutes of peaceful meditation before he began his journey home. They would have had to stare extra closely—maybe if they were sitting in my pew it would have been obvious—to see the tears on my cheeks.

It was as though I were fighting, struggling for my very soul with some unspeakable demon, embattled in a frightful new reality that had just been thrust unexpectedly and violently into my life. It was a violent new reality that, although on one level had ended some sixteen years before, had never been exorcised from who I once was or from who I had become.

Maria Ladillya. Maria ... Ladillya. Maria ... We were in love. We were to be married. And then ... and then ... every damn thing changed! Life changed! It ended! I made a choice; she made a different one. Damn that time! Damn that war and everyone who had anything to do with it. What was the whole thing for? Her brother, Tony, was killed. She believed that I had sold out. That I didn't have the same courage as she, to do what was right and fight the machine, fight the government and the soulless corporations. Eleven months of hell in fuckin' Nam! The better part of a fuckin' year spent God knows where. Damn you for your fuckin' principles. Why couldn't ... why didn't we ... Oh Maria! Maria! Maria ... my dearest, sweetest squirrel.

The memory of the Spanish word for squirrel, La ardilla, the name I called her during moments of great affection, brought a smile to my face. I remembered her whispering, playfully warning me that a squirrel was nothing but a rat with a fancy tail. Taking solace in that thought and the immortality of Maria's wit, I rose from the pew, breathing in the cathedral's beauty before my trembling legs gave way. Collapsing onto my knees upon the prayer cushion at my feet, I knelt, my hands clasped, my arms hanging over the pew, and bowed my head between the welcoming vee they created ... and prayed.

I did pray, remember! I did as you asked!

I was not a religious man, never had been. I could not recall the last religious service I attended. It was probably when our daughter...when Beth was killed. That was the last time I prayed...and cried. I prayed mostly for Maria that day, for the girl she once was when we were so young and innocent and in love with each other. The future was always going to be there for us. But I also prayed especially hard, the tears streaming down my cheeks, for Katya. I had been given a second chance when she found me. Somehow, someway I was lost again.

Sometime later, drained of all emotion, I left my short-lived sanctuary. Passing through the cathedral's doors and descending its steps into the warm night air, I found a contrasting cultural shock between the streets of glass and steel that I saw before me, in addition to the harsh, discordant sounds of late-twentieth-century Manhattan, and the serenity and mysticism of the Gothic superstructure I had just left. Meditation, reflection, musings, and all the meaningful, humanistic aspects of spirituality seemed to have no place in this fast-paced and crass, ultra-commercialized world.

Suddenly the shout and horn from a taxi driver brought me back to the moment. I watched the cab race down Second Avenue and disappear into the evening rush-hour traffic as I attempted to decide what I should do next. It was not an easy decision. I thought bitterly of everything that had happened, of all those events that, in their screaming bright red intensity, were never too deep below the surface. Partly out of reflex, but also because I was uncertain where else to go, I walked in the direction of our apartment, which was on Fifty-Second Street between Beekman and Sutton Place.

The white-gloved doorman greeted me when I entered the building and escorted me to the small wooden-and-brass elevator. The first time Katya and I had ridden in it, we had felt as though we were back in London at Claridge's. The art deco lamp that hung from the ceiling and the bronze Erte statue placed conspicuously in the lobby entrance suggested the same graceful and rich ambience.

I opened the door to the apartment and reacquainted myself with its warmth and charm and felt a sense of peace. Katya and I called it our Petit Bijou. I switched the air conditioner to its coldest level and then checked for phone messages. There were four. The first two were from Cindy. Her first message was straightforward. She was calling, she said, and this was very typically Cindy and not Miss Nettleton, to inform me that Ms. Lieber would be continuing to finalize the presentation slides for our meeting at corporate. The second was more a product of the day's events. She didn't mention anything specific; she just asked that I call her as soon as I could, leaving her home number in case I didn't have it.

The third message was from Katya. She had just received a very peculiar phone call from Cindy and wanted to talk to me about it as soon as possible.

The fourth, which was not more than twenty minutes old, was from Detective Hopkins. He left his number and said to call him as soon as I got his message. He sounded angry.

I ignored the messages for as long as it took me to shower and fix a cold drink. I dialed Katya first. With each ring, I became more uncertain about what to reveal. I was spared any deception when my voice at the other end thanked me for calling and announced our unavailability. I left word about where I was and then severed the connection.

I placed my next call to Cindy. She answered before the first ring had finished.

"Hello?"

"Cindy, this is Mr. Douglas."

"Oh? Oh, Mr. Douglas! It's you. I'm so glad you called." There was an unfamiliar nervousness to her voice. "I was worried about you after you left the office this afternoon. It was so … it was so sudden and not like you at all."

"Nothing to worry about." I paused, thinking of an excuse and knowing she kept a calendar of all my appointments. Damn, I was not very good at this sort of thing. "The fact of the matter is, after Clouseau and Kato's third degree, I just needed to get some fresh air," I said truthfully.

"Oh … Why … Yes."

"Well, thanks for your concern, but was there any other reason you called?"

Her voice tightened. "Mr. Douglas, that detective—Detective Hopkins—called me." Correcting herself, she said, "No, no, I don't mean that. I mean he was really calling for you. He said he had to speak to you about some woman."

She paused, her nervous tension apparent. "He told me the woman's name was Maria Ladillya and that you knew her. That was when he inquired as to whether I was familiar with the lady. I, of course, replied that I most certainly was not. Well, to be completely forthright about it, he first told me that they were one and the same. Ms. Kelso and this Maria Ladillya, that is."

I became as tense as her voice. My heartbeat accelerated, but I felt an emotion altogether different from the ones I'd felt earlier. It was more the sort of sensation I would sometimes feel when I was there—back there in Southeast Asia.

A feeling bordering on existential disconnection came over me in spite of what she was saying. Just like the mental imagery from that period that pushed its way to the front of my conscious mind and made me believe that I was back over there, certain external stimuli could seemingly do the same for my body. It was as if my body had a memory separate and apart from my mind. My body's memory was based on the metaphysical, visceral, and instinctive nature of its being; my mind's memory was more logical and rational. In this instance, my body was remembering something between the fear and the anger it once faced. It was recalling its own mortality.

"Cindy, what else did Detective Hopkins say?" There was a steeliness to my voice that had been missing before.

Her quiver diminished. "He asked me, Mr. Douglas, if I knew why you would say that you didn't know her—Ladillya, that is. I said I had no idea whatsoever." I didn't respond, and she continued. This time the tremor had found its way back into her voice.

"He also wanted to speak with you. He wouldn't take no for an answer." Her speech was nearly unintelligible, and she sounded ashamed and embarrassed, like a little child who had been caught in some forbidden act. "I think ... I think I made a mistake, Mr. Douglas."

I wanted to scream, to command her to tell me. My breathing was so heavy that I turned my face away from the mouthpiece.

"At first I told him you were in a meeting and it was impossible for you to be interrupted. But then he became nasty, threatening to have me held in contempt for obstructing police business. And a murder at that, he stressed ... Mr. Douglas? Mr. Douglas, are you there? You're so ... you're so quiet."

"Yes, Cindy. Go on."

"I was frightened of him, frightened of what he might do to me. So I told him you left the office immediately upon their departure." After a period of silence, Cindy went on.

"He wanted to know if I knew where you had gone. I think this was a mistake on my part, Mr. Douglas, but as I already said, I was ... was extremely nervous. I told him that you had no appointments that I was aware of and that you left rather unexpectedly. I said that was not like you and that you didn't seem yourself. Your face was ashen, colorless, as if you had seen a ghost."

I remained silent, letting her exorcise her own demons.

"I couldn't lie to him, Mr. Douglas, could I? He is a policeman, after all. I was confused, so confused. Oh sir, I'm so sorry if I said something that may have cast any doubts about you. I truly am." Cindy was sobbing, her voice filled with anguish.

Was it only that morning since we had become part of this Kafkaesque tragedy? A tragedy that now appeared to have the potential to entangle each of us? For certain, I was not the same person I was then. Sadly, neither was Cindy.

The buzz of the lobby's intercom interrupted my reflections. Muttering more than speaking, I told Cindy to hang on, cutting off her acknowledgment to allow the incoming call through.

"Mr. Douglas," the doorman said, "there is a Detective Hopkins here to see you. He said that you would be expecting him."

Hopkins! He had come here, damn it! "Yes ... yes, Gilbert. He's correct. I was ... expecting him."

I switched back to my once-unflappable lady Friday. "Cindy, listen to me. You didn't do anything wrong. I understand why you did what you did. I'll see you in the office tomorrow, eight o'clock sharp." The doorbell chimed as the phone slid from my hand, Cindy's apologies fading.

Moving in slow motion through the foyer and gallery, I wished I had time to compose myself. I was still wishing for time when I opened the door and saw the smiling face of Detective Hopkins.

I forced a smile and tried to act surprised. The surprise was easier than the smile. "Oh, Detective Hopkins, please come in. I had just come in and was about to return your call when ... Well, here you are." Reentering the living room, I motioned for him to take a seat on the sofa.

"Can I get you something to drink?" I said, trying to act as if we were old friends.

"No, thanks," he replied curtly, confirming that we were not friends. His eyes gazed about the room, and he nodded his head in apparent appreciation. "Nice place you have here—nice block. Must have cost a pretty penny."

I nodded. "How can I be of assistance, Detective?"

His eyes met mine. "Why did you lie to me about the Ladillya woman?"

God knows I thought about that question that day after I ran out of my office—that question and a score of others. But mostly I thought about why she had been murdered. And what was she trying to tell me? And why that Kelso name and not Ladillya?

I fought to maintain my composure. "As unusual as this might sound to someone in your line of work, to answer you honestly, I really don't know." I could see by his widening eyes that my response was not expected. "I asked myself the same thing a hundred times this afternoon. I can only believe that it was the shock of hearing that name ... I hadn't heard it spoken in at least ten years or more, and the context in which it was introduced ... combined with some other unrelated business setbacks ..." Unable to complete my thought, I shrugged my shoulders and repeated my initial comment: "I really don't know."

"Really now, Mr. Douglas, you have to do better than that," Hopkins said sarcastically, the notebook reappearing in his hands. "I don't know, Detective Hopkins." He mimicked me in that affected whine of his and shook his head from side to side.

"Listen here, Detective Hopkins. What I just told you whether you believe it or not is the God's honest truth."

What I said next was something I had not said since the early years of my marriage to Katya.

"What I'm about to tell you will hopefully help you better understand why I did what I did. When you told me her name, I was stunned, as though I had been suddenly kicked in the stomach."

There was no reaction on his part, only the same silly-assed, closemouthed smile frozen on his face.

"Detective Hopkins, Maria Ladillya and I ... You have to understand, it was a long time ago." *Such a long time ago. The image of Maria's smiling face on the beach when I asked her the three questions filled my mind.* "We were going to be married. I haven't seen or heard from her in nearly ... since 1969," I said as Maria's image began to fade.

The insipid smile disappeared from Hopkins's face. "That's some admission, Mr. Douglas. I can tell you that's a new one on me." Hopkins hesitated. I wondered if he was deciding whether to offer condolences or to maintain his original remote-yet-cynical bearing. He surprised me with his answer.

"I guess I can kinda see why you might be shaken up at hearing this." He continued to stare at me. "Okay, I guess I can believe you, Mr. Douglas." Then he added his own version of a corporate disclaimer. "At least, let's say, for the time being. How about Kelso? I assume you know now that she and Ladillya were the same person."

"Yes." I dropped my eyes from his. "Cindy called and told me you informed her of that fact." Back in my office, I had wondered whether I should answer his questions without an attorney present. Up until then, I had dismissed that notion as just another paranoiac overreaction on my part. Upon further consideration, this seemed as good a time as any to ask Hopkins a few questions of my own.

"Detective Hopkins, please don't misunderstand me," I said cautiously, "but, I mean, what exactly is my status with you? With the police, I mean. Do I need a lawyer?"

"Mr. Douglas, I can't tell you what to do. If you feel or believe that you need an attorney, well, that certainly is your right. But if you're asking me if you're a suspect in this case, I learned a long, long time ago that everybody's a suspect until a conviction comes down." He smiled. It was the way someone smiled when he knew he had you where he wanted you.

"But like I just said," Hopkins went on, "I believe what you told me about why you lied. Strike that." He grinned, seemingly reveling in my discomfort. "Let's say instead that you didn't tell me all you knew about the deceased."

My sixth sense, which had been napping for a good part of the day, woke up and told me it was time to end this interrogation. I rose from my chair and, with as courteous a manner as I could muster, indicated that the session was over.

"Listen, Detective, this has been one helluva day. Would you mind? My corporate headquarters start their quarterly reviews on Wednesday, and, well, I really blew it today. I've got a ton of work that needs to be finished before I fly to Greenville, South Carolina, on Wednesday."

He looked at his watch. "Yeah, I guess you're right. It is later than I thought."

As we walked to the door, I knew I wouldn't be able to rest until I knew the answers to some of the questions I had been asking that day. Placing my hand on the doorknob, I turned to him.

"Detective Hopkins, I know this may not be important to you, but I loved Maria Ladillya at one time. Can you tell me anything about her? I mean, did she … Was she married?"

"Yeah, she was. We notified her husband, and he flew in from Paris a few hours ago. He's claiming the body and bringing it back for the funeral." His eyes narrowed. "That is, after we're finished with it."

Paris? Her husband? But then another thought hit me. It was so sudden that I spoke it before it could even take final form in my mind. "Her husband … maybe he knew something about this, perhaps what she was working on."

Hopkins nodded.

If I hadn't stopped him, if I hadn't asked him, the son of bitch would've never said a damn thing. I would have zero connection, zero understanding of what is happening.

Finally he broke the heavy silence. "Mr. Douglas, you just asked me about whether you needed a lawyer. Well, now I'll tell you my opinion. Take it as free advice. If I were you, I think I would talk to one." He removed my hand from the doorknob, opened the door, and crossed into the hallway.

"Oh yeah, one other thing. That was a good question you asked." He turned to face me. "Her husband did know what she was working on. He told us this afternoon when we met him at the airport. I think you'll find this interesting, Mr. Douglas." There was a smirk on his face. "You see, she was writing an article about big-business corruption. You know, what everyone refers to as white-collar crime— the so-called completely bloodless type where nobody gets killed. Or so that's what I've been told. Not at all like the cases I would normally find myself involved with."

All this was a prelude to his finale.

"Like I told you, Mr. Douglas, I would see a lawyer if I were in your shoes. You see, there was this one particular company she was focusing on. And guess what? You're a bright boy. You figured out that Kelso and Ladillya were one and the same—and without any phone call from your secretary."

He paused for a moment as if to let the effect of his words

penetrate. "So take a guess," he said, nodding his head as though urging me to comply, "which company it was that she was after."

I could only listen to his monologue.

"Well, as you said, it's late. See you around, Mr. Douglas."

Chapter 6

THAT NIGHT ALL I thought and dreamed about was Maria.

The year was 1963, and Maria and I were seniors at Baycity High School. It was a time when it was easy to be a kid, although, like most generations of high school kids, we weren't quite aware of that fact.

Maria had known since she was little girl that one day she would be working as either a big-city newspaper reporter or a freelance writer with some avant-garde magazine. Sometimes, when she was feeling especially good as we talked and dreamed about the future, she said she would write a book, be a novelist, and tell the world about our lives together and why we were special and would someday make a difference. But for me, outside of going to college, I wasn't at all certain of my life after graduation.

So Maria proposed her solution to my dilemma: "Why not write?" In her mind, she was coming to my rescue. She said that someday the two of us would not only be married but also make a great professional team. My steadiness of purpose would provide us with a regular income, enabling her to explore all sorts of fringe subjects. I kidded her that she would be covering the decline of European colonialism in what was then the Belgian Congo and I would be writing some mundane, do-it-yourself manual.

In reality, though, the odds were that I was going to get a degree in something more practical, such as economics, go to graduate school for my MBA, get a job with some corporation, marry Maria, and live happily ever after.

Maria, however, was not going to be denied. She was smart as a whip, and once she made up her mind about something, she was a five-foot-four, 105-pound ball of tenacity.

That's one of the reasons she was the class valedictorian. So I made a deal with her. For the next few months, I would write about anything and everything that came to my mind. We both agreed that if she felt I was a prospect at the end of that trial period, then I would treat journalism and economics as dual majors in college.

Well, the trial period flew by, and Maria was losing heart. She wasn't about to concede defeat, however. She had far too much riding on this bet. Well, as luck would have it—I believed in luck in those days—our fortunes changed. The change was not enough, as Maria had wished, for my future day job to be determined, but it was enough of a change for her to win the bet. "It was the Zapata change," Maria said whenever she would teasingly refer to it later.

I had entered a contest a few weeks earlier to write about the life of Taras Shevchenko, a famous Ukrainian poet and someone my grandparents revered as part of their Ukrainian heritage.

One Saturday in mid-May, after another great day at the Jersey Shore, Maria and I returned to my house for dinner. My dad spotted us in the driveway, broke into a huge grin, and shouted, "You won! You won!"

To my amazement, my essay on Shevchenko had come in second, which, in my dad's opinion, was the equivalent of winning. The $500 prize that came with it made him even more ecstatic, as that would cover a good part of my first semester's tuition.

I remembered Maria kissing me on the cheek, whispering in my ear, "I love you," and then swearing passionately, "Now we will be together forever and ever, my sweet, dearest Christof." She slid her head off my cheek, stared into my eyes, and said, "But this Shevchenko you wrote about, whoever he was—always understand that he was no Zapata."

I could still see her face.

Her greenish-brown eyes were aglow with life, her lips parted and moist as she continued to stare, as though examining my soul. I ignored this playful reference to one of her own national heroes and whispered, "I love you too, Maria. I will love you forever, my beautiful squirrel."

Years later, I would think of that day and recall it as one of our happiest. I didn't know then, none of us did, that we were on the brink of one of the greatest social upheavals our nation had ever faced and that all of us who were celebrating our newfound good fortune that day would find in the future, along with most Americans, that those happy days would never be the same.

*****

"She's got legs, and she knows how to use them!"

I twisted on the bed and stretched for the radio alarm, pressing the off button to halt ZZ Top before they could describe any other part of her anatomy. It was six thirty in the morning. I backtracked over the past forty-eight hours to determine which day of the week it was. I decided on Tuesday.

By the time I rolled into bed the night before, it must have been two o'clock. My aching head reminded me that I'd broken my agreement with it. I tried to sort out the images from last night into which were dreams and which were memories. Unable to distinguish between the two, I decided it didn't matter. Both were equally scary.

After a quick shower and shave, I was in the kitchen, wolfing down a second cup of coffee and knowing I had to call Katya. But what would I tell her? Could I honestly tell her that I was involved with a police murder case? One in which the victim just so happened to be someone I was once about to marry?

"Of course, Katya," I imagined myself saying, "you know who she is—was. Why, it's my old fiancée, Maria. The girl I was in love with before I met you." How about that for openers?

Then I could toss in for good measure, "The funny thing about the whole situation is that she may have been killed because she was digging up some dirt on the company I work for. Can you imagine that?"

Adding the pièce de résistance, I could say, "Oh, I almost forgot. This is for your ears only, but not to worry, I'm certain the truth will eventually come out and your husband will be exonerated. It seems there's this one sticky detail with the NYPD and their silly suspicion that I might have something to do with this whole mess."

Not knowing what to say to Katya, I rationalized that it was a bit early for her to be up.

Fine, I'll call her from the office later.

Fifteen minutes later, as I was leaving the apartment, the telephone rang. I lifted the phone from its cradle.

"Chris? Chris, is that you? Are you all right?"

Uncertain how to respond to her question, I ignored it. "Oh ... Kat? I was just about to call you. I didn't want to wake you, though." I tried to control the flow of the conversation. "By the way, where were you last evening? I called around seven, and there was no answer."

The concern faded from her voice. "Libby and I went out for dinner. We drove up to the Highlands to Doris and Ed's."

After the past few days, it was easy to read things into what was said. I was becoming, as Slaus would say, "a flaming, certifiable, paranoid cuckoo." Still, there was such a thing as a too-pat alibi, wasn't there? Disappointed at this newly discovered mistrust, I eased my conscience and told her everything.

Almost everything.

"That's nice; I hope you had a good time," I began. "Listen, Katya, I, ah ... Well, there is something crazy—something terribly disturbing—that happened to me yesterday."

Her tone reverted to her original one of concern. "What is it, Chris? What happened?"

Why did I sense that I had altered her intended, perhaps even rehearsed, conversation? I gathered my courage; I found what I was about to say difficult. God, it was difficult.

We both knew it was over between us at that moment.

"Remember the gal who called my office Friday—Kelso?"

The sound of her heavy breathing quickened. "Yes. Yes, I do."

"Well, what can I say? She was murdered over the weekend. And the police came to see me about it yesterday at the office."

"Murdered? The police? Christof ... Christof, that is horrible. But ... but what have you to do with any of this this?"

Conscience be damned! There was no way I could bring Katya

into this situation beyond what was necessary—not now, anyway. There would be time later when we were alone, but not now.

So I slipped further down that slippery slope.

"Nothing, of course," I answered, bending the truth. "She called my office on Friday," I went on, now breaking it, "the same way she had been calling other businesses, trying to arrange an interview with whatever key executives she could for the story she was writing."

When the time was right and I told her the truth, I could only hope Katya would understand why I couldn't tell her at that moment.

I continued. "The police found my office number in the telephone records of the hotel where she was staying, and, well, they wanted"—I forced a laugh in order to downplay the seriousness of it all—"to question me about whether I knew her."

I was a little surprised at what Katya asked next. It didn't seem to be the response a wife would have when told her husband was not a suspect in some murder investigation.

"What did you tell them?" She repeated her question, this time with a bit more incredulity in her voice, as if she were softening the perception of any hardness. "I mean," she said, stumbling over her words, "was that the only reason she was calling you? To get an interview?"

Each question she asked made it that much more difficult for me to extricate myself, as well as for her to forgive me for my lies. "Katya, all I can tell you is what the police told me. She was calling because she was some kind of reporter, and she was working on some book or article on corporate America. And she had a list of executives and was contacting them in order to interview them for whatever she was writing." I paused to let what I'd said sink in and then added, hoping to terminate this misbegotten conversation, "Anyway, that's what they think."

"What happens now?" she asked. "Does this have any effect on your South Carolina trip?"

Glad to be past the subject of Maria, my tone became lighter in spite of my deception. "That's the first question I can give you a factual answer to. No, it doesn't. Actually, Kat, I need to get to the office pronto to finish my presentation for the DFT headquarters brass."

I had one last hurdle to overcome.

"Oh, Chris, one other thing I almost forgot," Katya said as soon as I finished. "Cindy called yesterday evening and left a message on the answering machine for you to call her."

I had forgotten about that call. But with all the practice I'd had the past few days—shamefully so, I thought to myself—I was getting quite good at lying. But I didn't want to think of it as lying. I preferred a less-damaging description: fencing with the truth. So I dismissed Cindy's call as insignificant.

"Cindy, oh yeah. She called here also. No big deal. She got a little confused about something I asked her to do for my trip. You know, after the police and all quizzing us about—" I caught myself in time. *Which name was I about to utter?* "Anyway, I spoke to her later in the evening from the office. Everything's taken care of."

Katya sounded confused. "Chris, I hope there is no ... You know what I'm trying to say ... no real problem."

With all my heart and soul, I loved Katya.

"Kat, listen." My voice became softer and much more relaxed as the image of the smiling, beautiful woman from our early days together floated through my thoughts. "I have loved you since the moment we met. You know that." I began to trip over my words. "It's just ... I guess it's just ...I guess what I'm trying to say is that a lot of things are going on right now. What with the company and all."

I stopped and turned away from the phone to regain my composure.

I couldn't.

"Katya, listen, I really have to go. We'll talk more about this later."

I could always sense when Katya was about to cry.

"Chris ... tof," she sobbed, her voice breaking.

I breathed hard, my face again away from the mouthpiece, my eyes tightly shut as I waited for her to say something besides my name.

There was deadening silence.

"Yes. Yes," she said at last in halfhearted agreement. "You're right. I guess ... Yes, we'll have to talk later."

I heard the high-pitched humming of the disconnected telephone line.

It was some time before I put the phone down.

Chapter 7

WHEN I ENTERED MY office, I was surprised to not see Cindy there. I began sorting out my mail from the stack of papers on her desk. After a momentary detour to make a pot of coffee, I sat behind my desk and searched each page of the *Times*, *Post*, and *Daily News* for any information on Maria's murder. All I could find was a paragraph or two recapping what had occurred. The phone interrupted me as I was finishing my search.

"Chris, good morning." It was Marilyn Usher, assistant VP of human resources.

"Good morning, Marilyn. What's up?" I stuffed the newspapers into the wastebasket.

"I just wanted to let you know that Cindy called and said she won't be coming in due to illness."

Damn, that's not like her. She's never out. And why didn't she call me directly?

"Did she say what was wrong? It's not like her to miss a day."

"Not really. Just that she was, in her words, 'a tad under the weather' and would probably be out for the next few days. If you don't have any objection, I'll have Rose from legal come up and sit in until Cindy gets back."

"Sure, whatever." I wondered if Cindy were really sick.

I spent the morning with Lieber, finalizing my presentation for corporate. I also spoke to Andy, who was at our San Francisco station, about whether he'd heard anything further on the Great Air negotiations. He hadn't. As for the Geo Computer contract that had shown up on my desk the previous day, he was as much in the dark as I was.

"It didn't pass my desk," he said when I told him how I'd found it, sans tags and all. "That's pretty sloppy work. Whose initials are on it from my department?"

"Good question. Let me find the file." My eyes scanned the top of my desk for the folder. After I spent a few frustrating moments looking through each desk drawer and the wastebasket, in case it had been tossed by mistake, and mistakenly calling for Cindy for help, I gave up.

"No matter, Chris. I'll find out when I speak to my secretary," Andy offered before we ended our discussion.

The first thing I asked Cindy's replacement to do when she arrived was to track Weitzer down. After checking with a number of people, she told me no one had heard from him since his voice mail yesterday. He was really on my nerves now.

Although I couldn't concentrate as well as I would have liked on the DFT presentation data, with thoughts bursting into my head about Maria and Katya, my submergence into the various charts and reports was a welcome distraction. I didn't realize how much of a distraction it was until, at precisely 12:15, Cindy's stand-in poked her head into my office, looking nervous.

"A Mr. Paulson is on the telephone, Mr. Douglas. An extremely irritated Mr. Paulson," she timidly announced. "He says he has been waiting for you at Le Bernardin since eleven fifty."

With all that had been going on, I'd completely forgotten about Billy. I jerked the phone from its cradle, and before even placing it to my ear, I could hear his four-lettered tirade.

"Whoa. Slow down, Billy," I broke in. "I'm on my way. I'm on my way."

"Goddammit, Christof," he snorted. "You better get your sorry ass down here ASAP. You hear me, trooper? ASAP!" I heard him slam the phone down.

Despite the chaos of the past few days, I had to smile. I told Lieber to take a break and meet me back in the office around three, and I was out the office door before she had a chance to protest.

Weaving my way through the heavy lunch-hour traffic, I hailed a cab and thought about Billy Paulson. I could not describe our relationship, nor give it the justice it deserved, for to simply say we were old friends would lose everything in the translation.

We had been introduced to one another under the most severe of human conditions in the hell known as Vietnam. But it was how we met that perhaps was more important than where.

Along with Katya, William Paulson III shared the dubious honor of having saved my life. And, whereas Katya's claim to me was more spiritual, Paulson's was as fundamental as it got, as he'd literally ridden in on his white charger to snatch me from the jaws of death.

The helicopter I was flying in was an OH-13B, or Loach, the nickname for a light observation helicopter. We were looking for the enemy, just as we had been for the last eleven months, in a place called the A Shau Valley, near the Laotian border. And to the best of our knowledge, that enemy was no longer just Viet Cong troops but also some elite regiments of the North Vietnamese regular army.

The OH-13B weighed less than three thousand pounds; it was light and maneuverable and perfect for this objective. Its identifying, distinctive feature was the plastic bubble that enclosed the two-man crew. Its main drawback for the pilot and copilot, or forward spotter, was that it was effectively defenseless. All that separated the occupants from a well-aimed, armor-piercing AK-47 round was less than half an inch of "not quite good enough," as we sometimes joked, steel beneath the seats.

One day our ticket was punched when we took a number of rounds to the engine, killing it. After doing his best, auto-rotating the dying propellers to slow our fall, my friend Dickie Lake was killed when we slammed into the ground. I was more fortunate, suffering a dislocated shoulder, a fractured ankle, and various odd lacerations over my face and body, including a six-inch gash running across my upper cheek and forehead.

The cacophony of Midtown traffic snapped me out of the unforgettable nightmares. As I shook my head, visions of Dickie Lake as he lay dead in my arms gave way to the sounds of the horns and cars stuck on Broadway. My cab had moved only a few blocks since I had gotten in. I paid the driver and bolted from the car, the sweat pouring from my body. It was 12:40 when I arrived at the Equitable Life Building on Fifty-First Street.

When I passed through its revolving doors, all thoughts from the past were gone and I was transported into one of the more elegant restaurants the civilized world could offer. I announced myself to the maître d', who smiled at me with that all-too-familiar look that insinuated, "Your party has been here for some time. He's just ordered his third double martini, monsieur," and he motioned for me to follow him.

We were no more than twenty-five feet from our destination when I heard the raspy voice.

"Jesus, Douglas. It's about time."

The maître d' ignored the disturbed stares of the surrounding crowd and slid my chair from the table and handed me the menu.

Billy took advantage of our arrival by ordering another round of drinks. "Monsieur, un autre Absolut martini, s'il vous plaît. Et tu, mon ami? La meme chose?" His prior army duties, and now his position with Air France, required him to remain fluent in French. I ordered a glass of the house Australian chardonnay.

As soon as our host departed, Billy switched to English to read me the riot act. To my relief, he did so in an appropriate manner for the plush and gentile environs—controlled and understated. To the tony pair sitting a few feet from our table, he could have been explaining the latest theater opening. Two minutes later, all was forgiven.

"So now tell me, Chris. What was so important that you kept your old buddy waiting for almost an hour? I hope she was worth it."

His last remark was said totally in jest. He knew that I was faithful to Katya. I believed he was even slightly envious of our marriage.

I laughed off his wisecrack and was about to say something in kind, but my spirit for this sort of byplay wasn't there.

We spent the following minutes catching up, exchanging the most current family and career news. Billy, who was senior vice president of operations, or some such title—he would always give me a different business card with a different title and address whenever

I asked him for one—traveled extensively, more so since his divorce the previous year. Travel agreed with him. While I was beginning to show evidence of wear and tear, he looked the same as he had when we'd last met and still maintained the same 180-pound, six-foot frame that he'd carried with him in Southeast Asia.

"Exercise and proper diet," he boasted, bursting into laughter as the waiter set down another vodka martini.

We saw each other three or four times a year when his business brought him from France. We usually met over lunch between travel connections to his primary DC destination. We tried our best to stay in touch by phone or by mail, and I received some form of correspondence from him from some remote or desolate spot on the globe once or twice a month. Only in my current mental state could I have completely overlooked our luncheon engagement.

We paused in our conversation just long enough to order lunch. His flight schedule didn't leave us a lot of time, and he was leaving for the airport directly from Le Bernardin. Billy ordered for both of us because he was familiar with the specialties of the chef after dining at his three-star Parisian restaurant.

While he ordered, I debated what I should reveal to him as much as I'd debated what to reveal to Katya. My desire for his advice, specifically as it related to hiring an attorney, outweighed any reservations I had concerning his involvement. Most importantly, I believed I could trust him without creating any conflicts in his loyalties. That was the reason I hadn't asked Andy, even though he had the right legal connections to assess my circumstances.

"Billy, I have a favor to ask of you," I probed discreetly as soon as the waiter disappeared. "The thing is, I'm not quite sure how big a favor it may turn out to be. But I need … I guess what I'm really trying to say is that I know I can trust you."

He hesitated only as a long as it took to place his martini aside. He stared into my eyes, his jaw tightening ever so negligibly. "What is it, Chris? What do you need?"

Had I any doubts that would be Bill Paulson's response?

I reminded myself of Cindy and her rambling, circumstantial narration to the NYPD as I divulged everything.

Billy listened. On occasion, he asked a question or nodded in understanding, but mainly he just listened. Through the first course of oysters and then through the monkfish entrée, pausing only when I needed to swallow, I revealed everything. By the time the waiter brought coffee an hour later, I had finished my tale.

"Well, there it is. What do think?" I said by way of summation. His reaction was not what I wanted to hear.

"What do I think?" he said, sounding like a loud echo. "What I think is that you're in some deep shit! Hell yes." His voice drew a nasty glance from a couple sitting nearby. "You need to damn well see a lawyer ASAP!" He bent forward; his arms rested on the table, and his left hand waved the waiter away when he appeared with the dessert menu. "Look, let's go down the list of what your problems are."

I nodded.

"For openers, I think it was a mistake—a bad mistake—not to tell Katya everything. Frankly, Chris, I'm really confused why you didn't."

How could I explain something I couldn't understand, or perhaps didn't really want to understand? "Billy, this may surprise you, but I'm not sure why either," I answered. I was thinking aloud more than explaining as I continued. "Partly, I believe I did it to protect her. And I guess to protect myself also. Maybe it was—still is," I corrected myself, "a form of protection from having memories from an unpleasant period played back. And partly, well, let me say it this way …"

It then occurred to me that what I was about to say had never been spoken. I had successfully suppressed it, as Slaus would have said.

"One of my problems—mine and Katya's," I corrected myself, almost embarrassed, feeling that I was making a habit of correcting myself. I hesitated, deciding on what exactly to say, staring at him uncomfortably.

For an instant, I didn't recognize who I was looking at.

The moment passed, and my nerve returned equally as fast.

"Well, what I'm about to tell you … I … Well, I would really appreciate it, Bill, if we could just let it pass. Move forward, okay?"

He nodded.

"Katya and I are having some problems." I dropped my eyes and watched my fingers swirl a spoon around my half-empty coffee cup. "We seem to be going through some very difficult times."

Neither of us spoke. I wasn't sure how long we were silent, but it couldn't have been as long as it seemed. His eyes narrowed in a way that made me feel, once again, as if I were looking into his face for the first time. He started to speak, apparently reconsidered, and closed his mouth. The muscles in his jaw clenched and re-clenched, his eyes never dropping from mine. I could tell he was angry. He was very angry—as angry as I could ever remember without physical danger threatening.

Finally he let out a heavy, defeated sigh, and with it, the tension that hung in the air dissipated as well.

"Whatever you say, Chris." A thin, pained smile took shape across his lips. "I understand. I'm one of the few people in the world who knew how much Maria meant to you. I …" He seemed unable to finish his thought and shifted his gaze. It felt as though he were looking at everything else in the room other than me. "What can I say? I hope everything …"

We moved on to my other problem.

"Okay, as I see it," he said, his tone resuming that earlier, cut-to-the-chase style, "your real trouble is that you lied to the police about Maria. Maybe you didn't mean to, but trust me, they don't like being lied to. Any doubts they may have had flew out the window when you bolted from your office right after they mentioned Maria's name to you. The question they're asking themselves as we speak is why. No matter what that detective, the one who showed up at your apartment, said about believing why you reacted the way you did."

I started to answer, wanting to defend myself, but the combination of his hand gesturing for me to remain quiet and not knowing what to say stopped me.

"And the connection between her and the DFT exposé, or whatever the hell you want to call it, points to you or someone in DFT as having motive. Circumstantial, I grant you," he said, shaking his open hand in a motion that seemed to convey 'maybe yes, maybe no.' "But one that clearly leaves a trail leading to someone like you."

He sipped his coffee. A disgusted expression appeared on his face. "Cold," he said, and he set the cup back on the table and continued.

"All this is as obvious as the nose on your face. What bothers me is that something or someone is bugging that cop who came to see you last night. Look, let's assume the police are not telling you everything, okay—like whoever else they may have talked to, what other notes or phone calls they may have traced, et cetera."

He stopped for a moment, but I didn't have any comments to make. After the brief silence, he resumed where he'd left off.

"I can't say I'm an expert on internal police matters, but don't you think it unusual that only one of those detectives met with you? Or that he badgered your secretary about her obstruction of justice when he called for you? Seems to me that's pretty strong stuff. Even more so when you consider the people he's dealing with here. We're not talking some low-life, two-bit street thug. Unless … unless …" He seemed unable to complete his thought and shifted back to original admonition.

"I don't like it, Chris. I don't like anything about it. It's like when I would go out on patrol and something didn't sit quite right." He shook his head as if to exorcise the haunting memories and return to the present. "You need to see a lawyer before this goes any further and escalates, and not some wimpy corporate type either."

I offered no reaction to his comments, though I had the same worried sense about everything that he'd said.

"Chris? Did you hear me? Do you know someone? If not, I know just the right guy."

"Okay, if you know someone, I'll go with him," I answered, trying my best to be positive. "Sounds good. How do you know him?"

"It's a long story, but the gist of it is that we were implicated last year on some nasty drug bust. Some Air France personnel here in New York were convicted for being tied in with heroin smugglers operating out of Marseille. Reginald Roquette — don't underestimate him by his name," he interjected when I started to smirk. "Likes to be called RR. He's as tough as nails, cleared us completely of any involvement. And he knows all the right people in the New York criminal system."

He checked his watch and signaled our waiter for the bill.

"Look, I've got to be going," he said. "Why don't I call him as we're leaving?"

'What else do I have to lose?' I thought.

That was the next step to my destiny.

Billy picked up the tab, annoyed that I attempted to pay. "When you're in Paris, it'll be your turn. Anyway, this is cheap by comparison."

I followed Billy from the table amid exaggerated "Merci, messieurs" from the restaurant staff and walked past the glass-enclosed kitchen to the public telephones. A few minutes later, Billy gave me a thumbs-up sign from inside the phone booth. After a few minutes, he emerged, smiling.

"You owe me big time, pal," he said, pleased with his success. "I explained the urgency of the situation, apologizing for such short notice, to get him to agree to see you at his office at six-thirty tonight." He grinned. "Of course, it doesn't hurt your cause any that we pay him a few million a year retainer." He scribbled the lawyer's name and address on the back of a matchbook and handed it to me.

We hailed a taxi as soon as were on the sidewalk. Billy turned to me, and although his mood was subdued, I could tell he was trying to offer encouragement. "Listen, everything will work out. Trust your old buddy. I'll call you tomorrow from Washington to find out how your meeting with Roquette went."

He placed his hands on my shoulders. "I just want to say again that I'm sorry, Chris. I remember many of the things you told me about Maria and how you felt about her."

I tried to express what I was feeling. "I know you are, Bill. I thank you now as I thanked you then." That was all I could say.

He tugged himself away and got in the cab, shutting the door behind him. He peered through the closed window, his features distorted by the shadows cast by the surrounding skyscrapers. It seemed as though his face were attempting to remember something he had forgotten. He rolled down the window, the pain still in his face.

"I'm sorry about this, Chris—and Katya too" were the last words I heard.

Chapter 8

I KNEW I HAD to meet with Mr. Reginald Roquette, but this time, unlike yesterday, I returned to my office to finalize my presentation with Lieber. I was pleased to find everything ready to go. Thanking Lieber, I reviewed it one last time and approved it for transmission to corporate. We wrapped up around six o'clock, and I left to meet with Roquette.

His office was on Park and Fiftieth in one of the ultramodern glass skyscrapers that lined both sides of the avenue along that stretch of Midtown. I got off the elevator at the forty-fourth floor and was buzzed into the law firm's anteroom. After introducing myself, I was whisked into counsel's private chambers.

Roquette was on the phone, nodding repeatedly and murmuring, "Hmmm." He motioned for me to sit in one of the two black, leather Breuer chairs in front of his desk.

Before I had a chance to study the high-tech, expensive surroundings, he was off the phone. He walked around his desk and shook my hand. "Reginald Rouqette," he barked. "Call me RR. And you're early."

I rose from my chair, but he didn't allow me the time to introduce myself. "Don't get up," he said curtly, and he walked back behind his desk.

I ignored his invitation to address him by a pair of stupid initials. I remained standing, my hands curling involuntarily into fists as they somehow found themselves resting on his desk.

"Listen here, Mr. Roquette. If my appointment with you is

inconvenient, I understand. Just tell me right now, and that way we won't waste my time or yours."

He smirked and raised his hands, palms opened in my direction. "Nothing personal, Mr. Douglas," he said, and then he sprang back into that short and not-so-sweet manner of his. "Bill Paulson briefed me this afternoon on what he called your circumstances, but why don't you tell me in your own words?"

I debated for a second whether to say the hell with it and walk out; however, instead I sat down and worked at overcoming the negative transfer I felt toward him. Calming myself, for the next fifteen minutes, I recited everything that had happened, including my old relationship with Maria. Roquette said nothing, nor did he take any notes. Finally I finished.

"I think the most important thing I can do right now, Mr. Douglas," he said after some seconds of uncomfortable silence, "is to determine your exact status with the police. They haven't charged you with anything, so I believe Hopkins was on a fishing expedition when he went to your apartment. Let's say, he wanted to see if you knew more than you had originally told him."

He shook his head in a way that reminded me of Hopkins.

"No, he knew you knew more. You knew who Ladillya was. He just didn't know how you knew her. But that's all water over the dam. I need to make a few calls and find out where the police are in this case. Make sure you call me tomorrow." He rose from his chair; apparently our meeting was over. "Around five. Hopefully I'll have something by then."

I remained seated, uncomfortable at this ending. "That's it? That's all?"

He walked toward the door. "Yep, that's it." As if noticing my discomfort, he added, "Look, don't sweat the small stuff. There's no sense in planning anything until we know what we're up against. Capisce?"

I left Roquette's office more dejected than when I had entered, and continued up Park until I reached Sixty-Fourth Street. I crossed over to Madison, not stopping when I passed the Plaza Diana Hotel. This time, I just glared at it and walked back to the apartment.

I was disappointed to find no messages from Katya. I automatically keyed our number, only to hang up in frustration once I heard the pompous ass who answered. That recording had to be changed the minute I got back. It didn't sound like me at all.

Some time later, having showered, changed into a fresh polo and jeans, and finished pecking at the sandwich I had picked up from the local deli, I redialed.

Damn it. I really had to change that stupid message. This time I left word that I had called and then slammed the phone down. It was almost eight o'clock. She was probably out having dinner. This instinctive justification excusing her absence was immediately overlaid by an uneasy, more emotional thought—who was she with?

I struggled not to fall into that trap and poured myself a cognac. I tried to concentrate on my notes for the next day's meetings but couldn't, as I found myself less and less focused on what I was reading. Forget it! I'll work on the plane, I thought, stuffing my notes into my briefcase before any other voices disagreed.

When Beth was murdered, there were two things I did to maintain my sanity. The first was flinging myself into my career, and, well, we know where that got me. The second was embracing my love and deep appreciation for music. For me, music was meant to be a personal, almost meditative experience. Time and again, either when I was away on business in an empty hotel room or when I came home and Katya was asleep, I gained an inner peace in listening.

As the years passed and the cold, icy, blue intensity of Beth's tragedy somehow began to blur around the edges, like some indirect mathematical correlation, my fixation for this form of contemplation grew equally. There were days, though, when this need grew exponentially. This was one of those days.

I refilled my cognac and walked over to the stereo and selected a Mozart CD. Turning off the ceiling chandelier, I stretched my body across the living-room sofa. Its bewitchment worked at once. I was captured in the web that the beautifully melodic violin concerto was weaving and began to drift through time and memories.

*****

Maria had just received a scholarship to Columbia. I could still see her mother's face smiling, her eyes sparkling as they filled with tears of pride at her daughter's success. Maria had tears in her eyes also, for in spite of her general self-assurance, there was a vulnerability to her that anyone she allowed to get close to her would discover.

In those days, I spent much of my life at Maria's house, initially because her brother, Tony, and I played on the high school basketball team and would practice there together after school. But after a while, as Maria and I got to know each other, our romance began and I went to her house to be with her.

Gradually, as we began to open up to each other, sharing our ideas, feelings, and future dreams, we drew closer until, by the end of our senior year, we believed we would be married.

When I got older, as the years all too rapidly sped by, I would look back and reflect, more often than not in sadness, at the summer between our high school graduation and our freshman year in college, now knowing that it was to be our happiest.

That summer, I dubbed Maria with her nickname, Squirrel. The name Ladillya was close to the Spanish word for squirrel, which is la ardilla. It was on the beach at Point Pleasant one July afternoon that I asked her to marry me. She kissed me passionately on the lips, her tanned arms draped around my neck, and accepted with the whispered proviso that we wait until our graduation from college.

She was wearing my school ring, but I also gave her a special jade ring that day. It was the ring my father had given my mother before he was shipped overseas during World War II, which she gave to me when I was certain about Maria. I promised to buy an engagement ring from Tiffany's as soon as I had the money, but we both knew the wonderful and loving sentiment that was attached to my gesture that day.

Things remained the same between us through our junior years in college. There was, however, one unwelcome harbinger of some future collisions.

I was enrolled in Saint Peter's voluntary Reserve Officers' Training Corps program, or ROTC. I enrolled not because I was some gung-ho GI Joe but because it provided a reduction in tuition that, in my dad's eyes, was sizable.

Whenever I tried to remember the dollar difference between

participating and not, I became confused. And how sizeable the reduction was became insignificant in retrospect.

Maria and I talked about my enrollment, at times heatedly, and she made it clear that she wouldn't accept my participation in the military. My dad, on the other hand, told me, "If you don't, then go ahead and come up with tuition yourself." It was settled when Tony, who was in his school's Air Force ROTC, cast the deciding vote in my favor. Under the weight of the three closest males in her life, Maria begrudgingly gave in.

I conceded to her, though, that before graduating and raising my right arm to swear acceptance as an officer in the United States Army, we would revisit the subject.

While this internal family debate was going on, Columbia was becoming a hotbed of anti-status-quo activities. For Maria, that fell right in line with her way of looking at the world. She was always involved with some demonstration or some rally. I agreed with her on most issues; I just wasn't as vocal.

Vietnam wasn't yet the centerpiece of the nation's unrest. It was just beginning to spill over onto the front pages and appear on the evening television news as American boys began to be drafted in larger numbers. But this was 1965. It was much too early for most of us to see what was lurking on the horizon.

Finally, 1967 came, and I had to make a number of critical decisions. I had run out of time and was faced with the choice of whether or not to reject my commission and deal with the heavy personal baggage that decision would carry with it—the repayment of past monies bestowed and the loss of my dad's respect. Such a choice might also lessen my chances of landing a decent job in corporate America. All of that played in my mind. As for the prospect of becoming some future Hemingway, well, let's just say it was, by mutual agreement, put on hold in favor of my economic studies. Maria could accept this latter setback but not the military. She was adamant.

"There is no way," she would threaten, "that I would ever marry someone who was in the United States Army!" In spite of her protests that "It might as well be for a lifetime," I eventually got her to acknowledge that it wasn't.

"It'll just be two years," I said, and I convinced her somehow that it would be over in the wink of an eye.

Adding fuel to the fire, 1967 was not 1965 when it came to Southeast Asia. The country was beginning to stagger under the weight of the casualty count the nightly news brought home each evening. It was a period that many considered to be not unlike the war between the states, with the nation's divisiveness serving as the common denominator.

And the Ladillya family was hit as hard as anyone.

Maria and Tony were estranged from one another. He was now an F-5A pilot, flying missions over the DMZ. Maria, meanwhile, had become assistant editor of *The Lion*, Columbia's radically left-wing student paper. With each publication, it seemed she would turn up the intensity level, increasing the vitriol of her language and its hard-edged assault against the war, Washington, and just about anyone who didn't agree with her version of the world.

I was an enigma to her. We still loved each other, make no mistake, and for the most part, we still agreed on most things, although not as strongly as before. Yet there was that one ominous black cloud hanging over us.

"Why?" she would plead. "Why don't you just dump all those John Wayne wannabes?" Maria would go on for hours in the hope of convincing me and saving us.

She knew more than I did where we were headed.

I tried to explain that it wasn't that simple. If I reneged on my contract with the army, I would be disinherited from my family. And, anyway, I would tell her, I wasn't cut out to be a rebel. I had neither the financial resources to attend graduate school nor a grant like she did for her graduate studies.

Ultimately, we reached an uneasy compromise.

"Okay, okay. Go and play soldier, repay your debt, and keep the peace in your family," she said dejectedly. "When you get out in two years, we'll get married. I'll think of you as a prisoner of war. That's how I'll survive. You'll be a POW taken captive by the country's special interests." To underscore her commitment, she agreed to continue to wear the jade ring as a symbol of our love. I was counting on the next two years going as swiftly as the last two. I prayed that before we knew it, we would be able to resume our lives and our dreams.

I prayed then. I was so, so naive. Maria and I would never be the same.

We did our best to spend the summer as we always had—together and at the shore. And there were flashes—brilliant and vivid flashes—when it was obvious that the old spark was there. We knew we would always care for each other and that she loved me as I loved her. Both of us swore that we would love one another forever.

"Until there are no longer poinsettias in this world," she whispered early one morning as we lay in one another's arms, watching a beautiful sunrise.

In September, when Maria went on to graduate school at Columbia, I was called up for active duty. For the next six months I was stationed in the south: eight weeks at Fort Benning, Georgia, and then four-plus months at Fort Rucker, Alabama, to be trained in my military occupational specialty, or MOS, as a helicopter forward air observer.

During those months, Maria and I wrote each other daily. Anyone who read one of our syrupy love letters would think that we were two twenty-two-year-olds hopelessly in love.

Before I went overseas, I was able to return home for a week on leave. Sadly, it was not a great homecoming. Most of the time, we argued, as neither of us wanted to admit to the frightful reality ahead. I remembered that we talked or argued about everything under the sun except the place I was being sent. We ignored it, as if saying "Vietnam" aloud would bring some ancient curse hurtling down upon our vulnerable heads.

My mom and dad gave a going-away party that week.

At the end of the evening, my dad gave an emotional toast for my safe and quick return. My mom broke down and left the room.

I will always remember as long as I'm alive the image of Maria staring at me.

When we were alone later, Maria's huge green eyes began to moisten, and teardrops silently fell onto her cheeks as her mouth slowly, soundlessly formed her words: "Don't go, Christof! Don't ever leave me!"

Maria cried that night in my arms.

*****

Whirrrrrrrr. Whirrrrrrrr.

In the eerie stillness of the apartment, the sound of the CD player attempting and then reattempting, in buzzing futility, to reseat one of the discs came as an intruder.

As I listened to the empty repetitiveness of that sound, it brought home the loneliness that now filled my life. I slowly lifted my body from the couch and shut the stereo off. In the partially lit room, I saw the iridescent green numerals 10:45 blink from the front of the stereo. Rubbing my eyes with the heels of my hands, I moved unsteadily into the bathroom; my body had not returned from my mind's journey in time.

A few more minutes went by. I remained motionless. My arms tenuously kept me upright as I stood over the bathroom sink, my thoughts racing in angry conflict over what to do. I studied my image in the mirror; it seemed I had aged ten years in the past few days.

Once upon a time, long ago—*Isn't that the way the fairy tales always begin?*—I would have known what to do. In those earlier days, it was easy. Katya appeared. The sound of her voice would overcome any emptiness, any depression I felt. Envisioning those memories, hearing her voice in my head, I moved toward the telephone. My heart raced faster when I keyed our number, realizing what a mistake I had made by not being with her these past two evenings.

After four rings, my recording came on. As I waited for the insufferable message to end, my eyes clamping tighter and tighter with each word, I crossed my fingers in the hope that she was there and just screening her calls. When I heard the beep, I opened my eyes and spoke with an urgency I'd thought I was no longer capable of.

"Katya, it's me—Christof!" I pleaded. "If you're there, please pick up. I need ... I must talk to you!"

I heard only the nothingness that one hears when listening to the airless vacuum traveling from one's ear to some distant receiver miles away. I broke the silence with a loud sigh. "Okay ... Okay. I was just calling, Katya, to tell you I love you. I miss you. I shouldn't have stayed in the apartment. I should have asked you to come with me."

I whispered, "I love you."

The following morning around six, I reached for the telephone. Not really able to sleep, I had been up and watching the sunrise, pacing the apartment for the prior thirty minutes. Taking a prolonged sip from my second cup of coffee, I listened impatiently and counted the number of rings aloud.

"Hel-hello? Who is it?" Katya's garbled voice confirmed that I had awakened her.

I spoke our names into the phone. "Katya, it's me, Christof." This time it was my turn to ask yesterday's question. "Are you … Is everything okay?" I said, spitting the suddenly sour-tasting coffee from my mouth and tossing the balance of the cup into the sink. I could hear the sheets rustling, and I imagined her shifting in our bed to a more comfortable, upright position.

"Oh, Chris, it's you. What did you say?" Her voice grew steadier as she spoke. "I dropped the phone and didn't hear everything you said. What's okay?"

"I asked if you were okay. I called you a number of times yesterday evening. The last time it was almost eleven. When did you get home?"

"Oh?" I heard another "Oh?" This one was a bit softer and away from the mouthpiece. "I must have come right after that call. Must have just missed it. I didn't exactly look at the clock." She added, "I was in bed by midnight. Fell dead to the world the instant my head hit the pillow."

"At least one of us got some sleep. Why didn't you call me? Didn't you get my message? I was worried sick about you." Before she had an opportunity to reply, I repeated myself. This time I wanted her sympathy rather than to make a point. "I couldn't sleep a wink, Kat. Why didn't you call me?"

Katya's response gave little satisfaction. Her voice sounded very tired, her manner almost mechanical. "Chris, it was late—far too late. So I decided not to return your call. And, anyway, as I just said, I was completely exhausted."

Since she did not voluntarily offer information about where she had been until such a late hour, or with whom, I posed the question we both had been avoiding. "Is it requesting too much of you to ask you to tell me what you did last evening?" As soon as the words were out of my mouth, I realized they sounded harsher that I'd wanted.

Katya was not the type of person who usually chose to be quick with a remark that was intended to hurt. In truth, she was by nature considerate, if not understanding and kind. What I heard from her was not normal. I was stunned by the intensity of her response when she spoke.

"No, Christof, it's not. But, quite honestly, if you were home … If you elected to be here with me," she answered, her voice rising as she drew out her words, exaggerating them as though she were lecturing some first-year foreign-exchange student, "these past few evenings, you wouldn't have to ask."

This was not how I wanted this conversation to go. Unhappily, I realized that whenever we talked lately, this was invariably how it went.

"But since you asked," Katya angrily continued, "I was over at Libby's. She was having a small, rather intimate party, and at the last minute—since you were away, Christof—she invited me."

I wished I weren't leaving for Greenville. I wished I were on my way back to Sea Isle.

I wished …

Katya wouldn't stop. "And guess what, Christof? I had a really great time. A really super, wonderful, fun-filled time. No arguments. No disputes on what I said, or why, or how I said it."

Her voice began to drift, as though her thoughts were a thousand miles from me, but the pain behind her words somehow remained.

"For the first time in a long, long time—too long, Christof—I was … God, Chris, it's been too—"

I interrupted her before she could complete her unspoken sentiment, a sentiment I could not bear to hear. "Katya, listen to me. I'll be home tomorrow night. As soon as I get back from Greenville, we can talk. It's all right. It'll be all right. I'm sorry I came to the city, came to the apartment." I apologized but knew in my heart Katya was right. "I understand now. It was a mistake. You're right; I shouldn't have left you."

She ignored every word. "Do you want me to say it aloud, Christof?" she cried. "Do you? Damn it, answer me!"

My eyes closed as I listened to her scream. It was as if that simple, physical act could suppress what was happening.

"Please, Katya, you know it doesn't do any good when this sort of thing happens and we try to work it out over the phone. Especially when I'm about to leave for a couple of days."

I paused, still hoping that somehow my words would have an effect. After five or six eternal moments of silence, I pleaded once more with her. "Please. Please, Katya, let's go on. Before you can blink, it'll be Thursday evening and I'll be back. We'll be together— alone. We can talk better then."

I could hear Katya breathing heavily.

Now speaking as much for myself as for Katya, I said, "Yes, we should talk. There's so much that's happened to me in the past few days; we need to be with each other and talk about it. Talk about everything."

I heard only the sound of her breathing.

It was neither a plea nor an order as I said, "Katya, answer me."

With unmistakable resignation in her voice, her breathing still heavy, I heard softly before the line went dead, "Yes, Chris. We need to talk—soon."

Chapter 9

A LITTLE MORE THAN an hour later, the buzzer of the lobby intercom reverberated throughout the apartment. I had been waiting for it since Katya hung up.

Judy Lieber was waiting in the limo. She looked as though she were the only executive in the world without a care. "Good morning, Chris." She smiled and shifted her IBM portable closer to her. "Looks like another great day. Weather should be ideal for flying."

I forced a smile. That was the extent of my agreeability, and neither of us spoke on the ride to the office.

"See you in a couple of minutes" were the first words I said, exiting the elevator onto my floor. She continued up to hers to pick up some last-minute slides.

The outer door to my office was open, and the gal from legal was sitting behind Cindy's desk. She was opening the morning mail. "Good morning, miss …" I said somewhat lamely, unable to recall her name.

She glanced up in surprise. "Oh, Mr. Douglas? I didn't expect you. I thought you were traveling to corporate." She seemed confused as she rose from her chair. "I'm a morning person and have a tendency to be in the office by seven. Is that okay with you?" she asked. Apologizing for any breach of protocol, she added, "I hope I haven't done anything wrong."

"Sure, I think it's terrific." I signaled for her to sit. "What's in the mail? Anything important?"

She handed me the stack of mail. I flipped through it quickly until, halfway through, I came across a plain white envelope that had been left unopened. Above my typed name and address, in heavy capital letters were the words PERSONAL AND CONFIDENTIAL. There wasn't a return address. My curiosity piqued, I tore the envelope open.

"Chris, I called my secretary, and she said she left the slides in your office."

"Excuse me? What's that?" I looked at Judy, who had just appeared.

"I telephoned my secretary at her home when I couldn't find the slides for the presentation," she explained in frustration. "Luckily, I reached her, and she said they were in Cindy's office."

Her eyes searched the top of Cindy's desk. "Aha!" she cried, spotting a package. "It's our baby!" Judy said, exposing its contents.

"Okay, let's get going. Let's not take any chances with the tunnel traffic," I said, stuffing the opened envelope into my jacket pocket. "We have a plane to catch."

Sixty minutes later, we were sitting in seats 2A and 2B with glasses of orange juice and coffee. Twenty minutes later, we taxied onto the runway and were in the air within five minutes. That was a signal for my traveling companion to open her computer. After apologizing that she needed to finalize some spreadsheets for corporate's chief financial officer, she was now lost in cyberspace.

As I watched her fingers flying across the keyboard, her thoughts seemingly preoccupied with complicated ROIs, asset–liability ratios, and net profit calculations, I felt guilty. I knew I should be reviewing my own notes, especially since I hadn't done a damn thing the night before. But as I watched her—so involved, so excited as she did something she was so good at: moving huge, impressive numbers about to wherever they made some sense to whomever they made some sense to—I realized I couldn't. It was no longer something that was important to me.

I felt the envelope in my pocket. Whether as an excuse to avoid work or to satisfy my curiosity, I took out the envelope before I changed my mind. I pulled out the beige writing paper, and a black-and-white photograph fell out. I lifted the picture, but I didn't see anything I recognized. It was a group of people dressed in formal evening attire at some fancy cocktail party.

Wait a second …Was that Katya in the picture? I held it closer and tugged the window shade down to eliminate the sun's glare. Yes. Yes, it was Kat. She was wearing the black Norma Kamali tuxedo evening gown she'd bought in Soho. But where was the party? There was no one else in the crowd I recognized. I switched my attention to the beige paper.

The name Plaza Diana, stenciled in bold crimson letters across the top of the page, leaped out before I'd even unfolded the paper. Just beneath those two words, handwritten in a finely penned script— *God, it was exactly the same*—was a letter addressed to me. A feeling identical to the one I had felt Monday morning when I'd read about Sammantha—Maria—began to creep up my spine.

PLAZA DIANA
75 EAST 64TH STREET
NEW YORK, NEW YORK 10002

July 12, 1987

My dearest Christof,

I am writing to you at this time, after all these long years, to warn you that you may be in grave danger. And it is I who may have inadvertently placed you at risk. I've tried to contact you directly, but I didn't think it wise to use my maiden name. You'll hopefully understand as you read on.

Forgive me for being so melodramatic. I didn't even inquire as to your health, etc., etc. I hope that your shoulder and leg have completely healed from that rather nasty incident you had overseas some years back.

My apologies again. There is so much we could talk about, but I fear I am running out of time and must alert you somehow before it is too late. I will therefore be brief and to the point.

About three months ago, I began a project delving into the world arms markets, specifically involving Western countries that were major suppliers of military weapons and biochemicals to so-called third-world countries. As perilous as this may appear to you, I did not believe it greatly different from many of my other undertakings. By the middle of June, my investigation brought me to the States—California, to be precise, and explicitly to the front doorsteps of Space and Technology, the multinational munitions and chemical conglomerate.

Christof, I knew then, of course, that DFT Ltd. was the parent of Space and Technology. I had no idea, though, that you were president of a sister division. But I digress.

My fingers rubbed my eyes shut, but I couldn't prevent my mind's eye from seeing the initials DFT exploding deeply within. The improbable juxtaposition of those letters with the concept of Maria—one signifying who I became, and the other who I had been—sent a cold shiver through me as if the 727 had disintegrated in midair and I was now floating in icy space. My eyes reopened instinctively. I was the moth drawn to the flame—the letter.

I uncovered some data indicating that the company in question had continued to violate a multitude of sanctions and embargos that either the US or the UN had levied against Iran, to name a primary offender in what I would charitably describe as grave transgressions. Suffice to say there were other eager non-post-Irangate recipients as well. One country in particular I know will be of extra special interest to you.

Shortly after I arrived in California, I began to receive telephone calls—all anonymous, of course—advising me to cease my research. Initially they were tepid in comparison to others I had received. But following my unsuccessful attempts to interview Jason Spire, whom I believe you know, and, more than coincidently, subsequent to my intrusion upon a luncheon between him and his superior, Rick Carlson, the threats escalated dramatically. It was more or less at that time that I came across your name in a DFT annual report.

Rick Carlson? Jason Spire? I read faster, my heart pounding.

When these calls reached the point where my life was threatened, along with the lives of anyone else I held dear to me, I decided to go into what you referred to as a holding pattern. Funny how that phrase just came to me. I remember, Chris, that was how you would describe your army life. It's funny, isn't it, how some things just seem to pop up?

I flew to New York earlier in the week, thinking that would act as an acknowledgment to my adversaries that their tactics were having the desired effect. I also needed a bit of a holiday. It hasn't been either.

Once, I was almost run down by an automobile as I was crossing First Avenue. The driver rode onto the sidewalk after me when he didn't succeed. Then, Thursday night while I was out, someone broke into my room. The person took nothing but disturbed the contents of the closets and drawers and disheveled my clothing and belongings.

I flipped to the next page. I couldn't believe what I was reading.

I reported the incident to the police. A detective came the next morning and wrote down tons of information. Odd feeling I got from the chap—a clear example of negative transference, as Charles, my husband, would say. So, heeding what has kept me in good stead, discretion being the better part of valor and that sort of thing, I made arrangements to fly back to London Saturday. But what happened next was why I had to contact you.

Friday, at exactly noon, soon after the detective left, I received another call. It was the same voice from California. He told me it was too late, that I had gone too far and there was only one solution to this problem; whether it was solved here or in London didn't matter to him. And then he said something that frightened me as badly as I've ever been frightened. He warned me, Christof, "And after you, Miss Ladillya, it will be Mr. Douglas's turn." Chris, he knew me. I hadn't used that name in years. He also knew about us.

I called the police as soon as he hung up and was advised to stay in my room until someone from their offices arrived. That's when I decided to get in touch with you.

My fingers trembled so badly I could barely grasp her letter as I turned to the last page.

When I telephoned your office, I used my professional name out of habit, but I was also concerned about revealing too much to anyone but you. I resolved that if I couldn't contact you before leaving tomorrow, I would do so from London—this time as Maria.

I also had the impression from the police that they would be getting in touch with you. I wasn't sure in my heart who should tell you first.

Christof, I'm mailing this to you in case I get cold feet or the police fail to notify you. You have a right to know. If you wish to call me in London, the number is 01-234-890-3655. If I'm not there, ask for Delacroix. He can be completely trusted. There, it's done.

Oh, the picture. I almost forgot about the picture. Delacroix took it when we saw your wife, Katya, at a premiere for some up-and-coming artist last year in Paris. I'll tell you when I get back how I knew who she was.

Always with love,
La Ardilla

PS She wasn't aware that he took it.
PPS Poinsettias are still my favorite, but I learned they no longer last forever.

Tightly clutching her letter in my perspiring palm, almost crumpling that which represented Maria's final grasp of life, I pressed my eyes shut, and my mind filled with a collage of blinding, distorted images. I vividly saw the scenes of our youth, as if they'd occurred but yesterday—vibrant, so full of the precious life that I once knew—cruelly interspersed with the cold, indisputable, harsh emptiness of what I now knew.

"Chris, did you say something? Are you okay?"

"Huh?"

"I asked if you were okay. You made some sort of sound, and I thought you were talking to me."

Opening my eyes, I saw Judy Lieber staring at me strangely, her lips pursed as if awaiting an answer. I shook my head, as much in response to my visions as her question. "I just need a glass of water," I said. I unbuckled my seat belt, disregarding her comment to "let the stewardess get it," and slipped around her legs and stumbled to the restroom.

I locked the door, stepped to the basin, and slammed down hard on the faucet handle. I breathed deeply three or four times with my eyes closed, and the drone of the engines and the sound of the water became hypnotic. I pressed my forehead so hard on the lavatory mirror that I thought the mirror would crack and shatter into a million pieces. When it didn't, I lifted my face away, stepped back, and raised my fist. For a second, I believed my fist would finish what my head had been unable to do.

I wished I were sailing on the ocean—drifting slowly, dreamlike, the boat bobbing ever so slightly. I could see it was twilight, and the sea was becalmed. The moon began to appear from beneath it, yet mystically it rose as though the water were an illusion not to be disturbed. I was close enough to land to hear the gentle lapping sounds the evening surf made as it fell upon and then retreated from the shoreline, its energy momentarily spent.

I don't remember everything that went through my head or what my body felt. Eventually Lieber became concerned and had a stewardess check on me. When I returned to my seat, she was packing her portable PC into its carrying case in preparation for landing. I dismissed her inquiry about what had happened as something I ate.

But I remember that I was filled with the same wild rage that I felt when Beth had been murdered.

Chapter 10

WE ARRIVED AT THE Greenville-Spartanburg Airport on schedule, just before eleven o'clock. The driver DFT had sent was waiting, and we were seated in a black Lincoln Town Car a few minutes later.

My meeting with Carlson was not until three, so I had the driver take us to the Hyatt, where we normally stay. I gave him instructions to return at 2:30 sharp and checked into the hotel. Lieber and I agreed to meet in the lobby a few minutes prior to the driver's arrival.

I didn't bother to unpack. I hung my overnight traveling bag in the closet and then sat on the edge of the bed and dialed London. I glanced at my watch and calculated the hour to be around five in the evening there. While I waited for the overseas connection to be made, thoughts about Maria's murder continued to flash through my mind.

Why? And by whom? The image of Jason Spire and Rick Carlson sitting together at a business luncheon when Maria burst into the restaurant and interrupted them replayed itself over and over as if to answer those questions.

"Allo?" a man answered.

I cleared the lump in my throat, and uncertain what to say, I began one of the most defining dialogues of my life. "Good … Good evening. I'm trying to reach a Mr. Delacroix. If this is his telephone number, may I speak with him, please?"

After a longer delay than the transatlantic connection would have caused, a man on the other end said, "Delacroix? Oui. Who is it that wishes to speak to Monsieur Delacroix?"

"This is Mr. Douglas, a Mr. Christof Douglas. I'm calling …" Suddenly I had to stop. How should I portray our relationship? "I'm calling regarding a friend," I lied. Was that all she was? "A Miss Sammantha Kelso." I then quickly added, "I knew her as Maria—Maria Ladillya."

There was a little less delay on that exchange.

"How did you know … Do you know either of these women?" he said, catching himself and switching tenses as he did.

I raised my voice, frustrated, as if speaking with someone who was not quite familiar with the language. "They're not two women. They're the exact same person. I knew Maria from when we went to school together. I knew her …" I paused and then dropped my voice and said, "A long, long time ago."

"Ah. Ahh! Je comprende. I see, I see, Mr. Douglas. Answer me one question, Mr. Douglas, Monsieur Christof Douglas, if you will. Did this Maria—this Maria Ladillya you claim to know—have any brothers or sisters?"

I knew I had found Delacroix. "Yes, she did. But he was killed in Vietnam. His plane was shot down over Laos. They never recovered his body."

Christ Almighty, both Tony and Maria were dead.

"What was his name, Monsieur Douglas—this brother you claim was killed over Indo Chine?"

"Antonio—Tony. He was her older brother. Her only brother."

An image of Tony, smiling and full of life as he stood in front of his F-5A fighter jet, dark aviator glasses shielding his eyes from the sun, flickered in and out of my thoughts. I remembered that Maria's mother had proudly displayed that picture of him in their living room.

As memories of Maria's family continued to fill my head, I kept on speaking. I was unable to stop myself. "It was just the two of them. And her mother. That's when Maria left—left home and disappeared. Right after Tony died." I paused to compose myself before sarcastically asking a question of my own. "Is there anything else you'd like to know about me or Maria, monsieur? It is Monsieur Delacroix, isn't it?"

If he was surprised by my question, he didn't reveal it. "Oui, c'est vrai." After her brother died, Maria came to London."

It was Maria I saw that time in London getting on the bus.

There wasn't time to reflect on this startling revelation, as Delacroix's cautiousness returned. "Why are you calling me?" he demanded. "Eh! What is it you want from me?" he snapped.

Since reading Maria's letter just a few hours ago, I had made up my mind to fly to London, hopefully in time for her funeral services. I didn't know if this were the right thing to do, or even wise; I just knew I had to go. And before going, I would tell Katya the truth about what had occurred over the past three days. But now what I wanted from Maria's friend was to find out what the arrangements were for the funeral. At least that's what I kept telling myself and what I told him.

"Monsieur Douglas," he said, when I had finished explaining to him the purpose of my call, "I've known Maria for many, many years. In those earlier years, she would talk to me about you. But, as you so aptly put it, that was a long time ago. Maria is—was—no longer the girl you remembered."

There was silence between us when he completed his statement. After a minute, I began to worry we had been disconnected or that he had decided to hang up. Eventually, in a tired voice, he said, "The funeral is scheduled for Monday morning. The church services will begin promptly at nine o'clock. If you must come—if I can't stop you—come to Paris then, not London. Maria has lived in Paris for quite some while, and that's where her final resting place will be. Do you know the cathedral Saint-Germain-de-Prés, Monsieur Douglas?"

I nodded my head.

"Monsieur Douglas, est-ce que vous etez ici?" Are you still there?"

Finding my voice, I whispered, "Yes. Yes, I am here. I am familiar with Saint Germain de Pres. It is right off the boulevard of the same name, near the heart of the Latin Quarter."

"D'accord. Tres Bien. When will you be arriving?"

I thought quickly. The earliest I could leave for Paris would be Sunday—Saturday if I pushed it with Katya, which I did not want to do. "Monsieur Delacroix, Sunday sometime," I whispered. "I'll call later in the week to confirm."

"As you wish. I will be departing London for Paris tomorrow. You can reach me there at 03-234-573-0998. Oh, one other detail. My name isn't Delacroix. That was Maria's ... How do you Americans say ...?"

I heard him talking to himself in a combination of French and English, stumbling for the precise translation of what he wanted to say. I thought I knew what he was trying say but didn't know the French equivalent. The closest I could come was nom de guerre. Frustrated, I said in English, "Her nickname for you."

"Ah, oui! C'est ca." His relief was obvious by the lightness of his tone. "Yes, her nickname for me. My real name is Magritte, Renaud Magritte." He laughed in delight at the irony of this and then said, his laughter disappearing, "Au revoir, Monsieur Douglas."

A few hours later, after a much-needed shower and a change of clothes, I was in the hotel lobby, waiting for Lieber.

Before I left the room, I called my office for any messages. Outside of a call from Billy, checking up on my meeting with RR, there was nothing that couldn't wait. I called Billy back, uncertain whether I should tell him of my trip to Paris. He was already en route to some place in Europe, so that decision was made for me.

I decided to fly to Paris on Sunday, instructing Cindy's stand-in to book me on the earliest flight over and to see if the Hotel Relais Saint-Germain had a room available. That was where Katya and I stayed when we were in Paris, and it was near the church.

I spent the rest of the time in my room rereading Maria's letter, staring at the photograph of Katya, and thinking about when, and what, I would tell Katya. My discussion with Katya would come down to how late I got home on Thursday. In any case, I would not go into the office on Friday, and we would talk about everything, including why I had to go to Paris.

As I waited for Lieber, I pulled out the photograph and tried to determine the circumstances surrounding it. Katya had been in

London last year on one of her business trips, but I didn't remember her saying anything about Paris. The whole thing was a total blank.

"Is our car here?"

"Oh. Judy." Melancholy visions of Paris disappeared as I slipped the photo into my jacket pocket and pointed to the black Town Car parked in the hotel's driveway.

She smiled and gave me a thumbs-up sign. "I got all my work done. We're looking very good." She eyed me. "You seem much better also. I was worried about you. It seemed as if you were—I don't know—air sick or something on the plane." She continued to study my face. "You didn't appear to be the same Chris Douglas that boarded our plane at Newark."

"It was nothing really," I replied, and I walked toward the waiting limo.

The trip to DFT headquarters was quick. After a brief stop to present our IDs at the gate, we wove our way up the half-mile, tree-lined park to the main office complex. Our driver dropped us off, and we entered the lobby, which was more atrium than office, and introduced ourselves to the receptionist.

"Mr. Landon has instructed me, Mr. Douglas, that you should proceed immediately to his office upon your arrival. And Ms. Lieber should proceed to the corporate finance conference room." We thanked her and did as Landon had instructed.

Landon's office was on the fourth and top floor and only a few steps removed from the corner suite of our mutual boss. As he liked to point out when it suited him, "That's a helluva lot closer than Midtown Manhattan."

When I opened the door to his office suite, Landon was sitting on his secretary's desk, his back to me. His face was a couple of inches from hers.

"Knock, knock. It's two forty-five; your guest has arrived," I said sarcastically, seeing the weasel in what might be considered a compromising position.

Landon hopped clumsily to the floor. A sneer formed across his thin lips. "Cutting it close, aren't you, Chris?"

"You wanted two forty-five, Carl; you got two forty-five."

His lips tightened even more. Then the sneer on his face broadened and became relaxed. With a dismissive, bored air, he asked me to have a seat. "I'll be with you presently," he said, and he withdrew into his office.

I smiled at his secretary, who dropped her eyes upon making contact with mine, and did as the weasel suggested.

After ten wasted minutes of twiddling my thumbs, I got up and headed for the executive men's room. A few minutes later, Landon rushed in. "Damn it," he cried. "It's three o'clock! We're late for the meeting with Mr. Carlson."

Quisling, weasel—if I'd had more time I would have come up with a dozen or more job descriptions that fit Landon. But what else could I expect? When a person brought nothing to the party, he had no choice but to suck wind and obey his master's bidding. My opinions aside, I opted not to aggravate his terminal condition any further.

"No sweat, Carl. If Rick says anything, I'll tell him I was the guilty party."

Without any indication that he had heard my proposal, he spun abruptly and, with an awkward, exaggerated stride, began to half run and half walk toward Carlson's office. I followed a few steps behind.

Carlson's secretary greeted us when we entered. "Mr. Carlson is expecting you. Won't you both please have a seat? He'll be with you momentarily. Would either of you gentleman care for some iced tea?"

"No, thanks," I said, smiling politely. Landon just shook his head.

At that moment, Carlson's door opened, and Jason Spire, my counterpart at Space and Technology, unexpectedly came out. Ignoring the weasel, Spire walked toward me.

He grabbed my hand a little too firmly and pumped it vigorously, his welcome reeking of too much bravado. "Chris, you're looking terrific," he stated, either lying or in need of stronger designer glasses. "Great to see you."

I suddenly felt compelled to ask him if he had ever heard of Maria or Sammantha. "Good to see you also, Jason."

He continued to clasp my hand, although the pumping had

ceased, and stared into my eyes. "I understand your presentation has been switched to go on immediately after mine."

"Yeah. Any idea why we were switched?"

He released his grip but not his stare. "I have to be in Washington tomorrow. Meeting with a few generals. You know, the guys who buy the five-hundred-dollar screwdrivers," he said, laughing. He punched me lightly on the shoulder.

I would have staked odds the bastard had heard. Each time I considered the absurd notion that Spire and Carlson had anything to do with Maria's murder, I tried every rationalization imaginable to dismiss the idea: It's pure coincidence. They're legitimate businessmen, not murders. Maybe she's wrong about DFT. Maybe someone else who had a grudge from an earlier exposé killed her.

These and a host of other theories, each more far out than the previous, ran through my mind. But as much as I didn't like the notion of my colleagues' involvement, as much as I didn't want to believe it, I could not reject its growing plausibility.

Why don't I ask him straight out? Now is my chance. Why don't I ask him if he knows who killed her? But sanity, or something else, stopped me. So instead I said, doing my damnedest to maintain an air of disinterest, "Yeah, you know what they say—the most expensive screw in Washington."

Spire's eyes widened, his teeth clamped together, and for an instant he resembled some predator about to spring. Then, just as quickly, the danger he conveyed disappeared.

"I like that." He laughed. "Screw in Washington for a mere five hundred dollars a whack." He punched me again, this time a little harder. "I like it. Can't wait to tell the boys that one."

"Gentlemen, pleassssse. Mr. Carlson is waiting." The weasel was holding Carlson's door open and motioning in an overstated, sweeping fashion for us to cross his master's threshold.

"Looks like it's your turn at bat. I'll catch you at the cocktail reception," Spire said, tapping me once more before he left. I walked quietly into Carlson's office.

"Mr. Carlson, Mr. Douglas is here as you requested," the weasel proclaimed.

Carlson raised his head from whatever he was studying on his desk and greeted us with his typical, disarming smile. Rising, his arm outstretched in welcome, he rolled my name invitingly off his lips.

"Chris, my boy. I am so delighted to see you. How are you? And how is Katya?" He engulfed my own outstretched hand in both of his. "Please, please, do sit down."

In spite of all that had happened, it was difficult not to settle easily into one of the two handcrafted wingback armchairs in front of his desk. The roller-coaster ride that passed for my emotions temporarily restrained, I finally returned his greeting.

I couldn't match the warmth of his tone, though.

"It's good to see you too, Rick. And Katya's—well, she's just fine. She's taken off for the summer from the museum and is doing research for her doctoral thesis." I shifted uncomfortably and forced a smile. "Her specialty, as I'm sure you recall, is the French impressionists."

It was harder for me to share the same animosity toward Carlson as I did toward Spire. Then again, perhaps it just wasn't as close to the surface.

The sincerity oozed from his pores. "Of course I recall. Thank her again for putting me in contact with that art gallery in London. Thanks to Katya, I picked up a fabulous Seurat, along with a couple of interesting paintings from some lesser-distinguished bohemians on my last trip across the pond."

He was all smiles.

"The black orchids you sent her were most unusual and thank you enough," I said somewhat stiffly.

"Nonsense. The next occasion I happen to find myself in New York, you must allow me to take both of you to dinner. Le Cirque is always entertaining. And if there is something worthwhile at the opera, that also."

"I'm sure Katya will be very excited when I tell her of your invitation," I lied, trying to sound interested.

Carlson turned toward Landon, who was standing motionless a few feet inside the office, seemingly hanging on to our every word. Carlson held his gaze just long enough to issue his command, a terse "Landon, that'll be all for now." With that, the weasel bowed and backed out of the room.

Carlson glanced at his Rolex. "Now, where were we? Ah, yes, yes," he said, answering his own question, "I'm sure she will be."

A moment of awkward silence filled the room. Carlson appeared to be observing me closely, perhaps deliberating on what he would say next. In my mind, I was asking him the same questions that I had been asking his buddy Spire.

I decided that if I didn't break the silence, I might begin to speak these bitter questions. And, at that moment, I was not yet prepared to accept the consequences—later perhaps, but not just then. So I played straight man and asked the obvious question of what it was he wanted to see me about.

"First, let me say," he began, "I took a preliminary peek at your sector's performance, and it is magnificent what you have accomplished. Why, Chris, you have those stations operating like a well-oiled machine." He gestured for me not to interrupt. A couple of loose strands of his silver hair fell over his forehead.

"No, no, I know you want to give credit to your staff and the rest of your organization," he said, pretending to scold me. "They're a good group, and they deserve recognition. For instance, I've heard good things about your CFO, Lieber, to cite someone whose name comes immediately to mind."

He paused, his blue eyes narrowing. "But, Chris, it's you. It's your style. That's why I had the good sense to hire you. You're the primary, if not sole, reason why the entertainment sector has made a complete about-face."

Everyone likes to be told by his boss that he's done a good job, but this was coming on a little too thick for my taste. "I appreciate your confidence in me, Rick, but it really has been a team thing, along with some good timing and catching a few breaks."

"Fine. If you insist, Chris, I won't discourage that type of loyalty on behalf of your colleagues."

More than thick—he was coming on like some snake-oil salesman. I wanted to say something, but he gestured again not to. I noticed something close to a frown appear on his face.

"As I indicated to you when we spoke earlier in the week, I wish I had a few more people like you in this organization."

With apparent effort, his whitening knuckles helping to boost his body, he lifted himself, as though the weight of the free world would cause him to tumble back into his chair. He stepped around the desk and walked slowly to the windows. He stood motionless and gazed out. The only sound in the room was the muted whirring of the groundskeepers' lawnmowers.

Two or three minutes passed before he spoke. It was not the voice I was accustomed to hearing. "Chris, I love this place," he said quietly. "It's been over twenty years since I moved here. Ah, those early years here. Those were the days."

A minute or two of silence went by before he turned to me. I sensed the change in the air. I sensed that whatever he had been thinking had disappeared. He strode toward his desk and sat down. The weight of the world removed from his shoulders, there was now facing me only Rick Carlson, chairman of a fifteen-billion-dollar multinational conglomerate.

His tone was a little harder edged when at last he spoke. "Hell, Chris, these are the days. Damn the old days." His face was now masked in a scowl that bore no similarity to his former, troubled frown.

"But I have a serious problem. No," he added, "DFT has a serious problem. And you can help me solve it." His head bobbed affirmation to his statement as if it were the minion of its vocal sibling. It was also a cue for me to talk.

"What exactly is the problem?" I asked warily.

"I have an offer to make you, Chris." He hesitated as he studied me. "Chris, I'd like you to be part of an executive task force. A small, elite group of at the most four, maybe five, people. Its full-time charter will be to determine the eventual disposition of the Apparel and Retail sector."

This time I spoke before the jolt of what he'd said fully registered. Not bothering to give Carlson the chance to elaborate—I should have told him then and there, "Piss off, I'm no rag merchant"—my corporate demeanor barely held as my voice rose just enough to be in sync with my blood pressure.

"Rick, tell me what you're talking about. How can I possibly help you with … with this? I'm a broadcast guy. What the hell do I know about … about …" As I groped for words less offensive than my thoughts, he completed my sentence for me.

"The rag trade?"

Hearing that less-than-corporate expression from the quintessential corporate man—or "suit," in Casey's parlance—only exacerbated my indignation.

"Yes, the rag trade," I shouted. "Look, Rick, you just told me you were pleased with my sector's results. Why rock the boat?" I asked, completely disbelieving we were even discussing this subject. "Especially with the precarious state we're in with respect to the FCC and the ongoing litigation. If we lose, we're talking an easy billion, maybe more, if the ratings continue to climb. I don't get it."

Glaring at the expressionless person sitting across from me, I realized that never had those few feet of polished mahogany represented such a wide schism between us.

"Chris," he answered in a patronizing tone, "if I were you, I would ask the same questions. I most likely would think, that blankity-blank, son of a bitch is screwing me. But I'm not. Quite the opposite is true. If anything, I'm asking this of you as a reward for the fine job you've done."

I heard the words, but I knew—and he knew—that what I was hearing from him was pure, unadulterated bullshit.

"Let me explain why I say this and how, at the same time, you can help DFT address some outstanding and rather sensitive issues." At the mention of the hallowed corporate name, Carlson leaned forward, his arms stretched out on the desk, his hands clasped together as though in prayer, and bore his icy, blue eyes directly into me.

This was now prime time—one of those rare instances in one's life when choices had to be made. It was the moment when I either signed on to the snow job about to come my way or kissed whatever brought me here good-bye. All this went through my mind, yet for the first time, I never had any doubts as to what I would do. I tried to stop myself from smiling as I recalled the phrase a former squadron mate would use when he returned from some particularly harrowing mission.

He would take his time, unhurried and unconcerned as to who might be waiting for his post-flight briefing, and methodically unbuckle himself; step out of his bubble with his charts, helmet, and log in his hands; and walk away from the landing pad. As he did, he would announce to no one specific, though we could all hear him over the fading, rotating chopper blades, "Things change."

The first time I heard him say that, I had just arrived in the country and needed to ask what he meant. "What changed?" I naively asked. I remember he stopped, lifted his eyes from the black tarmac, and, with a vacant stare, just looked right through me before continuing on his way toward air ops.

I never asked again. I had no need. I found out for myself.

"I've decided to drop all the legal proceedings with the FCC, Chris." Carlson's voice, like an engulfing net, dragged me back to our meeting. "I've cut a deal with Walker. A deal that I believe is in the best interests of our shareholders. Essentially, we stop opposing him—the FCC, that is—and sell the stations to those challengers Walker approves. Approves ahead of time, I might add, and for full market value. Everything is legal, and there's absolutely no reason why it can't be completed within six months."

Andy and I had discussed this possibility, negotiating some backroom deal to accomplish what Carlson had spelled out. The kicker was always Walker and whether he could be trusted. He had already reneged on his original promise, first terminating the pending legal actions and then reversing himself when DFT acquired those same stations. What was different now?

As though Carlson was reading my mind, he asked, "What's different?" He shrugged his shoulders and answered our questions.

"Circumstances," he said. "For one, we need the cash that will be raised from the sale. About a billion dollars, as you so eloquently stated, which will then be used to address some strategic issues in Space and Technology—issues that require an extensive capital infusion if we are to move forward into the twenty-first century and that need to be addressed immediately."

When he mentioned Space and Technology, my preoccupation with my own future began to fade, replaced with the image of Maria barging in and interrupting Carlson and Spire's lunch.

"Concomitantly, this time I have every faith in Walker's word,"

Carlson declared smugly. "It's not important for me to elaborate. Let's just say he'll keep his word this time."

They had bought the bastard off. How much was he getting from Great Air? Smart, very smart: Walker had worked both parties against each other, and it had worked.

Maria, you squirrel, you stumbled over this. You changed it all for me—for us.

"When the announcement is released sometime later today, it will contain something to the effect from Walker that although it should be viewed as a victory for the FCC—as they would have expected a favorable decision later in the year, blah, blah, blah—this settlement is a more equitable way of achieving the same goal but without allowing DFT to suffer any unnecessary penalties. And guess what will happen to the price of our stock?"

He didn't wait for my answer. "Share value will go right through the fuckin' roof! That's what will happen. Right through the fuckin' roof."

Carlson was right. Because of the FCC uncertainty, our stock had been languishing in the low fifties for the past year, and now the analysts would upgrade our status to "buy, buy, buy," especially when measuring our performance vis-à-vis the so-called industry leaders. But Carlson could have orchestrated this scenario before. We ran the numbers over a year ago, taking into account what we're discussing this very minute. Could it really be that Walker is the only wild card?

"And, Chris, you know what that means to our—to your—stock compensation program?"

Hundreds of thousands for me, and millions to you, you cunning bastard.

He resumed his earlier sell regarding the rag-trade task force. "Chris, I hope you now understand why I want you on this task force," he said, his face now looking so sincere that I thought I was observing a different person.

"No," I replied. "No," I repeated, just to make sure that both of the Carlsons heard me.

"I'm sure you're aware that, on rare occasions, we've moved executives from one sector of the company to another. Special people, for sure. Chris, you're one of those special people. I need someone who can bring a fresh look but still has the management experience and style to keep him from being out of his depth. Hear me now," he hastily said, lifting his hand to quell any objections I might have.

I wasn't about to say anything. And quite frankly, you can take this task force, along with your so-called special people and stick them in your ear, you wily son of a bitch. This has something to do with Maria. But what, damn it?

Carlson continued to extol the benefits of the task force with more arcane babble. I floated between listening to him and trying to fathom the Maria connection. Staring at the figure opposite me, I began to further understand what I would do.

The room became quiet. The old windbag was finished. Carlson rose and walked toward me. "I know this is all happening very fast for you. Take a few days to think about what I'm asking of you."

He made it seem like an afterthought when he added, "We'll need to discuss a few details. Like who'll be responsible for the day-to-day activities of Entertainment in your absence—that sort of thing. But that can wait. I know it's a big decision for you, Chris."

He placed his arm over my shoulder and guided me out of his office.

Chapter 11

"US AIR TERMINAL, SIR."

I rubbed the condensation from the window and gazed through the heavy rain to where my driver pointed. He glanced in his rearview mirror at his sole passenger as he pulled the Town Car up to the curb. "Hope there's no delay in your flight back to New York."

In spite of the weather, my flight was not delayed, and I didn't have to spend one minute more than necessary in Greenville. As we lifted off, the Lockheed's powerful engines whined as they strained against the earth's gravitational pull. I calculated we would arrive at LaGuardia by nine in the evening. It was going to be late by the time I got home.

Too late.

I cursed myself for driving the Bimmer into the city on Monday. If I hadn't, I would have flown into Newark and been back to Sea Isle an hour earlier. That would have given Katya and me enough time to talk.

Well, Lieber was the new chief operating officer of Entertainment. Carlson made that clear when he asked her to remain for another day to discuss some recent developments, as he tactfully put it. Plus, his parting comment right before I left for the airport was a suggestion that perhaps she should stand in for me during the coming week until I got back from my emergency trip to Paris. "Of course by then," he said, winking at me slyly, "you may have your hands quite full with all sorts of things."

I'd wanted to skip the cocktail and dinner party the previous evening but at the last moment had changed my mind. The idea of seeing Spire had kept eating away at me. So I'd unpacked my Brooks Brothers tuxedo and gone.

For the most part it was your typical, boring corporate affair. The one exception was my confrontation with Spire. As soon as I entered the otherwise festive room, I sought him out. He was completely caught off guard when the first thing I said to him was to ask if he had ever heard of Sammantha or Maria.

He didn't answer right away. He glared at me, the fingers of both his hands nervously straightening and then re-straightening the knot of his ugly, yellow silk polka-dot tie. I just stared back. Eventually he flinched and did say something. It wasn't what I had expected, but to me, it was the same as if had come right out and admitted he killed her.

"You're crazy! You're a fuckin' crazy loose cannon," he hissed. He didn't wait for my response after blurting out his evaluation of my mental well-being; he immediately spun on his heel and faded into the crowd.

I watched him weave his way through the packed and spirited assemblage to see if he were headed to Carlson. He wasn't; instead, he just blended in with a mixed group from the various units within DFT. Nothing out of the ordinary.

I actually took a step toward him, propelled more by the moment than any logical decision to do so. I could see him roll his head in my direction when I did this, but I had no intention of following through. I turned away and walked out the main ballroom door.

"Cocktail or cold beverage, sir?" the stewardess asked.

My attention jumped from the lightning-saturated black heavens, each shade of violent darkness vying for supremacy of the night, and the equally turbulent impressions of yesterday only long enough to order a double Finlandia martini on the rocks.

Before I left for the cocktail party, I called Roquette. He had nothing new to report. He did say that his usual sources in the police department weren't of any help, which he found highly unusual. "They acted as if they didn't have the foggiest notion of who you were," he said, sounding disappointed. "Call me tomorrow, and hopefully I'll have something more concrete."

Well, I called him right before I boarded my flight. This time I spoke with his secretary, as he was out of the office. "Nothing new, as per Mr. Roquette. Call back tomorrow," she relayed to me.

Although I was anxious, I tried to look at the situation optimistically. After all, if I were a suspect, wouldn't the police have cautioned me about traveling out of the metropolitan area, the way they always did in the movies? I wondered what their impressions would be if they discovered I was traveling to Paris this weekend. The thought that they might prohibit me from going crossed my mind, but I uneasily adopted Roquette's philosophy of "take it as it comes" and decided to deal with it if it became a reality.

Piinng..

I looked at the source of the sound and saw that the captain had turned on the seat-belt sign. Over the PA system, he said something about passengers remaining in their seats. The rest of the announcement, I surmised, was something about weather ahead. I started to bounce in my seat, and I saw the stewardess kneeling behind the service curtain, hurriedly restacking the dinner trays into steel racks. At moments like these, I was always grateful for the invention of the martini. I took a sip, toasting Mr. Martini, wherever he might be, and shut my eyes and allowed the liquid to take its effect.

There had been close to one hundred executives at DFT's quarterly meetings over the past two days.

Right before Carlson introduced me for my presentation, he informed the audience of the decision to settle with the FCC and to sell the broadcast properties. He also announced that I would be part of his so-called elite rag-trade task force. I just smiled and nodded like a stuffed toy dog mounted in the rear window of some bouncing car.

I didn't remember much of what I'd said; I was moving without a sense of who I was or what I was talking about. I was lost in the trance-like stupor that I found to be consuming me. It took less than ten minutes to labor through my moment of fame.

After I finished, Carlson congratulated me and insisted that I stay for the Apparel and Retail "dog and pony show." I stayed but didn't pay much attention. My mind was churning as quickly as my heart was pounding, the pair obsessed with what I had resolved. Occasionally, when Carlson slammed his fist onto the table, visibly upset at some remark or some disappointing revenue figure, I would be sufficiently startled and catch the drift of what was happening. "Unsatisfactory—totally unacceptable!" Carlson would bellow whenever the beleaguered presenter tried to make an excuse for not meeting plan.

This debacle contrasted with the earlier stellar, captivating performance by Spire. Stressing that Space and Technology was well positioned for the future—specifically with the infusion of two billion dollars suddenly raised, guaranteed capital planned for it over the next three years, and the new contracts worth ten times that amount with the military establishment—he boasted to the applauding audience, "I can assure the members of the executive committee and DFT's shareholders the highest rate of return they have ever seen."

For his session, I hung on to his every word. "Smart systems that are capable of negating supersonic, stealth aircraft," he bragged. "Satellite sensors and advanced ordinance systems capable of mass destruction and determent designed to satisfy the most sophisticated user. And even to satisfy some less-than-sophisticated camel jockeys if they happen to have a need," he added with a derisive laugh.

Words and terms I had only heard or read about were taking on a new, more-relevant meaning. Which of these programs—each apparently vital to the national defense, each the product of well-intentioned, responsible military and corporate executives—had Maria stumbled upon and found not to be as advertised? How and when did she come to the realization that it was my company involved?

It was apparent from the audience's smiling faces that they were pleased. I just sat by and absorbed the information, vowing that he would live to regret his part in this affair. After his presentation, right before he left for Washington, he glanced in my direction, making brief eye contact with me, but that was all, so we didn't have an opportunity to revisit his opinion regarding my sanity.

"Another martini, Mr. Douglas?"

"What? Ah, no, thanks. I'm fine," I lied to the stewardess, realizing where I was. I was dying for another, but I had a lot of driving ahead of me—and maybe a great deal of explaining to do—before this evening would be over.

As she raised the tray and placed my dinner on it, I noticed that the turbulence had subsided. Moving my head nearer to the window, I stared into the endless vastness to see if the rain had ceased. There was nothing—no stars, no rain, none of the flashing, jagged illumination from before. There was now just total blackness.

"Red or white wine, Mr. Douglas?"

One glass should be okay. "Red, thank you."

I hadn't eaten all day, so it took only about five minutes for me to devour the tasteless, over baked chicken breast and vegetables.

Had it been only two days since I had lunch with Billy at Le Bernardin?

In spite of the nourishment, I felt drained of my being. In its stead there was only overwhelming emptiness. 'What else? What's next?' I wondered, mouthing my thoughts quietly, more with a sense of hopelessness than fear. 'Is this what it all comes down to?'

Simple nothingness?

Never had I imagined that this would be the course my life would take. Confessing this to myself, I wished I could make some sort of arrangement, some sort of deal with whomever, to change things and start over, or even make different choices. If I hadn't gone to Nam, resigned before I was commissioned …

I leaned my cheek against the cold window and stared into the blackness as if there were some escape there, or someone with whom I could negotiate this wish. Instead I was thrust deeper and deeper into my own ever-expanding abyss and the struggle to understand the limitations of my mortality.

*****

When the helicopter I was in was wrenched from the sky that day in Vietnam, I did not have much time to think about what was happening. I was terrified, of course—scared out of my human or animal wits; that much I would always remember. But I was occupied with obeying my military instincts and, by inference, my survival. The whole damn thing took less than sixty seconds.

We were a few hundred feet above the tree line when we began to take on enemy small-arms fire. Dickey Lake was behind the rudder that day, and he was as competent a pilot as any in our squadron. He tried his best, using every trick he had been taught or had learned on his own to evade the incoming rounds, first darting away and then rising faster, almost at a right angle to the earth, higher and higher. But each of us knew that the Plexiglas bubble left everything to be desired. "Hung out," one might have said when describing our protection and our government-issued lives.

There was no need to tell me when we were hit. The sounds the bullets made when they penetrated our aircraft were followed instantly by thickening black pillows of smoke and violent shuddering beneath my feet. Words were not necessary to understand we had taken a fatal blow.

When the engines failed, Dickey employed autorotation procedures to try to stabilize our free fall and control our descent. The second this happened, I frantically began calling in our Mayday to flight ops, praying that it was received in spite of the constant, crackling static.

*****

"Mr. Douglas, more coffee?"

The voice brought my face from the window. I smiled and declined her offer but asked when we would be landing.

"We should be at LaGuardia in about thirty minutes, approximately ten minutes after nine. It will be a few minutes later than scheduled due to the turbulence," she replied. "Is there anything else you need before we land?"

I shook my head and turned to stare at the heavens. The evening sky was no longer solid black, as tiny pinpoints of light now punctuated it. I felt a renewed sense of security with the emergence of these natural, faithful residents. The storm had passed, and once again the heavens and the gods, unlike their human playthings, were at peace.

I recalled many a lonesome night in Vietnam when I would gaze at the heavens, searching for familiar stars. I remembered being fascinated with the notion that Maria would be watching the same stars in the same sky, except one day later, and wondered if they would sparkle more for her.

"Tomorrow, Maria, you will see what I saw tonight," I wrote to her after one brilliant celestial display. Then, as a postscript, I asked her, "Does this mean I can see into your future?" I could tell by the way she replied in her return letter that she was a little jealous. She didn't come right out and say it, but I could tell that she didn't care for the idea that someone else, even if that someone was me, could pretend to know her future if she didn't.

That was the last letter I ever received from her in Vietnam.

*****

It was early evening when we fell to earth. Twilight was beginning to comfortably settle in, and the sky had a red glow from the sun sinking into the horizon. Another few minutes and we would have turned the bubble around and been on our way back to base. In another hour, or as long as it took to fly back and file our debriefing reports, we would have been unwinding safely at our battalion's version of an officers' club, chugging down a couple of icy brews.

Instead Dickey was dead and I was in pain, crawling from the mangled wreckage of our helicopter, Cruising Lady.

Dickey's actions had reduced our drop speed, so we didn't fall like the two-ton stone we were. We were like some bobbing and weaving punch-drunk fighter, twisting and spinning in midair, his head first in one direction as he froze in place only to quickly rotate 180 degrees and freeze in that direction, searching for some imaginary foe. It was as if Dickey couldn't decide which direction to turn as we did this deadly dance. In the end, though, it didn't matter which way he turned or how much our drop speed was reduced, because neither would have prevented him from dying.

I knew he was dead as soon as I turned to him. I knew I was alive by the jolt of pain that slammed into my shoulder and my psyche when I saw his broken body, his head askew at a weird angle, wedged between the seat and unyielding brown earth. I was suspended above him, strapped in my seat in midair. It was Dickey's horrible fate that before we crashed, Crusing Lady caught her skids on some branches, causing us to smash into the ground on his side.

I often thought that if he had altered our fall, turned the rudder a bit differently, or pressed a bit more on the cyclic, maybe our places in eternity might have been reversed. Perhaps he knew what the risk was, I thought at those moments, but simply and courageously chose not to affect the outcome. Parcae told me that I tortured myself thinking about it, that she had explained a thousand times why he'd died and I hadn't.

It was longer than I prayed for, before I managed to half cut, half rip myself from my harness. I checked Dickey's pulse and other vital signs the way we were trained to do but hoped we never had to. He might have had other injuries as well, but none more obvious than his broken neck.

I suddenly became terrified that the bubble's fuel would ignite at any moment. I began to pull my friend's body from the wreckage and put as much distance between us and the helicopter as my pain-racked body would allow. I wasn't thinking of Charlie. I also didn't know that my ankle was broken. I learned that as soon as I stood.

I managed to crawl and limp through the tangled, heavy underbrush, dragging the lifeless twenty-three-year-old body of Richard Lake—sometimes behind me, sometimes under my good arm—some thirty or forty yards. That was as far as I could push myself, the throbbing pain in my ankle too great to go any farther.

Dropping to the dirt exhausted, I managed to pull my friend's body closer to me. When the blood started dripping into my eyes, I realized there was a nasty gash from my left ear to my hairline and back down to my left eyebrow. Cleaning it as best I could with my sleeve and canteen, I waited for the explosion that would signal the final moments of our other comrade in arms.

I never had the chance to hear it happen.

Within seconds, I heard voices, followed by the rush of leaves and branches snapping. The voices had that harsh, shrill-pitched inflection marking them as Vietnamese. I also knew from my preflight briefing that there weren't any Republic of South Vietnam, or RVAN, units operating out of this sector.

In the future, when I began to allow myself to think about that day, when I believed that, because years had passed, I could handle the haunting memories, the primary sensation that would fill my being was a numbing, primordial, cold-blooded fear. I would recall and freeze-frame the precise thought that passed through my mind when Charlie burst through the underbrush a few feet from my face, nearly as surprised as me but with enough presence of mind to have his weapon ready and aimed in my direction. It took years before I stopped shivering.

I was spent and bleeding. Dickey's body lay next to mine as three black-clad Vietcong stepped out of the swaying elephant grass. I knew they were going to kill me. I had my Colt .45 service revolver in my good hand, and I began raising it from my lap, taking aim as I did.

The last thing I remembered was seeing the blinding flash of an AK-47 and hearing its unmistakable, staccato-like burp, burp, burp.

*****

"Flight attendants, please take your seats; tower has cleared us for landing," the captain's voice announced, wrenching me back to the present.

I was sweating. I could feel my shirt sticking to the leather seat. My palms were clammy. My throat was parched. I caught the stewardess's attention before she could take her own seat and asked for a glass of ice water. The first-class cabin seemed hot and close. I took my handkerchief from my pocket and wiped my brow. Swallowing the water the stewardess had handed me did some good, relieving the dryness in my throat.

I didn't shiver, though.

Since Beth's death, I had recalled the Vietnam incident more and more. Sometimes in dreams it would come to me, although the dreams never compared with the haunting intensity that some conscious reminder brought.

It was ironic that although Billy was from that time, I never thought of him in that light. We never talked about Nam. We were always meeting in some elegant restaurant, such as Le Bernardin. I was his best man when he got married, and he was mine. We were practically brothers. Yet the first time we met, his face less than a centimeter from mine ...

*****

"Shhh. Listen up, and don't talk," a cold and emotionless voice commanded. A hand placed gently but firmly across my mouth ensured that I didn't. Stirring but dazed from a combination of pain and a stupor-like coma, unaware of who and where I was, I thought I was dreaming, my inner voice speaking. "Shhh. Listen carefully," the voice said, releasing the tension ever so slightly from his hand. "I'm an American—Special Forces. If you keep still and follow everything I say, maybe we can get you out of here," he whispered, his mouth an extension of my ear, not wasting his breath to add the word alive to the end of his sentence.

I saw two coal-black eyes and thought I was in hell.

"Can you walk?" He slid his hand onto my chin.

I realized then that this was no dream, and with that realization came the reality that this was hell. I was afraid to move a muscle, unsure if an involuntary noise would emerge when I did.

Two or three precious seconds went by. "Can you?" I saw his eyes enlarge as if to will me to answer yes.

I barely moved my head, indicating no.

I heard him say something under his breath that sounded like "Damn," and then he said, "Okay, no problem. I'll take you out." He swung his free arm and checked his watch.

"Okay, listen up." Something resembling a strained "Yes" tumbled silently from my parched lips. "In sixty seconds, two Hueys will touch down thirty yards east of here." He motioned to his right with his head. "There are only three VCs that we were able to place." He paused, his eyes narrowing, and I sensed a trace of uncertainty about him. "Roger?"

I struggled not to cough or to be too loud. In an unfamiliar, raspy whisper of a voice, I said, "That's all I saw. Jesus, that's all I saw, because they goddamn killed me before I saw any others."

"Okay then," he replied, the self-assuredness returning to his voice, "as soon as we hear them, or if we hear Charlie coming in our direction, I'll pick you up. Help however you can. Try to grab me around my neck and slide onto my back."

The weight of his body shifted, and I felt the tension of the ropes around my legs ease. "Turn over a little," he ordered, and his hands guided me to his command. My arms were freed at the exact moment a sledgehammer of pain shot through my shoulder.

"As soon as we move, all hell will break loose behind us as the rest of my team moves in and sanctions Charlie. Don't worry—we've been in far tougher situations than this cherry walk."

Suddenly I heard the familiar sounds of Huey rotor wash. At the same moment, my rescuer hoisted me onto his back, and two silhouetted figures leaped from the concealment of the high grass and fell upon two of my captors. That was all I remembered; I went into shock as we ran to the Hueys.

*****

"Mr. Douglas, I believe this is your luggage."

I took my luggage from the stewardess and walked to the exit.

"Manhattan, Eighth and Forty-Fourth."

The taxi lurched from the curb, its driver seemingly oblivious to the onrushing traffic. It was 9:25. I wouldn't arrive in Sea Isle until at least 11:00. Stupid, stupid, stupid! Why did *I* drive the Bimmer on Monday?

A half hour later, I picked up the Bimmer and entered the Lincoln Tunnel. As soon as I exited, I dialed Katya. I wasn't surprised when I heard my recorded voice. I almost said something sarcastic, such as reminding her who I was in case she had forgotten, but that would have added fuel to an already-blazing, if not out-of-control, fire.

"Katya, I just got out of the Lincoln Tunnel. I should be home around eleven." I was too tightly wrapped to close with "I love you."

The late-night traffic was light, and with the bomb averaging better than eighty, I was on the Garden State Parkway, approaching Cubbies Marina, in thirty minutes. As I passed the marina, I wondered if it had been a good week for them. Cynically I mused that if it had been anything like mine, the coast guard would have issued hurricane warnings—force five, or whatever was considered the fiercest.

I couldn't believe it! I couldn't goddamn believe it!

Less than a car length behind, its red lights flashing, was a New Jersey state trooper's car. I felt like beating my head against the steering wheel, but I settled for a half dozen open-fisted punches on it instead. For the umpteenth time, I cursed my decision to drive into the city. I downshifted and pulled onto the shoulder.

The officer's flashlight blinded my eyes. "License and registration, please." Although I couldn't see the face, I recognized the voice. I handed him the identification he'd requested.

"Well, looka here now. If it isn't as I suspected." He redirected the beam away from my eyes, confirming what I already knew. "Good to see you once again, Mr. Douglas. I told you I'd see you soon. And, shoot, you didn't disappoint me none. Remember what I told you when we last chitchatted? This here car of yours has got too much engine for these parts."

I was in no mood for his bullshit. "Look, Officer, if you don't mind, I can do without the small talk. If I was speeding, just give me the damn ticket and let me be on my way." More for my benefit than his, I added under my breath, "It's been one helluva week."

"Step out of the car, Mr. Douglas," the shark commanded, dropping all pretense of his down-home, good-old-boy, backwoodsy tone.

"What? What did you say?"

"I said, step out of the car. Now!"

What the hell was going on? Complying with the idiot's request, I somehow contained my rising anger by focusing on the genesis of my predicament and vowed to put the Bimmer up for sale, auction, whatever, as soon as I had the chance.

"Place your hands on the roof of the car." He kicked my feet apart.

Shock, more than anger, became my primary emotion. I realized that although he was an idiot, he was an armed idiot. "Listen, Officer, what's this about?"

He yanked my hands from the roof and, in one movement, handcuffed them behind my back. As I started to say something, he broke in over my protests and led me to his car, reading me my Miranda rights.

He shoved me into the rear seat of the cruiser. The handcuffs made it difficult to sit, and I twisted in place to find a comfortable position. I must have said something, because the shark interrupted his radio conversation and asked if I were all right.

"No, god damn it!"

His face on the other side of the metal mesh separator appeared surreal as the lights from the parkway traffic alternated on and off his cold, hardened features. "Mr. Douglas, now, now. I'm going to have to ask you to be a good boy and be quiet." He returned to his radio.

It was not easy to control my fury. I was steaming. Recalling my assessment regarding his intellectual capacity helped a bit. Balancing the two, I decided to appeal to his sense of decency. "Look, Shark—Officer—all I want is to know what's going on. Why am I handcuffed in your car like this? I'm not some vicious criminal, right?"

A second state police car arrived alongside us. I couldn't hear everything that was said, but I heard the shark say he would follow the other officer.

I was about to repeat my plea, when the voice on the other side of the steel partition spoke first. "Mr. Douglas, just sit back and relax. We'll be at the Asbury Park station house in a couple of minutes."

This unexpected soliloquy by my state-employed abductor shifted my balance to the steamier side of the equation. "Listen, Officer, or whatever your name is!" I shouted. "How can I relax when you pull me over, drag me out of my car, handcuff me as though I were a common, everyday criminal, and then tell me you're hauling my ass off to jail?"

A few seconds of quiet tension filled the cramped interior of the police cruiser before I cast caution to the wind and laced into him with both barrels blazing.

"For Christ's sake, what's the goddamn charge? I didn't do anything! And what about my rights? Jesus, what about them? Answer that charge. Fuck Miranda—I didn't do anything," I shouted at the back of the head sitting in front of me. The image of Roquette and his no-nonsense persona emboldened me further. "You'll hear from my attorney on this"—the only word I could think of was buster, so that's what I called him—"buster!"

To the shark's professional credit, and my frustration, he appeared unmoved by my tirade. "Mr. Douglas, I'd thank you to be quiet now" was all he said.

I was embarrassed by this whole situation. I was confused, angry, a great deal fearful, unbelievingly frustrated, and very embarrassed. I was exhausted, having had little sleep in the past week. Closing my eyes, I wished—I prayed once more—that when I opened them, I would find that everything had returned to normal—to the way it was last Friday. I was not greedy. Forget those thoughts about wishing I could start over. Friday was perfect. Friday around three—about the time I drove up the driveway and Katya called me on the car phone.

I was ready to sign up and replay everything over from that point, replay it as many times as necessary until I got it exactly right, when the horror of what I was asking hit me. No… no! I tried to erase the thought. Friday was no good. It was terrible—all wrong.

Friday was already too late for Maria!

When I opened my eyes, I could see we had left the parkway and were somewhere downtown in what was once one of New Jersey's most beautiful, desirable coastal cities.

Maria and I would ride the merry-go-round together at Asbury Park sometimes after leaving the beach—before things changed.

As the police station loomed ominously ahead, the shark—in a weak, perhaps even magnanimous, moment—apparently decided that I had been punished enough. Either that or he was saying nothing more than what he was required to say by law.

He was to the point. "Mr. Douglas, you should know I didn't arrest you for speeding." He shut the engine off and turned his head so that his profile was visible. "You see, Mr. Douglas, a warrant was issued for your arrest for the murder of Sammantha Kelso."

Chapter 12

THE HARSH, COLD SOUND of steel clanging against steel as the cell door slammed shut was what I remembered most.

I was allowed my one phone call. I debated whether it should be to Katya or Roquette. I decided on Roquette for two reasons. One, if I called Katya, she would have to call him afterward anyway. And two, more importantly, how was I to explain to her what had happened? I couldn't—not from jail, anyway.

Why didn't I tell her everything when I had the chance?

I was betting that some junior partner or some conscientious first-year law school graduate trying to meet his or her monthly billable quota would answer, but I caught my first break of the day when I was told to hang on for Roquette.

A few minutes later, he was on the phone and roaring at me. "Douglas, why the call at this hour? Didn't my secretary inform you to call me tomorrow? That maybe by then we'll have some news regarding your situation?"

"Tomorrow can't wait," I shot back, explaining my reason for calling.

"I'll have you out of there in less than an hour," he screamed confidently.

Approximately an hour later, my cell door swung open, my personnel effects were returned, and after signing some papers under the watchful eye of a local counsel that Roquette pressed into service, I was a free man.

"You were never free," Parcae would remind me.

I had not been under arrest for Maria's murder. That's what Roquette's toady told me as we walked out of the station. He said the NYPD had told him that my arrest was a mistake and that there was no record of me associated with her murder. All internal police references associating me to the murder had been expunged from the record.

I asked if that seemed strange to him and why Roquette's inside connections were all of a sudden able to sort through the red tape and find this out. "Very unusual" was all he said.

"What's the likelihood of these storm troopers arresting me again?" I asked.

He started to spout some pedantic gibberish, extolling the writ of habeas corpus and my inalienable right to be informed of the crime with which I was charged, among other nuances of the law; however, apparently noticing the angry look on my face, he cut his speech short and simply advised me, "You should take it up with Roquette." I wasn't certain which response he heard when I left, running toward the Bimmer—the one that said, "I would," or the one that said, "Fuck off"—because I didn't pay any attention to his own good-night ramblings.

When I pulled into the pebble drive at Sea Isle, it was somewhere between two and three in the morning. I walked quietly up to the moonlit house, my shadow flickering tentatively, if not stealthily, ahead. When I got to the porch and reached for the handle, I hesitated. Through the corners of my eyes, I saw that my shadow had somehow maneuvered itself behind me. I had an eerie premonition that Katya was not asleep inside—that she wasn't there at all and I would never be able to see or touch her again.

She was, though. She was asleep in our bed, her silhouetted profile motionless in the moonlight, beneath the thin summer sheets, her face buried protectively in her pillow. I lost all sense of time as I stood there, not moving, just staring at the figure before me.

It was as though it were the first time I was seeing her.

I undressed in the darkness of our bedroom, with only the light from the moon filtering through the curtained windows. Exhausted, I slipped into the bed, my head dropping heavily upon the pillow. My body touched my wife's. I kissed her tenderly on her bare shoulder and whispered softly, "I'm here, Katya. I'm finally here."

Some hours later, after another fitful night drifting between consciousness and a deep, dream-like lethargy, I woke to the sound of the bathroom shower. Rising reluctantly, my bones stiff from too much sitting, too much traveling, I managed to twist myself into my robe and stumble down the stairs into the kitchen.

As I counted the tablespoons and filled the coffeepot, I also prepared myself for what to reveal to Katya.

After the call to Magritte, I had also informed my office that I wouldn't be coming in for probably the entire next week and advised Cindy's somewhat-permanent replacement that I would be calling in for messages if anyone needed to contact me. I had planned that Katya and I would use Friday and Saturday to sift through the whole damn mess—Maria, the police suspicions, what was happening at DFT, and what our lives had become. We would talk about everything, and things would work out. Maybe our relationship would never be the way it was when we first married, but it would be okay. Even though things had changed, they would be okay.

I did my best to assure myself this would be the case, but there was something lacking, something wrong with everything I thought and hoped. Even as the scenario played itself out in my head, I cried aloud, "They have to!"

"Who are they?"

"Kat? Oh, Kat. I didn't hear you come down." Caught off guard, I watched, mesmerized, as she towel-dried her long, blonde hair in the kitchen doorway.

"What exactly do they have to do?" She removed the towel from her head and shook her hair in a quick series of exaggerated side-to-side motions, releasing any excess water still clinging to it. She draped the towel loosely around her neck; her terry-cloth robe separated to reveal her tanned legs as she walked to the kitchen counter. She poured herself a mug of coffee and leaned against the counter, holding the steaming mug tightly between her hands. "Evidently you're not going to answer me," she said. Her eyes met mine over the steaming vapors.

"Oh, that," I replied, waving my hand dismissively. "It's nothing.

Just some incoherent babbling that lately, it seems, I've taken to mouthing on a regular basis." I crossed the kitchen to where Katya was standing.

I took the mug from her and set it on the counter; I clasped her hands in mine and tugged her body to me. As she fell against me, my arms pressed our two bodies against each other. I felt her arms reach up as she searched for my neck and her head drop onto my shoulder.

No words were spoken. We just swayed in place and in each other's arms, my fingers loosely entwined in Katya's damp hair, tenderly stroking it, feeling her heart pounding against my chest. It was as close together as we had been in a long, long time. Finally, Katya moaned, breaking the spell.

When she lifted her head from my shoulder and gazed into my eyes, I saw the same sad expression that had become so familiar in these recent years.

"What happened to us, Christof?" she asked. "Why us?" She tilted her head, awaiting a response but she knew why in her soul.

How do I reply to questions that have taken years to formulate? Questions dating back to when we were different ... Before Beth ... Before things changed.

I found myself sinking further and further into memories long since buried, long since forgotten. I could no longer shut them out, unable to halt that dark slide into awakened emotions before ... before Katya.

Yes, I love Katya. Those feelings had mystically resurfaced that week as well. It was as though Maria's death had unleashed and freed her earthbound spirit from the deepest recesses of my tormented soul and allowed these feelings to be felt again.

"Kaya, I will love you forever," I whispered. Struggling with my inner demons and avoiding her question, I kissed her lovingly on the lips.

Her hands pushed against my embrace. She stepped backward, distancing herself, and her eyes stared angrily into mine. Neither of us spoke. I couldn't. The air was too heavy, my throat too dry. The moment seemed to stand still forever.

Finally it was broken. I could see her green eyes moisten as a tear formed in each, falling a few seconds later down her cheeks.

"I can't anymore! I can't!" she shouted, shoving me backward, her eyes now squeezed shut, her head shaking violently. "It's too late—too late for us now, Christof!" She spit out the words as her voice rose. "Why now? What happened all of a sudden to make you think that these newfound sentiments, whatever you believe you think they are, can just smooth things over, make everything right because now you feel it?"

"Katya, listen to me. We can go on. We can. We must!" My arms were outstretched, my hands open as I stepped toward her and pleaded for her to forgive me and told her how much I needed her. As though repelled, she stepped back. Her arms and palms were outstretched as well, but instead of a plea, the gesture seemed to be a move for protection and a signal for me to not come closer. "Go on. Go on!" Katya shouted, repeating herself, her face flushed, the veins on her neck bulging. "To where, Christof? Don't you understand? It's too late!"

This final fiery explosion, releasing emotions denied for years, was apparently too great a stress for her fragile psyche, and with a low, soft moan escaping from her lips, she collapsed onto the cold kitchen floor.

*****

It was April, the spring of 1972, and Katya was alive, although I had yet to meet her. I was just about to, though.

It had been almost three years since my discharge from Uncle Sam's army, and sleep still did come easily. I rarely slept through most of a night. I would often awake, my body covered in sweat after a restless few hours of tossing and rolling about, violent nightmares or past memories my constant, unsettling companions.

Spring break had just ended, and the final two-month stretch of my MBA program was about to start. It was supposed to be a tough two months, what with finalizing my master's thesis, prepping for finals, and trying to land a good job.

I was in luck with that last item. Or perhaps the gods, who over the past few years had chosen not to grace me with their blessings, took pity. Occasionally, at a weak moment, and with reluctance, I would cede that possibility.

Since Nam, I had developed a new philosophy, a hard-edged, prove-it-to-me attitude regarding all of the rotten things that happened in life, such as my euphemistic tour in Nam, the disappearance of Maria, and Tony's death. I felt that all those dots eventually connected like some paint-by-number scheme, only to result in a completed product that resembled Hieronymus Bosch's version of paradise.

And vice versa. Anything good, anything that meant happiness—such as my enrollment at NYU; my rescue by Billy, although I could argue that as a good or a bad thing; and my internship at the radio station WPMY—was part of a parallel and separate plan, maybe even another universe, one based on nothing but pure, unadulterated luck. It was a universe more in line with those eighteenth-century Turner oils of the gentle English countryside.

That day, though, whether it was God's smile or pure luck, it didn't matter. I got what I wanted.

The year before, I had heard through one of my professors about an intern position at WPMY. And although I was majoring in finance, I had developed an extracurricular appetite for broadcasting. I originally acquired a taste for it in Vietnam when I helped with the battalion's media radio operations; I then further fed my interest by joining the university's broadcast club. So I called WPMY and applied for the spot. Instead of mailing my résumé as the lady I'd spoken with advised, I went in person that same day. As luck or whatever would have it, I got the job—got it on the spot. As soon as I arrived and introduced myself to the unreceptive receptionist, a middle-aged, well-dressed executive type passed by a few feet behind me.

Coincidence or fate? Was luck the residue of design, or there but for whim of the gods go I? I got tired of debating the question with Parcae, because she would just tell me everything happened that day as though she were standing next to me.

"Christof Douglas, not Christian." I enunciated my name a second time, naively disappointed that I wasn't about to get an interview immediately. "And I can wait if that's okay with you." The moment I finished my statement, I felt someone grab my elbow and tug it as though to spin me around. Half expecting the security guard, I found myself looking into a face that could be described only as having seen a ghost.

"Mr. Lake, this gentleman was on his way out," the receptionist declared. She seemed unsure herself of what was happening but made it clear that she had been doing her job.

He gestured for her to stop. "What did you say your name was?" he asked, staring at me.

I had no idea who this man was, but it was obvious he was of some importance. Reverting almost subconsciously to my military bearing, I just about snapped to as I answered, "Douglas, sir. Christof Douglas."

The man gazed into my eyes as though he knew but couldn't quite understand what his next response would be. I felt his grasp tighten about my arm, and my shoulder began to throb.

"Did you know Richard Lake? Dickey?" He seemed to be struggling with his question and paused as if to gain his composure. "That was what his friends called him."

My mind was struggling also, searching through memory banks, not wanting to place the name it knew all too well.

"He was my son. He was a captain in the army," he said softly. He dropped his eyes from mine and relaxed his grip; the throbbing seemed to pass from my shoulder to his body when he painfully added, "He was killed in Vietnam three years ago."

I started at WPMY the next day, and by the time I met Katya, I had been there for a year. I would go on to spend another five wonderful years at WPMY before moving on after Dickey's dad passed away.

We talked a little about the past during those first few days, especially right after we met. Mostly we talked about what sort of guy his son was, never being too specific, never discussing my final moments with Dickey. It was as if we were probing each other, skirting around the edges. After a week or so, neither of us ever brought it up again.

I met Katya through my association with the station. Professor Tkarr, Katya's father, had just written a book that was climbing all the nonfiction best-seller lists. His book, *Yugoslavia, Country at the Crossroads: Ottoman to Breshev*, was being hailed as the definitive analysis of that country's role in shaping modern Western geopolitics, and as such, it was a hot topic for talk media.

He was at the time a professor at Princeton's Woodrow Wilson School of Political Science, having taught there since arriving in the early seventies with his wife, Katya, and her sister from London, where he had been head of Marshal Tito's unofficial delegation to England. He had already published a number of other books addressing the social and political issues facing postwar Eastern Europe, but this one had a wider, more general audience and was perfect for talk radio. "Its primary purpose," he later confided in me, "is to reach the American public and educate them by exposing the true insidiousness of the Soviet Empire."

When he accepted Mr. Lake's invitation to appear on one of WPMY's programs, I took it upon myself to read his book. And although I couldn't disagree with his premise regarding the Soviet Empire, my tour in Nam suggested that average Americans had more to fear from their own government than some foreign one.

It was our tragedy that both of us were right. I thought, believed ... we were unique ... Katya ... Maria ...

The morning was sunny and clear when I went to pick up Professor Tkarr that spring day. He was staying at the Hotel New Yorker, and it was my task to make sure he arrived at the station on time for his guest appearance. When I rang his room, I thought I had dialed a wrong number when a young woman's voice—I couldn't describe it as girlish, what with the accent conjuring up images of Julie Christie—answered.

"Ell-oh?"

"I'm ... I'm ... sorry. I-I was looking for ... Dr. Tkarr," I stuttered, checking the room number the hotel clerk had given me.

"This is Dr. Tkarr's room. May I ask who is calling?"

"Oh ... sure. Yeah ... Yes, that is. This is Chris Douglas from WPMY. I was sent ... I'm here to pick up ... Meet Dr. Tkarr and bring him there for his interview."

"Oh? Why, yes. Please wait a second. I'll get my father."

Months later, when we were engaged, we would be holding hands across the table at the White Knight Café in the West Village and thanking the fates for bringing us together. I didn't quite share her enthusiasm with respect to providence's intervention, but what the hell, we were in love.

"After all," I could picture her declaring, so full of young life, so radiantly happy, "if my spring recess were not the same as yours, I wouldn't have been able to accompany my father to New York, and we wouldn't have met."

At that time, I hadn't told Katya about Dickey Lake. Later I would, but I couldn't bring myself to do so just yet. She knew about my being shot down and the crazy things I did afterward. But I still had to keep Dickey for myself—Dickey and Maria. She knew about Maria, of course. As we were getting serious, she grew curious and speculated about who had come before. So I told her. I also told her I was over Maria—that she was ancient history as far as I was concerned. That wasn't entirely true, though. I didn't love Maria, not the way I had before; that was true enough. I couldn't. I felt too much anger over what she'd done. But I knew I would always wonder about us. Katya, on the other hand, brought less baggage with her because I was her first true love.

Katya accompanied her father to the studio that day, and I was completely mesmerized by her the instant I saw her approach the concierge's desk. There was no doubt in my mind that the gray-haired man with her was the professor—who else would wear a black, hounds tooth sport coat with a hideous red bow tie, defined by a bushy white mustache and beard?

When I first met Katya, I could sense that this was someone I wanted to be with. I couldn't come right out and say it was love or anything so definitive; I didn't immediately feel that she was the woman I was going to marry and spend my life with. It was far subtler. I felt as if I had known her, or some part of me had known her, from some other, very intimate place, or from some other time, and now, without knowing why, the two of us were reunited.

"You are Mr. Douglas?"

"I am, sir."

"This is my daughter, Katya."

I wanted to say something profound, but all I could manage was a meek "Hello."

She had an air of sophistication, a captivating allure that was impossible to resist. When she entered a room, heads would turn. "Charming, delightfully charming" was how Carlson reacted upon meeting her. He monopolized her that evening, making sure that she sat next to him at dinner, and the two conversed in French and discussed the hottest fads in the art world throughout the entire affair. She would have been equally at home speaking Italian or her native tongue—not that there would have been too many others in the room who would have understood her language, a form of Serbo-Croatian—as well as her adopted language, the Queen's English.

I didn't know all that then. I knew only that she looked, moved, and sounded like the most desirable, fascinating woman I had ever met.

Her fashionably long blonde hair, streaked with traces of auburn, swayed upon her shoulders when she walked purposely in my direction. From a distance, I thought her eyes were brown, but when she stood next to me, I realized they were emerald in color. She was about five foot five; the top of her head rested against my lips when we danced together. At our wedding, less than a year later, her head nestled under my chin, her heart beating against my chest, I kissed her head tenderly as we danced to our song, "The First Time."

And she was slender. Her weight was one of her most guarded secrets; she never told me, despite my pestering, how much she weighed. I had an idea—somewhere around 105—but it was one of those things, along with never telling me for whom she voted, that she kept to herself.

If only all her secrets were as harmless.

But what really made her Katya? What made her different? I sensed its presence immediately yet couldn't quite place my finger on it. But as the weeks and months sped by and we started to fall in love with each other, I came to understand the answer to this riddle.

Katya had a glow, a spirit, and ultimately a soul that very few were blessed with. It was something a person was born with or not. I didn't have it. Maria touched upon it at times but was too cynical to sustain it.

Katya had something about her persona that—along with her finely, delicately shaped face, the clipped British accent that she had developed at Miss Porter's School in the Cotswolds, and the way she spoke through that winsome smile of hers—reminded one of Audrey Hepburn.

If Christie were Pasternak's melancholy Lara, then Katya was Tolstoy's young, irrepressible Princess Natasha—or, for less royal tastes, a sophisticated Holly Golightly, or maybe even a metamorphosed Eliza Doolittle.

That was Katya to me.

I must have stood there not speaking, just staring at her, longer than I realized, for the professor finally took me by the arm and inquired, "Which way to the radio station?"

The professor was a hit with the staff that day, especially with Mr. Lake, who had an intellectual's curiosity in most substantive matters, regardless of how arcane they might be. He was a hit with the audience as well, based upon the extra heavy volume of callers for the time slot he appeared in.

Afterward, Mr. Lake invited the professor and his daughter to join him for lunch at Sardi's. He must have noticed my infatuation with Katya and apparently took pity, because he asked me to join them also. "Only if you participate in the conversation. And do try to refrain from appearing like some love-struck moon dog," he forewarned, whispering in my ear.

The memories from that day are so vivid, so powerful that I can still recall them as if it were yesterday and not—what is it now?—nearly twenty-eight years ago. It was as if that day I was at last able to close the chapter on one phase of my life and begin to write the next.

Katya and I listened attentively as her father and Mr. Lake discussed Cold War politics. I listened but was looking at Katya out of the corner of my eye. I found out that she was completing her master's program at Princeton in fine arts, having graduated two years earlier with the same major. I learned these facts as the professor traced his family's journey from the "old country to this new and wonderful America," to quote him.

When the bill came, I was both nervous and terrified. I was now staring at the realization that she might walk out of my life in the following minutes and I might never see her again. Thinking on the spot, I impetuously volunteered to escort them back to the hotel. I turned to Mr. Lake and noticed he was smiling. For an instant, I believed he was going to remind everyone that it was only around the corner or, even worse, request my presence back at the office.

I also discovered during lunch that Katya and her father were staying in the city for the week, as the professor had been booked on one or two other shows, so I jumped at the chance to offer my services again. The professor thanked me but declined graciously. He had a full itinerary planned, he said. He paused and glanced at Katya, and the two exchanged whatever secret code they were privy to. Before he could add anything else, Katya spoke.

"I'd be delighted to take you up on your offer." She turned her face from her father's and looked directly into my eyes.

And that was how I met my wife, Katya.

Chapter 13

SOMETIMES THE SEA SEEMS so inviting.

Royce and Betty Ingersten helped me put Katya into bed that July morning. I didn't want their help, but, well, with the windows wide open, they heard Katya's shouting, thought something terrible was happening, and came rushing into the house. I was sitting on the floor, cradling Katya in my arms, rocking her gently and stroking her damp hair when they burst in. She was awake, but her eyes were closed; her quiet sobbing was punctuated every so often by a deep moan.

"Oh. Oh no! Charlene was right. She was right; they are splitting up," Betty hysterically shrieked when she saw us. "What happened?" Not bothering to wait for a response, she took charge. "Here, let's help the poor dear to her bed." She reached toward Katya and lifted her from the floor.

We all sort of pitched in at that point, including Katya herself, who by this time was more embarrassed than upset. At least that's what I was hoping as this peculiar figure with eight arms and eight legs—like a pair of entwined octopi engaged in some grotesque dance, stooping and crouching sideways—wended its way up the stairs to our bedroom. By then, Katya was awake and alert and telling everyone, "It's okay. It's okay. I'm perfectly all right." But this strange procession had developed a mind of its own and just ignored her pleas.

I never did get to tell Katya that day about my plans to go to Paris.

It wasn't until the next day, when we were alone, that I would have a chance to do that. It was late Saturday night when I told her I would be leaving the following morning and would be gone for a few days. But I didn't tell her the real reason I was going. Instead I said that Carlson had dropped the legal maneuvers against the FCC, was selling the stations, and had requested I take part in this rag-trade task force of his. I even told her that the trip to Paris was an introductory step for me to become familiar with the entire apparel and fashion industry and was necessary for me if I were going to make any sort of contribution.

But I never did tell her anything about Maria. Or any of the related aspects, such as the police harassment and eventual arrest. As much as I had sworn I would, I never did. And I never told her what I was really hoping to accomplish by going to Paris.

Katya didn't say much. Once or twice she asked a question, but mostly she just stared at me, her face empty of emotion. It was as if I had already left. I wasn't sure if she believed it all—or, for that matter, any of it. The whole time I was telling this lie, my stomach was on fire.

I'd like to think that if I had come home earlier the day before from my trip to Greenville, I would have told her the truth. Or maybe if I didn't get that phone call from my office as we were bringing Katya into the bedroom Friday morning, perhaps as the day went on, when we were alone, trying to rekindle something that once was, maybe then I would've told her.

Since then I've thought a great deal—reflected, mused—about whether I would have told her that weekend, or when I returned from Paris, or ever, for that matter. After all these years, what was the point? I never did tell her. I would never get the chance. That was the harsh reality. I did get that call. The phone rang just as we were helping Katya into bed.

"Hello?"

"Chris, it's Mosely. You gotta get here ASAP! We got a major emergency in WXRA's studio. The damn place is going nuts!" I could hear a loud din in the background, underscoring his statement.

My initial reaction was that some deranged madman or terrorist group had stormed the station and taken hostages. "What the hell is going on?"

"It's Casey, Chris. Casey's gone ape shit. He's snapped."

"Casey? He's no terrorist!"

Mosely told me that maybe the Casey I knew wasn't, but the Casey who locked himself in his studio an hour into his show and wasn't allowing anyone in was. "He's got a .357 Magnum that he's holding against his head," he said. "The police are on the scene, negotiating with him as we speak."

Mosely told me all this and then repeated his prior demand. "Chris, you gotta get here ASAP."

What else could I do? DFT Entertainment was still loosely under my watch. And Casey was someone I had known for years, someone who had been an integral part of DFT and my successes. I didn't have a choice. If it weren't my responsibility to help resolve this thing safely, then whose was it?

I hung up and pulled Betty off to the side, out of Katya's earshot, and asked if she'd mind staying with her. When I explained what was happening, she agreed immediately and said she understood why I had to go.

She had said that, hadn't she? But that was so long ago I can't be certain anymore.

I told Katya that there was an emergency at the station and I needed to get there immediately. She seemed to understand, repeating her previous statement: "It's okay. It's okay. I'm all right."

I was out the front door before I had a chance to reconsider and jumped into the Oldsmobile 98, my company car, in case my friend, the shark, was out there and on the lookout for the Bimmer. I turned on the radio and heard Sean Casey's voice. It was his voice, but I knew he wasn't following what his program director had in mind for that morning's broadcast. He cursed and ranted at the callers he let on the air, and most returned in kind or better.

Mosely had said that Sean hadn't made any specific demands but had threatened to blow his brains out if anyone attempted to break into the studio or tried to pull him off the air. Listening to him, racing as fast as I dared toward Manhattan, I had the feeling he'd meant what he said.

I was shocked by the mean-spiritedness of the callers, who spewed forth their venom and seemed to become intoxicated with themselves upon finding a receptive forum. I was sickened by their viciousness. I was accustomed to the usual malcontents—those losers who called and, protected by the shield of anonymity, ranted against the government, their neighbors, and anything or anyone they didn't agree with. But I had never heard anything remotely as nauseating as I did that morning.

Normally, if such callers were clever enough to get by the screener, the on-air host tossed them aside once their messages became obvious. But Casey was not only encouraging these crazies, disregarding the on-air delay button whenever one violated broadcasting decency standards; he was taking calls only from their sordid ilk.

Sometime in the future, when the discourse of political and everyday life got crasser and uglier, inevitably polarizing our society, I would not have been as surprised at their calls. But this was pre-crash 1987, the feel-good-about-yourself years. Sadly, in the future, society would sink low enough to make this type of sick spectacle a media art form. I did learn later, when the fall book came out, that this fiasco had the highest morning-drive ratings Arbitron had ever recorded. What could I say? Sean was the consummate showman and knew exactly what he was doing when it came to his ratings.

When I got to the studio, it was almost eleven, and Casey had been going at it for more than two hours. I had had my fill of the crazies goading him, "Go ahead and blow your fuckin' brains out," or "Seek salvation and repent, sinner; it is never too late to find God," along with a score of equally bizarre, voyeuristic pieces of advice. I was just as fed up with Casey, who would randomly laugh at them; he exhorted one caller, "Remember me when I'm air history, and honor my memory by taking out some Wall Street cocksucker," and then admonished the next, "Go and find your own redemption, you godless prick." I couldn't help but wonder what the FCC's reaction would be when they reviewed the day's tapes—and what the impact would be on the deal Carlson was cutting with them.

As I took the elevator to WXRA's studios, I still hadn't figured out what I was going to say to Casey. My initial thoughts were to appeal to him about our relationship and stress the well-being of the station and staff, even assuring him that when everything was sorted out, he would be in demand and there would always be a place for him in radio land. Then again, recalling how our meeting had ended last Monday, I thought it best to play it by ear.

Exiting the elevator, I sped past the empty and silent conference room where I'd held my last staff meeting. Five days ago? Was that all it was? The contrast between then and now, and how my world had turned upside down, only underscored the isolated hallway. Instead of the normal midmorning hustle and bustle of people going about their business, there was just the eerie stillness, disturbed only by the echoing taps my shoes made as I ran.

I was headed toward four separate, soundproofed studios at the corner of the floor. Each had an adjacent glass-encased room to interface with the "live" studio, usually manned by a program manager or assistant who would screen calls, prompt the host as needed, and generally communicate with the host. In one of those studios, Sean Casey was holding himself and DFT hostage. I could picture Mosely and the police, staring at him through the glass from the adjacent room, trying to defuse the situation.

At the end of the corridor, before gaining access to the heart of these operations, it was necessary to pass through station security—first an outer set of steel doors requiring an ID card for entry and then a security guard seated behind a shatterproof Plexiglas enclosure. If a person had the required clearance, the guard would then buzz him or her into where the actual broadcasting took place. We sometimes joked that the security setup wasn't about security in the sense one usually thought of; rather, it was more a line of separation maintained to delineate the so-called talent of the business from the more plebian among us.

When I reached the end of the corridor, I was blocked by two beefy, no-nonsense NYPD cops. Their initial response was to tell me the area was off limits, only to reverse themselves when I produced my ID. I was then buzzed through the second set of doors by a familiar face. The moment I entered that inner sanctum, I was met with a surreal calmness that belied the underlying drama.

Directly down the hall, standing silently, watching the chilling scenario play out in front of them, were Mosely, a station engineer, two additional police officers, and Detective Hopkins. I was not surprised to see the latter. As I approached them, Sean Casey, the object of their concentration and the person occupying center stage, the way he preferred, came into view.

He had something resembling a small cannon propped against his cheek. He was sitting in his chair, glaring back at them, his sweat-stained shirt wide open to expose a huge and hairy chest. With his free hand, he was wiping the beads of sweat from his face. It was an exercise in futility. By the time his hand dropped back onto the microphone, fresh beads would appear.

In the connecting chamber, there were three other people. All wore headsets and were maintaining whatever level of communication with Casey he might grant. Sitting nearest me was Roger Mason, Casey's program manager, who was still performing some of his normal duties by taking incoming calls and then keying the lines they were on and their basic messages into the teleprompter. Next to him was a man I didn't recognize. Given what was happening, along with the cut and style of his wardrobe, I was certain he was an associate of Hopkins's. On his left, and farthest away from me, trying hard to maintain her composure, her red-rimmed eyes and tearstained cheeks betraying her, was Casey's wife and broadcast partner, Vivian.

Mosely was the first to notice me. His face appeared drained and stressed to the breaking point under the mounting tension as he rushed to greet me. "Damn it, Chris, he's crazy," he whispered. "He's really going to do it. He's really going to shoot himself."

"What the hell happened to him?" I whispered back. "Why is he doing this? Did he tell anybody why?"

Both of us were whispering to each other, yet neither of us could remove our eyes from Casey.

Mosely motioned with his chin toward the room where Vivian was sitting and dropped his tone lower as though afraid she might hear him. "She was asking for a divorce. Apparently they had been having marital problems for some time, and my guess is that she gave him an ultimatum: divorce her now, or she would go public and air on the next broadcast enough dirty laundry to destroy Sean's career. I don't think this is what she had in mind, though."

I shook my head. "No ... no, I don't think so."

My eyes darted between each of the rooms and between each of the protagonists. "Who's the guy beside Vivian?" I pointed with my chin in a manner similar to Mosely's.

"He's with me."

I ignored Hopkins's voice and continued watching what was unfolding on the other side of the glass partition.

"He's with me, Douglas." This time he said it a bit louder, a little more pronounced, especially the last syllable of my name. "His specialty is dealing with head cases—with guys who are candidates for the funny farm. You know the type. Guys from the TV and radio business who either are trying to blow their sick brains out or blow somebody else's out."

I spun around and saw the stupid, insipid smile I'd expected. "Hopkins, did anyone ever tell you that you're a real shithead?"

I saw his vulgar smile widen, and almost unnoticeably—I was positive Mosely didn't catch it—Hopkins raised his right hand slowly, his index finger extended toward me, his thumb cocked in a firing position with the rest of his fingers curled into a fist.

Our eyes locked. *Any doubt I had about you, you son of a bitch … You know something, don't you? There's a special interest you have in me far and above your official cop's duty. Do I have to beat your fuckin' head in to find out?* If eyes could talk, that's what mine would have said. It didn't matter, though; he knew what I was thinking.

"Chris! He wants to talk to you," Mosely yelled. Ignorant of the subplot developing around him, he was tugging at my sleeve and pointing at Casey, who—like some mirrored opposite—was pointing at me.

Apparently realizing he had my attention, Casey motioned with his gun hand, signaling for me to enter the live studio. Turning my back on Hopkins, I took a long, deep breath, trying to compose myself. Casey was still enthusiastically directing me to join in. I opened the studio door and sat down.

I flipped the mike to the on position and adjusted the headset that Roger had handed to me. I was amazed at my voice's calmness when I spoke. *Everyone else probably is too,* I thought, noticing that all eyes were on me.

"Good morning, Sean."

"Right on, Jacko. Right on. That's the spirit I like. Shoot the bastards."

For a confused moment, I thought Sean was speaking to me when he replied. "If you don't, they'll be coming for your mother and your wife, never mind your children and your dear, sweet eighty-year-old granny next, unless you stop them at the gates this instant," Casey raved at his caller. Listening to his ranting, I had not the slightest doubt that the man was crazy.

"Okay, I have to go now. Bye." He smiled at me and pressed the off-air button. Casey looked at Roger and then turned quickly back to me. He appeared to be debating his next move; a wide, furrowed frown replaced his smile. Suddenly he ordered Roger to break to a sponsor. "How about Geo Computer? They're our largest sponsor. We owe them the best performance we can provide for their money." He broke into a hysterical, high-pitched laugh. "Let's give them some bang for their buck, eh, Roger? And don't try anything stupid. I just need a couple of private moments to chat with my old buddy, Mr. Douglas, here." He shifted the .357 to his temple, pressing it against the sweaty flesh, seemingly to emphasize his warning.

There was dead air on my headset before Roger could find and activate the unscheduled commercial from the program cart. As soon as the Chaplinesque music introducing Geo Computer filled our ears, Casey's grin became less maniacal and more satisfied, a fat-cat-eating-the-canary sort of grin, and he flipped on the intercom.

Ignoring everyone else, he spoke to me as though we were alone. Like his grin, his voice had lost the hard edge and was more measured, more rational. "You know why I'm doing this, don't you, Chris?" he asked.

I began to breathe faster. Out of the corner of my eye, I could see the professional police negotiator staring at me without expression. Just think of this whole thing as two friends sitting across the table, having a conversation about cars, lawns, investments, whatever, but stay cool. Stay calm, I kept reminding myself. I couldn't hesitate forever, knowing that the commercial would play itself out in about a minute, and then who knew what was coming.

"I'm not sure, Sean," I finally answered, "but whatever it is, it can be worked out."

"Come now, I told you Monday, laddie. Your memory can't be failing you at this young age. Oh," he gasped, practically leaping from his seat, "it almost slipped my mind. Why, I do believe congratulations are in order." He laughed hard, and his large face reddened so quickly that I feared he would burst a blood vessel.

"I think I'll call you by"—he continued to laugh and snort even louder—"your new title." He was clearly enjoying himself. "Ladies and Gentlemen, I give you …" He paused, seemingly for effect, and then extended his gun hand to its full length, the Magnum waving in a mocking, celebratory flourish, before he pompously exclaimed, "The imperial … the exalted prince … No, no, wait a moment, my good ladies and gentlemen. Let's change that; let's make it sultan. That's a little more him, don't you think?" Casey didn't wait for a response; he finished his pronouncement in near hysteria. "I give you Christof Douglas, the exalted Sultan of Rags!"

Even though he was seemingly laughing out of control, he had enough presence of mind to anticipate the end of the commercial. He turned to Roger and, in a combination guffaw and snort, ordered him to queue another two or three minutes of commercials. "Pick something that's in keeping with me lad's new role in life," he roared.

Before he could offer some sarcasm as to what that role was, Casey looked at the wall clock and quickly changed his demand. "Check that. Just make certain it's less than two minutes. I need to be back live by then." He returned his attention to me, looking more and more like the fat cat. "Can't keep my loyal fans waiting too long, right, Exalted One?"

With everything that had happened since my meeting with Casey, I couldn't remember what the hell he'd said. And if it had been about his contract and the legal issues surrounding the sale of the stations, some things were better left unsaid. I looked up at the wall clock and forced a smile. "Listen, Sean," I said nervously, "we talked about a lot of things. Why don't we go back… go back to my office and discuss whatever it is…whatever gripe you may have or whatever you feel needs to be readdressed?"

Casey checked his watch. Then he turned to me, the commercial ending as he did. His smile had disappeared, leaving his face expressionless.

He looked so serene—so peaceful and relaxed.

Casey didn't waste a second of airtime. The instant the commercial ended, he flipped the on-air switch to live and, ignoring everyone else, refreshed my memory. "Suit, Chris! That's what I told you Monday. You're a suit. That's why you're the Sultan of Rags!"

He jumped up and glanced at his wife and then at the wall clock one last time. "Oops. It's fifteen seconds after eleven. Gotta go!" Then he added, almost as a second thought, "Sorry about running late. It's never happened to me before. Give my apologies to the mayor for delaying his broadcast."

I wasn't sure whether Casey acted first or the police anticipated what was about to happen and began to break open the studio door. It didn't matter. His blood formed grotesque patterns on the studio windows in front of me, and his body was on the floor. I screamed, "No! No!" and leaped from my seat. Other voices screamed the same word in perfect unison in my ear as though by sheer volume we could prevent what we were seeing from happening.

Hopkins made it a point to personally take my statement afterward, even though there was nothing I could add that he hadn't seen. He had lost some of the earlier smugness he'd flaunted when I'd first arrived, but he still had that simmering, underlying hostility as he took down my responses. He was the last of the police, EMS, and coroner's office to leave, and he couldn't resist one final cheap shot.

"See you again, Your Supreme Exaltedness," he said under his breath.

Well, he was wrong. After that day, I never saw Detective Hopkins of the New York … whichever para-military state department he worked for. I heard about him once or twice in the future, or in the past, depending on how one looked at it. But I never saw him again. I guess the same thing could be said for most of the people I've thought about.

I left Sunday morning from Newark International on a flight to Paris. From the moment I got back to Sea Isle sometime late Friday until I left for the airport, Katya and I didn't discuss what had happened between us earlier. I was also spared having to tell her all the gory details about Casey, because she had heard everything on the air. The one question she did ask me—"Why?"—I couldn't, or wouldn't, answer, which seemed to set the mood and curtail any other questions or thoughts she had.

We spent most of Saturday with a couple of her colleagues who happened to be down the shore that day and unexpectedly dropped in. They stayed for dinner at her insistence. The pair eventually left around midnight when all the cognac was drained and after a rather boisterous evening spent debating everything from the federal sponsorship of the arts to whether the influx of the Japanese yen and the resultant spiraling prices were good or bad for the art world.

Katya even joined in at times, arguing her points with her usual clarity, incisiveness, and wit. At moments, as I watched and listened to her, she reminded me of the old Katya—the young woman who was always so poised, so certain, and so comfortable with herself and her life.

Before the limo arrived the next morning, I was already dressed and prepared to go, having slipped out of bed while it was still dark. Katya was asleep as I pulled on a pair of jeans and a polo and crept down the stairs and out the front door. There wasn't a soul in sight as I crossed the highway, half walking and half trotting toward the beach, occasionally looking at our summer cottage.

As I stepped onto the cold sand, I could see that the sun had already begun its daily climb and was rising on the horizon, its bright golden rays of light shimmering enticingly across the waters.

I sat alone on the beach, almost never leaving it.

Katya was still asleep when I returned. She remained asleep until the car arrived and I leaned over to kiss her good-bye. I kissed her gently, first on her lips and then her cheeks; her green eyes slowly opened and looked into mine as I did. Neither of us spoke. We remained that way, just staring into each other's eyes—frozen in time—until at last the driver, evidently concerned about his schedule, shattered the moment with the car's horn.

That was the last time I saw Katya.

I was exhausted that day on the plane and slept most of the time. It wasn't a restful sleep. It was like most of my sleeping hours that past week; I drifted in and out of consciousness. I was floating in and out of the present, past, and future, interleaving each in such a manner as to disregard any sense of continuity of time. Mostly, though, I dreamed—or, when I was more awake than not, daydreamed—about the time before Katya, that brief window of time in my life when I'd lost Maria but had not found my wife.

Chapter 14

IN THE SUMMER OF 1969, I received a medical discharge from the army. For the three months prior, I'd been bedridden, convalescing in a San Francisco veterans' hospital after being transferred from one of its counterparts in Hawaii. The medical prognosis was favorable, and apart from some scar tissue here and there, I was told my physical wounds would heal and I would find myself as good as new.

The US military, however, had their own definition as to what "good as new" meant. In their view, I would no longer measure up to their demanding specifications, and so, with only a few months remaining on my enlistment obligation, I was told that as soon as the doctors signed off on my health, my military career was over.

The army wasn't about to get much of an argument from me on that decision. My recovery had been the absolute pits—a chest operation to remove an AK-47 round and another operation to reconstruct my shattered ankle, followed by tortuous physical therapy. But there was something else troubling me, and it was a thousand fold more unsettling than any of my physical injuries.

During those three months in the hospital, I had been unable to reach Maria. She did not return one telephone call or answer one letter or postcard. Instead most were returned unopened. My parents did everything they could to help, telephoning or stopping by the Ladillya home to relay my messages. Most of the time there was no one there. When someone did answer, it was some distant relative who didn't understand English well enough to shed any light on this increasingly frustrating situation. The only solace I had from my parents' intervention was in knowing that my letters had been hand delivered.

I was filled with despair when I finally learned that Maria's mother had moved and hadn't bothered to leave any forwarding address. That part I learned from my parents after they stopped by the house to deliver one of my letters and found themselves facing the new owners.

Years later, especially during that period when Maria was murdered, I learned everything—how fate had cruelly tied us all together. Like so many things from that early time, all I knew then was that this event also began with Tony.

The relationship that Maria and Tony shared, although tested during the Vietnam War, was an extremely close one. Maria told me that their closeness had a lot to do with the fact that their father had died when both were young children, and with how hard their mother had taken his loss.

"My mother and father were soul mates, Christof. They were like us," Maria confided in me the day she made her three wishes on the beach.

Worried about their mother's health, uncertain as to the permanence of their father's death, they made a vow to be there for each other no matter what the future brought. Even when they grew older and Tony became engaged, I could sense this bond.

When my parents called and told me her family had left without a trace, I started packing whatever belongings I had that still mattered. Hospital or no hospital, army or no army, I was checking myself out of that place. I could walk—with the aid of crutches—and I was determined. I didn't get very far, however.

After I screamed at the ward nurse, swatting at her with my crutches, she summoned the hospital's security, made up of military police. At my instigation, the rest of my fellow patients joined my personal crusade and escalated the whole thing into a near riot. I found tears of frustration, sorrow, and hate flowing freely, my emotions changing with each swing of my crutch, until I was pinned down and hog-tied. The others were similarly disposed of, and the ward resumed whatever normalcy wards of that nature could ever resume.

I was almost court-martialed for that outburst instead of medically discharged. But the army was facing enough embarrassment surrounding the war and didn't need to make an example of some minor war hero—a status I earned thanks to Billy Paulson. He pressured the appropriate brass into nominating me for the Silver Star. If they didn't, he said he would blow the whistle on what he was really up to the day he rescued me. He also told whomever he had to tell that there were even more politically embarrassing missions he would toss into the pot as well. So I got the medal.

Later, when I learned more about his missions, including the details behind mine, I knew he'd had the wherewithal to back up his threat. He didn't give a damn about his military future either. He'd had it with the army. As part of the deal for buying his silence and my medal, he resigned his officer's commission. That was no small gesture for a fourth-generation West Pointer.

But I digress.

Silver Star or not, the army had a last shot at paying me back before my discharge. The medical records said that I had contracted Rocky Mountain spotted fever and that it was necessary to place me in medical isolation with no mail or human contact other than meal delivery. For the next week, I depressingly dwelled on what my parents had told me when they'd called—what had become the catalyst for my outburst.

That was the period in my life when I changed, when I stopped clinging to whatever faith I might have had. Someone far more cynical than I was might say I grew up. My experience in Nam took my youth from me, and when I was released from isolation, I was never the same Christof Douglas again.

Tony was dead. His plane had been shot down while I was in the triage section in Saigon. He was killed on a strafing mission of a North Vietnamese position in the northern province of Quang Tri, just southeast of the Laotian border, when his F-5A Freedom Fighter took a direct hit from a surface-to-air missile and slammed into the mountainside at five hundred miles per hour. It was the same sort of mission he had flown fifty times before, basically providing air-cover support for combat troops. On the fifty-first mission, fate intervened.

My parents learned about Tony from the new owners of Maria's house. They had picked up bits and pieces from their real-estate agent, who told them that Mrs. Ladillya took it hard but Maria went crazy when the air force notified them about Tony. The last letter I received from Maria was in April, about a week before I was wounded. Even if Tony was dead, why had she disappeared without a word? And to where?

Why did I have to wait all those years—to that week in Paris so many years later, when I attended her funeral—to find out those answers?

I flew home on July 12, 1969, the day I was discharged from the army. By then I didn't need crutches, but for the next few weeks, my sometimes-lifeless ankle required the support of a cane. As an ever-present reminder, a thin reddish scar above my left eye, one that never quite tanned in the summer, would stay with me for life.

My mother nearly died when she saw me walking up the driveway. For the first time, and one of only two times in my life, I saw my father cry. But that day, unlike the day when Beth was buried, his tears were those of relief and happiness.

The only person who didn't seem happy at my homecoming was my grandfather. Oh, he was glad to see me; he was ecstatic that I was safely home. I remember him telling me, "What a son of a bitch Johnson is for getting us deeper into that goddamn war of his!"

He missed Maria. And he knew I did too. As time passed, when everyone else told me to forget her and get on with my life, he was the one who told me that I'd never forget her. He was, I would sadly learn, only too correct.

During those initial weeks home, I exhausted myself by contacting everyone I could imagine who might help me track Maria down. Did the post office have a forwarding address? How about the bank? Surely the Realtor who sold the house had a telephone number, an address? Anything! I contacted them all—neighbors, local merchants, former schoolmates, and so on. All my attempts ended the same way: I got nowhere.

I even wrote the air force in some quasi-official attempt to learn the address of Tony's next of kin. "Sorry," I was informed in bureaucratic governmental nonsense, "this is confidential information and only available to the immediate next of kin."

In desperation, I began hanging out at Columbia's off-campus hot spots, particularly the watering holes where the antiwar protesters gathered. It was difficult, if not impossible, to gain their trust. What with my hair still army fashionable and my choice of civilian clothes marking me as someone who viewed the Kingston Trio as radically chic, it became obvious that I was a square peg in a round hole.

A few students, if that's what they were, knew Maria. But when I began asking if they knew her whereabouts, their reactions were guarded; most gave only a nod or a terse no. Eventually, when I explained who I was and why I was looking for her, their responses became hostile.

"Who are you, some kind of cop? The FBI?"

"Hey, button-down, how many babies did you kill over there?"

"Why should I tell you, Dick Nixon–head?"

It was unsettling to return from serving my country in Nam only to be the brunt of epithets spewed by those who felt I was not part of the more tolerant, sensitive, and gentle political far left of the time. Ultimately, I walked away, no further along in my search than when I had begun.

Maria's family wasn't much help either. The relatives who had minded Maria's house were gone, and I knew few of her other relatives. I knew she had some uncles and cousins, but they lived somewhere out west in Texas, California, and even Mexico.

And Tony's former fiancée wasn't any help. I knew they had ended their engagement a year earlier, but I was hoping that there was still a connection between Maria's family and her. It was just another dead end.

"I can't talk about it," she cried when she opened her door, so upset at seeing me that she burst into tears, her hands covering her face. "Go away, Christof. Go away. I loved Antonio once. But that was then. He is dead, and it is over. I know nothing of where his family is."

By that time, I not only had arrived at the same conclusion as the protesters from Columbia, adopting the popular opinion that we should never have gone into Nam, but also had realized that I was a complete ass. I was wrong.

God, I was wrong to have gotten that fuckin' commission!

Whatever rationale, whatever financial incentives I'd had were insignificant. Yet they were nothing in comparison to what I had lost, to what I was going through. And I loved my father, would love him forever, but he was wrong too. I should have told him the hell with it—that I loved Maria and that her love meant more to me than anything else.

My only comfort during that unforgiving period was my relationship with Billy Paulson. Because of our dissimilar backgrounds and the general economic distinctions between us, it would seem that we had little in common. But, in truth, we shared something much more profound, more fundamental than societal or class differentials could ever artificially separate. In the future, our connection would come to be trivialized by the socio-babble term known as bonding—or, even worse, male bonding.

We didn't put a name to it, though. The two of us knew we shared the sense of surviving an armed, misbegotten conflict thousands of miles away from our homes. Each of us had dealt with the volatile fragility of our own mortality day in and day out, never quite sure why we were being asked to do so. And then, when we returned to the country we'd left, we found everything had changed; we found it no longer our home. It dawned on us that our country had betrayed us—fucked us—and would continue to do so for as long as we lived, and that experience transcended society's definitions of what constituted common ground.

How nice. How wonderful. Let's all stand up and cheer. I was so stupid. So brilliantly naive!

Billy Paulson came from a wealthy, conservative West Point military family who could trace their roots to when his maternal ancestors had fought on the Union side in the Civil War. Needless to say, when he decided to resign his commission, it didn't sit well with that bunch. And as if that weren't enough of a family insult, one morning he popped into his father's bank, surprised the hell out of him, and said, "Thanks, but no thanks. I don't think I'm cut out to be a banker." Then he walked off to see the world—an act his family viewed as real heresy. That was what he did, though.

It seemed like a pretty good idea at the time, so I decided to tag along with him. Of course, in my case, I had neither bank nor career plans, and my parents, although never condoning my decision, were on their own personal guilt trip when it came to their son's recent experiences and wisely didn't butt in.

Was I giving up on finding Maria? Absolutely not! That was the furthest thing from my mind. As part of our travel scheme, Billy and I were planning on pursuing a lead that Billy had cajoled out of one of his former clandestine associates. Aside from somewhere in the Laotian mountains, it was the most current address the military had on file for Tony. Billy's friend also told him that this was a new address, less than a month old, and that it had replaced the old Ladillya residence in Tony's files. So, without hesitation and without regard for any sequence to our travel itinerary, we flew straight to California.

We found Mrs. Ladillya living in a rented, two-story clapboard bungalow three blocks from the ocean at Manhattan Beach. Billy waited in the car as I climbed the stairs to the apartment number written on the piece of paper I held in my hand. Judging by her expression when she opened the door, Maria's mother was both shocked and happy to see me. She had also very noticeably aged. I was struck to find that her once jet-black hair was now white, and she was much thinner. In the little more than a year since I had last seen her, her middle years had tragically deserted her.

Any awkwardness we felt was quickly forgotten when, with tears in our eyes, I told her how saddened I was to have heard about Tony. She squeezed me and sobbed on my shoulder. When she finally stopped, she stepped back, looked into my eyes, and whispered, "She's not here, Christof."

I could only nod, afraid my voice would betray my words.

"No, Christof." She rocked her head, seemingly to emphasize her point. "She's not here. Maria is gone. She has left the country."

Her words made no sense. I heard her but didn't understand. I hadn't known what to expect or what I would find when I came here, and I was having difficulty registering what she was telling me. The one thing I knew was that my fragile psyche had just received another paralyzing blow.

"Where?" I could barely utter.

She continued to shake her head, her eyes closing as though that simple action deflected her pain. "I don't know. Dios mio, Christof. I don't know." She wept.

Maria hadn't been in contact with her for nearly a month. She showed me postcards from Hong Kong, Australia, and, most recently, London, all of which had the same message.

Dear Mama,
I'm fine. Don't worry about me. Yo t'quero
por eternaidade. Maria

It was Maria who had convinced her mother to sell their home and move to California to be near her mother's brother. I suppose Maria had it all planned, knowing she was going to take off the way she did. But she never told her mother any of this. It was all a secret. The only thing the poor woman knew was that Maria took Tony's death very, very hard. The fact that his body had not been found drove her crazy.

"You wouldn't recognize her, Christof," she said. "Then, one morning, soon after we moved here and without a word of adios or where it was she was going, she left. Over three months ago it's been. All I have are these postcards," she said, her voice a whisper as she waved the cards in the air.

I didn't stay long. I couldn't. But before I left, as we squeezed each other good-bye, I made one final plea. "Please tell Maria I love her. I will always love her. Tell her to remember the night when she told me the story of the poinsettias. Tell her to remember what we swore to one another that night, and tell her she must call me. Tell her that I will come for her, that I will find her wherever she is."

She called too late. We found each other too late.

And so, for the following year, Billy and I wandered across the earth in search of ourselves and Maria. After California, we went next to London, and from there our journey took us to Australia and Hong Kong. I didn't know whether I expected to find her; I just needed to feel that maybe she was somewhere close by, that maybe there was some chance that we were in the same part of the world together. My heart would beat a little faster, my pulse would quicken, and my whole body would become more alive. It was as though an electric charge had filled my being in some kind of subconscious anticipation that she might be near.

Maria always seemed to be one step ahead of us as we traveled throughout Europe and Asia. We would go wherever Maria's mother had last heard from her, though most of the time we didn't hear anything for weeks. At those moments, our drifting spirits could be found on the secluded coves and pebbled beaches of the Balearic and Greek Isles—on Majorca, Ibiza, or off La Costa del Sol—the jet-set and hippy meccas of the Mediterranean. Yet sun-swept vistas and blue waters aside, we always returned to Paris when in doubt where to head next.

Money wasn't a problem for us. I had saved most of my army pay for the time when Maria and I were supposed to be married, and it was more than adequate for the no-frills, low-budget lifestyle we were living. And if we really needed money, Billy's trust funds would be tapped.

I continued to stay in touch with Mrs. Ladillya by mail. Then, one day, I received a letter from my mother, telling me that Maria had sent back the jade ring in an unmarked envelope. I called Maria's mother and told her to tell Maria that I loved her, would always love her, and said good-bye.

I kept whatever sanity I had during that period by pretending that this seemingly endless odyssey was some sort of grand but ill-fated romantic adventure. In the process of our travels, I learned a lot about life and about myself. Nothing was more instructive, however, than hearing all the facts surrounding my rescue. And nothing was more chilling than understanding what the words "They stay where they lie" meant.

Originally I believed that my Mayday was received, my was rescue planned, and Billy and his team were sent to get us. I learned one night while somewhere off the coast of Majorca that nothing was further from the truth. I learned that it was a combination of luck, fate, and Billy's willingness to tell his superior officers to go screw themselves that saved my life that day.

He was part of an elite team of Special Forces Rangers whose mission was to keep contrary Republic of South Vietnam—and, by inference, anti-US political—activities from spreading faster than they were through the hamlets. They operated under a code name: the Studies and Observations Group, a benign, almost academic cover for what their job was.

The Tet Offensive, the first display of power by the Viet Cong and their North Vietnamese comrades-in-arms had taken place the previous year, and if nothing else, that meant his team would be working overtime. Up until that propaganda shocker, the US military high command had been under the impression it controlled the south—well, controlled it during daylight. And guys like Billy were doing the devil's best to also control the night. If we had been the Mafia, it would have been called intimidation, but since we were the good old US of A, it was euphemistically dubbed sanctions.

To put it simply, they killed people—and not just anyone.

They were very discriminating in targeting potential sanctions, unlike most of us in regular military units. Although our job was essentially the same—After all, what were we there for? To win the hearts and minds of the people?—we primarily had to differentiate between someone shooting an AK-47 and someone selling a rice ball or begging for a Coke before killing him. Although, the line between the two became fuzzier and fuzzier.

Billy's sanction team was on the way home after some such mission when he saw our helicopter fall, smoke trailing like some welcoming beacon announcing our position. Base headquarters never heard our Mayday that day, but Billy's radioman did. Billy broke one of the cardinal rules of engagement, as well as his unit orders, when he opted to break radio silence.

"I really don't know why I decided to do what I did, Chris," he said when he first explained what had happened. "Let's just say it was our karma." He also told me he wasn't surprised when he heard the tinny, static-enhanced voice reply, "Get your ass back home pronto, Black Hawk One! They stay where they lie! Copy and out!" No, he wasn't surprised, I reflected as I listened.

After all, death was his game, and he might have even been faced with the same decision before.

Maybe he had seen too much and it had finally caught up to him. On those nights drifting aimlessly in the Mediterranean, every star shining brighter than I had ever imagined, he would often confide this thought to me. Maybe they should have rotated him stateside when his initial tour in Nam was up. After all, such a rotation would have avoided the embarrassing confrontations that took place between him and the high brass. It would have saved his commission too. Of course, had that happened, I would have been dead for real.

Was it, as Parcae would say, our mutual destiny that day to have our future inextricably interwoven together—through the good times and the bad?

Maybe another time he would have simply replied, "Roger, I copy," acknowledged the order, and silently faded forever from my life into the tall grass. On those same seas, he also revealed to me that although he didn't have any regrets, he couldn't say with certainty that he would do it the same way again.

"It was a spontaneous thing, Chris," he said, continuing to smile.

I smiled in return, not speaking but staring at the starlit skies, thinking of Dickey Lake and the fact that he had stayed where he lay.

It was early in the summer of 1970, and we had just crossed the channel, heading for Paris for the third time. In the past eleven months, Billy and I hadn't circumnavigated the globe, but we knew we'd covered the necessary twenty-five thousand odd miles to qualify for the Magellan Club. Except, in our case, our navigation path looked like inspiration for a work by Jackson Pollack.

We never talked about when our ride was going to end. We just knew that someday it would. And during the prior two weeks, I had started to become a bit antsy. It wasn't the kind of nervousness I would feel when, out of nowhere, I would see Maria's face before me or hear her voice in my head. No, that was a much more defined sensation. That was more a sense of the spiritual, emotional emptiness that I knew I would have to deal with forever.

This sensation was coming from the logical, rational side of me. It was as if some aspect of my pre-Vietnam self were trying to reemerge from its two-plus-year hibernation and lay claim once more to my life. The side of me that subscribed to the simple philosophy "if you take care of business today, the future will take care of itself" began to reassert itself.

We arrived in Paris late in the evening, checking in to our customary student and low-budget pensione, Chez Madeleine, before midnight. It was not too late, however, to join in the city's festivities and the magic that was nighttime Paris.

Chez Madeleine was located on the Left Bank, in the heart of the Latin Quarter, and it was the only place for young borderline insomniacs looking for fun to go. I qualified on all three counts. Billy qualified on two; he never had any problem sleeping.

The night air was clear and light and too electrified to waste by sitting inside one of the myriad of stuffy bars and clubs that were always booming in that section of the city. It was a perfect night, we decided, for one of the outdoor cafés and our third-favorite Parisian evening activity—people watching.

Les Deux Magots was our choice that evening. When in Paris, we invariably found occasion to stop by this venerable and beckoning haunt. It was only a few blocks from Chez Madeleine, but that was not the primary reason we tended to gravitate there.

Located at the intersection of the Boulevard Saint-Germain and Rue Bonaparte, across from the cathedral Saint-Germain-des-Prés, it never suffered a shortage of customers. All hours of the evening, the sidewalk café and the two interior chambers—the one upstairs was a private, intimate room that drew many of its patrons from the literary and art world, and its downstairs equivalent was generally filled with a younger crowd—rang with the sounds of Parisian society enjoying life to the fullest. That was closer to the reason I went there but still not the real one. Fortunate to arrive just as a small party departed, we were seated at once. We immediately ordered a glass of white wine for me and a bottle of Heineken for Billy. "If you're not going to have wine, don't ask for the French beer," he said with a laugh when he ordered. "And a dozen icy oysters apiece to help wash our drinks down."

We made ourselves at home, and I was pleased with our table's location. Although it was not directly on the boulevard, our green granite-topped table and red-and-white wicker chairs were only a table in from the street and facing the ancient cathedral. Close enough, I assured myself, to get an open view of the evening strollers.

That was the real reason I wanted to be there.

I still harbored a silly, romantic fantasy that one day I would be sitting there, sipping a glass of wine, not caring what the hour was, and staring at the faces walking by without seeing them, when suddenly Maria would appear out of the crowd like some unexpected apparition.

She would walk toward my table and, without saying a word, sit down beside me—not before kissing me affectionately, first upon one cheek, then my lips, and then the other cheek. I would order a glass of wine and cheese for her, and we would talk about the days' events since we'd last spoken. Everything would be as though our meeting were perfectly natural. As if time had decided to smile upon us and stand still and it was always this way.

Once I even imagined I did see her. I jumped to my feet, knocking over Billy's beer, and ran after the dark-haired young woman, Maria's name silently on my lips, only to apologize to the woman after I grabbed her arm and saw that it was not Maria. And why did I have the fantasy at Les Deux Magots and not at Le Café Noir? Or La Metairie or any of a hundred similar cafés and bistros? What was so special about that place? About that street in Paris, or that corner even? Whether it were those initial times in 1969–1970 with Paulson, or the many occasions years later when I would continue to come to Paris for the reasons that drove me to that city, I would always go out of my way to spend a few minutes there.

Perhaps it was because I learned that this café was where many of the literary cognoscenti would often come, local and international, famous and not so famous, whether they were authors, journalists, poets, or just patrons of the arts. Maybe, once I realized this, I felt a stirring in my soul—something that told me that even though she wasn't here or with me, that this was a place where she would have been very comfortable and would have come.

I could have asked Magritte about this. I asked him many other things about her, so this wouldn't have been that big a deal. I was positive he would've known what her feelings were when it came to Les Deux Magots. I never did ask, though. I much preferred to remember and cling to that romantic fantasy, the same one I had in '69 and '70, which now would be mine forever.

Chapter 15

KATYA AND I HAD been to Paris together, but when I returned for Maria's funeral, it was the first time I'd been back to the city alone since the summer of '70. God, was it seventeen years between the two times? Whenever I looked back, I almost forgot how long ago that was. And just like that time in 1970, when I learned so much about myself and life, I learned a great deal in 1987 as well. As I stared at the cathedral across the cobblestone courtyard that night, I couldn't help but think of that Bob Seger line, the one that seemed to play itself over and over in my head as I drifted further away from land, the one that prophetically says, "I wish I didn't know now what I didn't know then."

* * * * *

When I landed in Paris, I went straight to Magritte's loft. It was located across the street from the Delacroix Museum and only a stone's throw from Les Deux Magots. When I'd telephoned on Friday to confirm my arrival, Magritte hadn't said much; his attitude had been one of almost bored disinterest when he'd said, "If you must come. It is your decision."

As my thumb pressed down on the bell that had the letters *A&M* next to it, increasing the pressure each second it remained there, I realized that this was it. Up till then, I could have turned around and walked away and gone home. I was still crushing the bell when I heard the voice over the intercom.

"Oui? Que c'est ca?"

"Monsieur Dela—Monsieur Magritte?" I stammered, not

believing I was really here. "It is Monsieur Douglas. You know, Maria's friend. We spoke the other afternoon."

There was a moment of deadly silence before the squawky voice answered. "Ahhh, Maria's ami. I see. It's you. You came then after all. I see, I see." There was more silence. Then the squawk asked, "Tell me this, Maria's friend, if you will be so kind: What was the name only you called Maria? Your nickname, as you Americans would say, for her?"

When did Maria tell him?

I knew what he as asking. No other person on this earth could have the known the answer except me. But I didn't want to share with him what only Maria and I had shared.

"Monsieur Douglas? Are you there? Porqui … Respondez moi maintenant!"

"Look here, Delacroix," I answered, "or Magritte, or Renoir, or whatever you want to be called. Okay, whatever, that's fine with me. But I can't see what some … some personal name I called Maria is any of your business."

"Ah, Magritte is altogether fine with me." The sarcasm was wrapped around every word. "And, Monsieur Douglas, if that is who are, you either tell me or the gendarmes will be here tout de suite."

The son of a bitch had me. Damn it! All right, all right. I hadn't traveled three thousand miles to be sent back over this. "Squirrel," I practically shouted. "Squirrel. Got it?" Under my breath, I added, "Bastard."

"D'accord."

Unbelievable relief flooded over me when I heard the buzz, followed by a sharp click of the solid oak door unlocking. Before either of us could change our minds, I grabbed the handle and pushed my way into the downstairs vestibule. I took two steps at a time up the wooden staircase to his second-floor apartment. "Well, I'm here," I managed to utter between gasps of breath when I reached it.

"So you are," said the silhouetted figure standing at the end of the dimly lit hallway, half in and half out of the open door.

I walked slowly in his direction. My breath returned to normal as I wiped the beads of sweat from my face. Working to overcome any fear or uncertainty I felt, I called out his name.

171

"Yes, it is I. You've come this far, so you might as well come in."
He stepped aside and motioned for me to enter.

As I walked in, I quickly surveyed the apartment. It seemed
to run the length of the eighteenth-century building, maybe sixty
feet or so. It was narrow, perhaps no more than twelve feet, without
separators or rooms. The walls were unadorned, just bare brick,
except for one section near the door, which was covered with black-
and-white photographs. Past this gallery, there was an overhang with
a ladder leading up. I could see what appeared to be a cot, or some
sort of sleeping arrangement, on it.

"Please, Monsieur Douglas, follow me."

I followed him to what passed for his living room—two folding
chairs, a sofa that looked like a Salvation Army discard, and a couple
of snack tables. There was also a small television set placed against
the brick wall and a shortwave radio sitting atop one of the tables.
The radio appeared to be worth more than the rest of the room's
contents.

"Monsieur Douglas, please sit," Magritte said, and he sat on one
of the folding chairs across from the sofa.

I pushed aside some papers and sank into the sofa. With an
even, measured voice—my corporate voice, I'd like to think—I said,
"Look, Monsieur Magritte, I know you have some concerns, some
reservations about my coming here. But I'm asking you to understand.
This is very important to me. Maria is—was—very important to me.
You must understand all this."

"What is it exactly that you want, Mr. Douglas? What is it that
I am to understand?" He sat perfectly still, his eyes never dropping
from mine.

A few days earlier, I would have had great difficulty talking about
this subject, never mind proposing my own involvement. A few days
ago, however, I still believed that Katya and I could work out our
problems, that we would grow old together, and that I had buried
into the recesses of my deepest being those bitter memories of my
first life. So placing everything in perspective, talking about it, was
no longer a challenge.

"Monsieur Magritte, I came to Paris for two reasons. First, I had
to see Maria one more time." My eyes clouded over as I said this. It

occurred to me that what I had just told myself a moment ago was all bullshit. "And second, Maria told me … or was trying to tell me … I didn't tell you everything that was in her letter." I reached into my pocket and handed him the letter. "Here, you read it. It'll help you understand what I want to do."

Magritte took the wrinkled paper from my hand. A few minutes went by. Outside of an occasional nod, he made no other movement or sound until he finished reading.

When he finished, neither of us spoke. His head was bent over the letter. After an interminable time, he lifted his head and seemingly recognized my presence. His hushed voice had less of an edge when he spoke. "She was a very brave … a very determined and beautiful woman."

Another moment of silence passed, and then, in the same hushed tone as his, I explained my second reason for coming.

"Monsieur Magritte, what you must understand is that I want to help." He didn't respond to my statement; his eyes stared blankly, and his body was still. He continued to stare as I explained what I meant by helping.

"I want to help you finish writing Maria's story and find her murderer!"

He shot from his chair as though he had been blasted from it. He began to speak rapidly in French. Apparently noticing my vacant stare, he then switched to English. Either because he was not as confident in that language or because, in his estimation, I might not be, he proceeded more slowly, enunciating certain syllables as he spoke.

"Lis-ten care-ful-ly, Doug-las. Apparently it is you who does not un-der-stand! You may be a bright fel-low when it comes to your pro-fes-sion, but this is not about …" He hesitated, seemingly searching for the appropriate words in English. "Some unwelcome melding of one bourgeoisie establishment with another. Or some chanteuse or fast-talking con man who, for whatever idiotic, capitalistic reason, convinces some fools to buy his sponsor's dog food. Or persuades them that if they smoke a certain brand of cigarette, all the pretty little birds will flock to them tout de suite." Snapping his fingers, he repeated, "Tout de suite," and he sat down.

He leaned forward so that his face was just a few inches from mine. "You said it a minute ago. This is about murder. Do you understand, Douglas?" He nodded, tilted backward in his seat, and pulled a pack of Lucky Strikes from his trousers. Raising one to his lips and lighting it, his eyes locking on mine, he inhaled deeply and slanted his head in such a way as to blow the smoke over his shoulder.

"Go home, Maria's friend. Go home while you can, and forget about this nonsense." He took another long drag on his cigarette and repeated his prior motion. I felt that he was studying my reaction to his harsh warning, measuring my appetite for what might lie ahead.

Slowly, imperceptibly, I began to smile. I knew there was no hint of gladness in that smile as I felt it widen disdainfully into an angry sneer, the images of Spire and Carlson forming in my mind. "Oh, no, Monsieur Magritte. I won't go home. Not now. Not until I know everything that you know about what she was working on. Not until I know what you believe about her murder. Oh, no, Monsieur Magritte. I didn't travel all this way to be frightened off so easily."

I spoke freely, trusting him completely, because Maria had told me I could. When I mentioned my ideas about how I thought I could help, I could see the wheels churning. He seemed to be weighing his warning to me against his journalistic ambition for the possibility of another Irangate. I pressed on with my point.

"See here, Monsieur Magritte, Maria said in her letter that my company was involved in some sort of illegal sale of munitions and bio chemicals with rogue foreign countries. If that is true, I can help you get to the bottom of this. I know all the players, internal procedures, where to cut through the crap. I can be a valuable insider for you," I told him, naively more comfortable with the corporate term insider than its more draconian, cloak-and-dagger counterpart, mole. I also sounded more convincing than I felt, because I hadn't the foggiest idea what I would be looking for.

Magritte remained quiet, every few seconds blowing smoke toward the ceiling in that herky-jerky fashion of his. So I continued, willingly promising anything to avenge Maria. I had repeated that thought to myself so often that it was consuming me, but I also asked myself, would I feel the same if DFT were not implicated?

At last I had said my piece, and I waited for him to speak. But when the silence became deafening, Magritte seemingly content to stare peculiarly at me or to blow smoke into the air, I almost shouted, "Magritte, damn it, say something! Answer me. Admit it. I can be of help to you."

He reached for another cigarette, lit it, and exhaled the smoke into my face. "Oui," he calmly replied.

"Will you let me then?"

He nodded. A small, almost sly smile appeared on his face. And then he said, "I understand. Monsieur Douglas, I understand now."

Magritte proceeded to tell me what I wanted to know about the investigation he and Maria had been conducting, beginning with why heavy munitions and bio chemicals were the subject. He also explained how Maria had stumbled upon the closely guarded fact that DFT was immersed in the clandestine international arms trade, and he ended with what he hoped to accomplish.

"What bigger, more salient issue is there in the world than the arms race between the East and West? And one that is made even more entertaining by their third-world sycophants and surrogate toadies. The manufacture of military weapons alone, never mind bio chemicals that could be used in warfare, is a trillion-dollar global business. Ask yourself, Monsieur Douglas, who the leading munitions exporters are in the world. Then ask yourself who the main recipients, importers, and beneficiaries of these wares are."

I was somewhat familiar with most of what he explained—no more, no less than an average American citizen. The United States, France, South Africa, and West Germany were the major producers and exporters on the Western side of the equation. Israel, Saudi Arabia, South Korea, Afghanistan, and a host of other countries strategically important to the Western world were the legal recipients of those valued exports.

On the Eastern side, Bulgaria, Czechoslovakia, and, of course, Papa Bear—*Although Magritte did mention in passing something about Yugoslavia in this market*—did their capitalist best to compete and keep their vested interests satisfied on a more-guns-than-butter profitable footing.

The whole thing was sort of an updated, never-ending domino

theory similar to the explanation given to my generation, which I'd bought into—*Maria didn't*—for supporting the Republic of South Vietnam.

"Arm the buffer states," Magritte said, "and protect the motherland. Never mind letting them play with all the new gadgets and toys to work out any nasty wrinkles in the technology."

All this was pretty straightforward, almost boring stuff. The military-industrial complex was old hat as far as I was concerned. Sadly, most people didn't get excited about it. There were exceptions, such as when certain powerful lobbies felt there were too many toys slated for an old enemy, or when a hue and cry was raised about the government's military expenditures, particularly during tight budget times, while people were lying homeless in the streets or dying from dreaded diseases.

But all this was legal and nothing like the furor that would be created, or the heads that would roll in high government and private offices, if someone decided to bypass the legal procurement process—in this case, the laws of the United States Congress—and sell large-scale weapons to so-called outlaw nations.

"So Maria was right. You caught the suits at DFT gaming the system, didn't you?" I didn't wait for an answer. "How did she find out?"

"In light of all the notoriety that Irangate, as you Americans like to call it, has generated, it was obvious to anyone but the most naive among us that there had to be equally big stories waiting for someone to dig up. To us, it seemed pretty logical."

"But how did she know about DFT?"

"A source from some other project she worked on told her. Someone she had cultivated a relationship with over the years." He lit another cigarette. "Someone she met in Ho Chi Minh City tipped her off on this business. He told her that the US government had been sending military weapons to Communist Vietnam for the past couple of years in direct contradiction to their official position."

I was stunned. I wanted desperately to ask when she was in Saigon, but I didn't and forced myself to listen.

You were already stateside; it wouldn't have mattered.

"We were in Algiers," Magritte continued, "working on a story about the fundamentalist movement that no one in France wanted to admit was ready to explode. She said she knew a person who claimed he was now ex-KGB, if you can believe that." He stopped and snorted at the absurdity of the idea. "Said he was retired and living there. Sort of an expat like her, he told her. Retired!" He shook his head. "Once KGB, Monsieur Douglas, always KGB."

"This Russian guy—she met him in Vietnam?"

Magritte's eyes widened with surprise as he inhaled his cigarette. "Look, Maria had been around. She knew her stuff. She had a real good, almost uncanny knack for knowing when she was being used or cultivated for the other guy's purpose. Sometimes, but not often, we made a decision, vous comprendez, and let it play out. You know, as you Americans like to say, go with the flow. And, anyway, his information in the past had always proved accurate. This time was no different to us."

I bit my tongue, vowing to hold any questions until he was finished.

Even though the cigarette dangling from his lips was only half gone, he pulled another from the pack and lit it from the older one. "D'accord. As I was saying," he said, grinding the partially finished Lucky Strike into the overfilled ashtray on the floor beside him, "he said that he had been given access to some highly sensitive intelligence by one of his former colleagues. Former, he had the balls to say." He raised his voice and then mumbled, "Games. Il faut jouer son jeu."

His eyes darted back to mine, his mind apparently back in the present, and then he rose from his chair and began to pace the floor, his cigarette bobbing from his lips. "We had no reason to doubt his story's authenticity. As I said, his information had always been reliable." He stopped pacing and looked at me. "Maria was always the greater risk taker, and he was her contact, so it was her ultimate decision to trust him."

He turned and walked toward the closed door at the end of the room. His back remained toward me when he began to speak again. "He made the use of us." He paused, turned to me, squeezed one hand into a tightly closed fist, and, in a swift, chopping motion, brought it down hard into the open palm of the other. "He made the use of us and killed Maria." He opened the door and left the room, slamming the door shut behind him.

I remember sitting at Les Deux Magots Monday evening after Marie's funeral, staring at the cathedral, thoughts, images, longings all converging together.

"Monsieur, un autre espresso?"

"Non, merci … no."

I watched the waiter walk from my table to take an order from the two young couples seated at a table nearby. They broke into laughter at something he whispered to the pretty red-haired girl sitting there. The young men shook their heads, while both women smiled, their eyes sparkling in coquettish delight.

"D'accord. C'est bien," the waiter said, and he walked toward another table.

My attention returned to the endless stream of humanity flowing by just a few feet from where I sat. I had been sitting there for over two hours watching this parade. The crowd finally started to thin out as the evening grew late. I spotted my waiter and pantomimed the international gesture for the check.

Monday was long gone, I realized after checking my watch. It was now Tuesday morning, and I had been sitting here alternating, with no particular preference, my beverage intake among espresso, wine, and vintage Jean de Fleur Armagnac.

"Bonsoir," I blurted aloud, staggering to my feet. "And to all a good night." This outburst must have been a little louder than I'd intended, for the people at the surrounding tables glared in my direction. I rocked my way unsteadily through the aisles, offering sporadically, "Pardon moi."

The Hotel Le Relais Saint-Germain was a five-minute walk away, in the heart of the Latin Quarter on the Left Bank; it was where Katya and I stayed when in Paris. In fact, I was staying in the same duplex we always stayed at, the Moliere suite. I knew that was its name because there was a brass plate on the door proclaiming it to be. That was also how I knew I was in the right apartment.

I was halfway up the narrow and winding apartment staircase to the upper floor when the quiet was shattered first by the sound of breaking glass and then by a rustling sound, followed by a drawer slamming shut. Then there was silence.

I was frozen, unable to decide whether to retreat down the stairwell to the chamber's entry or to proceed the equal number of steps toward the sounds. Another ten seconds went by. I heard nothing from above. Come on, Christof. You can't stay here forever. Goaded by the side of my conscience that had urged me to serve my country, I lifted a foot. However, the part of my conscience that told me I was a fuckin' idiot for doing so placed it on a lower step. Inertia and bravado overcome, I duplicated this tactful retreat until I was downstairs and out the apartment door and by the hallway telephone. I lifted it and waited for the manager to pick up.

"Oui?"

"Monsieur le manager, c'est moi, Monsieur Douglas," I whispered in broken English and French. "Je suis … I am staying in la sale de Monsieur Moliere."

"Oui. What do you need, monsieur? Please be so kind as to speak up. I cannot hear you very well."

"Listen, someone is in my room," I answered, a little louder this time. "I heard something break when I approached my door. I heard a dresser drawer slam." I paused to allow the seriousness of what I was saying to sink in and then added, "I think we should call the police."

Monsieur le manager ignored my comment. "Stay where you are. I'm coming up."

Moments later, he was standing beside me along with someone he introduced as Mustad, a squat, muscular man whom I took to be the hotel's security. The shape of a small handgun protruded from Mustad's ample waistband.

"Please, Mr. Douglas," Monsieur le manager said, gesturing with his hand as he spoke, "if you would be so good as to remain here." Without waiting for a reply, he moved to my room and opened the door with his passkey. Mustad withdrew his revolver and slipped ahead of his leader. The two men ascended the spiral staircase out of my sight.

"Voilà!" a voice I was hoping was Mustad's called out. A light from the apartment came on.

The suspense was broken by Monsieur le manager's voice calling down the stairs. He said that there was nothing suspicious and that I should come up. "Here is your intruder, Monsieur Douglas." His hand was pointing to a shattered crystal vase lying on the floor. "And here is the perpetrator, as your American police like to say." His hand moved toward the open terrace doors. The curtains, lifted just enough by the gentle breeze, had draped themselves over the table where the vase had been. I watched this occur two or three times, trying to convince myself that the curtains were the perpetrator, as he had declared.

My eyes studied the apartment, suspicious of this ready-made solution to what might have occurred. If I had been in Paris at any other time, I would have bought it. But not now. I remembered Maria's letter and the intruder in her hotel room.

"Monsieur Douglas, if you are satisfied, Mustad and I will leave now." He waited a few minutes as Mustad closed the terrace doors and then swept up the broken crystal. The two left without any further words.

After they left, I looked through every drawer and closet to see if anything had been disturbed. I again thought about Maria's description of what had happened in her hotel room. But her intruder didn't give a damn about her finding out about his break-in. He wanted to leave a message. This was different. If someone had broken into my room, he had covered his tracks. My personal effects, my clothes, and everything else were as I had left them. I even looked out on the terrace through the closed doors. I saw nothing remotely suspicious. Just the same two chairs and table that were there when I had left for Maria's funeral that morning.

None of this altered my opinion, though. There was no way the alleged culprit, some table-hopping flower vase, could have created this level of anxiety. Certainly it hadn't slammed the bureau drawer.

I decided on an impulse to phone Magritte. He had to have arrived in Tunisia by then, having left for Algeria after the funeral services that morning. I called the number he had given me, but unfortunately some unrecognizable voice came on, speaking some unrecognizable language, so I hung up, not bothering to leave a message. In truth, I was obeying Magritte's instructions to speak to no one but him. That was part of his game plan, which he'd outlined last night after he returned from behind the closed door. The plan began with his meeting the ex-KGB agent one more time.

"We need to raise the stakes, sort of redefine the original arrangement we had. We need to reestablish it on a more clear-cut foundation," he explained. "What he initially offered Maria was a good beginning, like your company's entanglement. But that is just the tip of the iceberg. We had to take each of the clues he dangled and piece them together as if we were on some damn treasure hunt."

I said nothing.

"We don't have the time now for that approach. Names, dates, places—all the hard evidence of what's been going on. What we need is which countries with which American industrialists. In return, we can offer him front-page headlines exposing the entire subversive operation to the entire world."

"Why didn't he offer this information before? I mean, why should he do it now?"

"In this business, things change."

I was about to ask him to qualify what he meant, but he beat me to it. "Maybe he was unwilling, or afraid that if too much leaked out too quickly, it could be traced back to him. But with Maria's murder, who knows? Perhaps it is just a matter of time before someone shows up at his doorstep. That's why we can't waste a minute. This time I know he'll give us everything."

Blinded by my own thirst for revenge, I ignored or disregarded any inconsistencies in his explanation. But the more I listened, the more I realized that it wasn't just the story he was after. Nor was it the need for revenge—at least not a need like mine. No, there was something else there. Something I couldn't quite put my finger on.

Those thoughts were ricocheting around my head when he wrapped up by saying, "With those headlines, he gets the political fallout he could have only dreamed of: an international scandal and world-class embarrassment to his country's arch enemy, the United States of America."

Prior mistrusts aside, when Magritte said that, I had mixed emotions regarding this particular strategy—with most of the mix being negative. "Magritte, this is a Soviet—a Communist agent you're talking about. You may not be an American citizen, but I am. In some circles, this could be viewed as treason. Do we really need to involve this character any further? And you said he used you and got Maria killed in the process."

He didn't appear upset when I posed this dilemma. He nodded, lit another cigarette, and leaned forward in his chair.

"Heed me carefully, Mister Douglas," he said icily. "You have two choices. Which one you choose, you will choose solely on your own. First, you can get up, walk out the door, and forget we ever met—forget about everything we discussed tonight, and go home. Go back to America, Maria's friend."

We both knew that this was tantamount to me forgetting about Maria—something that I wouldn't do.

"The second option ... There are only two options, do you understand? Oui ou non! Yes or no!" He didn't wait for my answer. "The second choice is even simpler." He waved his hand above his head as if for emphasis. "It is to listen and then follow exactly what I tell you. That is my rule number one. These are very simple choices, n'est pas?"

Whatever Magritte's motivation, it seemed obvious he wanted to finish what the two of them had started. My problem was that I didn't give a rat's ass about any organization besides DFT. I wanted to see Carlson and Spire behind bars. I didn't give a damn about embarrassing them or seeing some weasel of a lawyer get them off with some monetary slap on the wrist. I wanted them—*That was not the first or hundredth time I'd thought the word*—I wanted them dead!

"I understand your terms," I said. "But before I tell you my decision, I must ask you one question."

He shifted his body backward into his chair. "What is it that you wish to ask?" he said, his voice still retaining the icy tone.

"Look, you said earlier that DFT was involved with her murder, right?"

He nodded.

"Okay, but you also said you didn't know who actually did it."

Another nod.

"So I assume this is one of the things you plan on finding out from … Let's call him Igor, okay?"

Magritte was crossing and uncrossing his legs. "You wanted to ask one question. You've asked two. And, quite frankly, I haven't any idea what your point is, if there is one."

"My point is," I shot back, "I need to know if you will be able to find out from this character—Igor—who killed Maria."

Magritte stopped crossing his legs; his eyes dropped from mine.

Suddenly it hit me like a ton of bricks.

"Son of a bitch! You weren't going to ask him." Leaping from my chair, I nearly knocked him off his. "Fuck you and your two simple choices!" I shouted. "You're not the slightest bit interested in finding her killer. You just want the fuckin' scoop. I understand everything now. That's all you want—the fuckin' story."

Magritte shook as he rose from his chair. "Christof, listen to me. It's not what you think. It's not that simple. You just don't walk in on a man like … like … Igor and ask for the name of a murderer." He took a step back as though uncertain what to say next.

"You listen to me, Magritte," I said, barely controlling my rage. "I want to help you. And with DFT involved, I can." I didn't back down. "I'll agree to your rules, listen to them, and follow them, but this is one of my own that you must agree with."

He hesitated, started to say something, shrugged his shoulders as though to mean "whatever," and then said, "D'accord, as you wish. I will ask Igor who killed her."

Sometime in the future I would know why he agreed. And I would know who her murderers were. That night, whatever the reason, I didn't care.

Chapter 16

THE ALARM SIGNALED THAT it was time to raise my fatigued body and face the new day. I had been awake, gazing at the ceiling, drifting in and out of my thoughts, for hours before the alarm's buzzing disrupted my reverie that Tuesday morning. I rang room service and ordered breakfast. While waiting for it to arrive, I telephoned Magritte again.

"Allo?"

Although I had reached him, I had to follow through with the prearranged, somewhat ridiculous exchange Magritte had devised before leaving Paris the day before.

Speaking in my normal "Pig French"—he insisted it was so unique no one else could duplicate it—I implied that he should call back. "L'oiseau est libre, ou est-il mange?" I left neither name nor number. My inquiry told him that.

A minute later, I was telling him about the previous evening's apparent break-in. Aside from a few "Hmmmps," he said little, quietly listening until I finished.

Magritte responded in his typical "maybe yes, maybe no" style. "This just proves without any doubt that they know of your involvement in this affair, and it was meant as a warning, possibly to even frighten you from going further. Then again," he backtracked, "who can say what their intentions are? Or what they know?"

He hung up after advising me that he would call the next day at my place of business, code for my hotel, and telling me that he was scheduled to meet "Le grand oiseau" himself sometime in the afternoon. His closing admonitions—"Be careful!" and something that I translated to literally mean "Don't take candy wrappers from strangers!"—wound my nerves tighter.

I wasn't sure if what I felt was a lack of confidence in pulling this caper off or just uncertainty about him, as if those two emotions could be separated. Still, something didn't sit right. Certainly his candor didn't help. If he had worked in my organization, the "maybe yes, maybe no" that he made part of his conversation would have been enough for me to fire him by now. But I wanted to believe and accept Maria's advice to trust him.

So I did.

He had, after all, anticipated that our communication might be compromised and demanded that all dialogue be exchanged in such a way that it would be difficult for our adversaries to foresee our next move, as he less than optimistically phrased it. And I understood why he wasn't going to come right out and ask Igor about Maria. Even I could swallow the cold reality of that after I settled down and thought it through.

I heard a knock at the door, and someone claiming to be the porter announced that my breakfast had arrived. I slipped into my robe and stepped cautiously down the stairwell. One hand froze as I was about to unlock the door's safety chain. The other flipped the cover off the peephole.

The porter's eyes met mine in exaggerated recognition. "Monsieur Douglas, breakfast as you ordered is here."

I unlocked the door but remained careful. Just because he was the same guy who'd delivered breakfast yesterday didn't mean he wasn't one of the bad guys. Or even the person who broke into my room. Stay alert; stay ready, I told myself, watching him roll the cart into the room. I followed close behind as he climbed the stairs, a silver serving tray balanced in his hands. I watched him as he arranged the breakfast service on the terrace table. It was then I realized I wasn't watching; I was staring.

"Bonjour, monsieur," he said when he finished.

I forced a smile, tipped him twenty francs, and watched him disappear down the stairs. As soon as the door closed, I walked to the railing and inched my head around the bend in the stairwell. I was alone.

Although I hadn't eaten anything since the previous morning, I had no appetite. After swallowing a few sips of the orange juice and toying with a couple of spoonfuls of the bitterly sour yogurt, I pushed the plate away. The tiled Mansard roofs lining the streets were the only objects capable of holding my attention. The early morning sounds of rush-hour traffic rising up the ancient four-story building underscored the reality that it was Tuesday and the poignant incongruity of my being here.

I had telephoned Katya twice yesterday—once in the morning and again later in the afternoon. To be precise, I called her six times—twice at the summer cottage, twice at the apartment, and twice at our primary residence in Jersey. The results were the same—no response. Considering the time spread between my attempts to reach her, as well as the time difference between Paris and the States, she should have heard my messages by now and called back.

When I return home …

As quickly as it had appeared, the thought was aborted and replaced with the haunting question that had been looming like some unwanted, vile intruder in the shadows of my mind for days. I had tried to include it with all the other questions, feelings, and sensations, tried to think of it as just another temporary, unanswerable one, but one that would resolve itself when I returned home.

Damn it! That one was not like them!

Leaping from my chair, I knocked the coffee service off the table and ran to the edge of the terrace. Leaning over, grasping the handrail, I could see the people below scurrying from one point to the next and could feel their frenetic energy even from these heights. It all seemed so random, so aimless as I followed first one, then another, and then a third before they disappeared from sight.

Suddenly I felt weak and then dizzy, my legs rubbery as if I were inflicted with a severe case of vertigo. *I heard a voice—a woman's voice. One that was unrecognizable, but then it was gone.* I needed to sit or lie down. With effort—it was as though my fingers were some stranger's and not mine—I struggled to uncurl the left and then the right fist from the railing.

I reached for a chair, the table, anything to steady myself, my other arm stretching toward the glass doors, and pulled myself back into my room to collapse upon the bed. My head was spinning, the answer to the question racing faster and faster, louder and louder in a crescendo. I wished I could shout it, scream it, cleanse it from my mind as its pressure became unbearable. Finally the pressure was too great, and it burst forth, filling the room with my maddening, wild cries.

"I don't know! I don't know!" I screamed. "Damn it, leave me alone! I don't know the answer. I don't know when I will ever return home."

I lay on the bed, my eyes fixed upon the whirling ceiling fan, its motion and drone hypnotic, my hands massaging my pounding temples. How long I lay there I was not sure, but it was long enough to see the morning become brighter and fill the room with its warmth. I lay there as the brightness shifted. Ever so slightly, the sun's rays became more filtered, passing through the curtains and forming shadows on the bed and floor yet still maintaining their brilliance. Eventually, the brilliance faded as the sun descended behind the buildings of the Latin Quarter.

As I lay there, I thought about an explosion of things. But mostly I thought about the previous morning, the day after my arrival in Paris, and my reason for being here. I thought of that morning, the morning after conspiring with Magritte to bring Maria's killers to justice, which was the same morning I began to doubt that my wife would ever call again. And I thought, continuing to stare at the ceiling, about Monday morning and Maria's funeral.

* * * * *

Magritte met me at the hotel in his battered, antiquated Renault. "Bonjour, monsieur. I trust you slept well." I'm sure he knew that the contrary was probably true. He shifted into first gear and leaned out the window, waiting for an opening in the traffic flow.

"Likewise," I grumbled to the back of his head.

The church was only a few blocks away, so when we turned the corner onto Boulevard Saint-Germain, we could see the cars for the funeral procession already queued. Magritte slowed the Renault to allow one of the ushers to come up to us.

"Comment appelez-vous, monsieur?" he asked politely. He squinted from either the sun's glare or an attempt to determine who we were.

"Je suis, Monsieur Magritte."

The usher nodded and dropped his head to his clipboard for verification of our position in the motorcade. I watched the vehicles continue to arrive. There were at least twenty cars aligned, not including the three Bentleys at the front of the procession. I watched this macabre dance, my face expressionless, as another funeral attendant motioned and jockeyed the cars back and forth, stacking them into neat rows in the churchyard.

"D'accord. C'est ici," the usher said. He gestured for us to advance toward the parking area. A few minutes later, we climbed the steps of Saint-Germain-des-Prés alongside other somber mourners.

Magritte ignored the signals from one of the funeral attendants as to which aisle we should proceed to and grabbed my jacket sleeve, whispering for me to follow. We walked around the church's perimeter and the wicker chairs that passed for pews, toward the wooden benches that lined the stone walls. Selecting a bench with a view of the altar and the front few pews, he sat and motioned for me to do the same. Beneath my dark glasses, my sunken red eyes searched the crowd.

There must have been over three hundred people there that summer morning. An eclectic crowd, I thought, observing the mix before me that surely was a metaphor for the varied and extreme lifestyles and circles Maria had traveled.

Scattered throughout the worshippers, with the heaviest concentration seated near the altar, were a large number of people dressed in the finest and latest fashions that Paris offered. Their hair was immaculately coifed, their faces were tan, and their jewelry conspicuously reflected the sun's filtered rays.

There was also an equal number of society's opposite—people who didn't know or care whether hem lines had risen or fallen in the past decade, who didn't care that their jackets were a bit threadbare at the elbow or that their hair was too shaggy. Those were the people, I remembered, that Maria had felt the most comfortable with.

Magritte, as though reading my mind, bent his body nearer. "Most of the people in the pews farther back, over there, starting with that column"—his hand discretely indicated where I should look—"are Maria's friends. People she worked with at one time. Writers, painters, all sorts of artists." He paused, his eyes, like mine, seemed to be searching the congregation. After a few moments, he whispered, "Many a night, she and I shared a bottle or two of wine with them—with our bon amis. Many a night."

I tilted my head in the direction of the apse. Still reading my mind, he continued with his remote introductions. "Those people in the front—those are her relatives." Clarifying, he said, "I should say, mostly relatives of her husband, Andre."

My eyes jumped from one person to the next, trying to pick her husband out. They came to a stop on a tall, well-dressed man who was standing in the middle of the first pew, with only two others.

On his one side was an older woman, maybe in her seventies. She was dressed in black. A black veil covered her head, so it was impossible to see her face. On the opposite side stood a young girl who could not have been more than ten; the man's arm was draped protectively around her tiny shoulders. Her petite body was snuggled into his side, her blonde head leaning against it.

Before them was Maria.

My eyes came to rest upon her closed casket, which sat at the base of the altar, surrounded by a display of exotic flowers. I was allowed but a brief reminder of why we were gathered in that sacred place that morning, because the congregation rose as one as the priests entered and blocked my view.

Saint-Germain-des-Prés, this awe-inspiring monument to Romanesque architecture, which was older than the venerable Notre Dame and had endured centuries of revolutions, wars, and plagues, transported me to thoughts that spared me the pain of the reason I was there. Only when I heard a heart-wrenching sob from the otherwise silent assemblage, or a rustling movement when they rose or sat during the service, did I return to the moment and its immeasurable sadness. And when I saw her coffin and its shocking, empty reality, I fought with all my strength to avoid sinking into madness.

After the services ended, we waited until most of the gathering had filed past her coffin. When there were only a few family members remaining, including the three from the first row, Magritte turned and whispered that it was time to pay our final respects. He rose from our bench and hesitated, waiting for me. When he saw no movement on my part, he shrugged and went on his own.

I watched him weave his way through the crowd and take his place at the end of the dwindling line of mourners. I continued to watch, my eyes narrowing behind their dark glasses as he neared her casket. I saw him stop, his back toward me, his head bowed. After his farewell and prayer were over, he walked by the man from the first pew and looked up at him as he did so. I stood quickly and walked out of the cathedral.

Magritte found me in the Renault. It was parked in the middle of the motorcade, which overflowed from the cathedral's courtyard and onto Rue de Bonaparte. Neither of us spoke as we watched the pallbearers carry the casket down the steps and place it into the hearse. Nor did we say anything during the twenty-minute ride to Cimetière de Passy.

When we arrived, I mumbled under my breath that I would remain in the car. I knew he heard me, because I also mumbled for him to give me a cigarette. He gave me the cigarette—my first since Katya and I had married—and then he shuffled off to join the others.

I got out of the car, leaned against it, and lit the cigarette with the matches I had pocketed last night from Les Deux Magots. I watched the ceremony from a distance. I couldn't see much, mainly the heads and backs of the reverent crowd. I waited and watched. Two or three times I raised the cigarette to my lips, not inhaling it; just feeling it touch my lips was reminder enough.

After fifteen minutes, the service was over and Magritte was sitting by my side again. We left immediately. He pulled away from the curb, jumping the long queue of cars ahead of us in our haste to depart and leaving the cemetery before everyone else.

About the time we crossed over onto the Left Bank, I asked him if the man with the young girl was Maria's husband. I was about to ask again, since we had driven a number of blocks and he hadn't answered, when, without taking his eyes from the road, he nodded. A few seconds more passed, and I asked if the girl was their daughter. This time he at once answered loudly, "Oui," but still kept his eyes fixed on the heavy traffic.

Passing the Louvre and approaching Notre Dame and Île de la Cité, he made a sharp turn by Quai Malaquais to enter one of the ancient side streets that was too narrow even for that period's carriage trade. Not slowing the Renault, amid the frenzied, almost suicidal jaywalking pedestrians and the oncoming, speeding motorists, he chose that moment to turn and face me.

Pressing extra long on his horn at some slow-moving pedestrians and rotating his head hurriedly back and forth from the street to me, he said, "She is nine years old. And her name is Genevieve. Maria called her Ginny."

Magritte dropped me off. "Remember what I told you. Make sure you follow it," he said as I got out. He sped away to catch his flight to Algiers without any further discussion.

I watched him disappear before I went into the hotel. It was eleven thirty Monday morning, or five thirty in the morning back home. I didn't leave my room until late that evening, when I returned to Les Deux Magots.

Before I left the hotel, I called Katya and also my office. I wanted to let them know that my original plans stood and I would be remaining in Paris for the rest of the week. I also wanted to know what the reaction to Casey had been. I tried to speak with Andy, but his secretary told me he had been summoned over the weekend to meet with Carlson about the Casey tragedy. I settled on having Andy's secretary fax me the latest news stories on Casey from the New York papers.

For most of the afternoon, I read and reread them, another person's loss diverting my mind. There was a picture of Casey in each paper. I was reminded of when Maria's picture had appeared in the papers. Unlike that one though, I recognized Sean.

For the most part, the articles said the same thing: he had taken his life after negotiations with police and associates failed. There was also unofficial confirmation that the Caseys had been talking about divorce. But the general opinion was that the potential sale of WKRA was the underlying catalyst, as Casey had been concerned that he would be phased out and replaced with a new breed of less-talented on-air personalities more in concert with Wall Street. Most of this I had read over the weekend before flying to Paris, so I knew what the overall tone and commentary were.

But in Monday's editions, there were some new updates that further unsettled me. The *New York Times* indicated that DFT was committed to challenging the FCC's authority as it pertained to their licenses all the way to the Supreme Court. That information was credited to DFT's vice president of public relations, Mr. Carl Landon. It was such bullshit. I had to laugh at seeing that blatant lie in print.

I didn't laugh, however, when I read what was said about my involvement in this calamity. Skimming quickly past the information about who I was, my position within the company, blah, blah, blah, I came to a comment by an unidentified police department source that got my blood boiling.

"It was only when Mr. Douglas appeared on the scene and insisted on speaking with Mr. Casey that the situation took a turn for the worse," the source said. "Perhaps it may have even led to him taking his own life."

The *Times* further stated, "Inquiries revealed that Mr. Douglas was questioned last week regarding the murder investigation of Ms. Sammantha Kelso, who was slain at the Plaza Diana Hotel. Telephone messages left for Mr. Douglas at his office were not returned."

I could have killed Hopkins. I knew he had to be the source.

The one phone call I received that afternoon did nothing to alleviate my mounting anger and frustrations.

"Douglas, what the hell are you doing?" Roquette barked as soon as I answered. "Why didn't you tell me you were planning on leaving the country?"

I had to control myself from barking back. "If I did, what would you have advised me? Not to go?"

"You're damn right I would have!"

"Then you've answered your own question."

"Listen," he said, "don't be a smart-ass with me, Douglas. If it weren't for the relationship I have with Paulson, I wouldn't have taken you on as a client."

I didn't want to get into a Mickey Mouse argument with Roquette. He had come through the other night when I'd needed him, and I was certain I would need his services again sometime soon. "Okay ... Okay, no offense intended," I apologized. "Let's just say for the moment that I'm here on necessary business. Anyway, you were the one who told me the police didn't regard me as a suspect."

He ignored my last comment. "Did you see the *Times*'s coverage of that big-time radio personality who killed himself at one of your stations?"

"Cay...cee was his name. Sean Casey."

"Thanks for finally giving me a direct answer."

"What about the article?"

"What about it? What about it?" he shouted. "Am I talking to a fuckin' idiot?"

"Yeah, well, what do you recommend I do about it? Hopkins obviously has a hard-on for me."

"Listen, Douglas, hard-on or no hard-on, he called my office last night and got my home number from one of my associates."

"So maybe he's got a hard-on for you too?"

"Look, one more wiseass remark like that and—Paulson or no Paulson—you can go find yourself a new attorney."

"Okay, okay." I apologized again, knowing I needed him more than he needed me. "It's been a bad few weeks." I took a deep breath, attempting to erase the images of the weasel and Hopkins from my mind. "I just read the article and haven't been able to put it in its proper perspective," I said honestly.

"If that's the situation, and it very well may be, you're not doing yourself any favors by not keeping me advised as to your current whereabouts."

I knew I'd most likely repeat that transgression in the future, so there was no reason for us to dwell on the subject. "What did he want from you?"

Roquette was nobody's dummy. I sensed that he knew his message had come across. Besides, if it did turn out that things changed and

I was charged with some trumped-up accusation, such as fleeing the country, or whatever the correct legalese was, it might be in his best interest to not know too much about what my plans were.

He couldn't pass up the opportunity, though, to slip in a reminder of what our expected roles were. "I thought I was the guy who's supposed to ask the questions, Douglas?" He then went on. "Hopkins wanted to know if you were my client and wanted to know where he could reach you, since this guy Landon told him you were out of the country. That's when I found out you were. He said he wanted to talk to you about Casey's suicide and also about the Kelso thing."

"She wasn't a thing."

"Huh? Oh … yeah." He sounded confused. "He also told me he didn't think it was such a good idea for me to keep you as a client."

"He said that?"

"Not in so many words. He had a little more sense than to come out and threaten me. No, I have to give the little prick credit for the way he handled it." There was a brief silence, and then Roquette said, "I can't go into details; it has nothing to do with your case. Let's just say that a few years ago there was a touchy situation regarding a client I represented—and still do. The whole messy thing was eventually settled out of court. It was a rather delicate, confidential situation that would be better left where it is—forgotten and deeply buried in the past. Hopkins took the opportunity to remind me of that fact in the same sentence he asked about our relationship."

I could have said that it was obviously not forgotten, but I didn't.

"So what did you tell him?"

A couple of seconds went by.

"The only thing I like less than comments from some wiseass are threats from some flatfoot. So I told him I wasn't sure where you were but I did have your home numbers if that would help."

I smiled and felt an urge to thank him. But I also wondered how he knew where to find me and Hopkins didn't.

Roquette continued before I could ask him. "When are you returning to the States?"

In spite of what he had just told me—maybe even because of it—I was not comfortable with that line of discussion. I could answer that question candidly and with certainty, however. "I really don't know," I replied. "How can I help you when you're not being honest with me?"

He started to yell something else, but I cut him off. If I didn't, the entire conversation would only repeat itself.

"RR, listen to me, will you!" I said, trying to control my emotions. "It's true. I'm not sure when I'll be back." More for my sake than his, I softened that admission. "Soon—hopefully soon."

There was a lengthy silence before he broke it. "You're not going to tell me anything more, are you?"

What more could I say? What was there for me to tell? "No … No, RR. Perhaps later, when I get back, we'll sit down over a couple of drinks and I'll tell you everything. Okay? Let's leave it at that. Okay."

I placed the telephone carefully back into its cradle.

Chapter 17

I FOUND THE CERTIFIED letter from Katya's lawyer under my door Wednesday morning.

It was all rather official, rather cold and detached, but it went right to the heart. To wit, she was suing for divorce. Her basis—and as much as I wanted to deny or disagree, I couldn't—was irreconcilable differences.

Just two words to condense fifteen years of marriage.

The letter stated that Katya would be moving from our residence, though it didn't mention where she'd move, and that any further discussions should be conducted through her attorney. Until everything was finalized, I was free to use either of our homes, as Katya had no desire to do so herself—at least until the estates' assets were divided.

There was also mention—to some people, I assume it was an important mention, but to me, it was just a number, devoid of any significance and merely a cold abstraction of life—of a monthly alimony figure, which I was to make available to Katya immediately.

Whether it was because of all that had happened in the past week or because Katya and I were not the same people we once were, I didn't react the way I thought I would. I felt no anger, no painful anguish—not even a misguided sense of rejection. Even though I didn't want to believe it, I had come to terms with it and realized that our marriage was dead.

The marriage was over five years ago after Beth was murdered.

Yes, I loved her. I would always love her. I could not explain that feeling, especially considering the way I had treated her the past few days. I also believed—very deeply believed—that she still loved me and would love me until the day she died.

"She always loved you, Jwah," Parcae would explain patiently whenever I would talk about Katya. "Even though you were her first love, her true love, it was not your fate to remain together."

Before I left the hotel that morning, I disregarded her attorney's instructions and called her. Just as I had on Monday, I telephoned all three of our homes but reached no one. I didn't leave any messages. I also placed a call to Slaus. To the extent I spoke with him, I was successful.

"Yes, I'm aware Katya is filing for divorce," he said, his tone perfect for his manic-depressive patients. "She told Marcy and me on Monday. She was extremely upset. I believe she said something about you leaving her to go to Paris on some sort of business trip the day before."

"What else did she say? Do you know where she is? Maybe it's not too late. Maybe I can … Slaus, listen to me. This is my wife we're talking about, not some damn patient of yours."

"She's in London."

"London?"

"She went to visit her sister." His voice remained tranquilizingly calm. "How are you doing, Chris? And where are you? You know, it would make a lot of sense for you to come home so that we can talk about all this."

"Yeah … Well, I'll be home soon." I calculated how quickly I could make it to London.

We left it with each other that I could call anytime, whenever the slightest need arose, and that he'd let me know if he heard anything more about Katya.

I also phoned Katya's sister, Laura. We had a brief but cordial conversation. And, as with Slaus, it was not very satisfying.

"Yes, I know about the divorce filing," Laura said guardedly. "No, I'm sorry; my sister is not here."

I thanked her and asked her to tell Katya that I had called and would be calling again.

I made one more phone call that morning. I wasn't sure why I hadn't tried to contact Paulson earlier, but I felt an impulse to do so after talking to Katya's sister.

As soon as I introduced myself to the secretary, I was placed on hold. A second or two later, a man other than Paulson came on. "Mr. Paulson is away on business," the man said, "and will be in the States a few days before traveling on to London."

I opted not to leave a message and said, "I'll call back next week."

I left my hotel suite right afterward, vowing that I was finished feeling sorry for myself. "Get on with it!" I shouted. I was so forceful in my resolve that I had to contain myself; I noticed people stepping off the curb and into the street as I neared them. I saw Saint-Germain-des-Prés before me, which helped to push the morning's phone calls to the back of my mind. Yes, as soon as I had Maria's address, I would get on with it.

I could have waited and asked Magritte for her address the next time we spoke, but I didn't want to involve him. I had also tried to get her address from the phone book, but it was unlisted. So I was down to my last resort and my reason for returning to the cathedral—to find someone associated with the funeral and hopefully obtain her address through them.

Finally luck smiled when I stopped a young cleric emerging from the stone rectory adjacent to it who spoke English. Self-consciously rubbing the two-day-old stubble on my chin, I explained, "I'm an old American friend of the deceased—missed the funeral, lost the family's address in the process—and I am desperate to pay my final respects." In a matter of minutes, with the address written on church stationery, I was in a cab and on my way to her home.

But why was I doing this? Why was this act's completion necessary in order for me to come to terms with my life? The only explanation I could propose—*then and to this day*—was similar to why I would always love Katya.

It wasn't a need I was fulfilling. I felt as if some unseen foreign or mysterious force were compelling me, pushing and pulling me, dragging me willingly or unwillingly to this end.

And what was this force? Could it have been nothing more than human nature? Maybe in combination with morbid curiosity?

A demand for some form of bereavement closure? Those thoughts sometimes passed through my mind. At other times, I wanted to believe it was part of the plan to catch her murderers and spot some suspicious character, or someone I recognized—like Spire or Hopkins.

I'm sure that some psychological or fantastic aspects played a part in why I did go, as naive as it might have been, but I didn't believe they were the real explanations. At best, they provided the illusion of a plausible basis or tangible logic, when, in actual fact, all they did was obfuscate the truth.

I didn't believe it then, and too much has happened since to change my mind. Parcae convinced me of that.

"The force, Jwah, which was pulling you to the place where she had lived was your destiny—our destiny," Parcae said.

It began to rain when I got into the taxi. The sky, which had been sunny minutes before, became overcast with black clouds that enshrouded the earth. The gloom brought by this change in weather was of no help in blocking out images and memories of Maria. Their vividness was in stark contrast to the day.

It was a short ten-minute trip to Maria's home. As I neared my destination, I became nervous and told the driver to stop at the intersection of Avenue des Champs-Élysées and Montaigne. The squirrel's residence—*once she was the epitome of the antiaccumulator*—was 5 Rue Francois Premiere, which happened to be in the Seventh Arrondissement, one of the wealthiest districts in a very wealthy city. The irony of those youthful debates we'd once had regarding the accumulation of wealth was not lost on me.

Images of Katya jumped back into my mind. I thought about when she and I would dine at the restaurant at the end of Avenue Montaigne, which had a romantic view of the Eiffel Tower.

The rain continued to fall, the canopies and awnings of the fashionable shops providing temporary refuge. About a third of the way down Montaigne, Francois Premiere would intersect, and I would be there.

It was then that my eyes saw a sight I had either forgotten or blocked out. In bold red letters, on a canopy almost identical to the one I'd found myself staring at last week in Manhattan, the name

Plaza Diana, like some nightmarish reminder, leaped out. I stood in the rain for a second or two, staring at the name, before I felt an urge to move on. But this time, unlike that moment in New York, I entered the hotel. I didn't stay long—five or ten minutes. As I walked about the lobby, I noticed that it looked no different in outward appearances from any other Plaza Diana, but the rage inside me intensified with each step.

When I resumed my original route and turned onto Francois Premiere, the rain had slowed and the sun was forcing its way through the clouds. The address I was looking for was at the end of the street, right before Place Francois Premiere. It was in a quaint, isolated residential square that even Parisian taxi drivers had difficulty finding, but it was one that Katya and I would often pass by after leaving the restaurant.

As the building numbers began to descend, I found my pace slowing, and then I halted at number 7. By then, the rain had stopped, and the sun's rays were shimmering in the puddles along the tree-lined street. The warmth I felt comforted me. I slowly began to walk toward number 5. I dragged my fingers deliberately over the iron gate surrounding the wildflower garden that led to the oversized entrance doors. An eternity later, after I had passed her home, I crossed the street and walked a few houses farther before stopping. I gazed at her building from what I believed was a safe distance, separated by the narrow street and three or four similar dwellings. I wasn't certain how long I stayed there, but years of memories cascaded through my mind before I was brought back to the present when one of the doors opened.

Four people emerged. Two were men—large men in dark suits, white shirts, and black ties. They reminded me of the security people at our broadcast stations, or the police with whom I had recently come in contact. The third individual was a woman. She was an older woman but wasn't the woman dressed in black from the funeral. She was taller and heavier. The last person to appear was the little girl from the funeral. The two men stepped aside, protectively allowing her to walk between them, and the woman held her hand as they walked down the steps.

I was too far away to see the girl's features, but I was envisioning which qualities of hers were Maria's. In less than a minute, the four entered the Bentley parked at the curb and drove away, and she was gone.

Just seconds afterward, I was on the ground, gasping for breath, my arms handcuffed behind my back. I heard the sounds of police sirens growing louder; the sounds ceased abruptly as I was hauled from the sidewalk.

I knew then who my assailants were; their police uniforms were the only introductions I needed as I found myself encircled by an ever-increasing number of Paris's finest. Cars were coming from everywhere—black-and-white patrol cars, unmarked cars, vans—descending suddenly upon what had been only seconds ago some sleepy bedroom neighborhood.

I opened my mouth and started to ask what this was all about, when it hit me. "Hopkins! The son of a bitch," I cursed aloud.

But I was wrong. This was my own stupidity. Sometime afterward, I would learn that the police had a twenty-four-hour surveillance on Maria's home, necessitated by the dangers that the police and the family felt until her murderers were brought to justice. That day, though, I felt Hopkins was responsible.

I cursed his name again as my captors dragged me to the nearest vehicle. Who knew what might happen next? At best, I would spend another night in jail before Roquette had me released. And at worst? Inches from being placed in that position, fate intervened.

"Christof? Christof Douglas! Dios mio! Is that you? Is that you?"

The woman's voice, although hushed, was loud enough when she spoke my name to turn all heads in her direction.

"Christof, it is you. Oh Christof ... Christof, after all these years! It is you!" The hold the police had on my arms relaxed. Their uncertainty about what to do matched my own.

As she approached, helped down the steps by the man Magritte had identified as Maria's husband, I saw that it was the elderly woman from Maria's funeral, the woman who had been standing on the other side of Maria's daughter, and I knew who she was.

When she placed her hand on my cheek and peered at my face, her eyes were full of tears. She didn't speak, but the tenderness in her eyes and her touch expressed more than words could ever say. At last, she lowered her weary gray head and placed it on my shoulder and whispered so that only I would hear the unbearable sadness of her words.

"She's dead, Christof. My little girl is dead. She is gone forever."

She was so old, much older than her years, and very frail. I could feel the bones of her ancient body as she held me around the waist, her head motionless on my shoulder. Whoever was in command must have taken pity on us, because I felt a new sense of freedom in my arms, and as though by some involuntary reflex, my arms sprang upward to drape themselves around her thin shoulders.

The police said nothing and waited until the woman's grief subsided. They were patient, maybe even sympathetic, but I knew they were also watching me. When I lowered one arm to reach into my trouser pocket, the officers on either side of me tensed. But the man who stood behind Maria's mother shook his head, and the officers relaxed.

I didn't speak a word to her, and she didn't say anything more. I knew of no words or phrases that could express my sorrow or ease her unspeakable anguish. As I withdrew my hand from my pocket, I used my other hand to nudge her head from my shoulder, and then I took her hand. While staring into her sad, teary eyes, I dropped into her trembling, bony palm the jade ring Maria had returned to me so many years ago.

The jade ring my mother had given me for Maria to have. The one Maria had worn proudly as a symbol of our love when that love—a love we believed would never die—was as innocent as we were.

The police released me. They didn't try to stop me as I walked away, reversing my steps back to Avenue Montaigne. I walked past Plaza Diana without stopping this time.

As with Saint-Germain-des-Prés, never to enter that building again.

Later that afternoon, Magritte contacted me. We raced through the cryptic questions and responses he had devised to ensure the other's authenticity before getting down to business. "Okay, he's agreed to do what I have requested," Magritte said.

"That's great. But could you tell me exactly what it was you requested?" I was trying not to come across as too cynical, yet I wasn't comfortable with trusting him. I didn't fear him—perhaps I should have—but I wasn't sure I could rely on him to live up to his end of the bargain. His response didn't help those concerns.

"No!" he said so hotly my ears singed. "You should have learned by now that our conversations have unwelcome guests. But you should rest your needless concerns. It is everything we discussed, including that which you desire the most."

I did my damnedest to avoid uttering the names of Spire and Carlson and confirming the fact that they had murdered her. "Is it the people we thought—those whom she spoke of? Did they—"

Magritte interrupted before I could go on. "Oui. It is them. Igor has given me all the necessary details for us to accomplish what we have set out to do."

Did I believe he had asked Igor? I had no way of knowing the truth. It didn't matter, though. He had told me what I wanted to hear. "What's our next step?" As soon as I said it, I realized it was a stupid question.

Magritte ignored me as though I hadn't spoken. "There is one minor item that needs to be resolved. Something"—he hesitated before continuing, his tone very different—"that Igor wants before he'll allow the release of all the information."

Did I hear him correctly? He did say before, didn't he?

"Allo, Chat?" he said, addressing me by my ridiculous code name. "Chat, are you there?"

"Yes, I'm still here. But see here, Dada," I sarcastically added, calling him by his equally ridiculous code name. "What does this mean? What does before mean? I thought you said you had what we needed in your possession. Do you have it, or don't you? Yes or no?"

"Aaaaah," he purred. "Unfortunately, life is not as simple as you and I would have it. But, to answer your question, yes and no. I have it, but I don't have it."

I felt as if I were listening to a magician; I was tired of his "now you see it, now you don't" routine. If Magritte had been sitting in front of me, I would have wrung his scrawny neck; whatever control I once had was now gone.

"Yes and no?" I spat into the phone. "Yes and no! What the hell does that bullshit mean?" His conversation was close to pushing me over the edge—if the exchange between Chat and Dada, full of yeses and nos, followed by "now you see it, now you don't," could even be called a conversation

His voice was as calm as mine was not. "Listen carefully to me. Listen, and remember rule number one. You remember rule number one, don't you?"

He didn't wait for my answer. "I will try to explain it to you as best I can if you don't remember. I feel I must also remind you once again that I will do so over unsecured telephone lines."

I restrained myself and told him to get on with it.

"Listen, and follow everything I tell you. But there is a corollary to that rule. That corollary is patience. One must have patience in all things in life. And one must have even more patience in my form of work, n'est-ce pas, mon Chat?"

I knew he wasn't expecting me to answer him—images of my hands clamping tighter and tighter around his Adam's apple running through my head.

"You see, Igor has revealed all the necessary documents, all the papers, even some photographs. I have read through this material he has compiled on our … our Santa Clauses." Magritte paused as if to make certain that I'd caught the code words. "I can assure you, as I already said, it is everything we want. Everything! But, as I also said, there is one small item that we need to work out."

I didn't know if he enjoyed hearing himself talk or if he didn't know how to tell me what the so-called small item was.

"Yes?" I finally had to ask him, his face now purple in my mind.

He cleared his throat with a muffled sound away from his mouthpiece. "Igor wants something from us. He wants us to give him something hard—and real—before he will release everything to us."

What is with this character? First yes and no. Now … forget it. I stopped myself from going down that road again, although I thought he had made more sense when he was telling me the "now you see it, now you don't" gibberish.

"Do you understand what I am telling you?"

"No, I don't!" I exploded. Magritte's lifeless body lay on the floor of my imagination. "No, I don't have the foggiest damn idea what you are babbling about. Cut the mumbo jumbo, and spell it out, damn it!"

"The lines, mon Chat. Remember the lines."

"Fuck the lines! Tell me what the hell is going on!"

As though offended by my outburst, the lines appeared to be sulking, pouting as they took my insult personally; their silence was deafening. After more silence, I realized it would be necessary for me to reverse our roles by asking Magritte if he were still there.

"Oui, I am here," he replied softly but indignantly. "Are you ready to pay attention for a change?"

Thank god he didn't recite rule number one. "Yes," I said, still hot under the collar but calmer since my eruption.

"He—Igor, that is," he explained, "wants us to provide some evidence—proof, if you will—to support his own data. He thinks it would add, and I agree, an undeniable pièce de résistance to the whole problem. In our opinion, without this evidence from us, we—he, that is," Magritte said, correcting himself in midsentence and beginning to confuse me again, "believes that there isn't enough to make it worth his while." Before I could hit the roof once more, he said, "Let me now spell it out for you."

When he continued, his voice was poised and his English was perfect. "Think about this, mon Chat. Think about who Igor is—or was. Now think about what the Santa Clauses will say. How they will respond to the outcry that will be raised after we reveal to the world their involvement in all their diverse … toy distribution. If you were they, how would you defend, perhaps even justify, your behavior if all the accusations, the alleged basis of their illegalities, arose solely from someone with Igor's background? Are you beginning to understand, mon Chat?"

Why did there always have to be these complications—euphemisms and corporate-speak? Fancy words used to cover and dull the real meaning and pain the truth caused. I wished he would call them what they were: merchants of death selling their weapons of war. Maria wasn't killed, strangled to death by some fuckin' Santa Claus. The sons of bitches killed her to prevent the world from finding out what she had uncovered. I wanted to scream back to her so-called friend that Carlson and Spire wouldn't have jeopardized their careers and lifestyles if she hadn't found something that left them no choice.

"I accept your silence to be an affirmative," Magritte said, breaking into my reflections just as I started to wonder how much Igor and he really knew about what Maria had discovered.

"They would deny everything. In fact, they might even be able to use the opportunity to exploit their own cause," he said, pausing briefly as if to let his words sink in. "How is that possible, you may very well ask? How could they change down to up, black to white?"

My head was spinning. He was turning into the magician again.

"Very simple. Their defense would attack the credibility of whatever documentation we presented. Most of it, they would claim, was part of a disinformation campaign sponsored by Igor's colleagues to embarrass their competition. Information that was doctored to support their goal, which was to destroy the legitimate toy industries of the Santa Clauses. Are you with me?"

"Yes," I replied, finally with him.

"Good. I am almost finished. Of course, it will not be as simple as I've outlined. There will be complications—inconveniences, investigations. The whole thing will drag on interminably long. In the end, though, the Santa Clauses will prevail. I know this to be the case because they are part of a powerful company, maybe the most powerful organization in the world. And, therefore, as I have just theorized, all the information Igor has acquired over the years would be wasted, causing him great unhappiness."

I thought I heard him say something under his breath about his friends being even more unhappy. "No matter," he said, now speaking to me. "Igor's unhappiness is not the problem here. The problem is figuring out how we can add something concrete, something that can't be refuted, so that we minimize the chance of that outcome."

As I was following his rule number one, I kept thinking about what Maria had found. That and the way he had said theorized. Did that mean there was an outside possibility we would go through with everything without more information from Igor?

After all, all I really wanted were two of the goddamn elves, and Igor had told Magritte they were involved.

"Mag—Dada, did the squirrel find anything? Anything close to what we need?"

"No! Nothing. She found nothing like what we need."

I didn't believe him. I had come to realize that Magritte only told me what he felt I needed to know, placing me on the short end of the stick when it came to the truth.

"You used the word theorize. Is there a possibility, after everything is said and done"—I paused before speaking the asinine terminology aloud—"that the Santa Clauses could lose? And that the people I am the most interested in could lose as well? So why can't we forget about Igor? You read his files. Granted, without them we're not in as good of shape as we are with them, but don't we have enough to at least cause some damage?"

Magritte exploded, screaming in French and then in English. "What is it with you, Mari—" He caught himself two syllables too late. "You just don't get it, do you? It doesn't work that way. We would be considered inconveniences if we were to proceed on our own. No. That is, yes. We have no choice. You—we—must show something that could be produced only by the North American Santa Clauses."

Chapter 18

BY THE TIME MY plane landed at Kennedy the next morning, a second surge of adrenaline had kicked in. As the taxi sped through the pre-rush-hour traffic to my office, my mind raced as well, first approving and then rejecting each of the strategies devised before departing Paris. The thought that I would be at my office soon only heightened my indecisiveness.

After Magritte and I had slammed our phones down, I had fought with my imagination for an idea to get us out of our stalemate. He was adamant that there was no alternative but to do as Igor demanded; I was equally adamant that we should proceed without Igor. By now it was also apparent that Magritte, or his shadowy alter ego, wanted something from me that only I could give them.

True, they hadn't come running after me; it had been just the opposite. It was only after I volunteered my services the eve before Maria's funeral, stressing my value in accessing confidential information from the bureaucratic labyrinth that was DFT, that Magritte had agreed to include me in this operation. It was just as true, according to Magritte, that Igor had used Maria. And the fact that Igor was KGB once—*Magritte did say there was no such thing as former KGB, didn't he?*—gave me more than a few moments of concern. But I was too blinded by my thirst for revenge to allow those facts to gain any serious foothold in my thought process.

So I blinked and called Magritte. That was when I told him about my plan to tap into Space and Technology's computer systems. "If we can access a few key files that the Santa Clauses use to maintain the children's orders, along with their"—I was at a loss for code words and just blurted out the real words—"billing and receivable records, we would have a chance of separating the bogus organizations from the legitimate, and we could give your buddy his hard evidence."

I was hoping that he would agree and not ask too many questions, as I had not quite worked out the details in my head.

"Brilliant, absolutely brilliant, mon Chat. I could not have done better myself," he said, congratulating me yet maintaining his code-speak. "We audit the children's letters, matching them wish by wish, child to child, until there are only a few naughty children that don't deserve their toys. Then we match them against Igor's list of bad children. And then when they do—bingo! He has what he wants. Bravo, Chat."

Brilliant or not, there were still a host of land mines in the way. The first and most lethal of them was Gerry Souk, my vice president of technology and the person with whom I needed to start this gamble.

Crossing the Triborough Bridge into Manhattan, I again went over the strategy that I felt had the best chance of success.

I would call Souk into my office, or whatever office I was now banished to, and explain that, as part of the new task force in the Apparel and Retail sector, there was a two-part objective for information technology.

The first part would require him to obtain for the task force all the sector's important historical reports and files regarding billings, inventory, and general ledger data. I would explain that this information was needed to help in our assessment of whether inventory levels, sell-through statistics, customer deductions, and all the essential data the business needed to remain competitive were up to speed.

I would further explain that this was one of the tasks I was responsible for and the reason why I had asked for his involvement.

I would tell him that all of this was legitimate, not prompted by covert aspirations; it was one of the myriad of responsibilities that fell under the group's charter. I also knew that Carlson's memo announcing my participation in the task force and asking for everyone's cooperation if needed would underscore my story's authenticity. It was the next step that would get sticky.

I would begin by cautioning him, impressing upon him that the next objective entailed a high degree of security. If this were the military, I would say, it would be top secret. For your eyes only, I would emphasize. I would take him into my confidence and reveal the industrial espionage that had been uncovered, which was the real reason for the rag-trade task force.

I would make it clear that the extent of this espionage was not known but that design secrets were copied or stolen, billings were not processed—or, worse yet, doctored—and merchandise was being lost at a rate far in excess of the normal shrinkage levels. Just as importantly, I would caution that this criminal activity was believed to be rife throughout the division's executive ranks and no one could be trusted. Borrowing a line from the magician, this would be Gerry's rule number one: everything had to be performed in complete secrecy and without the division's knowledge. And that meant he was to retrieve the data without help from anyone else.

I had confidence in my salesmanship abilities, and Gerry had been my protégé. In light of those two factors, I felt I had a chance to get past this initial hurdle. It was the implementation part that concerned me more.

I knew that this type of computerized access was usually extremely difficult, if not impossible, to accomplish undetected. But I was aware that there was a window of opportunity normally not there, due to the new corporate-wide system project that Gerry had updated me on just last week.

That project's goal was the integration of DFT's divisional systems, bridging the diverse computer platforms to allow DFT corporate online access to those systems. Gerry had mentioned at the staff meeting that the project was at a stage where files were transmitted and downloaded on a regular basis between locations. He'd said that although this transmission was occurring, it was still in test mode because the appropriate passwords and access security were not operational yet. So, if everything were a go with Gerry, I would slip in my real objective.

I would introduce it as an afterthought and add a slight addition to his task. Invoking the sacred name of our illustrious chairman, I would indicate how distressed the bag of shit had been over the whole Retail fiasco and how concerned he was that it could happen elsewhere in this great company of his. As though it were arbitrary, I would then toss out the names of a couple sister divisions, Space being one, and ask that Gerry retrieve the same information from them that I had requested for Retail. Carlson wanted to prove a point, I would emphasize, about how seriously security should be taken. Actually, what better example of a division taking security seriously than Space and Technology, a division so involved with our national defense? I would suggest off-the-cuff.

So that was it. That was my strategy when I arrived at my office. Happy to see that it was still my office, I summoned Gerry. He came immediately. We commiserated with each other about Casey's suicide, a tragedy that would have a great impact on the station's market price. And we talked about what a prick that cop Hopkins was to have said those things in the newspapers. Gerry made no bones about his own disappointment, wondering about the longevity of his career with DFT as a result of their decision to cave in to the FCC. That was when I segued into what I had just rehearsed.

To quote Magritte: "Bingo!" Gerry went for it.

However, I had my share of worries when, by the least likely source, the scales were tipped in my favor. About halfway through our discussion, as I was explaining the negative effect knockoffs were having on the business and how poorly everything was run, Lieber called. I tried to tap-dance around her request to meet, but she wouldn't take no for an answer and said she'd be up in a flash.

She was at my door before I could finish my pitch or escort my unwitting co-conspirator to the nearest sanctuary. She apologized for the interruption and said she could only stay for a second but wondered if I had a copy of the Geo Computer contract. Every copy had disappeared, she explained, including legal's, and there was some fallout beginning to take place with the client because of the negative publicity surrounding Casey. The heart of the issue, she said, was something about revisions that I had signed off on, enabling them to back out of their advertising commitment.

I didn't think this was the time to tell her, 'Go fuck off. I never signed off on the contract; go talk to Weitzer, if you can find the bastard.' So I lied and told her I knew what it was they were after. "Unfortunately," I also said, "I left my copy at home. The next time I go home, I'll bring it back with me."

My lies worked, because she didn't stay or ask any more questions. She did wish me well on my task-force assignment, adding before she went out the door, "How important Carlson felt its success was to the overall health of the firm."

After that remark, it was a piece of cake to convince Gerry. Any misgivings he might have had about what I was asking him to do disappeared on the spot. "And, yes," he said, "it can be done without anybody's knowledge."

He said he needed the better part of the day to review some of the computer integration project's documentation to be sure he grabbed the correct files. "Normally, if it weren't for this project, that documentation would never exist," Gerry explained. "But no sweat," he declared, his technical genes rising to the challenge. "I should be able to get what you need."

There was one thing he warned me of, however. Because the system was in test mode, the corporate technology group reviewed transaction statistics only once a week. That was the good part. "Usually every Monday," he said. "That means that by Tuesday people would learn about the security breach."

"No sweat," I replied, echoing his sentiments and walking him to the door, my own perspiration seeping through the underarms of my jacket. "I'll take care of that minor detail with Carlson ahead of time."

Damn it! Monday, I silently cursed, slamming the door shut. It was Thursday. That leaves today and tomorrow to get what I want. I decided not to rely on the weekend, as I had no idea if the computer system was available or if the risk of detection was greater. 'Take it easy,' Christof, a voice in my head reassured me. 'Focus on what we've accomplished. Don't panic now.' To the extent that I didn't jump from my office window, this little pep talk worked.

I wanted so desperately to believe I was under control and that I was still the same person who'd sat in that office for the past two years. But as I sat at my desk, staring out the window at the Hudson

River flowing into the Atlantic, in my heart of hearts, I knew I wasn't. I knew that despite my calm exterior, beneath it, *my soul was slipping from my grasp.*

* * * * *

Katya and I were married in 1972 in London, four days before Christmas and less than a year after falling in love. "Yes," we would both answer whenever asked if it had been love at first sight. We couldn't explain the full truth—that when our eyes had met, it was as though we had been magically reunited from some other place in space and time. That was too personal, too complex.

I had finally been able to put Maria and the bitter memories from that tumultuous period to an uneasy rest. I knew I would never be able to exorcise those demons. At best, I believed, they would lie dormant until some nostalgic connection occurred and aroused their furies. But I knew that I could restrain them and was content with that somewhat tenuous arrangement.

The story of the poinsettias would always stay in my heart.

Where better to officially recognize that love than London, the city of Dickens, during Christmas? It was also something of a homecoming for Katya and her parents, as none had been back since they had moved to America after her father was attached to the Yugoslavian diplomatic mission. The trip was even more of a homecoming because the Tkarrs' older daughter lived in Mayfair with her husband and newborn son. Katya couldn't wait to see them, especially since she had only seen pictures of her nephew.

It was one of the happiest times of my life. That was the period when I was so lucky, so fortunate to have Katya's love. And I thought this time was different and our love would last forever.

"You were neither lucky nor fortunate. It was your destiny," Parcae would remind me whenever I talked to her about that time in my life.

We were married in Christopher Wren's architectural wonder, Saint Paul's Cathedral. There were hundreds of poinsettias in the church, just as Maria had wanted for our wedding. In spite of the morning sunshine, it snowed, as I had wished. It wasn't a wild, blustery, cascading snow but a gentle, surrealistic version instead. It was the kind of snowfall that teased you, barely covering the dirt and grime of the city, hiding the bleakness that winter seemed to hold, and leaving behind the pristine promise of new, heavenly white.

Katya told me in bed that night that when she was a young girl, the people in her country would say that on days such as these, the fresh snow was an angel on its homeward journey to heaven. Its promise for a white Christmas now kept, it would part the skies to allow the sun an admiring peek at its blessed creation.

Our reception was held at the exclusive Saint James Club. Katya's father, I had grown to realize, had no end of important and influential contacts in the diplomatic and academic worlds, which made this extravagance possible. It was an elegant reception, with the premium on quality, not quantity, since the guest list was under eighty.

Billy was my best man that day, and Laura was her maid of honor.

Ironic, isn't it? Especially the toast he proposed that day and how important that date would turn out to be.

Billy stood and clinked his glass to get everyone's attention, and then he lifted his champagne flute. "With all my love and with all my best wishes," he said, "to my closest and dearest friends, Mr. and Mrs. Christof and Katya Douglas. May they always be as happy and as in love as they are this twenty-first of December. Health, prosperity, and the Lord's blessing should always be your destiny, and may every future anniversary always remind you of the love you have today."

He stepped back and looked at the happy couple; the hushed gathering awaited his words. "May you be so blessed," he said, "to have as many beautiful little Douglases as you so wish. Godspeed!"

More and more often over these last years, Billy's words have come back to haunt me. I always imagined that if Beth hadn't been murdered, we would have wanted the same kind of wedding for her. And I also knew— believed in all my fantasies—that she would have been as beautiful as her mother.

* * * * *

"Mr. Douglas? Mr. Douglas, did you hear me?"

Cindy's replacement called my name once more before I forced myself to turn my thoughts away from the past and the rushing water far below me to face her.

"Mr. Douglas, I'm sorry to disturb you, but you weren't answering your intercom."

"What was it you wanted?" I asked, images of Katya's smiling and radiant face, her fingers wiping the wedding cake from it, locked in my memory.

"It's Mr. Kiner. He called and wanted to talk with you," she nervously explained. "I tried buzzing you to let you know he was on hold, but when you didn't answer, I thought you'd left your office without my noticing. I just came in to leave this message." She dropped the note on my desk and left without any further comment.

It was awhile before I picked up Andy's message. I smiled after reading it, especially when I got to the part about me getting a raw deal and that if I needed help to let him know. I had always liked Andy, but I couldn't bring myself to call him. I stood and walked out of the office. Having completed my only purpose for coming in today, there was no way I could remain or speak with him.

"You were different, Jwah. When you left Paris, you were no longer the person you had been. Nor was your life any longer yours."

I left my office building minutes later, pausing only to instruct the temporary Cindy that if Gerry needed to reach me, he should call my apartment. As for anyone else who might be looking for me, I told her, *"I'll be back shortly,"* and I raced out the office never to return.

I spent the remainder of that day alone at the apartment. I called the office two or three times out of habit, checking in case Gerry had called, but there was nothing. Well, there was something, but nothing from him and nothing I wanted to hear. Mr. Wilson Bloome, the independent consultant whom Carlson had appointed as the rag-trade chairman, had telephoned. He left a message that he had scheduled a kickoff meeting for Monday morning to discuss the materials he had forwarded to each committee member. I hope he appreciates how dedicated I am, I thought smugly, remembering the assignment I had given Gerry earlier. But that thought disappeared as quickly as it had come when I realized what his message meant.

Damn. If internal security didn't discover Gerry's unauthorized access, then Bloome wouldn't be too far behind. Dedicated or not, there was no way I would be able to explain why I had jumped the gun and gone after that information without his formal approval.

Everything was closing in faster than I had planned. As tired as I was, the fear of failure far outweighed any sluggishness from jet lag or the overall fatigue my peripatetic week might have brought on.

So I continued to wait for the telephone call from Gerry, my anxiety growing by the hour. I waited much as I had earlier in the week for a somewhat similar call from Magritte—alone, with only the reflections of a life once lived. As I waited, my trepidation mounted and my optimism spiraled lower and lower, the seeds of frustration and helplessness taking root and giving succor to my approaching madness.

* * * * *

Katya and I spent our honeymoon week after Christmas at Claridge's, once proudly acknowledged as the finest, most prestigious hotel in London. It was quite a week, that first week as husband and wife. We truly had a storybook beginning to our marriage. One morning, we watched through our hotel windows as the snow fell upon the bedecked holiday city, and I thought that I was the luckiest man in the world and that dreams did indeed come true.

"But I am your dream too, Jwah," Parcae chastised me when she heard me talk in that manner. "I am your woman, but I am your dream as well."

And although we spent that week at Claridge's, we did, when the spirit moved us, venture forth and mingle with the other holiday celebrants of the city. On New Year's Eve, one of Dr. Tkarr's former diplomatic colleagues invited us to a black-tie dinner party, and Katya insisted we go.

"He and father knew each other, fought the Nazis when they were winning. How could I possibly say you would rather skip it, Christof?" Katya said, and then she asked if she should wear her hair pinned back or allow it to droop around her shoulders the way she did before coming to bed.

There was also one evening when Laura invited us to dinner. "Oh Christof, we promised we would go," she said when I began to balk and attempt to weasel out of going. "And you know how much I like to see and hold baby Jason. And besides, your mother and father and everyone else from your family will be there."

I would always remember that clipped, very upper-crust British accent of hers as she reminded me in that innocent yet beguiling way of hers what I had agreed to do. I would also never forget one incident from that week that illustrated how much our privacy meant.

Katya and I were window-shopping one brisk afternoon, strolling along Basil Street on our way to Harrods, when all at once she yanked my arm so hard she practically pulled it from its socket.

"Christof, don't move," she whispered conspiratorially, jerking me into the nearest shop alcove. "Shhh," she whispered. She held her finger to her lips as she stood on her toes, her head peering cautiously above and then dipping below my shoulder. "Shhh," she repeated, although I had yet to utter a word, and pushed me with an even greater sense of urgency deeper in the store's entranceway. "Your parents! It's your parents!" she cried. "They're walking this way."

We turned to one another and, without any further exchange, like two syncopated, silent movie villains who found themselves with the posse breathing down their necks, knew the moment had come for a speedy retreat.

Katya tugged the beret she was wearing tighter over her hair, tilting it at such an angle as to shield the side of her face that was exposed to the oncoming invasion, and raised her coat collar, her chin sinking deeper into her chest. And then we ran like the very hounds of hell were after us.

As we raced down the street, doing our best to avoid bumping into any of the startled shoppers in our path, we began to laugh. At first it was just a playful sort of giggle. But as we ran on and it became obvious that we had saved our privacy, our laughter grew louder. Eventually it became uncontrollable.

Finally we halted, out of breath, and fell into each other's arms. As we lost our balance and toppled against the fender of the parked car behind us, Katya was laughing so hard that tears formed in her eyes, and her laughter gave way to hiccups. I spent the next few minutes trying to frighten her, hoping to still the hiccups. Then I pulled her nearer to me, and my lips did what my words could not.

An incident the following evening at her sister's dinner party added to the humor.

"Were the two of you anywhere near Harrods yesterday afternoon?" my mother asked.

We both simultaneously and somewhat conspicuously blurted out a resounding "No!" and my mother proceeded to tell us, "Two people who had such a remarkable resemblance to you and Christof, Katya, raced down the sidewalks outside that department store, laughing hysterically the whole while."

In the corner of my eye, I could see Katya unsuccessfully trying to stifle her mounting giddiness. She began to hiccup, her face reddening in embarrassment, and rose from the table, excusing herself to flee to the sanctuary of the powder room.

Later, when we were safely nestled in the coziness of our bed and each other's arms, we roared yet again, imagining the looks on my parents' faces when they first spied us dashing madly down the avenue.

There were two incidents from that week, however, that did their damnedest to test that euphoria.

One day, toward the end of that week, as we were walking together, arms intertwined, Katya leaning into my body as much for protection from the icy air as to be close, an almost forgotten sight appeared.

I had been in London a couple of times with Billy during the period between 1969 and 1970 when we sometimes searched for Maria as we drifted through Europe. On our second stopover— *it was after Maria had returned the jade ring*—we picked up two hippie types and found ourselves as part of an audience at a Tim Buckley concert.

Buckley wasn't really one of my favorites, but during that period, when I was at one of those events, between the smell of pot and the half-naked girl grinding against my body to the music, an "us against the world" sensation would inevitably take hold of me—especially when the performer was singing one of the more powerful antiwar anthems of the time.

So there I was, one of a few thousand people listening to the music, sliding into the mood his twelve-string guitar and plaintive voice were creating, when it happened. All of a sudden, I understood that he was singing about me. It didn't matter that half the audience was probably thinking the same thing I was. That wasn't important. What mattered was that I knew this was my story. The song was "Once I Was," and it would be played a few years later as part of the soundtrack that set the tone for Bruce Dern's character to make a suicidal dash into the California surf at the end of the movie 'Coming Home.'

And sometimes when I would think back to then, to those moments, I would even try to sing its last verse, but all I was able to do was mutter, almost mindlessly, "Do you ever ... ever remember me?"

"Queen Elizabeth Hall." I exhaled aloud.

When Katya asked what I'd said, I told her about that day with Buckley and the concert. I even told her about the two girls we'd met, but I couldn't bring myself to tell her about the spell that song had cast. I would tell her that someday in the future.

It was a couple years later when I told her, when we had just walked out of the movie 'Coming Home' and she wanted to know how I felt. By then she knew—well, she knew most ... some of the things—about Maria.

"Did you identify with Dern, about the loss of his wife after Vietnam?" she asked, squeezing her body closer than I had believed possible.

So I told her. "Yes, once I could identify with him. I could identify very strongly with him, but that was then. I don't anymore," I said, completely believing that lie myself.

The second incident that occurred during our honeymoon week was even more disturbing. It was so startling and unreal that it left me shaking. It occurred on Bond Street as I waited for Katya to come out of Burberry. I was watching the people walk by, when, fewer than fifty feet away, a woman caught my eye.

She was about to board a bus when my eyes were drawn to her. At the moment they came to rest upon her, just seconds before she entered the red double-decker vehicle, she hesitated and then jerked her head toward me. Her action was so hasty, so unnatural, that it looked as though someone from out of nowhere had slapped her face. Our eyes locked for a split second, neither of us moving, and then I saw the poinsettia in her hand.

I began to walk in her direction, initially slowly and then, realizing she was turning and entering the bus, quickly.

Oh God! Oh God, no! Why, Parcae? Why?

But I was too late. By the time I got there, the bus had sealed its doors, and it began to pull away from the curb.

As it picked up speed, I began to run alongside, hoping I would somehow be able to see her face in the crowd packed inside. I ran to the following corner, arriving about the same time the bus did. It didn't stop. I ran faster, trying with all my soul to keep up, hoping it would stop at the next corner. I started to fall behind, the steam from my hot breath coming in shorter spurts, my ankle throbbing as it began to fail me. The bus sped past the next intersection and, instead of slowing, gained speed and pulled farther and farther away. She had disappeared again.

Maria was gone.

As I retraced my route, my heart was pounding, but not from exertion. When I arrived a few minutes later at Burberry, Katya was standing, shivering impatiently outside. The confused look she wore on her face disappeared when she saw mine.

I tried to smile, bent my head toward her, and whispered, "No, it wasn't a ghost I saw," in answer to her question as her hands touched my cheek. "It's just the cold. And maybe—maybe it's time for us to be going home," I said, pressing her so tightly against my chest that it was impossible to tell one wildly pounding heart from the other.

Chapter 19

TO QUOTE MAGRITTE ONCE more: "Bingo! Double bingo!" Gerry called early Thursday evening and said he had the information. However, he sounded a little like the magician when he explained that he didn't have everything in his possession but was in the process of downloading it from DFT's host computer to ours.

"I still need about an hour or so before I'll be finished," he reported. "The files are large, especially Apparel and Retail's, which I'm working on right now. They must have a thousand customers in their database. Not anything like Space and Technology, which has maybe a hundred at the most. I zipped through that baby, Chris, in no time."

I was tempted to tell him to abort the remainder of his download and bring me the files I wanted immediately. I was tempted, but I restrained myself, balancing the risks of being caught by some security check with suspicions that Gerry might have if I rescinded the basic cover for the operation.

'Be patient, mon Chat,' a voice within me instructed.

And, more importantly, the fact that Space and Tech's files were so small would only make it that much easier to ferret out the illegal transactions in question.

"Okay, whatever you say; you're the expert," I said to Gerry.

"We'll probably wind up with better than a dozen floppies, but that's the best media for your use."

It dawned on me that maybe it would be a good idea to have a second copy in case things got hairier than anticipated. 'When they get hairier, not if,' the same inner voice corrected. 'You have no way to tell what the fallout will be after this information hits the newspapers and the rest of the media.'

"Give me another hour to make a duplicate set," Gerry said after I told him I wanted copies.

Approximately three hours later, I had the disks and was dropping them off at the nearest Federal Express office. Within twenty-four hours of the plan going into effect, the data was on its way to Paris, and we now had what we needed to expose DFT's illegal dealings to the world, and ultimately bring the downfall of Carlson and Spire. I dialed Magritte to tell him of my success.

"Allo?" the all-too-familiar, nasally voice said, echoing in my ear.

"C'est moi, le Chat, ici. J'ai manage l'oiseau," I said conspiratorially, obeying his instructions to converse in the stupid code he had devised. The code was particularly important, he warned, whenever I was referring to names or our plans. Actually, I was beginning to enjoy being addressed as "the cat." It had a certain cachet to it, especially for one who was in the cloak-and-dagger business—an idea I'd found completely absurd a few days ago, but one that I had now become deeply immersed and lost in.

'Don't get too carried away with yourself,' my inner voice whispered. 'And you'd better hope there is more cloak than dagger to come.'

After a lapse, I heard the excited, nasal voice. "Oui, oui. Bienfait, mon Chat. Igor will be tres heureux. Est-il tous ca nous avons pense?"

I had to pause a moment to find the French words that meant "I don't know if it's everything we thought, but I know what we need is there."

"Why are we talking in French anyway?" I mumbled. But what the hell? If "yes and no" was an acceptable answer for him, it was certainly acceptable for me. "Je ne sais pour certainment," I answered, "mais je sais c'est."

There was a long pause. Then I heard a murmur that sounded like "C'est o n'est pas?" followed by a louder "Quand? Quand?"

I must have made my point about continuing in French, because he switched without warning to English. "When will I be able to see its feathers, mon Chat? The feathers of the bird that you have just eaten?"

I rifled through my wallet for the Fed Ex receipt and the package's tracking number. It was nested within Maria's letter and the photograph of Katya that Maria had taken. Shaken, I said, "Sometime late tomorrow it should be in your hands," and I began to read the tracking number to Magritte.

"Shut up, you dumb Chat! How many times must I tell you? The line is not secure. Do not give me the number. Do not give me any name. If I don't receive it by tomorrow, I will call you, and we will decide what we must do. Comprende?"

This was one occasion when I realized he wasn't overreacting. It was stupid to broadcast that confidential information.

"Listen, Dada," I started to apologize, "je suis une dumb Chat. Okay, I understand. Tomorrow it will be."

"Tres bien, d'accord," he replied, his tone still indicating his displeasure.

I wasn't sure if our conversation was over in his mind, but there was one more thing I had to ask him, and I needed to make certain he was aware of the tight timeline we were under.

"When do you think …" I hesitantly asked, gun-shy from his last outburst. "That is, when will I be able to see the results of our efforts?"

This time, I interrupted him before he got too far into his diatribe on "amateur Americans who should have remained at home, minding their own business instead of asking too many unanswerable questions" and told him, "By Monday or Tuesday of next week, the bird, the feathers, the whole damn aviary will be missed, and the gamekeepers will know that I was the hunter." I wasn't certain if those were the right code words, winging it the way I did, but it didn't matter; he got the message.

The telephone went silent. For a moment I thought the temperamental lines were pouting again. And then I heard him calmly say, "D'accord. Monday or Tuesday, ce ca."

That's it? That's all you have to say after what I just told you? Before I could ask Magritte that question, as though reading my thoughts, he interjected, "Chat, we will talk about this more tomorrow. I am thinking that maybe it will be best for you to return to Paris. But let us not be too hasty. Let us decide what to do when we talk tomorrow. I must go now."

Just like that, he was gone. I was now faced with another twenty-four-hour period of waiting before I would learn my fate. I was also exhausted. The chimes from the mantle clock struck their maximum number, reminding me how late it was. Now that this difficult task in our plan was completed, all the energy I had so forcefully pulled together seemed to have evaporated the instant the phone went dead. Mercifully, I hoped that this exhaustion would enable me to sleep and replenish whatever strength remained within me. But, even more importantly, I hoped to waken and find I was that much closer to my final objective.

Since it was now Friday, I poured myself a brandy, my first drink for the day, and fell into the Eames rocker. My eyes closed as I leaned my head against the soft leather. I placed the Baccarat snifter on the cocktail table, moving aside the duplicated set of precious disks and the photograph of Katya, and reached out for sleep.

* * * * *

During the first two years of our marriage, Katya and I lived in a rent-controlled, junior-sized one-bedroom apartment on the Upper West Side of Manhattan. Katya still had a few months remaining before she would complete her master's program in European impressionism at Princeton, so occasionally, when her reverse commute would get to her, she and I would stay with her folks. They lived a couple of miles from the university, where her father was a professor. I remembered those early years together much the same way I remembered that honeymoon week in London—a story book fantasy that had come true, with two people living their dreams.

I was now employed full-time at WQXT. I had started as soon as I received my MBA from NYU during the spring. I knew how much in debt I was to both Dickey Lake and his father, Richard. In Richard's case, that debt began when he offered me the internship the day I showed up at the station. From that day on, although he never raised the subject of his son again, I could sense that he took a special interest in me. To some extent, I became the son he no longer had—in some ways, perhaps the son he never would have had, for Dickey had told me he had zero interest in the broadcast business.

Dickey had said he was going to move out west. He was going to catch a plane for Wyoming or Idaho the day after his tour in Nam was up and go work on any ranch or cattle spread that would have him. That was his dream, he'd told me.

His dad took me under his wing and helped teach me all the nuances, all the ins and outs of the radio business. I knew that without his guidance, I would have never made it as far as I had.

At the time I started my career, WQXT had revenues of $5 million. Thanks to Richard Lake's stewardship and the purchase of stations in Boston, Chicago, and DC, during the six years I was at the station, that number for his mini–broadcast empire would grow to $25 million before he himself fell victim to the acquisition game.

To raise the capital for those acquisitions, the suits not only owned him; they eventually killed him.

Prior to that turn in our fortunes, I was appointed general manager of QXT. I remember Mr. Lake telling me I was ready and that he needed someone he could rely upon, traveling as often as he did to visit his new properties.

"I can trust you," he said, "to keep an eye on things here, because I know that they can change when I'm away at one of the other stations."

And if my professional career seemed to have taken off, my life with Katya was even more fulfilling.

Katya obtained a much-sought-after position as an associate art appraiser with Shoal and Whitney after her graduation from Princeton. They were a well-respected art boutique on the Upper East Side of Manhattan. Their specialty was twentieth-century abstractionists, but they were looking to expand their sphere of expertise into the area of European romanticists and impressionists, an area that Katya had majored in. The only reservation we had with the position was the travel required, as Katya would have to attend and participate in some of the most prestigious art and antique shows around the world.

But, in the scheme of things, we decided it was a minor

inconvenience we could live with. Like so many couples of our generation, we felt that being apart was a small sacrifice, and one that needed to be made if we were to grow in our dual careers and our lives.

It wouldn't be forever. Katya said that she wanted to have a child before thirty; she insisted that that was always her real dream and, with me, all that mattered in her life. So, in the third year of our marriage, we moved out of our one-bedroom apartment and into a larger two-bedroom on the Upper East Side, in anticipation of the impending event in our lives.

Aside from the week when I took time off for our honeymoon in London, I didn't take any vacation during those early years at QXT.

Katya was more fortunate. She was usually able to tack a few days on to her trips to London or the Continent and spend some time with her sister, or use the opportunity for her research on her esoteric subject matter. That was an enviable perk her chosen field had over mine.

My earliest chance for a vacation came in the late summer of 1973. That was when Katya and I went to Bermuda. It was our first trip, but it wouldn't be our last, we both vowed as we were departing those idyllic pink islands.

Bermuda was for lovers; perhaps for some it still is … The ocean pounds harder and harder against the battered hull; the white-capped surf rages, its salty mist crusting the slits that were once my eyes.

Some two years later, to celebrate our wedding anniversary, we took our second holiday. For this occasion, we went to Peter Island, a tiny and secluded pinch of land in the British Virgin Islands. We also decided we would be a little more adventurous and chartered a sailboat for a few days.

It was my first time sailing since Billy and I had searched for Maria.

We sailed throughout the BVIs for three days and then arrived at Peter Island to spend the remainder of the week regaining our land legs. We made the most of those three days, sailing and snorkeling inside the Sir Francis Drake Channel; our vacation was all we hoped for and more.

"The weather is perfect. Everything is so perfect and romantic,"

Katya said one evening as we gazed at the twinkling heavens above.

That night was extra special, for that was the night, Katya believed, that Beth came to be. "I just know," she would say with a smile when I asked her how she could be so certain. "A woman just knows," she replied, her beautiful, tanned face adopting that conspiratorial look of hers.

That night, as wonderful as Peter Island was, was anticlimactic. That night, I knew that Maria and the past would now just be that— the past.

Chapter 20

THAT NEXT DAY WAS Friday. It had been only two weeks to the day since my life began to unravel, every aspect of it collapsing as I slid further into my own hell. It was the last day that the being I once was remained within me, the person the world took forty-two years to create, to mold and form, and who, despite a rash of involuntary actions, could yet be recognized as Christof Douglas. For after that day, whatever tenuous restraint or thin patina of civilized society had once existed was discarded, shed like some dried, worthless layer of dead skin no longer of any value to its host organ. In its stead came the madness that would cling to me to until my very end.

I awoke that Friday morning refreshed. I tried to call Katya, forgetting what my world had become. A smile appeared on my face when the image of her beautiful face and the sound of her voice drifted through my mind. For a moment, I believed that this morning was not any different from earlier mornings in our life together when we'd found ourselves separated, with the telephone as our only link.

But reality set in. I almost took my hand from the phone and let it slide into the cradle. "What the hell!" I said to the empty room, staring at the picture of the two of us on the fireplace mantel, holding hands and smiling, glad to be in Bermuda.

I might as well have let the phone fall from my hand when I reached that insufferable bore giving instructions for the caller to leave a message at the beep. It was the same person who answered at the cottage at Sea Isle. I listened until the bore was finished and then left word for Katya that I was at the apartment and that she should call me as soon as possible. I also told her I loved her.

I telephoned my office even though it wasn't business hours and left a message on Cindy's—or, more likely, Monday's—voice mail. That was the name I had taken to calling the new gal in acknowledgment of Cindy being my gal Friday all those years. Monday seemed as good a day as any for her replacement to start. Besides, I had forgotten her name.

I let Monday know I wouldn't be in the office until later in the afternoon, if at all, and I also told her not to make arrangements for me to fly down to Greenville for the task force's kickoff meeting on Monday, as I would handle it. I had zero intention of doing either, but in my mind, these were necessary lies. I wasn't certain what I was going to do except wait. My next discussion with Magritte would determine any future actions, but I knew it would never be business as usual for me again.

What I did know was that sometime the following week, DFT would be aware that their systems were compromised and that confidential data had been stolen. At that time, Carlson and Spire would understand that their fictitious database was now in the hands of someone who had the power to destroy their lucrative and illegal game. It would be just a matter of hours before they would then learn that that someone was me. How they dealt with that fact would dictate what I would then do.

I couldn't see them contacting me directly, keeping it under wraps and away from the media as they appealed to my common sense or company loyalty. I couldn't picture Carlson, the old snake that he was, magnanimously offering—pleading was more like it—for me to return everything like a good old boy, insisting all would be forgotten and forgiven. What did he need me for? Another suit for his rag-trade review?

In all likelihood, they would send the same sick character after me that they had sent after Maria. Or, dropping the melodramatics, they might be willing to take their chances, as Magritte seemed to think, and send some weasel who was on their payroll—like Hopkins—to charge me with stealing corporate secrets and betraying national security.

Which of these two permutations they decided to pursue hinged, in my mind, on what was happening some three thousand miles away. If Magritte and Igor were able to extract the information that I desperately wanted to believe was on those diskettes before DFT personnel discovered that their system had been breached, then I felt I had some leverage on which variation Carlson would exercise. Under this scenario, I might even make initial contact with them, catching them by surprise, telling them of the serious security flaw in their system. I would advise them—however, they would know I was threatening, not advising—to keep their goons far at bay unless they wanted this sensitive data of theirs finding its way to the world media.

But each time that illusory notion of grandeur entered my increasingly softening skull, it was followed by a more cynical and pragmatic notion.

'Bullshit' was how it usually began. 'Get a grip on yourself, Christof,' my inner voice would chide me in the discomforting, third-person, schizo manner that was developing in my mind. 'You're dreaming, filled with self-indulgent and cockamamie illusions and all too willing to mistake yourself as some sort of James Bond character rather than the scared, insecure toady you have always been. If you were stupid enough to tell them you had their precious data, there would be a bunch of goons knocking down the apartment door before you even finished getting the words out of your dumb mouth.'

'No way, Jose. As much as you don't want to face it,' this more and more frequently surfacing voice concluded, 'any way you slice it, you have to vamoose and get the hell out of here. Disappear from sight and leave the country as fast as your sorry ass can get into gear. And in no manner, shape, or form, the voice warned, fading from my thoughts, could that be a minute later than Monday.'

Whatever renewal my body had felt when I awoke just a few hours earlier was gone; wrestling with this demon more than sapped my strength. And staying cooped up in the apartment was driving me crazier by the hour. I was like some penned animal circling eternally about its cage, forever condemned to spend the remainder of its captive existence in meaningless pursuit of the nearest corner. I had to get out.

That's when I decided to go to our house in Jersey. I could contact Magritte from there just as easily as from the apartment.

And, besides, I hadn't been back to our primary residence in over a month. The thought of not knowing whom I might stumble into clinched it.

Before that know-it-all voice got wind of my decision and had a chance to second guess me, I was on the phone with Hertz, reserving whatever they had available, which turned out to be a Ford Taurus. My usual mode of transportation, the Bimmer, was either with Katya or baking its too-well-known finish down to the metal on a hot shore driveway. Anyway, in light of the shark's attraction to that car, I would be better served with an unknown vehicle.

Ten minutes later, I was at the rental agency. However, two things happened on the way over that left me feeling more than uneasy.

When I walked out of my apartment building, two men standing opposite my entrance began to walk toward the cul-de-sac at the end of the block, away from the direction I was headed. Normally I wouldn't have even noticed them. But as I reached the corner and turned uptown, I saw that they had reversed themselves and were heading in my direction.

Any doubts I might have had about being followed disappeared moments later. When I was crossing First Avenue at Fifty-Third Street, I stopped in the middle of the street as though I were unsure where I was going and then retraced my steps back to the sidewalk. That was when I knew for certain.

For the next sixty seconds, or however long it took for the light to change, I controlled my mounting nervousness and shared the curbstone with them. Although neither said a word, their shoes did more than enough talking for them, telling me clearly who they were as I stared at the ground. The last time I'd had this type of conversation had been just a week ago, so I was well versed with the message. That conversation was with Hopkins, who had been wearing identical footwear, which no one with any sense of fashion would wear. I smiled, beating that smart-alecky voice from whispering, 'People don't wear Dr. Scholl's for their sense of style.'

When the light changed, I crossed the avenue. This time I reversed myself, backtracked toward Fifty-Second Street, and entered the local video shop. For the next ten minutes, I divided my attention between the entrance door and the current movie rack. Finally, feeling reasonably safe that I had lost or embarrassed them, as I was sure they realized I had spotted them, I walked out. They were nowhere to be seen.

But the Gucci brothers had done their job. That incident only added to the tension I had been able to contain thus far, which had the possibility of exploding at the least likely turn of events. Fortunately—or was it luckily?—the second incident that day wasn't that catalyst, even though it happened only a few minutes later.

When I entered the Hertz office at Sixty-First Street, the salesperson was with another customer, so I took a seat and did my best to wait patiently for my turn. When she signaled to me that she was ready, I noticed a double-parked Chevy outside the rental-office window. Two men in dark suits were sitting in it.

I stared at the car as I stepped to the counter, half expecting to see the Guccis, when it sped off. Then again, I thought, smiling at the clerk as I handed her my license while fighting to stifle the voice within that was taunting me and calling me a 'fuckin' idiot,' perhaps it was just time for them to drive away.

I mumbled, "I would have known the answer if I saw their shoes." The gal behind the counter asked if I was all right. She continued to stare alternately at my face and the photo on the license for what seemed an eternity before finally handing me the paperwork to sign and giving me the car keys to the Taurus.

I kept well below the speed limit on the drive to New Jersey. For a while, I thought I was possessed, but then I realized it was nothing more than a nervous twitch that kept making me turn around and look to see if the Chevy was following. Once, crossing over the George Washington Bridge, I thought I saw something resembling the Chevy, but I lost sight of it and never saw it again. The remainder of the hour-long trip to the Rose City was otherwise uneventful.

The Rose City. I always liked that name. Katya and I moved there from Manhattan another lifetime ago when Beth was born.

As I pulled around the corner of the two-story stone colonial house and drove up the tree-lined, herringbone brick drive, my heart beat faster at the thought of seeing a familiar car parked outside, but the driveway was empty.

I parked the Taurus on the side of the driveway usually reserved for the Olds, got out, and slammed the door behind me.

For a second I hesitated, unable to decide whether or not to check inside the detached garage.

'Neither of you have used that building for years, at least not for your cars, so what are you thinking of?' the voice asked, unexpectedly reappearing. "You're right," I whispered, disregarding its advice and walking to the garage. "There is absolutely no room for them, because Beth's toys, clothes, and furniture are all there."

I rose on my toes and peered through the garage windows. It was just as the voice had said it would be. "See, are you satisfied, you dumb fool?" I said aloud to myself. The darkened enclosure was empty. I saw only the same objects that had been gathering dust for years, their shadowy forms dimly visible before my searching eyes.

"Chris? Is that you? Christof Douglas? Oh, it is you," a woman's voice said.

I turned away from the painful memories lying in front of me to face this sudden intrusion. When I saw who it was, I forced a tiny smile, as much out of courtesy as the irony of both her question and her belief in its answer. There was no sense in confusing her, so I concurred.

"Yes, Abigail, it's me ... or I. Forgive me, but I always forget which is the correct usage."

Our next-door neighbor, Abigail, ignored my comment and remained next to the Taurus, some twenty feet away, as I walked toward her. "I didn't recognize the car that pulled up your driveway, so I came over to see who it was. I must tell you ... That is"—she began to stutter—"your appearance caught me completely by surprise."

Abigail—along with her husband, Harlan, and son, young Harlan, as everybody called him—had been entrusted with the daily surveillance of our soon-to-be-deserted domicile. Because she had taken her job so seriously, I figured there was no advantage in telling her that her job was a candidate for restructuring and her department had been eliminated.

Our cheeks touched in polite greeting. "Yeah, well, I haven't been too happy with the old Bimmer lately," I said truthfully. I stepped around her and walked up the porch steps. Abigail must have felt obligated to give me some sort of house-sitting update, as she trailed behind.

I was tired of her nosy presence and inane questions, so I took the offensive and repeated some of my more polite thoughts aloud.

"In case you're wondering why I'm here, Katya forgot some things she needed for the weekend—cooking things. Like a special pot for her … **Ragoooo**." I turned to her and pursed my lips in an exaggerated fashion when I said the word.

Her jaw dropped. Good, there was no way I wanted her to get too comfortable. Since I had her on the ropes, I let her have another hint of whom she was dealing with. "As soon as I get the **Ragoooo** and make a phone call, I'm out of here. I'm history."

That was the second truth I'd told in about the same number of minutes, since I did intend to get out after calling Magritte. Well, it was the second truth if I considered the question as to whether I was Christof just too perplexing. My answer to that question qualified equally as both the truth and non-truth, and therefore I had to exclude it.

Abigail didn't say a word as I fumbled with the lock on the door inside the porch. For a heartbeat, I believed that the locks had been changed, but then the door swung open. That was when she asked me how Katya was. My veracity percentage plummeted after that question.

"She's fine, just fine." I tossed the keys onto the island counter the way I always did and wished she would disappear.

"Fine," I repeated. "She's simply marvelous." My eyes hungrily took in everything. It was as though I hadn't been here for years, though it had been only a month.

"Harlan and I read about that shooting the other day at your radio station. How dreadful that must have been. The nerve of that detective to talk about you like that. Why, he was just horrible."

'Why is she still here? Go away, lady!'

I must have asked her something, for I heard her say, somewhere in the distance, "I said that it was terrible what happened."

"Yeah … Yeah," I echoed sympathetically, hearing Beth's and Katya's silent laughter fill the room.

"Harlan and I also read about your company selling all its radio and TV stations."

"Yeah," I said under my breath, responding much more quickly to that question. I walked out of the kitchen and into the living room. "That's what I heard too."

Abigail followed closely behind. This time, she asked me to repeat myself.

'Beat it, lady,' I almost let the voice tell her.

"I said you shouldn't believe everything you see and read," either the voice or I told her, each of us over enunciating every syllable as our combined patience quotient reached its limit.

As I circled the room, my fingers touched and lingered over treasured remembrances. I paused by the Louis XIII marble fireplace and stared at the picture of the two us in Bermuda—the same picture that sat on the mantel in the apartment—and then continued my circuit.

"Chris, I can assure you that everything is exactly as you and Katya left it," a woman's voice said. "No one, not one single person, has been in this house except for Harlan and me. And one time, when Harlan and I were away for the weekend, young Harlan was here to water the plants and make sure everything was okay. Well," the annoying woman went on, "to be perfectly honest, young Harlan was here twice."

About the time she was somewhere between young Harlan and Harlan, I stopped pacing and turned toward the irritation.

"Listen, Abigail," I said, cutting her off before she had a chance to recall any other exceptions to the rule, utter that stupid name again, or, worse, reassure me once more, "if you don't mind, I'm expecting—"

A shooting pain in my head forced me to pause and rub my forehead, smoothing out the crease lines as I did. "Listen, Abigail, I'm expecting a very important phone call any minute, and I need some time to prepare for it." I continued to massage my temples while the voice shouted in my ear to tell the pencil-necked nuisance to get the hell out. Then again, maybe it was the other way around.

Whatever I said only seemed to confuse her. Her head kept tilting, rocking back and forth between her shoulders. I was beginning to feel seasick watching her, my own head following her lead, transfixed by its rhythmic motions.

"Chris, are you all right?" she finally asked, her body swaying from side to side. "You don't seem yourself. You seem so—so different."

Aha! That was it. That was the final straw! At that moment, I was overwhelmed by the need to explain philosophically to her the metaphysical nature and true meaning of her statement, her discovery that I was different and not myself. That was what I felt, but the only thing that came out of my mouth was a simple, basic scream for her to get the fuck out. In the future, though, I would make sure she understood that it had been a case of mistaken identity on her part, that she had erred in her assumption that someone who happened to look like me was, in reality, me. When I heard both doors bang shut, I felt that I had also been mistaken about Abigail. She could take a hint after all.

Now that I was at last alone, in a place Katya and I once called home, I asked myself why I had come. Did I think she might be here and I would surprise her? In my mind, I saw images of Katya alone, quietly packing her clothes and personal effects, followed by noisy images of uniformed men streaming in and out of the house and loading a large van parked in the driveway with furniture, cartons, and anything and everything that was ours.

As I opened my eyes, that commotion-filled nightmare was just that—a nightmare. There were no moving men or truck in the driveway. There was only me, sitting on the couch, staring into emptiness. Yes, I ironically reassured myself, everything is, as Abigail so confidently stated, exactly as we left it. I shook that equally disturbing illusion from my mind and walked toward the hallway stairs, which led to the second-floor bedrooms.

When I saw that the door to the master bedroom was closed, something we never did, I sensed that something might be wrong. I opened the door slowly and, at the same rate of speed, pushed my head into the gap forming behind. What I saw was beyond my wildest nightmares. If I had seen a room that was barren except for the memories it once held, evidence of her desertion, I would have been a thousand fold less jolted.

To this day, whenever I think back to that moment, I still become more confused, rather than less, trying to understand the intent of the depraved and perverted message I beheld that summer afternoon.

If it were meant to frighten, it succeeded. If it were meant to provoke, to bring me to the next level of rage, which somehow I might yet be holding back, it did. But if it were intended as a warning or a threat to back off and force me to retreat from my goal of seeing those responsible for Maria's murder brought to justice, it failed miserably. And if provocation were, in truth, its primary aim, compelling me to act with greater irrationality or driving me further into madness, why even bother? A patient man would realize only too confidently that I would ultimately come to those ends.

All of those assumptions aside, as valid, as tormenting as they were, to this day, I can only believe that the act was the handiwork of some depraved, sadistic messenger—one who took immense delight in leaving his mark behind. And someone whose message was of secondary importance to the enjoyment his actions brought him.

That day, I found only one place—the cedar personal walk-in closet, which normally contained Katya's clothing—that somehow had been spared and that remained unsoiled by the psychopathic madman's actions. And, quite contrary to both Abigail's and my beliefs, nothing was as it once had been.

I didn't know where to look, so monstrously savage was the destruction. My eyes fell to the center of the room, where I would have expected to see the king-sized bed. Instead my eyes came to a shocking rest upon its remnants. Fragments of splintered mahogany, strewn bits of foam rubber and mattress stuffing, ripped silks and linens, shredded into a thousand pieces—the destruction before me was total, even down to the bed's feathers. They were everywhere: on the walls, on the carpet, in the air. They even somehow managed to float upward and cling to the ceiling. I saw shattered shards of crystal and glass. Splintered pieces of wood from Katya's dresser and my armoire and other sundry items of furniture were intermingled in violent disarray with the contents they once contained.

As I sleepwalked my way into the room, shuffling more than walking, my heartbeat and breathing quickening by the second, my eyes were drawn to the bedroom walls—the walls that were closing in on me. Unlike everything else I saw, the walls were still intact.

What had once been covered in a grass-textured celadon fabric was now awash in a dull brown-and-red tone. The entire room, I realized as I turned full circle to stare at each wall in that all-too-familiar space, had been transformed into that ghastly color. I lifted a hand, reaching from both morbid curiosity and horror, to touch a feather. The feathers had assumed the color of the walls as they clung lifelessly and repulsively to them. It was then that I realized what the reddish-brown substance was.

Blood ... God in heaven ... Blood.

I wondered if the feather, along with the walls and the rest of the room, had been chemically treated in some fashion to minimize the decomposing smell of blood, but it didn't matter. I knew as I was holding it, gagging and struggling to control the agonizing, involuntary dry-heaving reaction that nearly brought me to my knees: the room was coated in blood.

As I held the feather delicately between my thumb and forefinger, trying desperately to reject that macabre notion as too inconceivable, I began to tremble. I rubbed those two fingers together, the blood from the feather discoloring them as I did so, and continued deeper into the room.

Maria's blood! Maria's blood!

Those two hideous words repeated over and over in my head as I stared at the bloodstained message splashed across each of the dozen or so newspaper pages hanging from the wall.

Maria's blood! Maria's blood!

I wasn't sure how long I stared at those newspapers, each one reporting Maria's murder, insanely mesmerized, body trembling and heart pounding, before I was able to break the spell. Or maybe I didn't. Maybe it was the other guy within me—the one whose voice kept popping up more and more lately, and who seemed to have more presence of mind when it came to these situations.

'Downstairs. There's another phone downstairs,' the voice reminded me as I stood with the broken remains of the bedroom phone in my hands.

Moments later, the live dial tone in my ear truly sounded like music. The same reflex that caused me to lift the instrument from its cradle, however, also caused me to slam it down.

There was no way I could call the police that day.

But then visions of Katya flew into my head and cast my hesitance into oblivion. I was overcome with soul-crippling fear that Katya was in harm's way—a captive of that demented monster, or worse. I could not bear the thought of anything worse; I re-lifted the telephone again and punched 911.

It took three rings for the emergency service to answer; by then, I had already changed my mind. I disconnected the call when I heard the person at the other end of the line.

'Don't panic, you fool,' the voice had warned while the phone rang. 'If you get those gumshoes involved, you're dead meat. There's no way you'll be able to continue working with Magritte, and her murderers will go free. And, if you don't believe what I say will happen, just remember that bozo Hopkins.'

All right, all right, but only if one last thing checks out the way I hope, I agreed, compromising with the reasonable suggestion. Otherwise, Hopkins be damned, I would have to call the police.

Racing back up the stairs to the bedroom, I warned myself—and anybody else who might be listening—that each minute's delay could be the difference between life and death for Katya. I repeated that warning as I crossed my fingers and stepped through the debris toward the cedar walk-in closet.

It was amazing what the human mind considered lifesaving.

If it had been just that very morning when I opened the closet door and saw what I did, it would have been as though another stake in a seemingly endless array of such barbed weapons had been plunged into my already-savaged heart. But now it was the opposite. Now what I saw, or what I didn't see, provided much-needed relief from the shock that was coursing through my system, and, as such, I viewed the sight as good news.

The closet was empty. There was nothing—no clothes, no boxes, no shoes. Everything of Katya's was gone. There was not a trace of evidence that the evil outside the door had touched this inner chamber.

Thank God, I remembered crying.

That means she was here before anything happened.

'Well, probably here before,' the voice smugly corrected before letting me continue.

Otherwise, I reasoned, her clothes and her personal effects would have been scattered about with everything else. She must have taken her belongings with her before the weirdo arrived. It didn't make any sense that he would ransack one room and not bother with the other, or at least cause some harm and toss her clothes and whatever else into the mess outside, right?

After a minute of disappointing silence, I realized no one was going to answer my question, and I raced back downstairs to the phone. There was one last thing I had to do before I would be completely satisfied that my assumption was correct and that Katya was safe.

Laura's husband, my future ex-brother-in-law, Oliver, answered my overseas emergency call. "Hillo?"

"Oliver, it's me, Chris." Just in case he had forgotten or wiped from his mind who Chris was, I clarified my statement. "Oliver, this is Christof Douglas. You know, the guy who's married to your wife's sister."

The delay before his reply was so long that I thought he was having difficulty figuring out who his wife and her sister were. I was about to explain the subtlety of our relationships to him once more when he finally said, "Oh? It's you!"

Dismissing any smart-assed retort as being counterproductive, I bit my tongue and asked to speak with Katya. After another lengthy pause, I heard in the distant background undertones that sounded like "It's him. What in blue blazes should I tell him?" And then in a louder undertone, "She's not here."

I assumed the "She's not here" was intended for my ears and shot back, "Where is she then?"

"She's unavailable."

A reply like that earlier in the day might have sent me ballistic. Instead those words signified that maybe, just maybe, it was going to be all right. For Katya, that was. But, at the moment, she was all that counted.

"Oliver, listen carefully. I can't explain everything, but give me the benefit of doubt, will you? I desperately need to know where Katya is."

When he started to say something that sounded like "It's none of your blooming business," I repeated my plea.

"No, Oliver, you're not listening!" The intensity of my voice stopped him in midsentence, ceasing his rant about ex-brothers-in-law. "Forget what I just asked. I don't want to speak to her, nor do I care where she is." My lie must have caught him by surprise, because he ceased babbling. "All I want are assurances that you know where she is." I had to bite my tongue to prevent the voice within from substituting, 'if she's alive'.

I could hear voices in the background again, and I caught echoes of my previous remarks. Oliver cleared his throat and started asking questions and then giving his own answers, such as "Why?" and "She doesn't want to see you." I cut him off.

"Let me talk with Laura."

When I heard nothing from his end, I assumed he was having the same difficulty connecting with her name as he'd had before, so I repeated my demand—this time even more loudly.

"Laura, damn it! Remember her? She's your wife, for Christ's sake. Let me speak with her this moment. And don't tell me she's unavailable or that you don't know where she is!"

After a short silence in which I imagined Oliver handing Laura the phone, Laura shaking her head, Oliver nodding, and then Laura finally giving in and taking it from his hand, Laura came on the line.

"Christ...off, what is it that you want?" Laura asked, skipping over the introduction and emphasizing her annoyance. "It was just the other day that we spoke, and I informed you that Katya was not expected to join us until next week. Why are you insisting on behaving so badly and continuing to annoy us?"

I almost lost it when she added, "That's not like you at all." But her characterization of what I was now like didn't quite have the necessary cachet to elaborate upon my theory of mistaken identity. And, anyway, I had more pressing priorities.

"Laura, listen. It's very important that you listen to me." I composed myself enough to dull the sharpness that I'd used with

Oliver. I also caught that damned voice in the nick of time before it mentioned the danger Katya might be in. "Shhh, not now, you idiot," I whispered, stifling the voice by explaining that those words could be misunderstood as some form of threat on my part.

"Christof? Who are you whispering to? Which is it? Do you want me to listen or not?"

"Laura, all I want to know is this: When was the last time you spoke with Katya?"

The silence on her end might have signified that she was in the process of aping her husband but was more adept at covering the mouthpiece, but I hoped she was simply deciding how to respond. For the umpteenth time over the past few days, I crossed my fingers.

"An hour ago."

"What?" My ears did not believe what they'd heard. "What did you say?"

"I said, an hour ago." I heard her exhale in capitulation into the telephone. "I spoke to Katya an hour ago. She called from Kennedy before she was about to board an Air France flight for London."

An hour ago from Kennedy! That meant she was safe. That she was alive! I calculated the time it would take to travel there, and I sighed in relief, feeling confident that it was absolutely, unquestionably true. That meant she would have most likely taken her clothes with her before the intruder struck.

Don't even think it, you disgusting son of a bitch, I told the resurfacing know-it-all voice, shaking my head in disbelief at what I was imagining. This was the act of someone completely insane.

'Or someone insanely vengeful,' it said, flip-flopping my words a little too effortlessly before it sank back to wherever it sank back to.

"Katya was not capable of such destruction," I replied. "Don't twist everything around so cleverly that way."

"Christof, what are you talking about? Did you hear me? I said Katya was waiting an hour ago to board a plane at Kennedy. What in God's name is wrong with you?"

I would have let the voice respond, but I wasn't certain I could trust it. I feared that it would tell her, "Fuck off, lady," which would not do my case any good, so I ignored Laura's question and the voice's pleas to be allowed to state his opinion as to what was wrong with me and pressed on.

"Laura, did Katya say anything about her personal effects? Like her clothes and stuff?"

"I'm not sure I understand you. What exactly is it that you wish to know about my sister's clothes?"

"Look, I guess … Well, I'm calling from our house in Madison, and it seems … it seems that Katya has taken all her clothes. Or so … or so it appears."

"Well, they're hers, aren't they?"

I almost said something that I knew I would regret, thought better of it, and continued. "Do you know when she took them?" I asked, rechecking my watch and recalculating how long it took to drive to Kennedy and when Laura said Katya had called her. "Does she have them with her?"

For an instant, it seemed we were back into playing pass the telephone. I heard bits of what I'd just said interspersed with "You take it" and then "No, you talk to him. He's your sister's husband."

After the third round, Laura lost the game and was back in a position she clearly didn't want to be in.

"Chris…toff," she began, and although she emphasized my name differently this time, she nevertheless signaled that I was still in for trouble. "You said you only wanted to know when I spoke to Katya last. Well, I seem to recall that I gave you that information already. And, quite frankly, I must be going." And she hung up.

I didn't place the phone down; I just pressed the disconnect button and then dialed overseas. What did it matter when she had been in our home? Katya was safe and on her way to London, which was probably the best place for her to be, considering everything. Had I not lost my patience with that eraser-head neighbor of ours, I probably could have gotten an answer to my question. Images of Abigail's pointy nose peeking over the driveway hedges as Katya pulled up were quickly shattered as I heard a recording in French.

I checked Magritte's number and redialed, pressing each number carefully. The same recording came on. Panic spread like some fast-moving virus through my tensing body as I dialed for operator assistance. The moment the operator answered, I explained what had just occurred and impatiently told her to place the call directly. As I waited, I could feel sweat forming across my face.

'You know what this means, don't you? This whole thing was misbegotten from the get-go, jerk-off. Oh … oh, I'm sorry. I forgot; you're Christof.'

I was about to tell him to leave me alone and get out of my life, that I'd never asked for him to come butting in the way he had been, when I heard the operator's voice.

"Mr. Douglas, thank you for using AT&T."

I froze. The virus that was spreading unchecked halted as though it too were listening, its fate riding upon the news about to be delivered.

I managed a passable, "Yes?"

What I heard was brief and to the point—just a few words, but more than enough for me to lose whatever fragile grip I had on the remaining threads of my sanity.

"The number you requested, Mr. Douglas," the operator explained, "has been disconnected at the customer's request. I'm sorry, sir; there is no forwarding number."

Chapter 21

"WHY, I WOULD MEET with any of the French impressionist artists I could. What a silly question to ask, Christof, when you already know the answer."

We were sitting on the Left Bank and in the heart of the Latin Quarter at one of our favorite bistros. What more fitting place, I thought, to pose my question?

It was July 1976, and Katya was seven months pregnant. The due date her doctor had given her was any time after the third week of September. The betting crowd placed odds it would be either the twenty-first or twenty-second. We toyed for a brief spell that if it were a girl, we would name her Summer, but we were never that serious about it.

That trip to Paris, unlike Summer, was unplanned. Katya had been asked just the previous week if she'd mind crossing the big pond one more time, considering her condition, to appraise the most recent collection of twentieth-century artists that would be available for the upcoming fall auction. Normally this was much too short a preparation period for such an event, especially when the featured group of artists—Matisse, Braque, and Mondrian, to name a few of the acclaimed masters—was not within her principal area of expertise. But her boss, old Whitney, had faith in her—a faith that had been borne out of past expeditions where her uncanny ability to assess and set a value for the art market's future favorites before the competition had helped make millions for him and his partner, Schoal. Unfortunately, she was ahead of her time. Ten years later, that profit figure would jump exponentially as the unchecked growth of greed replaced population in that equation.

At the time, though, the future value of money didn't matter. Between her salary and bonuses and my general manager's compensation, we were well over an annual income of $100,000—a figure well beyond what I'd imagined was possible a few years earlier.

"Christof, why is money that important to you?" Maria would argue whenever we discussed our future. "Your ancestors, just like mine, were lucky to survive day-to-day, yet they produced something much more important than all the wealth in the world. In their own way, they lived for us. They gave us our lives."

"Christof, why did you ask that question?" Katya looked at me quizzically as the waiter set the red wine, assorted cheeses, and a bowl of sliced pears and apples on the table.

"Pour Madame." He handed her a glass of Perrier and bowed at the waist in a show of Gaelic respect at her imminent motherhood. He placed the half-empty bottle and a plate of lime twists on the table and repeated his deferential motion, this time with a bit too much exaggerated flair for my taste. I envisioned him bursting into a rendition of "Thank Heaven for Little Girls," but he must have forgotten the words, because he left without any further fuss.

I savored the rich, full-bodied taste of the Bordeaux before replying. "Well, it may seem silly to you, but I don't believe I have ever asked you that question. But, then again, your answer was no surprise. I mean, outside of us and our families, that impressionable bunch of anti-technologist, paint-by-number, connect-the-dots bon vivants are those you love more than anything else."

Katya slapped my arm, the smile on her lips betraying any sense that she took my comments for anything other than what they were—the deliberate misquote of one of her lectures to me on the essence of impressionist art.

"Now you are being silly," she said. She let her hand remain on my suntanned arm and playfully twisted its blond hairs. Her eyes gazed into mine.

That had been my first trip back to Paris since my previous life there. Katya had been to Paris on numerous occasions before our marriage, had even been to Les Deux Magots with friends, but that day was the first time we sat together at that familiar bistro. And although I no longer dreamed about Maria walking up to me, I still couldn't keep my eyes from the passing crowds.

Amid a discussion I'd started about which of us was sillier, I asked Katya the question about her three wishes, with the proviso that none of her wishes could be in any way associated with our families. So instead of health, happiness, and love ever after, I heard without any indecision whatsoever her desire to meet the people who reinvented the way the world viewed the relationship between life and art.

"Yes, I guess I am, at that," I replied, agreeing to her recent assessment. "I am quite silly, madame. However, since I didn't have the foresight to exclude those bohemians and lump them together with the rest of the in-laws, you've used up one your three wishes and I've yet to find out some of your hidden little secrets or desires."

A serious look came over Katya. Her eyes flickered as though in recognition of some greater, much deeper understanding as to why I was in truth asking this of her. Perhaps her somber expression only reflected my own—an expression far different from the tone conveyed by my voice or lighthearted banter.

Her smile was now gone. I noticed her brow furrow and her lips purse in the manner they would whenever she was troubled or deep in thought. I felt her concentration intensify.

I turned my face toward the afternoon crowd and awaited her response. I saw someone who looked like Catherine Deneuve walk by, her long, flowing blonde hair contrasting with the black dress she was wearing. Heads spun as she passed, as if to reaffirm who she was, so perhaps I was correct.

I saw no one else who was even remotely familiar.

"I think … No, I know." Katya's correction brought my attention back to her, my eyes meeting hers. "I wish … I wish, Christof, with all my heart and soul that peace will be my country's destiny. That somehow Muslim and Christian, Serb and Croat will be able to set aside their differences."

She took a sip of the bubbling water, her eyes shifting to gaze at the people walking by. When she turned to me, I knew her tears reflected the pain and the sadness that would always be there whenever remembering her birthplace.

"I wish that somehow those things that the good people have in common will overcome that which they do not. I wish that the killing will not start over again. That it will never begin again."

Her voice faded as she repeated her last sentence.

My hand reached across the table and covered hers; our eyes locked in understanding at the depth of her wish. I knew that the wealth and education of Katya's family had been unable to spare them; they were similar to the people of her country—tragically affected by the losses of relatives and ancestors to the centuries of mindless wars in that region.

Her wish brought back a conversation I'd overheard at our wedding, between her father and one of his many English acquaintances. They were discussing the book that Dr. Tkarr had published before his guest appearance on WXQT. The other chap was attached to the British foreign office and in complete opposition to the strategic importance of Yugoslavia specifically, and to the Balkans in general.

I would never forget, especially because my own brush with death had been just a few years removed, the icy detachment of his tone as his entire supercilious stature converged into the outstretched, admonishing finger that poked disrespectfully into Dr. Tkarr's tuxedo when he quoted Bismarck.

"That's the damn problem with you intellectuals," he blustered, so satisfied with his argument that he forgot that the man he was addressing was one of his country's most decorated freedom fighters. "Remember what Bismarck warned the West nearly a century ago," the pompous ass said, going on with his lecture and not bothering to give Katya's father the courtesy of a chance to reply. "Nothing—and, I quote, nothing—my good man, in the Balkans is worth the healthy bones of a single grenadier."

I was about to intervene, my own index finger assuming the appropriate dueling position to challenge the insolent son of a bitch, when I felt a gentle, restraining tug at my elbow. Of course it was Katya. She shook her head delicately and, clasping my arm tightly in hers, led me away.

No, my sweet, dear Katya, I thought, forcing the anger of that memory from my mind, neither of us believes that any genie could fulfill your wish.

"How about a bullfighter?" I asked, attempting to break the heaviness in the air.

"Excuse me?" Katya seemed caught off guard.

"Well, young lady, you've exhausted two of your wishes, and although we both desire that last heartfelt request, it was too close to the proviso that I specified regarding family."

Waiting to make certain she was with me, I asked my question again. "As a wish, didn't you ever want to meet a bullfighter?" There was no percentage in asking about her desire to meet a Buddhist, as her previous response had contained enough religion for one afternoon.

"But I have already, Christof," Katya replied, surprising me with her answer. "In Spain. When I was still in public school, Mummy and Daddy took Laura and me on holiday there, and we saw a bullfight. I must say, though, once was more than enough for me."

The sour expression on her face changed to a sly grin.

"The funniest thing," she said, giggling, "was the crowd. There were thousands packing the stadium, and all of a sudden they started to chant something. At first it wasn't all that clear what they were saying. But then Daddy began to laugh. All the people around us began to laugh." Her giggling became louder with every word. It was as though she were now simpatico with the spectators, as if the present had become the past.

"Toro! Toro! Toro!" Katya cried. "All at once I realized what they were shouting."

She was laughing now, her eyes misty. I imagined fantastic images of a huge Castillian bull standing erect upon his hind legs and dancing to Sabicas, castanets snapping crisply on his forehoofs, in celebration of his newfound fame.

"'Toro! Toro! Toro!' they continued to shout." A hiccup punctuated the second call of "Toro." "But what I remember most about that day was afterward, when friends of Daddy's took us to meet the bullfighter, a man who, despite the converted aficionados, was one of Spain's most acclaimed matadors."

Katya paused and sipped her Perrier. "So I met Manolete, or

whatever his name was," she said, resuming as soon as she swallowed the water. "You can imagine what kind of mood he was in after that fiasco. But he was so handsome, so romantic looking. And he was so very nice to me."

A tiny curl of a smile appeared about her lips, a smile that was very different from the one that had just disappeared.

"No, Christof, I'm not interested in meeting any more bullfighters," Katya declared, her eyes looking directly at me as her mood seemingly shifted back to the present, the hiccups disappearing.

She never did tell me her third wish.

* * * * *

"Where the hell is it?" I shouted for the millionth unanswered time. My hands ripped the cartons apart without resealing them. The garage, which just minutes ago had been meticulously organized with neatly stacked box upon box, row after row of storage, now resembled my own unraveled life.

I repeated the profanity, struggling with another reluctant victim. After breaking through its cardboard defenses, I tossed it aside when I saw that it contained only Beth's clothes.

"Where is it? Where is it!" I screamed, reaching for another carton with one hand while the other wiped the sweat cascading down my forehead. 'Perhaps if you asked nicely, softened your approach, and appealed to the sense of camaraderie you once shared, you might find it,' the voice, who hadn't said a thing since that phone call to London, offered. Immediately afterward, the words were gushing sweetly from my mouth.

"Come to Papa," I sang, my own voice unrecognizable in its weird lilt. "Are you in there, my pretty? Don't be shy now; come to your papa."

It had been less than a half hour since the operator told me that Magritte's number had been disconnected without any forwarding information. I'd spent most of that time here, in the sun baked, usually bolted, and always-off-limits garage. I was searching, so far futilely, for my service revolver—the one I didn't shoot that Viet Cong with the day I was almost killed.

I'd had enough presence of mind to use the rest of that half hour to call Thursday. That was Monday's new name. I had given her a greater day of importance after she had been resourceful enough to obtain Spire's plans for the next few days—something I desperately needed, especially since the other Bobbsey twin, Carlson, was out of the country. If she had been able to find out where, she would have jumped right over Cindy and become Saturday.

So Spire would have to do.

It seemed my boy Spire was scheduled to be in Greenville over the weekend, Thursday informed me, to receive some sort of reward—of all things, a Man of the fuckin' Year Award for the greater Spartanburg-Greenville area. I didn't bother to ask her how someone who no longer lived in the area was able to be honored in such a fashion. I bit my tongue and wrote down everything necessary for me to find and kill the bastard.

I was through playing the weak-kneed, indecisive prince. I would finish him off, and then administer the second coup d'état to that other worthless piece of garbage, and send the so-called trustworthy magician to wherever it was that his ilk disappeared. But I couldn't do a damn thing without my gun.

I knew it was buried somewhere in the garage—buried amid all the rest of the memories. But, unlike most of the others, I had kept this souvenir locked in the past. This time, though, I swore it would be released.

Sweet-talking my shy subject out of retirement was getting me nowhere, so I reverted to my earlier tactic. 'If nothing else, screaming at the top of your lungs will make you feel good,' the voice whispered as I began filling the hot, mildewed garage air with one expletive after another.

By then I had torn open two dozen boxes, or about half of the total, and still hadn't found what I was seeking. As I pulled the next carton from the top of the pile, tension and doubt gained a firmer foothold within my crazed mind.

"God damn!" I yelled, throwing the heavy box to the ground as though it were a stuffed doll. "It's here somewhere. I'll find it sooner or later."

The instant the box flew open, I knew I had struck pay dirt. I felt the air in my lungs escape in an orgasmic, involuntary gasp as my eyes found the page from history I had been seeking.

I disdainfully tossed aside the box's contents—first my class As and then the khakis packed beneath. I felt the coveted object before I saw it. With prayerful reverence, I knelt beside the cardboard carton and, with both hands, extracted the cigar-box-sized package from its tomb. It had to have been at least fifteen years ago, shortly after Katya and I married, that I'd last held it. Since that time, it had been shuffled from place to place, laid away with whatever military nostalgia I, for some mysterious reason, had elected to keep.

Eventually it found its way to our garage and what I imagined to be its final resting site.

Funny isn't it. Life I mean. There I was sitting on the concrete garage floor, unfolding the plastic outer wrapping, then gingerly unzipping the leather bag designed to protect the weapon, and removing the wooden container that housed the revolver—and I prayed. I prayed that the weapon was in working order, prayed that it would be able to discharge so that I could kill a man—or, to be more precise, kill two men.

I wasn't thinking about luck or fate.

"How could you, Jwah? You didn't believe in anything during that time in your life."

I was praying—for only the second time since Beth. Strange as it might have seemed to some, it made all the sense in the world to me. It was all quite elementary. In a nutshell, I reasoned that everything rotten, terrible, and evil in my life could be placed at the feet of Almighty God, or the gods, what greater evil could there be than to murder someone? So I wanted his blessing. Just like some ancient warrior from some pagan culture, I was asking God to give me strength and grant me his blessing as I went out to do his bidding.

I didn't care about the notion that God was good or that I might have been a little mixed up with which angel was which. If I were wrong, so what? I had both bases covered. And I didn't care about free will either. I had always been more impressed with Ivan Karamazov's argument than Alexei's when it came to the question of what kind of god would take the life of an innocent child. When someone could explain to my satisfaction what sort of free will a murdered infant was privy to, then maybe I would give some credence to his brother's perspective. Anyway, by then I had reached the stage in my life where complicated philosophical or religious and moral conundrums, dancing angels on the head of a pin, and that sort of thing were things of the past.

So I prayed, for once confident that my prayers would be answered and the Colt .45 would be ready.

Although the container hadn't been hermetically sealed, the gun had been protected from most of the elements, except heat. In the summer, the garage most likely reached in excess of one hundred degrees, and that was my one concern when it came to the weapon's functionality. I thought back to the temperatures in Nam and how they often soared over the hundred-degree mark. The army drilled the importance of daily maintenance into our heads. But I also knew that the greater threat of weapon malfunction came from the rain and dampness, especially during the rainy season, when the water penetrated everything.

When I opened the interior container's lid, my body quivered as flashbacks of the past flooded my consciousness. The pistol trembled in my hand as I lifted it. I closed my eyes, squeezing them shut in an attempt to exorcise the demons filling my head.

Suddenly a sharp crack exploded next to my ear. Then, just as abruptly, I heard nothing; the images were gone. The room was silent. The putrid, acrid smell of Vietnam, resurrected from its decaying past, drifted to my nostrils. I opened my eyes, hoping that the horrors would not return. I found only the Colt .45 in my hand, my knuckles white with tension, my index finger coiled loosely around the trigger, and traces of smoke floating from its muzzle.

My eyes dropped to where the gun was aimed. Any doubts about its utility were eliminated when I saw the jagged hole in my army uniform—all my uniforms, I discovered. The bullet had traveled through both sets of khakis and the class A's on top. Its penetration had finally halted as it came to rest partially lodged in the steel helmet at the bottom of the box. It was a clean kill; the bullet had hit right where my name plate had been on the uniform, just above the chest pocket. I saw vapors rising from the opening that had just obliterated that identification.

Seeing that erasure of self was a brutal reminder of why my weapon was still loaded. It hadn't been fifteen years since it was last in my hands, I remembered. It had been five—five short, eternal years.

'It was less than a month after Beth's murder,' the voice reminded me. Katya was staying overnight at Princeton with her mother. You went up into the attic. It was almost midnight. You started to look through your old army stuff the same way you were just doing, except then you were neat about the whole thing, placing each item back into its box exactly as you'd found it. You had a few drinks that night, something you would have never dreamed of doing a short time before.

'When you found it that night, you also had to search through additional boxes for ammo. Then you had to unlock the steel case where the weapon was stored. You were very careful those days, very protective that a loaded gun didn't wind up one day in her hands by mistake. You remember loading it now, don't you? the voice persisted. But you don't remember how long you sat there. Holding it in your hand, thinking about the reason you came there that night.'

"Jwah! Jwah! No! Not this time! You will lose!" Parcae's scream broke through the storm and my thoughts.

Yes, Parcae, you're right, as always. This will be my last time. I always liked the way she said my middle name. That was the only name she called me, refusing to speak my first name aloud. She claimed she couldn't because it was the name of my god. So she pronounced it in the French manner. "It's supposed to mean joy," I explained sarcastically to her. That was a better answer than telling her it was also my father's name. Although, he was always Joseph. Can you imagine if I told her that? There was no way she would believe I wasn't the son of God.

* * * * *

We moved into our new home after returning from Paris. On September 23, 1976, Elizabeth Chloe Douglas entered the world—all wonderful seven pounds of her.

Not long after Beth's birth, I switched companies, leaving behind QXT. It was about the same time that Richard Lake lost control of the company after allowing the venture capitalists to back him. That was also, not so coincidently, about the same time he died.

So we had a new baby, a new home, and a new job for each of us. Katya had no intention of taking maternity leave; instead, she quit her position, with no plan to return to the marketplace in the near future. We began the second chapter of our life's journey together.

Our second era began, with one notable exception, on as high a note as imaginable. The one sad note during this time was the death of my friend and mentor, Richard. With Richard's death, only Billy Paulson remained to remind me of that painful part of my life before Katya. My former life was becoming ancient history, and that haunted past rarely reappeared during the following five years.

During those five years, I changed companies three times. With each change, my compensation, responsibilities, and experiences grew. The last move came in 1982, when I landed my first corporate president's position. It was with Blair Holdings Inc., a media and entertainment powerhouse with holdings in the radio, television, print, and motion-picture industries.

I was hired as president of the radio and television division, having acquired what Blair's Board deemed the necessary amount of TV management experience since leaving QXT to qualify for that position. In their view, radio was the poor stepchild of television, having neither the glamour nor prestige that the tube commanded. That meant that radio was always toward the bottom of the pack when it came to budget reviews and appropriations. TV's review process wasn't quite as bad, but the fact that we had only two stations suggested it wasn't yet considered a core business.

What the hell am I talking about? Why am I even remembering that distant aspect of my life? Core businesses ... Budget reviews ... Appropriations ... Aaaaah ... It was Maria, wasn't it? I remember now. Yes, I had nearly forgotten. Between Parcae's screams ... and the gun and the ... wind ... I remember now ... Magritte.

* * * * *

The first evening that I met Magritte in Paris, I found by chance the article she had written. We discussed my reason for being there, and he agreed, although somewhat hesitantly, to my joining him on the

DFT exposé. Then he left me, entering the closed door at the rear of his studio—making that chopping movement with his hands, which I took to be an expression of his anger toward the way he and Maria had been used by Igor. Before he reappeared sometime later, I discovered the article.

For the first few minutes after he left, I sat quietly, deep in my thoughts, rehashing the implications of what we had just discussed. After a time, when he still hadn't returned, I became impatient, even called out his name. After a second yell, I was more anxious than impatient. I ran to the door and pressed my ear against it. I was about to shout his name, my fist raised as though to batter the door, when I heard a muffled voice. His words, translated in broken English, were "Maria's friend needs to restrain his ponies."

I was relieved to hear his voice. Relieved but impatient, I decided to kill some time by exploring the loft. I wasn't looking for anything specific as I walked randomly down the steel-cased aisles. I was surprised, though, when I saw that Magritte's files seemed to be in alphabetical sequence. I had assumed everything would have been cryptically encoded as an integral part of their security measures.

'Dummy', the voice chastised in that contemptuous manner it was prone to use whenever it had doubts about my intellectual capacity, 'how do you know that an A is really an A, smart guy?'

"Well, we'll find out soon enough," I replied. I slid open the drawer with the letters C and D marked on it. "Aha," I victoriously whooped, pulling a manila-colored legal-sized folder from the slot indicated as DFT Inc. "I don't know if an A is an A, but it seems that a D is a D." I rubbed this tiny victory in the voice's face. That was all it was, though—just a small, minor triumph—for the only thing the folder contained was last year's annual report.

'Go ahead', the voice prompted, not bothering to congratulate me for besting it. 'Explore further.' But where? In spite of its order, I was perplexed. I stood without moving for a minute or two. The prolonged absence of my buddy finally moved me to action. "Douglas should be close to DFT," I murmured softly, flipping through the Pendaflex tabs.

"Aha." I reiterated my earlier exclamation—but not with the same degree of confidence this time. Yes, a D was a D, and an annual report was an annual report as well, I saw, disappointedly lifting the folder's sole content: a corporate statement identical to the one in the previous file.

My associate seemed to be nursing a grudge—a practice that I sensed was occurring more and more often—as it rather meekly, and without any mention of my previous success, hinted that maybe there was a connection or some data that might be worth our while cataloged under the names of my previous companies.

"What the hell," I agreed, briefly turning my head toward the door Magritte was behind. It was as good an idea as any, so I opened the cabinet drawer with the Bs.

Unlike the other files, the name Blair had two folders. The second was labeled "Blair 1981–1983," which dovetailed with the period that I had been with them. I withdrew it and began to flip through.

"Is there something I can do for you?" Magritte's voice resonated through the loft the same moment I picked up the magazine article that had Sammantha Kelso's name emblazoned across the top. "Didn't your mother teach you any manners, Maria's friend? Didn't she tell you it was not polite to go through other people's belongings without their permission?"

His manner was strained, but I couldn't help wondering why his idioms were correct and his English was perfect whenever he wanted them to be. I didn't want to aggravate him any further—he was now running toward me—and made a note to ask him later.

"Eh! Give me that!" He snatched the folder from my hands.

"See here, Magritte." I used an expression I had never in my recollection used before. Then again, maybe it was the other guy reacting. "I think it's my business when my name is part of your library filing system."

That stopped him in his tracks. He started to speak and then, apparently reconsidering, waved his index finger at me, allowing "touché" to pass over his drawn lips.

So he showed me the article. He didn't let me go through the rest of the file, dismissing it as "unimportant, bourgeois red tape" and a contract Maria once had for the publication of the article in question. For that matter, he never allowed me access to any other files, and I never got the chance to covertly look at them after that evening.

I read the article with Magritte hanging over my shoulder and tossing in one anecdotal comment after another whenever he assumed I was at the corresponding point in the story.

"This was one of many that the two of us wrote together on the difficulties that postcolonial governments faced after their European masters departed. This story on the impact that Islamic fundamentalism had on Algerian politics was one of our earliest published in the mainstream press. We were in the process of doing a follow-up on the same subject, since it had been over four years …" He stopped, seemingly unable to complete his sentence.

After a few seconds, he continued. "You know, what I mentioned before to you about when Maria and I were in Algiers at the beginning of the year. We—she, that is—met up with that ex-agent, the one she so foolishly trusted. C'est la vie," he said when I didn't offer a response. "C'est la vie," he repeated, shrugging his shoulders and returning to the article.

It took awhile for me to get through the story. With his interruptions—including descriptions of what they did and saw on the trip, and recounts of the arguments they had with the Blair editors regarding journalistic censorship—each paragraph I read was accompanied by five minutes of anecdotal nostalgia. Some of the reminiscences, in fairness, were my own. In contrast with Magritte, however, I chose to keep mine to myself.

I was particularly jolted when he used the word postcolonial, as it sent shivers up my spine, taking me back to when I'd told Maria about her future writings on the postcolonial Belgian Congo. I nearly interrupted him to tell him that, but I remained in my own recollections.

It seemed ironic to me how often our paths crossed, missing one another by some infinitesimal degree of time or space. We were like travelers in parallel universes. Where was I those days when she was arguing with the editors from my company? Perhaps we were separated by just the floor between that division's offices and mine. Or maybe we were even in the building lobby at the same moment. And maybe …

"No! No! It could not have been that day. Not that one! Don't tell me it was … Parcae, don't tell me …"

"Yes, Jwah, it was the day your daughter was killed."

I felt an urge to explain all this to Magritte but didn't, tears falling down my cheeks. Instead I mimicked a page from his book—the one on fatalism, the one in which I was all too well read. I shrugged my shoulders and repeated to myself, "C'est la vie, La Ardilla. C'est la vie."

Chapter 22

I GLANCED INTO THE rearview mirror and saw the sun setting in the distance. I had been driving south on Interstate 95 for more than four hours and was approaching the outskirts of Baltimore. It had felt like a quick four hours, with thoughts, ideas, and assumptions about killing Spire filling my head. And although I hadn't resolved every detail of that subject, I wasn't upset. When it came time for me to deliver the goods, as my rag-merchant colleagues liked to say, I would. If there was one thing I was certain of, it was that fact.

As far as rental cars went, the Taurus was adequate for my modest needs. After all, all I needed was an inconspicuous vehicle to get me the seven or eight hundred miles down to Greenville. Well, even more, what I needed was for it to get me inconspicuously back a few miles to the airport.

We made a good pair, the Taurus and I. Since everyone I met insisted on telling me how different I looked, that I wasn't myself, no one would ever recognize either of us. It gave me a huge advantage, this ability to remain incognito without going through elaborate gyrations, such as pasting on a mustache, dying my hair, or donning thick glasses.

"Maybe I'm as crazy as a loon, but I'm not dumb." I began to sing, impishly repeating that phrase to remain in sync with the up-tempo Mozart Violin Concerto No. 5, which was playing on the radio. When it ended, as though on cue, I yelled, "They're not crazy?"

I lowered my voice, my enthusiasm for Mozart fading to a more restrained level now that I had my own undivided attention. "Are you going to sit there and have the unmitigated balls to tell me those bastards are not crazier than me? Some demented beast breaks into the house," my voice said, rising with each word, "does a Picasso on the bedroom walls in blood, and destroys everything, and you don't believe that's not the work of a crazed madman? Someone, or something, that's not a thousand times more loony tunes than me?"

Shaking my head in indignant disbelief at the stubbornness and ignorance of my reticent and invisible antagonist, I mumbled, "Schmuck," under my breath but loud enough for him to hear, and tabled the subject.

It was a couple of minutes past eight in the evening, and Washington was less than an hour away. What I had in mind wouldn't take long. Taking that stop into account, I should arrive in the greater Greenville-Spartanburg area between three and four in the morning. That should give me plenty of time to find some flea-bitten motel, catch whatever sleep I could, and finalize my plans, including getting a better feel for the lay of the land around the Hyatt, which was where my girl Thursday had said Spire's award ceremonies would be held. Since I had stayed there just last week and was familiar with the overall area, I felt that that part of the operation shouldn't be a problem.

That's how long ago it was? Only one week before?

Even though I didn't think my task would be a problem, I needed to ensure a few details. After all, this was my first trip to the area to kill a man, so I was positive some logistics remained to be ironed out if I was going to Paris afterward to kill the magician.

When I left our house, I made two stops before setting the Taurus's cruise control on fifty-five for the long journey down I-95.

My second stop was related to the getaway logistics. Unless this crazy loon I had become unexpectedly sprouted a pair of wings, I needed to book an overseas flight pronto. After discussing my options with the gal at Continental's ticketing counter, I made reservations to arrive in Paris Sunday evening. In fact, with one difference, it would be the same flight I had taken last Sunday. That one difference, or complication, however, was to make certain that my flight connections from the south had me back in Jersey in time for its overseas departure.

"No problem, sir," she assured me. "There's a US West flight leaving Charlotte, North Carolina, at eleven thirty that evening that'll have you in Newark at two o'clock Sunday morning."

No problem for you, lady, I almost said. You're not the one who has an appointment to shoot someone. "Book it," I told her, and I handed her my passport and American Express Platinum card.

For a tension-filled moment, I thought something was wrong with one or the other, as she also requested a current driver's license. As soon as she compared the name and photograph to the passport, she issued the tickets.

"Sorry, sir," she apologized. "They—well, your pictures, that is—don't quite look like you."

"No problem," I replied, grinning at her discomfort. "I hear that from just about everyone nowadays."

My first stop had gone even better.

That's what you believed at the time.

The cemetery where Elizabeth Chloe Douglas was resting was not far from where we lived in Madison. Although it wasn't exactly on my route, I needed to visit it. Originally, my purpose for going there was to tell her good-bye—to let her know that I loved her and that I always would, no matter what happened, no matter how far away from her I might one day find myself. I told her all that and more, much more. That day I swore to her that, unlike the last time, this time I would not fail.

Her stone was so small. It was almost doll sized and didn't belong there.

That was the reason I went to the cemetery that day, but since my old friend Magritte had disconnected his phone and crawled back under a rock somewhere, I wasn't sure what to do with the duplicate set of diskettes. The dilemma was giving me no end of agita. I knew that if I had any leverage in this crazy venture, it would have to be with those files. The brainstorm to bury them near Beth came to me about the time I was pulling through the cemetery gates. What sold it in my mind was that I knew the exact spot where this unauthorized digging would take place. "Yup," I said, quickly taking full credit for the idea before the other guy could put his two cents in, "right at the foot of that humongous pin oak, the one that towers over Chloe forever. That's where."

Beth's resting spot was toward the back end of the cemetery, which bordered an undeveloped, state-mandated preserve. The delineation between the two was rustically marked by a wooden split-rail fence, the bottom half of which was overgrown by a mixture of wildflowers and tall, reedy grasses. Katya and I had selected this section because it gave the impression that we were somewhere else, someplace not quite so terrifying. If we were able to forget why we were there, we thought, we might even imagine that we were out in the country, surrounded by the tranquility that nature at its purest brings. We consoled ourselves with that belief every time we came, but we both knew we were never able to have what we pretended. We never dreamed that its out-of-the-mainstream location would one day provide me with this opportunity.

It took about twenty minutes and a loss of half my body fluids to accomplish my objective. The tree was a perfect accomplice; its immense girth shielded me from any prying eyes.

The ground surrounding the oak, hardened by the summer, was rough and rocky, and what I used for tools left much to be desired—a tire iron, a piece of broken glass, and my hands—but the outcome was never in doubt.

In a foot-deep hole, wrapped in a double layer of plastic garbage bags I found in a nearby trash can, I placed the metal box containing the diskettes. As I re-shoveled the dirt back into the hole, tamping it and the surrounding area to minimize the disturbance created, I kept an eye out for the Gucci brothers. Luckily, I noticed nothing remotely suspicious—or with their bad taste—in the vicinity.

I dusted the dirt from my hands and trousers, walked toward the car, and got in. I rested for a couple of minutes, regaining my breath and calming my nerves, before turning the ignition on, my eyes never leaving her name.

Those two stops I had made were five hours in the past—ancient history, the way my life was fast-forwarding by. I saw that it was now time for my third and final detour as I noticed the exit sign ahead.

"Anyway, it's not up for discussion. It needs to be done." I shouted my thoughts aloud to that reclusive, no-longer-to-be-found intuitive voice. Intuitive—that was the word he used to describe the special knack he had when it came to these matters. "And where were you when I really needed you? When there was manual labor to be done, and not your typical backseat, second-guessing advice? I didn't see you digging any holes with me!" I argued, making certain that the same clown with whom I had debated the merits of my relative sanity just a few minutes ago understood my position.

It was twilight when I got out of the car. It was only three blocks away from the reason I was there in DC, I remembered thinking, steeling myself to what lay before me. The doubts, the questions, and the memories … Oh, the memories began racing through my soul. I could hear its agonizing cries when I finally stood facing its much-too-long, much-too-dark surface. How had I resisted its deafening screams, ignoring them and never coming before?

And why hadn't I? With the FCC hearings and DFT's FM radio station in DC, I probably flew to Washington twice a month. I knew in my heart of hearts what the reason was and why I had been able to withstand those haunting calls. I had often reflected that if 'The Wall' had been built in the seventies, I would have been to it often—someone who would have been broadcast, reported, and written about to the world as just another soldier, another casualty from just another war.

But I met Katya. And it wasn't built. By the time it was, she was there. A godsend. A buffer to absorb or repel their cries however she magically, mystically was able. But I was alone that night. I could resist them no longer.

When I reached the Wall, I was surprised, given the late hour, at how many people were there. There were hundreds—people of all ages, of all colors, suits and non suits—all moving in a surrealistic tribute to the century's latest memorial to war and to whatever cherished longing recalled, incommunicable to all except their own innermost remembrances.

As I walked closer, down the short flight of steps that led to it, I noticed that every so often people would stop their quiet shuffling, their goal in sight. They would stand in front of that section or name, oblivious to everyone around them. Occasionally, I would notice individuals break their catatonic state and lay some personal memento where they stood. When I got to the bottom of the steps and began to walk alongside the monument, my arm sometimes reaching out to touch it as my fingers traced the etched stone names, the manufactured substitutes for once-living flesh, the screams ceased.

There was suddenly nothing, only eerie silence.

I walked for much longer than I would have liked, staring at my reflection as I searched the columns of names for any I recognized. On my way to my own private and personal destination, I looked at some of the items others had left behind: a teddy bear, military medals, letters, a pair of woman's panties.

When the year 1969 appeared on the Wall, I slowed my pace. For an instant I believed I would stop, lose my nerve, or whatever was forcing me to continue, and turn around to race back to the car as fast as I could and forget this damn thing. 'This was not the reason you were traveling south,' the voice kept reminding me.

Somehow I didn't retreat and was able to struggle past January, February, and March, my hand, like so many others, rising instinctively, fingers tracing the beckoning list of names.

ANTONIO LADILLYA
RICHARD D. LAKE

I saw them both at the same moment. Oh God. God! They were next to one another. Their names were immediately next to one another. I never thought ... I never imagined. How could this be possible? For as long as this testimony to the madness of war stood, the two would be fated, like so many others who had touched my life, to remain eternally entwined.

"They were killed on the same day, Jwah," Parcae said. *"That's why they're next to one another. That was their destiny."*

* * * * *

When Beth was four years old, Katya and I took her over the Christmas holidays to Vermont. We hadn't skied since her birth, but both of us were decent skiers and familiar with Mount Snow, so we felt confident that our ski legs would bounce back enough to teach her some of the fundamentals. And we knew that that particular resort was among the best when it came to pre-bunny-trail toddlers like her.

It was Katya's idea more than mine. I preferred returning to the Caribbean, spending our vacation the way we had the previous year, charting a fancy sailboat and providing Beth with her second lesson on seamanship. Beth, who usually voted lockstep with her mother, agreed once again. "Just another little Democrat in the making," I would tease them whenever I wasn't able to get my way.

"We'll take a holiday this summer and go to Bermuda," Katya proposed. "She's not been there, and the waters there are ideal for sailing. That'll be the place for you to instruct her. And, anyway, Christof," she pressed on, likely knowing that I was weakening, "she's at the right age to learn to ski."

There, it was done. The mention of her age was the deciding point. And I couldn't argue with Katya, considering she was probably twice the skier I was, having begun to ski at the age Beth was then.

For that occasion, unlike previous trips to the area, when we'd stayed at the Inn at Sawmill Farm, we rented a newly built three-bedroom house on Chimney Hill. It was a bit more of a ride to the slopes, but the comfort and privacy it offered more than made up for the inconvenience, in Katya's opinion.

"It would be better for Beth," she coyly suggested one night as we lay in bed studying the rental brochure. "It would almost be a second home to her. This would be her winter palace. She would have her own room. We could even build a snow family for her on the deck."

Katya didn't fool me. Before Beth was born, we skied every weekend we could in Vermont. She said it reminded her of when she was a young girl and her parents would take her skiing in Sarajevo. I knew that she had an ulterior motive for wanting to buy that year-round chalet in this special part of the world.

So the week between Christmas and New Year's 1980, the three of us went on a ski holiday to Vermont. Beth learned to snowplow, and by the end of the week, she even went mid-mountain with us. "She's a natural, Christof." Katya beamed, nudging me with her elbow as she pulled Beth's restraining cord, preventing the budding Picabo Street from schussing too far ahead of us.

That Christmas, I told Beth the story of the poinsettia, the flower of the Holy Night—or '*Flor de la Nochebuena*,' as Maria had called it when she told me the story our first Christmas together. It was the story of a little girl not much older than Beth. The girl, who came from a poor family, didn't have any gifts to give her mother or father, so she was sad. As I told the story, I could see that Beth was becoming a bit sad herself at what I was saying, so I hugged her more tightly. "Don't worry, darlin'," I whispered. "Daddy would never tell you a fairy tale that would hurt you."

And so I told her about how the little girl, on her way to church that Christmas Eve, met an old woman who gave her wild green weeds from the hillside. The little girl—"Let's call her Chloe," I said to Beth—was surprised because they were only weeds to her.

They were nothing that she could give to anyone. But the old woman shook her head and said, "No, that's not true, Chloe; these weeds are beautiful. All gifts, no matter how great or small, are beautiful, because they are given." Chloe was a good little girl, so she took the weeds from the old woman and thanked her and wished her a merry Christmas, and then she continued on her way to church.

When she reached the church, everybody looked at her strangely; some people began to snicker at Chloe and the bunch of green weeds she held in her hand. But the little girl remembered what the mysterious woman had said. So she went right up to the church's altar and placed them there as her gift to the baby Jesus.

When she laid them there, they burst into a thousand flowers, their petals shining atop the green weeds like brilliant red-and-white stars. It was as though a thousand candles had been lit in the church, the light was so intense. And when the people left the church, the light appeared even brighter, for all the weeds on the hillside had been turned into the same brilliant red-and-white stars.

"*Like our love, Christof*," Maria swore after she told me the story. "*As long as there will be poinsettias, it will burn por Eternidade.*"

Katya, Beth, and I took holiday in Bermuda the following summer. It was our third visit back—Beth's first—and, as always, it was wonderful. I would forever remember Beth sitting on my lap, her arms outstretched before her as she held the wheel in her tiny hands, mine firmly holding hers, as our yacht skimmed over the frothy whitecaps.

"I'm sailing now, Daddy, aren't I?" I could still hear her asking, her enthusiastic voice sounding so much like a younger version of her mother's.

"Yes, you are, my little sweetheart. You're a real sailor now," I proudly answered, removing one of my hands from the helm to playfully tousle the beautiful blonde head.

She would have made a great sailor when she grew up, but she was never to grow old.

* * * * *

Katya was driving the Volvo station wagon that day; her mother and Beth were sitting in the rear seats. Everyone was wearing her seat belt. Beth had reached that in-between age where she was too big for the child's car seat she had used as a toddler but not quite big enough to look comfortable in a seat belt. But that was irrelevant; her wearing a seat belt wouldn't matter.

The date was August 29, 1982. It was your typical August day in New Jersey. The time was a little before two o'clock in the afternoon, and Beth was not quite six years young.

Katya would tell me later that Beth had just asked her another one of her questions about when she would be going back to school and whether Melissa and Amy, her two closest friends, would be with her in her first-grade class that year. Katya was about to answer her—*She would swear to me over and over as the tears fell down her cheeks that she never took her eyes from the highway*—when it was over before it ever began.

Cindy didn't bother to knock when she opened the conference-room door that afternoon, an omission on her part that alerted me immediately that something unusual was up. There were eight of us in the room, mostly TV executives, including me and the newly appointed president of Blair Holdings Radio and Television division. We were discussing whether to reopen negotiations for a package of Magnum P.I. reruns for the following summer season's program offerings when Cindy frantically signaled for me to come outside.

Cindy relayed everything the police had told her. "There was an automobile accident, and your wife, daughter, and mother-in-law were taken to Morristown Hospital. They said you should come immediately," she told me, her concern evident by the tears forming about her eyes.

The driver had run a red light. How many times had I read or heard those all-too-familiar words? The driver had run a red light, and his blood alcohol level had been nearly twice the legal limit. How about those words? *The driver of a late-model minivan ran a red light, drunk out of his fuckin' mind, and he killed your daughter.* Now, those were words I had never seen or heard before in my entire life.

That's essentially what the doctor told me that afternoon when I arrived at the hospital. "Your wife and her mother will be all right," he said, offering whatever good news he could. "Minor cuts and bruises for both, but nothing serious." It was their luck that the bastard was approaching them from Beth's side when he sped out of control and slammed into the rear passenger door, next to where she happened to be innocently sitting.

By the time the ambulance raced upon that horrible, tragic scene, the jaws of death were already busy at work. *Or maybe it was vice versa; it gets a little foggy to me by now. Whatever—it doesn't matter, does it? They knew she was dead.* At least that was what the doctor implied when he tried to console us by saying, "Her death was most probably instantaneous; she didn't suffer."

Katya and I buried her three days later.

The driver, James Watson Jr., was released on bail the day of the funeral. Our attorneys argued against it, but his daddy, some local politician, had the money and pulled the right strings to get his son back out on the highway despite their objections. The judge didn't seem to care that this was good old Jimmy's second DWI. What mattered was who he was.

I didn't need much to make up my mind. That was also about the time my self-aggrandizing, innermost friend initiated his conversations with me. When both of us were advised of the judge's decision, we vowed to ensure that James Watson Jr. would forfeit his bail by guaranteeing he would be a no-show for his trial.

Billy Paulson and his wife, Michelle, flew in from France after I called and told him what had happened. He seemed to sense what

I was thinking and tried his best to talk me out of it. I listened to everything he said, nodded, and even smiled a little, but I had made up my mind.

There was no way I would not have personally killed the bastard.

For the next three weeks, locked securely in the glove compartment of the old Bimmer, the Colt .45 became my faithful companion. I found out that Watson lived in Chatham, which was just a town or so over, and on a couple of occasions, I even drove by his house, ignoring our attorney's advice not to do so, in the hopes he would appear. Worst case in my mind, if I didn't get the chance there, I would kill the son of a bitch the minute he showed up outside the courthouse.

Then, one morning, as I opened up the local newspapers, I realized my vow had been fulfilled.

It would have been good old Jimmy's third DWI if he had lived. This time no one else was injured. This time, the article went on to report, Watson lost control of his vehicle after a high-speed police chase and killed himself as he struck one of the ubiquitous stone walls in the area.

"So in self-infliction, for those who steal my due, lay retribution," Parcae said.

Chapter 23

"SO THAT WAS IT. It was all over," I muttered with tired resignation to the empty room. I pushed my weary body from the torn and stained La-Z-Boy chair to pour myself another vodka.

Since I'd checked into the motel at four in the morning, I'd been drinking Smirnoff and thinking about old comrades who were no longer with me. Tony, Dickie, Maria … Spire. Spire? Well, let's consider that bastard an honorary member, someone who will soon be sponsored for full charter membership. Hopefully when he arrived for the initiation, it would be with a different club.

The memories of Beth haunted me most of all.

"I wanted to kill the son of a bitch." I fell down into the chair, the vodka spilling across my legs. "I would've," I continued, undeterred by the chilling dampness spreading beneath my body. "Just like Spire. But Jimmy was too quick, killing himself like that. Served him right."

Taking an extra long sip of the vodka, I closed my eyes and continued to recall the first time I was going to kill a man. "No, dummy!" I shouted. "That time in Nam doesn't count. And, anyway, you damn ignoramus, it was the other way around. They killed me! Remember?"

It was close to one o'clock the next day before I dragged myself out of bed. "Not much of a room," I grumbled, stumbling toward the bathroom and seeing it in all its glory, illuminated by the daylight. No big deal. I wasn't planning on being there long enough to get on a first-name basis with the resident cockroaches. ' Ish a palm … metto bog,' the voice slurred and corrected me. "Right, a palmetto bug ... that's right," I concurred, and stepped into the shower.

An hour later, I was in the Taurus, searching for the closest diner for something to eat. Owing to my body's inability to move at a rate faster than thirty-three revolutions per minute and to some rather interesting discussions I had with a few of the more sophisticated palmettos, it took me twice as long as it would have normally. I also needed to make a phone call. I almost used the motel phone, but that sobering voice in my head convinced me not to. 'No sess making it easier for them to cash you than nethassary,' it advised.

"Okay," I agreed, flicking one of my conversation partners off the receiver and surprising the voice by my quick compliance.

The telephone call was to change my flight connections to Newark. Somewhere between visiting the Wall and checking into the Palmetto Towers, it had dawned on me that I was cutting it close to try to kill Spire and still make my flight from Charlotte. I made the call from the lobby phone of a Cracker Barrel roadside diner.

"I'm sorry, Mr. Douglas," the reservation clerk for Continental politely said, "but the ticket you purchased is nonrefundable and nontransferable."

I counted to ten, attempting to remain calm in light of what the bimbo had just told me. "Listen, quit the bull—just tell me which flights depart after midnight but still get me into Newark in time for my flight to Paris. Even if that means I have to buy another damn ticket, lady!"

Get a hold of yourself, Douglas. Somehow my left hand was able to maintain its grip on the phone. And since there was no slurring to my thought, I also knew it was my advice and not the other guy's.

"There's a twelve forty-five departing Charlotte and scheduled to arrive at Kennedy at two twenty-five."

"Lady, who said anything about mother—Kennedy?" I yelled. I lowered my voice and tried to avoid the nasty stares of the Billy Bob family passing through the lobby. "Newark! I said Newark, lady!" She must believe she's dealing with some sort of dumbbell.

"Yes, mister, I understand you that you asked for Newark," the woman said, showing some indignation. "But unless you have a way of flying there on your own, there aren't any other flights out of Charlotte that will get you there in time."

Resisting the urge to tell her the story about the loon and the dumbbell, I told her, "Book it."

Sometime later I was circling the Greenville Hyatt parking lot. I wasn't sure what I was supposed to do or what to look for, but in keeping with my earlier instructions, I believed I was getting the lay of the land.

'Not too many times with this circling, Douglas,' my intuitive friend warned, finally over its hangover. 'Twice around should be sufficient for someone with your keen intelligence to become familiar with the hotel's egresses.'

"Yeah, if I keep circling, the car will run out of gas or you'll become dizzy." I laughed. Humor aside, the last thing either of us wanted was for someone to recognize me or to take unnecessary notice of the Taurus.

Somehow I had to catch Spire outside of the building. No way was I going to do it in his room or the hotel; the noise from the gun would be heard throughout. And it had to be done after the bastard received his fuckin' Man of the Year Award. If I did it earlier, he would be missed, and then what would happen? And it had to be no later than eleven thirty if I was going to make my flight. Why all these complications? Unless …

"That's it!" I stepped on the gas pedal, aborting my third circle around the lot and exiting. "Brilliant. Utterly brilliant. Honesty, that's it." Complimenting myself for the idea, I sped off the hotel grounds. For some reason, even after a full pot of coffee at the Cracker Barrel, I still felt the urge for another.

"It's all very elementary, all very simple, this killing business, once you put your mind to it." I continued to compliment myself while retracing my route back to the Cracker Barrel. The voice started to ask some specifics about what I meant by honesty, but I cut him off. "Let's not get hung up on unnecessary details," I replied to Mr. Doubting Thomas, falling back on a phrase from my corporate training that I used whenever I needed to stall for an answer. "Anyway, here's the diner; there's time enough later to work out the details."

More awake than earlier, this time as I pulled into the parking lot, I noticed that I had the dubious distinction of possessing the only out-of-state license plate. Mine was also the only car; the other vehicles were pickup trucks. "No sweat," I mumbled, tapping the Taurus as I got out. "I'm sure most of your parts are American made. You'll be okay with these good old boys. It's your buddy here who probably won't fit in that well. Probably the only guy in the whole place with a designer suit, attaché case, and matching revolver."

Four or five heads spun in my direction as soon as I walked in. Ignoring their stares—observing nevertheless that my prior sartorial assessment was right on the money—I took a seat at the farthest end of the counter.

A pretty young thing emerged from behind the swinging doors that all diners were apparently required to have. I ordered the largest cup of coffee they had and then did my best to be one of the boys. Without missing a beat, I stared straight ahead, my gaze landing somewhere between the blueberry pie and something greenish in color that I assumed to be key lime pie.

At about the moment the waitress served my coffee, the game we were all so intently playing came to an unexpected end. "If that's your Taurus, mister, I think you got some trouble with your radiator." The voice had an accent like that of my old nemesis, the shark.

I wanted to keep playing the game, so I didn't stop staring at the key lime pie. My fingers instinctively fiddled with the attaché's clasps, first springing them open and then clicking them shut. A few seconds went by before I heard the same person, now next to me, say, "Excuse me, mister, for not minding my own business, but that is your Taurus, ain't it? The one sitting out front with a New York license plate?"

On second thought, despite the accent and possible fetish with license plates, it wasn't the shark. It was far too polite to be him.

"Mabel, I'll have a cup of your coffee," the man said. "And bring me a slice of that delicious, homemade key lime pie of yours while you're at it." He sat down on the stool to my left and dropped his Clemson Tigers baseball cap on the counter.

Well, the game was over. Mabel removed the object that my eyes had been focused on, and in its stead, appearing on the mirrored backsplash, I saw a person who reminded me of me. Except something wasn't quite me. The face in the mirror looked different. There wasn't time to verify the identity of the person, as the man addressed me once more.

"Seems to me like you got a leak in your radiator. There's what looks like coolant all over the ground under your car."

As I angled my body in his direction, opening both clasps of the case as I did, he shook his head and made a face in commiseration.

After a brief reprieve, which was punctuated by noisy, slurping sounds he made as he drank his coffee and devoured his pie in three overflowing forkfuls, he returned his attention to me.

"That's your car, ain't it?" he repeated. He seemed determined that sooner or later I would be forced to answer that it was. He wiped some remaining crumbs from his mouth with a paper napkin and looked at me. "I know everyone else here, so it's gotta be yours."

Damn! The last thing I needed was for some local to remember this out-of-towner and the car he was driving. 'It's a little late for that concern now, dummy. You should have known this would happen when you were in the parking lot, admiring what those good old boys consider transportation.'

I started to say something to the second-guessing pain in the ass about him not being there when I needed him, when—like a flash—an idea came to me. Is there no end to my brilliance? I thought, grinning smugly in the mirror at what I was about to do. Without wasting another moment, right there on the spot, I went ahead and nominated myself for Man of the Fuckin' Year.

"Jason Spire," I said proudly, the name echoing throughout the restaurant. "Pleased to make your acquaintance, sir." I extended my hand as though in acceptance of the award, an ear-to-ear grin on my face, and rose from my seat. "Sure sounds as if it's my car." I walked over to the window to look at the Taurus.

In the background, the man said, "Gary Owens, but call me Chauncey; everyone else does."

The green-colored coolant had formed a large puddle beneath the Taurus. "Yeah, that's mine all right." The dejection in my tone flowed out with the coolant.

Okay, I thought, continuing to look through the window, the muscles on my face forcing a shit-eating smile, you are now Jason

Spire. That's good. I like that. He murders himself—an act very often referred to as suicide. But even a suicide needs transportation. Even the Man of the Fuckin' Year needs wheels! Shaking my head in dismay, I returned to my stool.

As though he were reading my thoughts—once he knew whom he was dealing with, he probably wanted to pitch in and help—the man everyone called Chauncey surprised me and volunteered his version of a solution to my dilemma. "I know an automobile mechanic in town. Name's Bucky. Right now he specializes in Fords, too. Although, with the new BMW plant opening up around here, things may change for him in the future."

That settled it. A man wise enough to understand that things change must know something about radiators, I thought. So I concurred with his insightful advice.

"Mr. Spire, your car is too hot to drive, so I'll call Bucky for a tow truck."

I shrugged my shoulders. Chauncey apparently took a liking to Spire, because he also offered to drive him to Bucky's.

"You're dressed too nicely, Mr. Spire, to ride in that old grease bucket he's gonna send," he said with a warm, friendly smile as we climbed into his vehicle.

The trip to Bucky's took almost two hours even though the shop was only ten miles away. Normally it was a short drive of twenty minutes, and only that long if you were stuck behind some farmer's truck on the single-lane road leading there. We took the circuitous route that day—a sort of backwoodsy, "when we get there, we get there" route, one that I had never traveled despite my many business trips to the area. My eyes were finally opened as I at last understood that I was not a suit after all.

Never meant to be one, Sean—to finally answer your question.

The day before, when I had embarked on this one-man crusade to kill Spire and Magritte, a part of the old me—the suit—had still remained. But now the events of the past two weeks—beginning with Maria's murder and culminating with Katya's departure, the destruction of our home, and the disappearance of Magritte—all combined to plunge me deeper into this compulsive, maniacal madness. I held on to a façade, which gave me some grip, tenuous as it might have been, on my identity.

I lied when I said that there wasn't a vestige of the old Christof Douglas that remained. There was. But that was all it was. The hopes, the dreams, the morality, and the love—everything that made a man more than he was, that gave him a sense of goodness and decency, an understanding of right from wrong—were gone. What remained was the façade: a vacant, empty shell for my flesh and bones, or a suit, but definitely nothing more than just another corporate executive in his uniform.

That day, though, as Chauncey Owens and I rode those South Carolina back roads, driving past one abandoned textile mill after another, I listened to his story. I kept hearing Maria's warnings echoing over and over in my mind. I had never heeded the second of her warnings.

"You're too decent a guy, Christof," Maria said, playing her trump card and desperately trying to make me understand her real meaning. "Much too nice a man for the corporate world. You will only lose your soul to them one day."

We hadn't been driving more than a couple of minutes, and I wasn't quite sure what I said that got us started. I think I maybe babbled something under my breath about how hot it was and how the density of the kudzu—I couldn't see more than a few feet in from the road—reminded me of someplace I once had been given a paid vacation to. And Owens was an easy going person, so when he began to talk, it made me feel as if I had known him my entire life.

Chauncey Owens was four years younger than I. In 1967, the day after he graduated from high school—the first in his family to do so, he proudly said—he obeyed Uncle Sam's beck and call and enlisted in the army. "Hell," he said, downplaying anything special about his actions, "they were about to draft me anyway. There was a war going on, you know, Mr. Spire. So I just figured that I'd do as the man said and enlist, and maybe I'd have some say where it was that they would send me."

"Did you?" I asked, certain I knew the answer.

He took his eyes from the road and looked at me. "Yeah, believe that one and I got a textile mill which will make you a million bucks." He turned his head back to the road.

"Nam, First Air Cav," he said. "I was sent there in four months, right after completing AIT."

I self-consciously fiddled with the clasps of the attaché case on my lap and stared at the overgrown kudzu countryside. How does it grow so fast? I asked myself, the forgotten military term 'advanced infantry training' returning to my mind simultaneously.

"Served two tours in Nam," he continued. "In between the two, Sarah and me got married." Chauncey paused. I saw out of the corner of my eye that he was facing me. "My high school sweetheart. The missus and me, we been married nineteen years. Here, take a look at this."

Shifting my gaze away from the window and toward Owens, I smiled and reached for the open wallet. His finger pointed out where I should look.

"We were nineteen when we got married. Lived half my life with my Sarah, Mr. Spire." He sounded as content as the happiest newlywed. "Flip that there plastic," he said, stretching across the front seat and doing it himself. "Yeah, that's it. That's my son, Gerald, on the right. We call him Sonny. He's gonna be a junior at Clemson this fall. On full scholarship as a defensive back for the Tigers."

I was counting ages and subtracting anniversaries in my head and kept on coming up with a number around twenty or twenty-one for Sonny's age, but before I could solve this problem on my fingers, Chauncey interrupted. "And this beautiful-looking young lady there," he said, his face beaming, "that's my daughter, Mary. She's gonna be a freshman at Furman."

"Nice family you have. You're very lucky." I flipped through the plastic inserts to see if there were any more photographs. "Very nice family," I repeated even quieter when I saw that there weren't.

"Got any kids of your own, Mr. Spire?"

I waited a few seconds before I replied. "It's okay to call me ..." For a second I almost said Christof. "Spire. No need to be so formal." I handed him back his wallet.

He must have noticed something different about me, for he

changed the topic. "Ever been to a textile mill? A finishing plant or weaving mill, Mis—Spire?"

If asked that question two or three weeks from then, there was a possibility my response would have been yes, what with the rag-trade task force scheduled to review DFT's operations in the Carolinas. Then again, in two or three weeks things could change.

Who the hell could predict the future?

"Why, I can, Jwah. Why do you always question me that way?" Parcae would tell me, gently holding my head in her hands, her pale blue eyes staring deeply into mine whenever I would ask how she knew about me. "I knew this was our destiny. To be together with her, with our daughter and tell your story."

"No," I answered. "Can't say that I have."

"I know your car's gonna take a few hours to fix. What say I give you the grand tour?" Chauncey looked at me for my reaction. "Anyway, you don't appear to be in such a big hurry, Mr. Spire," he said, apparently forgetting what I had just told him to call me. "Anybody dressed the way you are who stops in at the local diner on a Saturday afternoon … seems to me, shoot … Well, he was not someone in any big hurry to get wherever it was he was headed."

I shrugged. "Yeah, well I do have a few hours before killing." Whether he heard me correctly didn't matter; he understood my response to be in agreement with his offer. He probably thought I mistook one preposition for another anyway.

Chauncey nodded, pulled the pickup onto the highway shoulder, shifted into reverse, and floored the gas pedal to speed back up the hundred yards or so to the intersection we had just passed.

"Once upon a time, not long ago, there used to be more mills in this county than Burger Kings. But not today. Not anymore. Those days are long gone," he said, sounding every bit the experienced tour guide as he swung the truck onto the side road.

"A mile or so down here, there's a finishing plant that, in its heyday, employed some two thousand people. Seven days a week, three shifts around the clock that baby cooked. The fabrics we made—or goods, as we all called them—were used for all sorts of ladies' clothing. Skirts, slacks—that kind of thing. We couldn't make the fabrics fast enough. We even got paid overtime. Can you believe that?" he asked rhetorically. "Overtime!"

I started to ask what had happened. But that would have been insincere, stupid small talk, as I knew the answer.

"There it is, Spire. Look, down there over on the left, just past that Getty station."

My eyes followed to where he pointed, and I saw three large smokestacks towering above the deserted Getty station.

"Me and Sarah worked there for seventeen years. No, that ain't right." He shook his head. "Sarah worked there starting right after graduating from high school, so it must be twenty, twenty-one years for her."

"Where do you work now?"

"Don't." He smiled. "Well, I do odds and ends. Carpentry, plumbing—that sort of handyman, jack-of-all-trades thing. Between Sarah working at Cracker Barrel …" He saw the look on my face and laughed. "No, no, Spire, that gal was Mabel. She and Sarah are first cousins, easy to get the two confused. I was dropping Sarah off for the four-to-midnight shift when I seen what was happening to your car. Next time you're passing through, make sure you try the key lime pie. It's the best in the Carolinas."

"I will," I mumbled. "I'll try to remember that."

"Anyway, as I was saying, between her and me, we make enough to make ends meet." He slowed the car as we approached the massive, vacant building, and he pointed toward its far end. "Those loading docks were where the greige goods came in." He looked at me. "That's what they call the raw material in a finishing plant." Chauncey turned back to the road and then to me again, a puzzled expression on his face. "Spire, do you know what a finishing plant is?"

Before I could tell him that I had been enrolled in a fairly high-level graduate school course on the subject but that, at the moment, he had me at a slight disadvantage, he answered his own question.

"Whoooee! Hot damn! This may take longer than I thought." However, for the moment, he stayed with the story of his own life, resuming where he had left off. "That far end is where I worked. I was in charge of the first-shift quality-and-control department."

"Sounds pretty important," I offered, attempting to redeem

myself and convey some sense of scholarship regarding the textile organizational hierarchy.

"I was at that, Spire. I was at that. I was employee of the month, for your sweet information. Three times. Three times—now that says something."

It took a few minutes to drive past the remainder of the deserted building to the end of the road. Seeing that massive structure lying silent and idle was an eerie experience; it had to have been as large as a city block. The concertina wire on the top of the chain-link fence that surrounded the property reminded me of the vacation spot I'd alluded to before. Chauncey was turning the truck around when he said, "What it says, Spire … What it says …"

He seemed unable to finish his sentence and stared at me, a trace of a smile evident as he confessed. "What it says, Spire—I gotta tell you, buddy—I ain't got the foggiest notion anymore."

He looked away and shifted the vehicle into second quickly, the tires squealing against the gravel. He said nothing until we were back at the intersection for the main highway. As we slowed to turn onto it and resume our original direction toward Bucky's, his eyes focusing on the hot asphalt ahead, he asked, "What about you, Spire? Do you have any idea what it means?"

Yeah, I knew what it meant. But there was no point in spelling it out. Anyway, he knew the answer. With visions of my former squadron mate, the old philosopher who understood only too well the mutability of things that appeared to be permanent, dashing about my head, I said, "No, Chauncey, no, I'm just like you. I haven't the foggiest idea anymore either."

Well, that was pretty much the way the rest of the afternoon went. Neither of us had anything better to do—certainly Spire didn't—so there wasn't any objection on my part when Chauncey offered to continue with his grand tour of the neighborhood.

"When we finish," he said, having regained his previous upbeat spirit, "you'll know the difference between a finishing plant and a mill, between plain and greige goods, and a whole lot more textile jargon." Joking, he added, "Maybe it won't be as much as I know, but it'll sure be more than enough for you to apply for some management job."

Sometime during that afternoon, we stopped and called Bucky's to find out the status of the Taurus. The radiator did have a leak, but Bucky said that he would be able to seal it "well enough" for me to pick the car up later. "Not well enough to get you back up north, Mr. Spire," he warned, "but enough to get you back to the nearest car rental."

"That's well enough for me," I echoed, and I thanked him.

Six or seven abandoned plants and mills later, Chauncey said, "We would need more than an afternoon to see all of them." Even if I wasn't clear on their differences in products, I knew he was correct; besides, I was more than qualified for that management position. I sure as hell couldn't do worse.

For a fleeting, empathetic moment, I was tempted to tell him my real name, the one that Sean Casey had dubbed me—the Exalted Sultan of Rags—but upon reflection, I didn't think it wise to tip my disguise and let him know he was driving around the country side with royalty.

He dropped me off at the garage, and as we were shaking hands good-bye, I wanted to ask him what had caused him to do what he did. Why would he pick up a complete stranger, someone he had never laid eyes on, and decide to spill out his heart and soul to that someone?

I wanted to ask him that question, but instead I just shook his hand, smiled, and wished him and Sarah all the best in the future. I did tell him. Well, maybe he didn't hear me; he was already in the truck, and that engine of his was noisy. Didn't he know how lucky he really was? "After all, Chauncey," I almost told him as I slid into my own car, "there are some things in life more important than rags."

Sometime later in the evening, when the other Spire's testimonial was in full swing and an hour or so before I would confront him at last, I telephoned London. Oliver answered after a dozen rings.

"Ellooo?"

"Oliver, it's me, Christof." Recalling his earlier confusion with my name and feeling certain that I had just roused him from bed, I once again clarified who "me" was. "It's me, your brother-in-law, Christof Douglas."

If Big Ben were his personal alarm clock, it could not have roused him any faster than the realization of who I was. "You! What the blue blazes are you doing telephoning at this hour? Have you any idea what time it is?"

"Oliver, I'm truly sorry. I know it's late, but I have to talk to Katya."

"Late!" he yelled, disregarding any mention of why I was calling. "It's not late, you bloody loon. It's damn early. It's four o'clock in the morning here."

I was glad he hadn't confused me for a dumbbell and almost thanked him, when I heard a shout in the background. "It's bloomin' Christof; that's who the hell it is."

Before we started to play pass the potato again, I interrupted. "Put Kat on the phone. Put her on right now!" He was making a habit of disregarding anything that sounded like the name of my wife, for all I heard was silence.

"Oliver," I said, my voice beginning to lose whatever remaining control it had, "did you hear me? Put my wife on. I must speak with her!"

It was too late. They were playing pass the potato, a game they seemed to enjoy no matter what hour it was. "Oliver, Laura, whoever is there, stop this bullshit and let me speak with Kat!" I was about to shout again, when Oliver surprised me.

"She's not here."

"Come on, buddy. That flight from Kennedy landed at Heathrow hours ago."

"Listen here, Christof. Believe anything you wish. It won't change a thing. She's not here."

Any respect I might have felt toward Oliver for recognizing me as the loon that I was had now been shattered by his equal lack of understanding when it came to the dynamics of how things changed. It was a good thing he wasn't in the radiator business; otherwise, my car would have still been at Bucky's.

"She's gone to the Continent."

"The Continent? The Continent?" I repeated. "Where on the Continent?" I screamed. "Where, for Christ's sake?"

"Good-bye, Christof."

283

Chapter 24

AFTER OLIVER HUNG UP, I waited more impatiently than ever to get on with my objective. Some forty-five minutes later, the arrival of a caravan of stretch limos at the hotel, followed by the emergence of the area's most prominent politicians and businesspeople, signaled me to action. The ceremony was finally finished, and it was time for Spire to collect his reward.

Once I decided that honesty made the best policy, my plan became simple. Why create complications or cumbersome details? My spirits lifted as I recalled the expression about the devil being in the details. After all, my arrangements were with the other guy. Why bring in someone he might take offense with? I was confident that my money should ride on my namesake. So I decided to come right out and tell my boy the truth.

I realized that I was betting the farm, especially when it came to telling the truth to someone such as him, someone completely unaccustomed to the very idea. But what else could I do? I had run out of time and harebrained schemes that the loon had come up with. Like the idea that I would go to Spire's room, tell him I was Carson's new chauffeur, and say that Carlson needed to see him downstairs toute de suite.

'Not to worry', the loon insisted, 'he won't recognize you'. After listening to that one, I wondered if the loon and the dumbbell weren't cut from the same cloth after all.

So I told Spire the truth and said that I knew all about the illegal arms and chemical dealings that Sammantha was trying to expose and he should meet me after the ceremony in the hotel parking lot. I was surprised a bit when he agreed as quickly as he did.

Three hours later we met.

"For your sake, Douglas, I hope you know what you got your self into," Jason Spire spat. His condescending arrogance nearly caused me to blow his fuckin' Man of the Year brains all over the hotel parking lot.

"Yeah, well, like I said to you on the phone, if you want your dirty little secret kept a secret, just keep your mouth shut, and I'll show you exactly what I'm into." The nervous edge to my voice betrayed the façade I was struggling to maintain.

"Here, put these gloves on, and get into the driver's seat." I shoved a pair of latex medical gloves, which I'd picked up after Owens dropped me off, into his hand. With my revolver, I motioned where he should sit.

"No, don't touch that handle." Grabbing his wrist with my free hand, I prevented him from leaving his fingerprints on the Taurus. "The gloves, Spire—put them on first."

He glared as he stretched the gloves over his fingers, and then he opened the door and slid in. After slamming the door shut, I walked around the front of the car, watching him in case he had second thoughts and decided to get out.

"Where are we going?" Spire asked as I got in. "And what's with these gloves? You didn't say anything about wearing gloves when you called."

"Start the car and drive to the end of the access road; make a left, and then follow the signs toward I-84 North. When we get to where I have the diskettes I told you about, you'll find out." Now that we were on our way, I felt more confident that my plan was going to work. "Not too fast either. Just make certain you stay within the speed limit."

Spire started the engine and drove away from the hotel. "You know, Douglas," he said, when the hotel disappeared from view, his tone not quite as cocky, "I'm not sure why I'm doing this. Maybe if you keep treating me like some enemy captive instead of who I really am, I may decide to stop this car and get the hell out."

He paused as if expecting an answer. When I didn't give one, he continued. "If it were anyone but you, Douglas, I wouldn't be sitting here. You know that, don't you?"

How dead on the money you are, I thought. "Make the left up ahead and get onto the interstate," I said.

He followed my directions and shook his head in exaggerated amazement. "I never imagined you for a blackmailer," he said. There was a smirk across his lips. "Mind you, I'm not saying that what you alleged on the phone—accusing Carlson and me of being, well, gunrunners, I seem to recall was the word you used—has any truth to it whatsoever. But those diskettes?" Spire shook his head again, this time seemingly in disgust, and accelerated to merge with the interstate traffic.

"Just keep driving straight ahead until I tell you something different. And remember what else I said." Images of where Beth rested intermingled with my further warning. "You better keep it in your head what I said about that second copy."

"Hey, I'm a quick study." He raised his hand in mock surrender as the onrushing southbound traffic headlights caused his eyes to narrow. "You made it perfectly clear. Anything happens to you, or if I don't get you the million dollars in cash by the time the banks close Monday, your lawyer releases the diskettes to the Feds."

I nodded and congratulated myself once again for my perceptive estimation of where his IQ fell. "I always knew you were a smart boy." Our eyes fell on the gun that rested half on my lap, half poised in Spire's direction.

"Say, Douglas, do you mind pointing that thing a little to the right?"

I eased the gun away as he returned his gaze to the highway. He appeared more relaxed when he began to talk about the diskettes. "You should understand where I'm coming from regarding the diskettes you swiped. This bullshit about illegal arms trafficking is just that—bullshit! Probably a cover on your part to justify your own actions."

Oh, oh, here it comes, I thought, remembering Magritte's lecture on why additional proof was needed to expose the Santa Clauses.

"Yeah, Douglas, you may believe this little charade you're playing will fool some people, but the only person that will be fooled when everything is said and done will be the person I'm talking with right now."

Amazing, utterly amazing. His performance was precisely as Magritte had foreseen.

"Listen, why don't we level with each other?" Spire said, seemingly gaining confidence by the second. "We've known each other for some time. Work for the same boss, same company. Let's cut the crap." He swung his head toward me, a conspiratorial smile replacing the smirk. "I know, and you know, what this is all about."

I almost killed him right then. My index finger tightened against the trigger as I angled the gun a few degrees in his direction. If he breathed one syllable of her name, I swore, driver or no driver, I would do it.

"It happens more than you realize. Maybe not in your line of work, but in the defense and technology business, people selling internal research secrets, buying information from competitors, that sort of thing happens quite a bit." His voice was regaining that earlier cockiness. "Hell, look at that task force you're on. That kind of thing is rampant in the rag trade."

Although Spire, or the Santa Claus he was becoming, was staring at the highway, he might have sensed that the gun was re-aimed in his direction, because he made it clear what he believed I was after.

"Look, Douglas, tell me the truth about which company set you up and wants to buy Space and Technology's engineering secrets, and we'll cut a different deal. There's no gain, I can assure you, in getting yourself any deeper involved in some half-baked industrial espionage scam."

So that was what he thought this was about? Old-fashioned corporate industrial espionage? As I started to reevaluate my prior perceptions about where Spire would fall on the Stanford-Binet IQ Scale—pegging him now in the lower third percentile—I realized it was only Saturday. The security violation of DFT's computer systems would not be known for at least thirty-six hours. Could he be telling the truth? Maybe … Maybe this was all wrong … Maybe Maria was …

"Fuck you, Santa Claus." I heard a voice like the loon's, its intensity shattering any doubts playing in my mind. "You're only fifty percent correct as to what sort of scam I'm talking about. And to make it easier for you to guess where hot or cold is, industrial is close but no cigar."

"What? What did you say?" Spire's face was white.

"I said, industrial is close but doesn't get you the cigar. You're pushing my patience level, so pay attention."

"Not that smart-assed comment, you bastard," he snapped, further indicating he was not as self-possessed as he wanted me to believe.

'He's unraveling. You've got the Santa Claus now,' the voice whispered.

"What did you just call me? What was that name?" Spire asked again. He seemed distracted and confused, unsure whether to watch the traffic rushing by him or his passenger.

I then realized that it was not my rejection of that obscene offer of his that had stunned him. It was the unexpected usage of that supposed code name.

"Oh, that," I said, relishing the shocked look on his face. "I think my exact words, if my memory serves me, and I do like their ring, were, fuck you, Santa Claus." Grinning ear to ear, I went on. "It does have a certain cachet to it, doesn't it? Fuck you, Santa Claus. Eh, what do you think? Will it play?"

It was hard to understand what he said. It was a mumbled undertone, punctuated with obscenities, but I thought I heard Carlson's name interspersed along with some others I couldn't place, as well as something regarding my mental state.

Quite frankly, I didn't understand why he was so mad. I had done exactly as he'd demanded. I listened to him and cut the crap, and now we both knew that the other knew that each of us knew. More simply stated, he now knew that I was serious when it came to my gunrunner accusation, and I now knew that he knew what the name Santa Claus stood for.

The fact of the matter was that I was afraid he might convince me to believe his crazy tale about industrial espionage or, more importantly, maybe even smooth-talk me out of the whole purpose for our get-together. Whatever else one might say about Magritte, he had been right on the money when it came to the Santa Clauses and their ability to make the world seem up, or flat, when it was really down, or round.

Well, it was something like that; the gist of it all was to confuse you. On further reflection, that modus operandi fit Magritte.

Some minutes passed before Spire broke the silence. For the first time, he used my given name. "Listen, Chris, whatever it is you want, you got it wrong. I'm not the guy you should be talking to."

"Oh? Pray tell, Jason, who is this guy I should be having this delightful conversation with?" I remained on guard, wary that this might be another ploy from the bag of tricks the crafty Santa Claus had at his disposal. "Might that someone be our dear, mutual superior, Mr. Carlson?"

"You want a million dollars? Is that what you want?" Spire answered, ignoring my question. "Okay … Okay, you got it." Our eyes locked; his face was bathed in sweat. "But I need a couple of days to raise the cash. Monday is too short, too soon for me to get it." He wiped his face with the back of his hand. "What's it to you anyway if it's Tuesday or Wednesday at the latest? Eh, old buddy? Nothing sacrosanct about Monday, right?"

When I didn't answer, he continued. "Okay, I'll do as you instructed on the phone and take the diskettes." He wiped his forehead again, his eyes back on the road. "And verify that they contain the billing data." He paused and then interjected his own variation to my plan. "Although, to tell you the truth, Chris, my suggestion is to forget the diskettes for the time being. I believe you have the info that you claim. Let's return to the hotel so that I can make the calls to raise the million."

He looked at me. "Mind you, I'm not admitting that what you're saying has anything to do with me."

There he goes again. "I have what you claim, but I'm not sure what it is you claim." "It is, but it isn't," I mumbled.

Spire asked if what I'd just said was an okay. I cut him off and told him to take the next exit. He said something about making the jug handle to reenter I-84 south so that we could go back to the hotel, but I interrupted. This time I told him to shut up and follow the signs to Buffalo. He mumbled to himself but did as I told him.

"Here," I ordered a few miles later. "Pull off onto that side road right after that gas station." I pointed with my gun at the deserted Getty station. A minute later, we reached our destination.

"Stop here. Shut the car off, and get out."

Spire's hands fumbled with his seat belt as though he were re-strapping himself in rather than getting out. A hard poke into his ribs with my .45 convinced him this was not the time for heroics.

"Okay! Okay. Take it easy with that gun, will you?" he yelled. His eyes regained that earlier glare as he unbuckled and slid out of the car. "Let's get these goddamn diskettes and get the hell out of wherever we are."

I got out of the Taurus and walked up to him.

"And here I was thinking all along that you might like to visit one of DFT's former profit centers."

"What the hell are you talking about, Douglas? First it's gun runners. Now its profit centers. Next it'll be … How … How the hell am I supposed to know what you'll want next?" Spire seemed to be at a loss for words as he retreated into the shadows of the abandoned finishing plant Chauncey had shown me that afternoon. "You know, you really are freakin crazy," he raved, repeating his original diagnosis as to my mental health.

Well, at least he was consistent. 'He was … No, he was not … Well, maybe he was just a little crazy, but not too much,' the voice of the loon, which had remained quiet and sulked since I had rejected its earlier plan, babbled in my ear.

"Congratulations, Spire. Brilliant deduction," I answered, a wild grin across my face as I thought of the loon's playful antics. "But not freakin crazy. Crazy as a loon would be a more fitting description."

As soon as I said those words, a tremendous weight of doubt and misgiving engulfed me. It was so strong that I wasn't certain why the two of us were even standing there. I was confused, not clear where we were. I recognized the voice screaming at me, shouting about Santa Clauses, toys, and other stupid, meaningless codes and weird phrases. I stared into the darkness at his shadow, my eyes searching, my ears listening, but nothing connected.

'Could you really go through with this and kill this person?' a soothing, rational voice asked, the meaning of why and where beginning to return. 'Any person, Christof Douglas?' it probed.

At that moment, I recognized that the man in the shadows was Jason Spire. His mad screams—"We didn't kill her! We would have, but someone beat us to it!"—broke through my fog. I heard what sounded like a car approach from behind. I swore that as I turned toward the noise, I saw headlights, but there was only blackness and silence.

"Douglas, they're out there, you know." Spire's shout refocused my attention to where we were and why we were there.

"My guys are out there. You didn't think that I'd come without some backup, did you? I told you before; you'd better know what you're getting into when you mess with a Santa Claus." He laughed and pointed one hand at me and taunted, "Chris Kringle."

The next few seconds were a slow-motion blur. As soon as Spire said "Chris Kringle," I saw something black and shiny appear in his hand. Then I heard a clicking sound, followed by a loud, deafening bang—two loud bangs.

I didn't know if Spire were dead when I walked toward his fallen body. I just knew I wasn't. And although I aimed the Colt .45 at him, I wasn't sure why. There was no way I could kill him if I hadn't done so already.

Spire ... God, Spire was dead.

His white tuxedo shirt was changing to a dark, ominous red. Blood flowed from a small black hole high on his forehead, down his cheek and onto the ground beside his head. There was a pistol in his right fist.

I jerked away, revolted at what I saw, and stumbled from the lifeless form to the car. In half the time it had taken to get there, I was back on I-84 and racing out of control in the direction of Charlotte's airport.

'Calm down. Calm down, and slow down,' the voice said. 'This is not the time to be pulled over by the police.' I was physically fighting with my leg, which was pressed hard against the gas pedal, attempting to lift it to reduce my speed, when I realized that cruise control was a surer solution.

Somehow I had enough presence of mind to check my watch and calculate how long it would take me to get to the airport before I set the control to fifty while wrestling my leg from the pedal to allow cruise to kick in.

'It's over. You killed him, Christof,' the rational, soothing voice declared.

"I had to, damn it! There was no other choice. He had a gun. What did you expect?" I shouted. I squeezed my eyes shut, attempting to block the image of Spire's lifeless body from haunting me. "Don't you understand? If I didn't pull the trigger, it would have been just like that time in Nam again. Except today, there was no Billy Paulson to save me."

A prolonged warning by the car in the adjacent lane, a lane that our two cars were suddenly sharing, snapped me back to the moment. "I had to, don't you understand? I shot him because I had … because it was either him or …"

It was as though Spire were alive and had punched me in the face; the thought that had interrupted my appeal was that startling.

"You only fired once, Douglas," I yelled, the images of Spire's chest and head soaked in blood dancing eerily in my mind. "Only once," I repeated, stretching across the seat for the Colt .45.

Keeping one eye on the traffic, with my free hand I removed the cartridge and ejected the unused rounds. I counted and recounted the ejected bullets, paying special attention to make certain there was not a round still in the chamber, and then I recounted them again.

"Six! There are six," I yelled again, confirming my shocking realization from a few seconds ago. "That means it was a car I saw." I was confused and uncertain as to what it really meant. "Those were headlights I saw. There are six bullets left. Only one was fired. That means … that means someone else shot Spire."

Chapter 25

"WHY DID YOU COME back?" Katya coldly asked, her tone more appropriate for a formal interrogation than an old friend and lover.

But Maria fit none of those descriptions in Katya's eyes.

"Why didn't you remain locked in his past?" She persisted with her confrontational questioning. "He exorcised you from his being years ago. What could you possibly expect to accomplish by returning into our lives?"

Maria made a small gesture with her hand in polite defense to Katya's hostile inquiries, her mouth opening in protest, but the appearance of the waiter caused her to pause.

"Rouge pour Madame." The waiter, I was shocked to see, was the spitting image of Dickie Lake, even to the unnatural tilt of his neck. "L'absinthe de la maison pour l'autre Madame."

He set a large snifter filled with a watery yellowish substance in front of Maria.

Maria waited until Dickie was beyond hearing range before she replied. "No, Katya. I don't mean to be disagreeable with you, especially with us finally meeting, but what you stated as fact is simply not true. Christof," she said, her voice decidedly more amicable that her luncheon companion's, "has neither forgotten nor forgiven me, so I don't quite see how you can claim he is free of me."

Katya's green eyes flashed as she sipped her wine. She stared at Maria over the glass, and in her heart, she knew only too well that the words Maria had spoken were, sadly, true.

After that initial exchange, the two sat quietly, withdrawn and deep within their thoughts. Occasionally one would raise a glass to her lips and take a sip of her drink, but neither spoke a word, each content with her own private assessment of her eternal rival.

Observing the two, seeing them together, I was struck at how dissimilar they looked and how unlike the other I knew each to be. Everything about them—from their unique lifestyle and nature, to their physical appearance, ethnic background, culture, and family ancestry—was as different as one could possibly conceive. There were only two things, I belatedly realized, that they shared—the color of their eyes and me.

To underscore that notion, all one had to do was gaze no further than the dresses they wore. At the risk of oversimplifying that point, their attire reflected all that and so much more.

Maria, relaxed and seemingly calm despite the circumstances, was wearing a khaki safari-style outfit similar to the one in the newspaper photograph printed on the day she was found murdered. Katya, on the other hand, was strikingly beautiful, as always. Although outwardly mirroring Maria's tranquil composure, I knew Katya was nervous and uncertain, but the elegant Norma Kamali dress she had on when Maria snapped her picture that day in London was overshadowed by her perfection.

I asked myself for the thousandth time, why are they meeting? Katya began to say something but hesitated. Perhaps she thought better and reconsidered what she was about to say, or maybe it was nothing more than the reappearance of Dickie Lake that stopped her.

He placed their lunches on the table and left. "I believe the chicken is yours," Katya said, her tone unchanged, and she switched her plate with the endive and arugula salad Dickie had mistakenly set in front of Maria.

The arrival of their lunch gave each an excuse to continue avoiding conversation. Although it was clear that the pair wanted to speak their minds, it was also obvious that neither was comfortable nor certain how to proceed.

I thought that moment would be the perfect opportunity to attempt once again to join them. Plus, if I didn't move from this window seat soon, the blistering July sun would boil me to death.

I couldn't understand why the café still had these cold-weather partitions up in the summer and hadn't converted to alfresco dining by now.

In the blink of an eye, I rose from my chair, walked through the café's entrance onto the cobblestone sidewalk, and found myself—the whole scenario repeating itself exactly as it had earlier—sitting again in the same window seat, the merciless sun beating upon my face. What in God's name was happening?

"Katya—that is your name, isn't it? I hope you don't mind me calling you that and not Mrs. Douglas," Maria said, her voice temporarily causing me to cease whatever concern I had about my seating predicament and listen to what they were discussing.

"To be completely honest with you," she said, "I find it somewhat difficult to address you in that manner. You do understand, don't you?"

A smile surfaced on Katya's beautiful face. It was a smile I was very familiar with—the one I often saw appear whenever she was privy to an intimate, personal secret.

"Yes, I do understand," Katya replied. "I understand quite well." That was the first time her tone lost some of its hard, guarded edge.

Although she didn't reveal it—*I knew everything they thought*—I was positive Maria sensed that subtle difference in Katya.

"But you asked me a question," Maria said. "Perhaps it was merely rhetorical on your part, but, quite frankly, I do feel I owe you the courtesy of a response."

Katya smiled and nodded, motioning her to continue.

"I came back," Maria went on, her face taking on a haunted glow, its color draining as she spoke, "because it was my time. Because I had no choice, no say as to whether I wished to or not." She paused. The two stared into each other's identical green eyes—*They knew they were soul mates at that moment*. And then she continued, surprising Katya a little by what she volunteered.

"I didn't want to come back, if you really must know. I never wanted to return. No, my sweet, dear Katya, the answer to your question is the other way around. It was I who had forgotten him."

"No, Maria," I shouted, leaping from my seat and rushing toward the café door. "Don't ever say that. It's not true. You know you are lying."

It didn't matter. Despite how fast I ran, the instant I touched the cobblestones outside the café, I found myself back behind the windowed partition and in my chair, helpless, forced against my will to observe all that transpired beyond that glass. It was then that I noticed the others. I'd been so entranced with Maria and Katya that I had not perceived them before. It was as though I were seated at their very tables, for I heard all that they said.

"Is she telling the truth, Doc?" Hopkins asked, the contemptuous grin still plastered across his mouth, his suit as disheveled and unkempt as when he had visited the apartment. "You know, in my opinion, she looks shaky. Kinda like the sort of person I see on a regular basis in my line of work. Now, the other gal—she looks very classy. Someone, my instincts tell me, to put your money on."

"Well, I do believe this is more up your alley than mine," Slaus answered, not bothering to look at Hopkins. He continued to study the subjects at the adjoining table, occasionally shifting his attention to the small notebook in his hand whenever he felt the need to write something. "What I suspect, though, is that neither is a pathological liar—a condition which is often a symptom of some greater, more complex, and deeper psychological flaw than either of these two women, in my professional opinion, possesses."

Completing his analysis, Slaus looked at Hopkins. "Mind you now, I'm not implying that one or the other isn't telling the truth. It's more that I believe, in this case, you would be the more qualified to judge."

As soon as Slaus finished, Richard Carlson, dressed as another French waiter, arrived at their table. Hopkins addressed him first. "What hot tips do you have today, Whiterock?" he asked, referring to Carlson by his middle name, which only his closest confidants knew.

"Great Air," Carlson whispered, flicking the luncheon crumbs off the red-checkered tablecloth. "Their stock is guaranteed to quadruple in the next thirty days and go through the fuckin' roof. It's not too late, my boys, to get in on the action if you move with dispatch and act while it's still a steal!"

"Put me in for a thousand shares," Slaus ordered. He didn't care in the least what the price was. He signed a check that had mysteriously appeared on the table and handed it to Carlson.

"Too rich for my blood," Hopkins said. He shook his head and watched Carlson pocket the binder and slither away to another table.

I desperately wanted to return my attention to Maria and Katya, but I couldn't, as someone, or something, was restraining me. Instead it was Sean Casey's roaring baritone I heard next.

"Don't stop here, you pompous suit," Casey advised the waiter, recognizing who it was. "There's no room for your sordid ilk at my table." His words had the effect he desired, because Carlson vanished into thin air before everyone's eyes.

It was then I became aware of Cindy. She was dressed in some cheap 1940s or '50s French streetwalker's costume. She had perfected the look, including the garish, exaggerated Barbie-doll face that came from too much pancake makeup and too heavily rouged cheeks. She wore a tight angora sweater and figure-hugging skirt, complete with thigh-high slit and black fishnet stockings. She even wore a slanted black beret. She was perched on Casey's corpulent lap, a cigarette dangling from her red lips; her fingers tickled the bullet hole in the center of his forehead.

"Well done, Shamus, mon cher," she complimented him, the mixture of Irish and French accents adding to her grotesqueness. "Here now, laddie, somebody should have done that to him sooner, if you ask me."

"Forget about that prick," Casey boomed. "His time is long past. The much more pressing question in my mind, honey buns, is which of these two fair lassies is telling the truth?"

Cindy whispered into Casey's ear, and with a conspicuous leer on her face, she slid off his lap. He rose, and they walked away arm in arm and began to fade from sight. "Even though she's got a snippy way about her," I heard Cindy's voice say, their images now barely visible, "she's got my vote. I never did care for her Ladyship Mrs. Douglas. Her nose was always too high in the air for her own good, if you ask me. Always gave me the feeling she thought she was too high falootin' for us peons."

"You want me to believe what you just told me?" Katya asked, her voice freeing the spell I was under and enabling me to return to their table. "You must take me for a complete and utter fool!"

Her open hostility caught Maria by surprise.

"Listen, Katya—or Mrs. Douglas—it doesn't matter to me what your name is, okay? Or even that he's married to you and not me. You must believe me. I swear I'm telling the truth. I didn't want to … I didn't wish to come back," Maria pleaded, leaning across the table and, for the briefest of moments, placing her hand over Katya's in an unexpected show of affection. "You must understand I had no choice and was ordered to do so."

Katya, furious at what she was hearing, jerked her hand away, rose, and, losing all control, began to scream, "Garçon, garçon, attendez-moi, toute de suite, toute de suite." I saw her eyes beginning to tear. Maria's were too, I realized.

"I advised you, if you recall, that she should never have married that draft dodger," an unfamiliar voice asserted. "She should have married Milovan as originally planned. He was a warrior, a true leader of men."

Though I tried to resist, my effort was fruitless; my attention was dragged to the table where the voice had come from.

I recognized two of the men. Tony was wearing the same aviator flight suit that he wore in the photograph his mother displayed so proudly in her living room, along with black sunglasses that protected his eyes from the crowd, as they once had from the sun. Sitting beside him, his head bowed, immersed in the stacks of paper spread about their table, was Katya's father, Dr. Tkarr.

"Yes, Josip," Dr. Tkarr said. He didn't lift his head but nodded his agreement as he studied his papers. As soon as he spoke the third man's name, I knew that the other person was Tkarr's old friend and mentor, Josip Broz, or Marshall Tito.

"That certainly may be true. But my daughter, as you know, has more British blood in her veins than Croatian. And when one takes into account the blue Hapsburg blood which runs in them, it leaves no more than an eighth that Milovan would have believed pure enough for his comfort."

"Who cares anymore in this day and age about blood lines? She should have married him anyway," Tony interrupted sharply, siding with Tito. "Then Christof would have been free to marry my sister. Although, to this day, I can't understand for the life of me why he disappeared and deserted Maria at a time when she so desperately needed him."

Dr. Tkarr looked up from his papers at his daughter and her companion.

"No!" Tony shouted. "Don't pay any attention—never pay attention to what you just heard. She's lying! Hell would freeze before she would have forgotten her beloved Christof."

Tony became almost incoherent in his fury as he continued to shout. "And me? What about me?" He recounted his own twisted interpretation of our past. "You would think that my boyhood friend—I introduced him to my sister, the girl who was destined to become his wife—would have come to my aid, to my rescue … I was in such pain—such great pain!"

Tito tried to say something, words meant to calm him, but Tony wouldn't listen.

"The two of you know from your own personal experience what I'm talking about," he cried, his head nervously snapping from one to the other. "They put each of you in prison and tortured you the same as me. Except, for me, it was for four insufferable months before they finally had the decency to let me die."

As soon as he mentioned his own death, he collapsed in a sobbing heap onto the cobblestone ground, his glasses falling from his face to reveal two sunken and vacant dark holes where his eyes had been.

As Dr. Tkarr and Tito sprang from their chairs to aid their stricken companion, the icy Brahmin accent of Billy Paulson resounded across the courtyard. "Leave him. Leave him where he lies," he warned them. "He knew what kind of deal he was getting into when he signed on."

"And if he didn't know?" another familiar voice rang out. "To quote a famous friend of mine," Magritte said, appearing alongside Paulson, "c'est la vie. C'est la vie, mes amis."

Before either said anymore, the heart-wrenching sounds of Maria crying compelled me yet again to look in her direction.

She was on her knees sobbing, her hands tugging on Katya's

wrists in the hopes that those actions would somehow prevent Katya from abandoning her. "Katya, I beg of you." I saw the words form on her lips. "Don't leave us now. Please believe me. We both need you to remain with him forever."

"Leave him, Katya," Paulson said.

"Yeah, leave the stupid Chat, ma cherie," Magritte rasped.

Shaking her head, Maria shouted, "No! No!" when she recognized who the men approaching them were. "Katya, these are the men who killed me! Can't you understand what I'm telling you? It was only after they murdered me that I was forced to return. Don't you see? They're the ones who murdered me!" Her voice became shriller with each repetition of her accusations.

"Kill her, Magritte," Paulson coldly ordered. "Kill her again, but this time, make damn certain it's permanent."

I lost track of how often my feet landed on the cobblestones outside the café. But what did that count matter anyway? I would always find myself seated back in the café window, soaked in perspiration and unable to do anything to alter the macabre spectacle confronting me.

Katya began to back away, pulling herself free from Maria's grasp. Magritte obeyed Paulson's command and moved toward the two women. I yelled for him to stop; my fists beat upon the window. I picked up a chair and did the same. It was useless. There was nothing I could do to save them.

I was helpless.

It was then, when I felt this total and complete sense of powerlessness, that I beheld the strange young woman. Somehow I also understood that she had been there from the beginning, hovering at each of the tables, her ethereal presence undetected and unseen, which had enabled me to hear all that had been spoken.

Everyone must have sensed her presence, for all voices and movements halted. Magritte, Paulson, and even Katya, who ceased her frightened retreat, were still as the woman glided over the stone courtyard and approached them. At first I thought she wore a mask, so distinct was the contrast between the whiteness of her skin and the black strip that covered her eyes. But as she drew nearer, I realized that she had no mask. It was only the markings of her skin. Oddly, despite her look and the mysterious aura she conveyed, I was not afraid of her.

"You were drawn to me," Parcae whispered in my ear.

When she reached the place where Maria was kneeling, she stopped and peered knowingly into my eyes. I watched her mouth form my name, feeling the intensity of her words without hearing them.

"You are mine, Christof. Both Maria and Katya are wrong. For I am their fate. I am your fate. I have always been your fate."

Whether we stared at each other for only a few seconds or for a few hours, I could not know. Eventually, everyone else began to disappear. The last thing I heard was the sound of Katya's sobbing voice as I finally learned her third wish.

Katya wept mournfully, her image fading as she spoke, her words burning my very soul. "I wished that day in Paris, Christof," she gently said as she looked into my eyes, "that Maria would never come back. I wished and wished and wished that she would forever remain buried in your deepest memories, never to appear again. For I feared, my dear, sweet Christof, with all my heart and soul, this would come to be if she returned."

The dream was over, but it was to be as Parcae foretold.

*****

The warm Paris air had turned cold. Thoughts of the bizarre nightmare that had filled my sleeping hours on the previous day's flight sent shivers through my psyche. I was sitting on a bench in the Jardin du Luxembourg, and it was late the next afternoon. Slaus must see a lot of crazies if he could write a check, price unseen, and hand it to a stock-hustling waiter who looked like Carlson. I tried to make light of some of the dream's absurdity but couldn't. And as much as I wanted to forget it, the vision replayed itself over and over in my mind. Why wasn't Beth in it? Or Spire? And who was the mysterious woman who appeared right before I awoke?

"Wish fulfillment." Slaus counseled Katya and I when we started going for therapy after Beth was murdered. "Symbolically those dreams which the two of you are sharing nightly represent how you want your life to be," he explained patiently, even though he knew we knew exactly what they were.

That last recollection, although accurately and succinctly summing up my condition, given the instability of my overall state, was too great a dose of reality. "Enough already! Let's get on with it!" I barked, and I leaped up from the bench and, once again the prince of perpetual action, raced toward Magritte's loft.

There was one positive thing about that dream, though. It served as a sort of catalyst, somehow helping to restore whatever vestiges might have remained of my sanity. It was either that nightmarish fantasy that had reawakened my sanity, or the cold, chilling realization that I had indeed killed Spire. Regardless, my battle for restoration was a losing battle.

"Damn it." I twitched as I visualized Spire dying in his own blood. "What the hell does it matter which? The fact that the loon was exorcised was the good news."

'Forget about the loon,' a voice like the loon's said. 'Why the hell are you always concerned about him? He was never anything but a whimpering piece of second-guessing gray flannel. It's the other guy you should be concerned with. The magician was always your enemy.'

After clearing customs at Orly Sunday afternoon, I had made a beeline for his place. When he wasn't there, I had returned an hour later. Then a third time in the early evening. I wasn't certain what I would do if I did happen to catch him there. I had temporarily shelved my original plan to strangle his scrawny neck, about the time I murdered Spire, but there was something he owed me: the truth.

All three times I rang the bell marked A&M. Each time I battered the door with my fists and, when that failed, stepped into the narrow street to shout at his second-floor window to let Le Chat in. It was all for naught. The only responses I received were the stares of occasional passersby, no doubt wondering about this character who kept shouting, "Le Chat est ici. Monsieur Delacroix, Le Chat est ici."

Those three exercises are now part of yesterday, I kept reminding myself as I sped down Boulevard Saint-Germain toward my destination. Today is another day. And with the new day, I hoped to have another twenty-four hours of freedom to find my nemesis. In reality, though, I knew it was not just another day. It was Monday. And Monday meant the unauthorized computer access would be discovered at DFT. It probably also meant that if someone hadn't come across Spire's body by then, or if he hadn't been missed by whomever might miss a sleeze ball like him, his absence from his office would be a signal for someone to track him down. So, in my now somewhat lucid state of mind, it meant today was probably the last day to find the magician.

Well, today might have been another day, but the results were the same. Just as the overseas operator had said, Magritte was gone; he had disappeared from sight, as I had feared.

"He took everything with him when he left, monsieur. Like a thief in the night—files, cabinets, papers. Whatever wasn't nailed down, he took," the man who lived on the first floor of Magritte's building said in English. "He didn't pay me the three months' back rent either. One moment he was here in his apartment, and the next—poof—he vanished into thin air. If you find him, tell me, so I can collect what the little merde owes me."

So that was that. The only other thing I could think of was to fly to London to see if I could track him down using the original telephone number Maria had given me when this whole damn horror had begun. And if Oliver hadn't told me that Katya had left London for the Continent, I might have gone. But I had already tried that number a half dozen times, always hanging up in frustration when a recording of neither Maria's nor Magritte's voice would come on and tell me to leave a message. Going to London to try to track the number would have been as crazy as directly calling Hopkins. If the loon were still in control, I might have gone anyway, but as he wasn't, I retraced my steps back to Hôtel Sainte-Beuve to rethink my options.

I did make one stop at a kiosk where I purchased every French, English, and American newspaper to see if there was any mention of Spire's murder in them. I was hoping that nothing had been reported just yet. Certainly I wasn't expecting anything in the French dailies, but since my sanity had somewhat returned, it was cautioning me to be aware and alert.

No doubt some of my common sense had also returned, because if the incident that followed had occurred a day earlier, my reaction would have been different.

It happened at the corner of Rue du Four and Rue Bonaparte after I bought the newspapers. As I waited for the light to change, my eyes searched the crowd for anything or anyone that looked suspicious or recognizable, and I found someone.

She was walking at a lively pace, her shoulder-length, strawberry-blonde hair blowing ever so lightly in the gentle summer breeze. She was weaving her way through the heavy sidewalk traffic on the other side of Rue du Four, perhaps twenty yards from where I stood. Instinctively, I started to call out her name, but I was able to restrain myself. Yesterday, unquestionably, I would have shouted at her, that restraint nonexistent. Yesterday I would have run after her as well, calling out her name until she turned to face me to prove it was or wasn't her.

But that was yesterday.

I watched her from afar, the traffic light changing and then rechanging as she continued to thread her way through the crowd. The twenty yards between us quickly became thirty and then forty, her blonde head becoming difficult to spot. And then, just like that, she was gone. She had vanished from my sight, leaving me fascinated with the thought that someone else on earth could look so much like her.

Even though Oliver had said she had gone to the Continent, which meant she could be somewhere nearby, I knew that wasn't her. No, that woman might have reminded me of her, especially the way her hair fell about her face and the manner in which she carried herself. But that woman was too old to be Katya. She was much, much too old, I concluded, nodding my head as I began to cross the avenue. Maybe an older, long-lost sister, but she was definitely not my Katya.

When I returned to my room, I called London again. There was no other option. I could regroup and rethink whatever I wanted to think about till the cows came home; this was my best chance of locating Magritte. Perhaps I could stop off at Katya's sister's place when I got there, I thought, doing my best to maintain a positive attitude in spite of the telephone continuing to ring unanswered. Maybe the real Katya might even be there when I did, I allowed myself to fantasize.

"Okay, let's fall back to plan B," I muttered, the fantasy fading when I hung up after twenty unanswered rings.

Plan B was a plan I'd attempted before—trying to wheedle out of the operator an address or name associated with the unlisted number I was dialing. I'd always met the same fate when using that tactic to obtain Maria's address here in Paris. But I never did find out if plan B would have worked this time.

'Forget about plan B. It's nonsense. Check the newspapers,' a voice remarkably like the loon unexpectedly warned. 'Check them now, and try to determine how long you have before someone with a badge and gun comes knocking at your hotel door. Or, worse, someone without a badge.'

I was disappointed that he had resurfaced and wanted to argue with him out of a natural, self-protective resentment for having forgotten about the newspapers. But I dropped all thoughts of plan B for the moment and heeded his advice because, for once, his plan made more sense. I almost made one other phone call, though.

I had debated many times recently the pros and cons of speaking with Billy Paulson. I must have thought about picking up the phone and speaking with him a hundred times that past week, but for some inexplicable reason, I never did. Once I came close, hearing his voice on the other end of the line when his secretary was away from her desk and he answered. I guess I was not as prepared to talk with him as I'd thought, because as soon as I heard that distinct New England accent of his, I panicked and hung up.

And to what did I owe this reluctance? Why shouldn't I have spoken with him? Confided in him? After all, he was my oldest and dearest friend, someone to whom I owed my life. Was this reluctance nothing more than a desire to not get him involved? Or, at the very least, involved any further than he was already?

When you told him that afternoon at Le Bernardin about Katya and you, about Maria, you had a funny feeling—a weird feeling. One that kept telling you, 'Don't,' each time you reached for the telephone to take him any further into your confidence. So, once again, you listened to that feeling and didn't.

The *New York Times* was where I stumbled across the article. I almost missed it because I was so preoccupied with ferreting out any information pertaining to my own murderous activities. It was buried on some back page, and I did a double-take when I saw the headline: "DFT Denies Illegal Munitions Allegations."

"What the hell? What the hell?" I could only repeat that phrase, incredulous at what I was reading, as I leaped randomly from one sentence to the next.

Reading on, it slowly dawned on me what this was about. As I realized what had happened, what mistake had been made, I began to snicker. And then I began to laugh, the laughter rising in intensity and becoming hysterical in wild abandonment the further I read. It was as though the loon had returned, this time welcomed with open arms as it resumed its residence within my being, its laughter intermingling insanely with my own.

'The mistake was theirs, not yours,' the loon finally interjected, timing his interruption for the moment I had to pause and come up for air from my hysterical outburst. 'Don't you think those idiots who released this information, believing it to be factual, made a fatal blunder much greater than yours?' it asked, catching my attention with the astuteness of its statement.

'Here, dummy. Now that I have your undivided concentration and you appear to be calmer, let me spell it out for you. To begin with, we all know that the names the *Times* printed of the so-called bogus companies that DFT created to cover up their illegal arms and chemical sales were completely in error—Neiman Marcus, Bloomingdale's, Saks, Dress Barn. Those outfits can be accused of an enormity of things, but munitions dealings is not one of them. The two of us do know, however, that the balance of what was printed was essentially right on the money. The allegations that DFT has violated numerous international arms and chemical embargo sanctions, selling confidential military data to Vietnam, Libya, Iraq, and Syria, to cite some of their prominent business outlets, will have to be addressed now that they have been raised in the light of day.'

I babbled something about it not being my fault that Magritte and

Igor hadn't realized I'd given them the Retail and Apparel diskettes in error, that somehow what I'd believed I was keeping—a duplicate set of both Space and Technology and the Retail sector—was instead a combination of each, and that somehow Gerry Souk had mislabeled them before he had even turned them over to me.

The loon was surprisingly quiet and not at all what I recalled him to be as he listened patiently to my explanation and excuse.

When I had finished, he asked, 'Are you finished?' but since each of us was generally capable of anticipating the other's next move, he didn't wait for any response and continued with his prediction of what all this meant.

'That's all very well and fine—wrong diskettes, idiot Soviet KGB agents confusing the Gap with a purveyor of smart bombs, incompetent assistants, all the usual excuses, yada, yada, yada. The bottom line, my dear Christof, is that you have two very pissed off organizations, and you are number one on their shit lists. Oops, sorry for mixing my scatological metaphors. Whatever, I think you understand my meaning. And if that's not enough of a challenge to test your staying power, you have also failed miserably to accomplish your main objective.'

"What do you mean failed?" I shouted defensively. "We killed Spire, didn't we? Maybe there's still time to get the magician. In a couple of hours I can be in London, and then we'll see who has failed."

'Remember what Magritte warned you against, Christof,' the loon answered, his tone professorial in its calmness. 'Remember, he said, that without the proper data, the Santa Clauses may yet be able to reverse all this to their advantage. In the long run, no matter what has been reported in that paper, DFT and Carlson may go on with business as usual. Maybe even with more power and a greater, wider arms network than exists today. And if that happens, my good friend, Maria's murder will all be for naught.'

I started to object, but he wouldn't let me.

'But that issue is of secondary importance. Because, my sweet Christof, in addition to the United States authorities after you for Spire's murder, and the FBI or CIA hunting you down for whatever federal security violations they'll come up with, I would be most concerned with the other organization. The one you referred to a few minutes ago as idiots. Or was I the one who said that? No matter. The point I'm making is that you might as well forget about London. There is no need to go there in search of Magritte. Why, I'm quite certain, Christof, he'll save you the trouble by coming here for you.'

Chapter 26

"WAKE UP, YOU STUPID bastard," Magritte yelled, spilling a pail of cold water over my head. He didn't allow a moment for its chilling effect to accomplish its work, slapping me hard across the face with his hand. "Come on. Respondez-moi maintenant. Get up!"

I had involuntarily snapped my head erect when the water hit, so his action nearly had the reverse consequence he'd intended and practically rendered me unconscious again. Grabbing me roughly by the chin, he jolted my system a third time as he squeezed my face in such a way I was forced to suffer the garlic upon his breath.

"Where are the diskettes, smart guy? Eh? Answer me, you worthless merde."

Regaining my senses, I began to understand that in spite of my assailant greeting me with unfamiliar code words, I was not mistaken; it was the magician speaking. My eyes blinked, adjusting and refocusing as they strained to dissolve the blurriness before them. Locating my tongue for a response was easier. It felt parched and swollen, and it somehow poked its way into a spot that a few of my front teeth had once occupied.

"Diskettes? What diskettes?" I mumbled innocently, my sight sufficiently restored to recognize Magritte staring down at me. The answer I gave was a sincere one. If anything, it was his fault that my brain needed some time before it caught up with the other members of my body and began processing his arcane question.

Unfortunately, Magritte believed otherwise.

"Son-of-a-bitch wiseass," he cursed, leaping off his chair. I could sense from the corners of my eyes something resembling a fist cocked in position, ready to descend in my general vicinity.

Instinctively I shut my eyes, waiting for the blow to land. Any doubts I had that this was Magritte were now gone. There was no one else who would first call me stupid and then, only a couple of seconds later, call me both a smart and wise guy.

I waited, terrified, recoiling backward to the extent the constraints binding my body would permit. Before he struck again, however, my brain finally decided it had a responsibility to join this party and inform me how I came to find myself in this predicament.

It couldn't have been more than five minutes from the moment the loon had so perceptively advised that Magritte would save me the wear and tear of searching for him when there was a knock on the door. After being assured by the recognizable voice of the manager that it was most certainly he, I cautiously opened the door and ... Well, that was it. There wasn't anything else to remember.

"Enough," a man's voice ordered.

I jumped in my chair as though Magritte had in fact disobeyed that command and smashed his fist into my face.

"That's enough, Eugené," the man repeated. "Even you can see he doesn't have his wits about him. If you continue with this tactic, we won't have any way of determining whether or not he ever did possess the information we seek."

Eugené? Reopening my eyes, I saw the outline of a second man hovering near the person I swore was Magritte. "Good God," I shouted when I raised my head and saw his face. What is Julio Iglesias doing here? It can't really be him. It must be the beating I've taken. I blinked my eyes in amazement at the personification of what had to be a perfect hallucination. If my hands had been free, I would have rubbed my eyes, wiping the moisture and cobwebs from them, attempting to erase this illusion of Iglesias standing there.

"What do mean 'enough'?" Eugené or Magritte asked, clearly annoyed at being given that order. "I just started to have fun with this chatte."

Julio ignored both his irate comments and the deliberate mispronunciation of my code name. He leaned over and stared at me in careful examination. "So this is the son-in-law of Tito's former comrade, the infamous ex-Communist, Dr. Tkarr," he said, continuing to inspect the face he grasped in his smooth hand.

The guy might have looked like Julio Iglesias, but I'd be damned if he sounded like him. Further contributing to my confusion was that I couldn't recall Katya's father ever mentioning that he was a member of Julio's fan club. Even in my foggy, unstable mental condition, I began to understand that Julio might have known Katya's father from someplace else.

For a second, I thought about asking him to break out into the song of his choice and settle who he was once and for all, but a little voice warned me it might not be such a prudent idea.

'Remember how Magritte', the voice said, 'reacted when you pleaded ignorance to his question of where the diskettes were? Now is the time to keep those ideas or answers to yourself.'

Before I had an opportunity to debate the issue, Magritte interrupted. "Vladimir, please? We don't have all—"

Julio moved so quickly Magritte didn't complete his sentence. "I told you never to speak my name when there was company present." His fingers' tight grip on the magician's windpipe caused him to gasp for air. "Must I forever teach you the proper etiquette, dummkopf?"

My desire to perform the identical procedure on Magritte flickered through my mind and nearly elicited a bravo for the man who looked like Julio but was called Vladimir, when everything suddenly came back to me. Everything. All the pain and torment I felt hit at once. I was spared nothing—from Maria to Katya, from Casey to Spire, to why they wanted the diskettes and why I was here. I even realized who the man strangling Magritte was. As bad as it had seemed when I didn't know what this was about, I now knew it was infinitely worse.

I now knew they would kill me.

As though in confirmation, Magritte sputtered, "I swear. I'll never do it again. I'm sorry … Stop … Enough already; you're chok … ing me to death. And … anyway, he's not leaving here."

"That's not the point, Eugené," Vladimir answered, releasing the grip on his repentant associate's neck. "If you make that mistake now, you will most probably make it in some more, how shall we say …" He paused to re-straighten Magritte's shirt collar in a rough, exaggerated way and then said, "Much more delicate situation."

"What should he call you then? Igor?" I was unable to remain quiet any longer. The words tumbled from my lips before I could prevent them.

I saw a smile spread across Vladimir's handsome features—the same sort of smile that had caused me to mistake him for Julio Iglesias—when he turned his head in my direction.

"Igor? Very, very good, Mr. Christof Douglas." The smile changed to a smirk. "Very good. Yes … yes, Igor will do just fine for now."

"Where are those fuckin' diskettes?" Magritte screamed hoarsely, magically reappearing by my side and elbowing his way back into the act now that he believed he was in Igor's good graces. "What do you take us for? Eh? Sending us those ridiculous diskettes and pretending they contained the information we needed. Do you have any idea who it is you're fooling with, you trou de balle?" Repeating "asshole" in English, he made certain I understood his attitude when it came to our relationship.

Unfortunately, I knew only too well with whom I was fooling. The memory of a story I'd told Katya soon after we met came to mind. It was a time in the early sixties. I was still a teenager, and my family, Maria, and I were on the beach at the Jersey Shore when my father spotted off on the horizon a huge, transoceanic balloon drifting in our direction. It was far enough away that we couldn't quite make out the people in it, but whoever they were, they began to wave.

Maria—I never did mention to Katya that Maria was there—and I started to wave back. My father, though, as soon as he saw us do that, pulled my arm down and said in an urgent voice, "Christof, Maria, let's get off this beach right now!" Maria and I looked at each other in surprise. Confused, I started to protest. My dad cut me off. "There's no time to discuss this. Let's go; they're KGB agents."

My dad was not prone to non-sensible, irrational statements. Normally he was exactly the opposite sort of person. But at that moment, Maria and I did all we could to keep from bursting into wild laughter at what he'd just said as we reluctantly left the beach.

After telling what I believed to be a hilarious incident, one that I said reflected a combination of my father's own anti-Communist paranoia as well as the country's, I laughed and said to Katya, "Can you imagine anything more ludicrous than that? Of all things, KGB agents in a balloon at the New Jersey Shore?"

Katya listened the entire time I told the story to her, nestled comfortably on the sofa, in my arms. When I finished, she pushed herself upright, and I could see her eyebrows furrow and her head tilt in that funny, quizzical way of hers. Surprising me, she said, "But, Christof, you should always listen to your father. He was right that day. They were KGB agents."

"What's the matter with you? Answer me! Answer me!" Magritte raised his arm over his head. Apparently, he had either forgotten or was about to ignore Igor's command and resume his sadistic game with me.

Before I could find out whether he was bluffing, I heard the bang of a door slamming, followed by a heavily accented woman's voice in English. "Here is the item which you have requested, my colonel."

If Igor were concerned about the use of that rank in my presence, he didn't evidence it. Maybe he was even frightened of the large, brutish woman. A real Igoress if there ever was one, I thought when I saw her massive body dwarf her refined and slender leader. My initial reaction was an involuntary utterance of "What the hell?" as soon as I spied the threatening medical syringe she held in her hand.

Carefully, almost delicately, the man I now thought of as Colonel Igor reached for the syringe and said something that sounded Russian to the Igoress. He turned to address both Magritte and me. "This simple but highly sophisticated instrument will be far more effective with our Mr. Christof Douglas, Eugené, than your barbaric efforts will ever hope to be."

He stepped quickly toward me. His two associates moved equally as fast to my side, further supplementing the existing bindings, and the powerful Amazon, in one motion, ripped apart my shirt, exposing the flesh. "This won't hurt a bit," Colonel Igor lied, and he drove the needle deep into the fleshy part of my shoulder.

For a few minutes, or a few seconds, afterward, however long as I was able to maintain some level of consciousness, I struggled against the hands that restrained me and the drowsy, relaxing sensation spreading through my being. I believed my eyes were more aware of what was happening than my mind when I heard the colonel's soft voice. "Christof, can you hear me? If you can, please respond by answering yes."

"Yes," I replied without the slightest compunction, my eyes narrowing the moment I saw the face of my interrogator.

"Christof," he asked, his own eyes peering into mine, "do you know where you are?"

"Yes."

"Where is that? Where are you?"

"In some KGB building."

The colonel lowered his head. I thought I heard Magritte whisper something, followed by a loud "Shhh" from Colonel Igor. Then Igor raised his eyes to meet mine again.

"Do you know who I am, Christof?" the colonel said, resuming his questioning in the same smooth tone.

"Yes. Why, you're the man in the balloon."

"I told you, Vlad—" Magritte stammered, catching his mistake in midsentence. "This guy is nuts! Let me have one more go at him, and I guarantee you, I'll show him who the man in the balloon is. If he prefers, I'll even show him the fuckin' man in the moon."

"Eugené, enough with your nonsense already."

My head was pounding; the combination of whatever narcotic was in my system, the beating I had absorbed, and the tension that was transferred from the people hovering about me was lethal in its effect. I closed my eyes, wishing that the drowsiness I felt would mercifully turn to sleep, or at least make the faces and voices disappear.

"Christof, where are the diskettes? It is very important for you to tell us where they are. They will help you find what you are looking for."

The soothing, calming tone of the colonel's voice first subtly intermingled and then, after gaining that initial, precious foothold, more aggressively superimposed itself and replaced those sorrows he knew lived within. Those dark sorrows ... within.

Forcing my eyes open, with images of wildflowers, tall, reedy grasses, and rolling fields of open meadows fixed nostalgically in my mind's eye, I listened to my voice respond dreamily, "Under the oak tree."

For what was a relished, interminable period, there were no further questions. My eyes were allowed to reclose and revisit those tranquil, inviting visions of the bucolic countryside.

Sometime later, whenever it was that the interrogation renewed, there was a marked difference in the manner the questions were posed. It soon became evident, even to someone in such a stupor-like state as the one I was in, that time was running out and Magritte had convinced the colonel that his method was not working.

"Christof, listen to me," the colonel ordered. The sudden harshness of his voice shattered my trance and caused my eyes to snap open. Gone was any semblance of Julio Iglesias's smoothness. "Are you telling me that the diskettes are buried under some oak tree?"

"Yes."

"Where?"

"In a park ... or in a cemetery? I'm not sure which."

"Think! Where did you bury those diskettes?" He said this so loudly, his face so near mine, that the words were almost deafening, and more confusing than helpful. Instead of the answer he wanted, one that I knew I should have known, I could only repeat, "Under the oak tree. I buried them under the oak tree."

"Forget this pseudoscience of yours, Vladimir," Magritte interrupted. Surprisingly, in spite of his disregard for the earlier warning to not use Igor's real name, the magician sounded under control.

"This nut cake has made fools of us once already," he said. "If those diskettes aren't in our possession soon, and we are unable to expose the double-dealing that the Americans are engaged in, our comrades will be doing to us what I believe we should do to this idiot." There must have been some truth to what he said, because no one offered a different opinion.

I also noticed his customary cigarette now dangling from his lips. Ignoring me as though I weren't there, and seemingly emboldened by the implied agreement the silence brought, he continued with his version of argument and alibi.

"Even though we only had a few days before DFT would have discovered that their security system had been compromised, causing them to embark on an urgent damage-control campaign, we should have waited. We should have waited even if it meant that our information might have been counterbalanced by such an effort. If we had been more thorough, if we had checked our data more carefully, we wouldn't have been in this no-win race against our comrades right now."

The colonel started to reply in Russian and then quickly excused himself. "Pardonnez moi, Eugene," he said sarcastically. "I forget sometimes that you can't speak Russian." The hollowness of his tone lacked both the smoothness of Julio and the harshness of Igor. "We were thorough, Eugené. As you just stated, we didn't have much time. The diskette we printed and reviewed was correct. It did have the names of the shell companies that they used when they created their false audit trail. The information is not completely worthless," he asserted, attempting to rationalize their situation.

Magritte made no effort to conceal his sarcasm. "Ce sont des conneries! Oh, pardon moi, Vladimir, sometimes I forget you don't speak French that well. Therefore, for your benefit, allow me to make it plain to you in English what I think." He paused to blow some smoke in my face and then added in the following breath, "That's a load of shit."

Even in my sorry state, I was shocked at what I heard. A few minutes ago, Magritte would not have had the nerve to speak in such a manner to the man standing opposite him. I saw Vladimir lift his arm. At first I thought he did so in anger, but then I realized it was to restrain the Igoress from coming to his defense. "Please, Eugené," he said, surprising me by his calmness as the woman halted menacingly by his side, "please do continue."

Magritte didn't need any coaxing. Apparently, in his mind, this was now the disastrous conclusion, the final leg of a much-too-dangerous journey. A journey that began the second he'd decided there was a great deal of money to be made—more money than what the freelance photography and journalism professions were paying Maria and him—and allowed himself to be recruited and compromised by the man he was now insulting. He also seemed to have realized—unfortunately for him, too late—that he wasn't made for it. So when he began to speak, his voice reflecting whatever self-control he still possessed, the urgency and recklessness of his words only betrayed him.

"Hear me out, Vladimir. Forget the diskettes. They won't be of any use one way or the other. We are already dead men."

Whether the drug in my system had worn off or the cumulative effects of the tension in the room had served as some sort of antitoxin, the incongruity of a wide, blossoming smile appearing on his face when he made that statement was not lost on me. Neither were his words that followed.

"Kill this fool, and let's get out of here. Kill him just like we did that sentimental girlfriend of his when she got us into this whole damn mess. If you had listened to me when I told you that she would double-cross us the moment she found out that he was part of that company, we wouldn't be in this situation."

Those were the last words Magritte ever spoke. I guess even colonels didn't like to be made sport of when it came to how well they did their jobs, never mind being verbally abused the way he had been. The next thing I knew, without any warning, without any further discussion, he shot the magician as soon as he finished speaking. He didn't shoot him once or twice, the way I recalled shooting Spire; he shot him over and over. When he finished shooting him, the Igoress handed him another pistol, and he shot him some more.

"Poor Eugené," Vladimir said when he either was tired of shooting him or had run out of bullets. "He always seemed so unsure of his behavior whenever it came to proper business etiquette. That last bourgeois utterance by him was so typical." He shook his head in mock disgust at the crumpled body lying on the floor. He turned to me and said wearily, "Oh well. C'est la vie."

The colonel pulled up a chair and sat down, facing me less than a foot away. The large woman stood motionless next to him. "You know," he began, invoking once again the unmistakable voice of Julio Iglesias, "in spite of what I just did, Eugené did have a point, Mr. Douglas."

When I didn't answer, he breathed an almost bored, tired sigh and leaned his body nearer. He took out a small flashlight from his jacket and lifted my chin with one hand; he flicked the light back and forth from one eye to the other. When he had completed this little exercise, his diagnosis apparently satisfied, he politely announced, "Come, come now, Mr. Douglas. It appears the effects of the Sodium Pentothal have worn off. No need to look so confused, so upset. The dose Sabrina gave you was only good for an hour or so." Checking his watch while I blinked my eyes at Sabrina, he said, "That was almost two hours ago."

Two hours? What did I tell them? What did they ask me?

Seeing the puzzled look on my face, he misunderstood what I was thinking and volunteered to clarify his previous statement.

"No, no, not about that former associate of his, that girl ..." He hesitated, either having second thoughts about this open conversational style of his or, more likely, having forgotten her name.

"Anyway," the colonel continued after an awkward pause, apparently deciding that there was no harm at this stage of the game in discussing this subject, "as usual, Eugené misrepresented the facts. It was his idea to let her go off and investigate your company to expose your government's selling biological weapons and arms to our allies. It was not mine. Let the record state that I was opposed to it. Especially as I knew that she would find out Dr. Tkarr's son-in-law, her former fiancé, was associated with it."

"Why did you then?" I asked suddenly, surprising both of us by my boldness, not to mention removing any doubts he might still have had concerning my alertness.

"Ahh! The cat does have a tongue after all."

"Why did you?" I repeated, ignoring his play on words.

The colonel leaned back in his chair, his eyes fixed upon me, and muttered something in Russian to Sabrina. It brought a smirk to both.

"Why did I?" he asked rhetorically. "Okay, I'll tell you, but only because Sabrina just agreed that I could. But before I do, let me finish my original comment about Eugené. You know the point he was making about wanting to kill you? I believe his words were something about killing the fool and getting out." The colonel's smirk widened into a dazzling smile. "Well, my dear Mr. Douglas, we may still do what he requested unless you provide those diskettes."

I was afraid and in a great deal of pain—when my senses had returned, the throbbing pain from my beating had returned as well.

But what he had just told me was nothing more than what I had already come to expect. The moment my mind was clear enough to understand who these people were, I believed they were going to kill me sooner or later.

"A kopek for your thoughts."

I almost answered that I was wondering who the man in the balloon really was, but I caught myself, as there was no advantage in making it sooner rather later. Then again, what was the point? There was no Seventh Cavalry coming to my rescue.

"Her name was Maria, you know," I heard something that resembled my voice say. My breathing became more pronounced the second her name passed my lips. "Why did you let Maria do it then?"

"To borrow an apropos Western expression, have you ever found yourself between a rock and a hard place?" he offered sarcastically. "I had no choice, given the circumstances. You see, Sammantha was the best there was." He shook his head and said something in Russian to Sabrina. "Do you read the papers, Mr. Douglas? Have you been following what they report as happening in my country?"

"On occasion," I replied. Katya read everything she could when it came to that part of the world and kept me well apprised whether I was interested or not.

"Good. That's very good," he said, nodding. "Then, unlike the majority of your countrymen, you will better understand what it is we're discussing. Perhaps if I explain the seriousness of my own situation, you will have a greater appreciation for yours."

I sat as still as the pain would allow and waited for him to go on.

"It is just a matter of time before it will be over for us." His smile became noticeably forced as he pointed to himself and then to me to make his meaning clear. "For us as well as the Soviet Union. We can no longer compete. This escalation, this co-opting of our valued and long-standing customer base—North Vietnam, Iran, Libya, Angola, to name a few." He sounded like some chastened corporate CEO who had just been fired by his board of directors. "It has driven us into complete financial bankruptcy."

He motioned for Sabrina to come closer, and he whispered in her ear. "Do you understand what it is I'm referring to?" he said when he returned his attention to me. He didn't wait for an answer. "Do you mind if I address you as Christof?" he asked pleasantly, the smile again more natural. "Considering our circumstances, I believe we can drop this pretense of formality. Don't you?"

"That's fine with me, Igor."

The smile tightened, but Julio quickly reappeared. "So, to continue where I left off, we had to stop your country from stealing our customers. We would lose all control, all influence over them if we were to allow this business to go uncontested. As you can well imagine, being the astute businessman that you are, our customers would become extremely upset with us if they found out we were about to do such a thing. That was where Sammantha came in. Actually, that was where Eugené came in."

"Listen, Igor, since we're getting so cozy, first names and all, I'd appreciate it if you would refer to her as Maria. Okay?"

He shrugged. "Whatever makes you happy, Chris."

He leaned closer. He tapped me twice with an open palm across my cheek and went on with his story. "Once Eugené convinced me to let Maria be the one to expose this story, we both knew she was as good as dead. But if you ask Sabrina, or if Eugené could speak, they would confirm that I was never one for silly sentimentality, and so I thought, why not?"

The pain my body felt paled in comparison to the anguish raging through it. It was over. Igor was right. It was over for everyone. There was no longer any way I could contain my grief, and tears fell down my cheeks.

If he noticed my tears, he didn't comment. "If I'd had someone else, someone who was not associated with my organization, and someone half as good as her, I would have overruled that feckless opportunist." He turned his head to stare at Magritte's lifeless body. When he returned his gaze to me, his eyes had narrowed. "So I gambled—and lost." He added softly under his breath, "You lost."

Sabrina leaned over and whispered into Igor's ear. He said something in Russian, and she nodded and reassumed her menacing stance.

"Her objective, Chris," he went on, checking his watch quickly while shaking his head disappointedly, "was to expose what your country was doing, embarrass them in their high and mighty hypocrisy, and, at the same time, by doing so, return our customers to us."

For the next minute, he spoke in Russian, shaking his head. Sabrina nodded or shook her head, following her cue as dictated by whatever he was saying. "She would have succeeded, you know, Chris," he said, switching back to English. "She was the best at this sort of thing."

Apparently noticing my tears, he admonished me. "Come, come now. Get a grip on yourself. This maudlin display of yours will accomplish nothing, I can assure you. And, anyway, it was you, if I recall correctly, who wished to know why it was I let Sam—Maria go on this assignment. But who's keeping score at this point?"

"You let her go, you bastard, even though you knew she would be killed?" I would have plucked his heart from his chest if I could have, my hatred and pain so intense.

He leaned backward, too late to avoid the spray from my mouth, and calmly wiped the spittle from his chin. "No—well, yes, then again, I guess you might say," he answered, sounding like his deceased associate. "What I'm trying to tell you is that once she went on this operation, we would have killed her regardless of the outcome."

"Bastard," I spat, struggling against my straps and continuing to yell, damning his soul with every curse imaginable.

"You know, you are beginning to try my patience, Mr. Douglas," he warned. "The truth of the matter is, you should feel honored about this whole experience. There are not too many people I know— certainly there is no one that comes to mind in my profession—who gave up her own life rather than obey an order. Or disregard her own lifelong instincts and quit on an assignment, knowing that she would only face the same realization."

In spite of my attempts to scream over him, I heard his words but became only more confused.

"You still don't understand what I'm talking about, do you?" he inquired politely. "You see," he began, and he leaned closer, seemingly unconcerned with any further saliva spray, his voice assuming a conspiratorial tone, "I knew that once she found out about you, she would have severe reservations about going through with her assignment. That it would most likely end the way it has."

He nodded, and a smirk reappeared on his face when he saw my mouth drop open, the curses I'd been wildly shouting a moment before ceasing. "Oh yes, Christof. Unlike Eugené, who was driven by material wealth, especially these past few years, and who didn't understand any longer the power of love—or principle—I did my research and knew about Maria and about Dr. Tkarr's son-in-law." His smile broadened when he linked the two names. "I was certain that she would attempt to warn you or, at the very minimum, balk and create, how shall I say ... unnecessary complications." He checked his watch and turned to Sabrina. "Get the car now. It is time to leave," he ordered in English. She pivoted on her heel and disappeared.

"Oh, don't worry, Chris," the colonel interjected when he returned his gaze to me. "You're coming with us. We wouldn't be that rude and leave you like this. And, anyway, we have a couple of hours left to extract what we need from you. Now, where was I?"

"Why did you let them kill her? If you knew this was probably going to be the result, why did you let them, damn you?" I yelled as nightmarish images of Spire dead on the ground intermingled with those of Maria.

"Because I had no choice!" he yelled, dropping any semblance of Julio and startling me with his ferocity. "She was the best. And, as I already informed you, it was a calculated gamble."

He jumped from his seat, knocking it over. "I was gambling that she would obtain the necessary documents we needed before she found out about you."

For a long, eternal moment, the room was deadly still, and then he broke the silence and repeated his fatalistic remark. "I lost ... You lost ... We lost."

The room became eerily quiet. The man I thought of as Igor stared coldly into my face. I saw his head shake in what appeared to be complete, abject disbelief.

"Christof, Eugené told her she would be killed if she were to stop her investigation before she had what was needed. You know what she said to him? Huh? You know how she answered?"

Everything from that point on became total chaos. I heard

shouting, followed by the sound of gunfire. The room began to spin in front of my eyes.

But I could swear that before I lost consciousness, the colonel said, "She said she'd made a mistake once in her life when she was younger and she wouldn't make it again."

Epilogue

THE MONTHS LEADING UP to the winter of 1999 in Paris were bitter and brutal. I heard that wherever people went—in the cafés, on the boulevards, or even in the fancier hotels, such as the Plaza Athena—the only topic on people's minds was how cold Paris was that year. Every time people picked up a newspaper or turned on the television, they were told it would be the coldest winter in the past eighty years, or since the end of the Great War.

It didn't take for me long to arrive at that same conclusion. The moment I walked through the doors leaving Orly, the icy, bone-chilling winds that slammed into me got my attention . I was particularly susceptible to those harsh temperatures, as I had become accustomed in those past twelve years to tropical temperatures that rarely ever dipped below eighty degrees.

Luckily, I wouldn't be sampling the weather for too long. It would be later that afternoon when I would be shepherded back onto the special supersonic jet for the second leg of my journey. That was more than enough time. Except for one compelling reason to return, there was nothing else that remained here. Then again, that could also be said about the rest of my life.

The ride from the airport to Cimetiere de Passy was about thirty minutes, but it felt as though it took forever. As soon as I spotted the long black limousine waiting at the curb, it all rushed back to me. Everything, including the tragic remembrances of the man I once had been, resurfaced; the rest of the time those haunting memories stayed buried along with the forgotten identity, numbed by the growing madness within.

Why had I come back if it were that painful? Why did I even remember to do so, given my deteriorating and fading mental state? Parcae, the name I gave to the mysterious woman who came to live with me—sought me out, she claimed—after Katya and Maria were murdered, said it was all preordained, that it was my fate, just like everything else that happened in my life, including her being with me.

That's why I called her Parcae—or Lachesis, or Clotho, or Atropos. Or, when I was too drunk to remember what to call her, just plain old Fate. Because perhaps she was right; there was no other reason that I could understand.

Maria had been dead twelve years, and Katya for almost that long. It would be eleven years since her death the day after tomorrow, the first day of winter. It was the anniversary of Paulson's demise as well.

Both he and Katya were killed, along with hundreds of innocent victims, when the airliner they were on together exploded over Scotland in direct retaliation and revenge against Paulson.

Maybe that was it. Maybe that was why I did go back to Paris and then from Paris to the States to spend a few hours with Katya and Beth. Maybe when I'd found out about Katya's affair with Paulson, about how they died together, I'd felt responsible. Maybe I was really the one who was guilty of killing her. If I hadn't gotten involved with Maria's murder, or Magritte and Igor, perhaps I would never have become entangled in Paulson's web and there would have been no reason for Katya to be on that plane.

But, then again, as Parcae would say whenever I would talk this way, I was wrong. It was never my fault. It was only their destiny. Just as it is hers and mine to be together now.

Sometime after my rescue by Paulson, which proved me wrong, as indeed there was a Seventh Cavalry looming in the wings, I learned at last what I had done and who I had become involved with. To paraphrase the magician, Paulson was an elf to Santa Claus and always had been. He was a member in good standing—fairly high standing, actually—within the company that dealt with distribution

325

of the toys that Maria, and then I, was so intent on revealing. DFT was merely a distributor, a willing and exceedingly well-paid pawn for the real company, the very organization that Santa Claus himself presided over, which was the only one that counted in this entire tragedy.

Paulson told me everything. Maybe he did it because he was feeling sorry for me, what with the friendship and the trust we'd once shared, never mind my soon-to-be ex-wife. Maybe he even felt a little guilty. Whatever his reasons, I guess he felt it didn't matter if I now knew. There was no one I would be able to tell the tale to anyway.

For a while I even thought I would never be allowed to leave the sanatorium—or the "resort," as he referred to it—alive. But then, just about the time when my physical wounds had healed and my very presence was becoming embarrassing for everyone, he arranged for my participation—as good a word as any—in a unique program his company would selectively sponsor. In some ways, it was similar to the FBI's witness protection program—a person assumed a new identity, relocated, that kind of thing—except the company's version was a bit more stringent in its rules, bearing a closer affinity to a twentieth-century version of Robinson Crusoe in exile.

So he told me the whole story.

He told me how they'd found out about Maria, used her, and fed her whatever data they considered appropriate to keep her digging further. Paulson said they'd had to be careful with her. She was very good at sensing the difference between what was real and what was disinformation. They didn't want her to believe that it was a setup and cause her to back off and compromise their main goal, which was to capture Igor and destroy his network and credibility. One time, they almost blew it, he said, when both she and Magritte showed up at some art show when he was in Paris. "She didn't know who I was, though," he said.

And, just like Igor, my good buddy was concerned about how she would react once she found out about me. Would she warn me, get me involved somehow, or, worse, drop the assignment before compromising her control?

There must have been something in the milk those guys in the toy business drank, because—again just like his KGB counterpart—he also told me that if she had done anything that could've tipped Igor off that they were on to her, he was prepared to end the game immediately.

"Our guys weren't the ones that killed her," he quickly added.

Paulson reminded me of the magician when I asked, "Wouldn't Igor have been tipped off after he lost contact with her?"

"Yeah," he said, shrugging his shoulders, "Vladimir would probably know we did it, but he wouldn't be one hundred percent certain. And, more importantly, he would never know how much she revealed to us."

Paulson also told me—I didn't believe him—that Maria wasn't just an independent, "do good, save the world" journalist. She was on their side. He said she was no different than Magritte.

When I asked him why, if that were true, she had called the police after she was threatened, he said she never had. He told me that it was a lie on her part, all part of her cover, and that once she decided to write the letter to me, in his mind, she was going through with the assignment. "She was using you, Chris, to be her insider and get the information she needed."

If my arms hadn't been strapped to the bed and I hadn't been sedated, I would have killed him on the spot.

"We didn't kill her," he emphasized. "They had her sanctioned because they had a different opinion. Magritte didn't believe her when she told him she was going to use you to get the data, and he told the colonel so. Her death caught us a little by surprise as well. That's why I recommended Roquette for your lawyer—to help keep tabs on you. I did it for your own protection," he admitted, disregarding the fact he had revealed to me that he had put Hopkins on my case, necessitating the need for a lawyer.

So when Maria was no longer available, he'd used me next.

Although he hadn't put a gun to my head, forcing me to pick up after her, he'd gambled, knowing about the instability of my personal life and my relationship to Maria, that I would fall neatly into his trap.

He had known about—planned, actually—Roquette, Hopkins, Spire, and even the diskettes that I'd buried. And his plan had worked. Well, sort of, because he was dead and I was alive, if life was what one would call it.

He had even killed Spire. "I couldn't very well let him shoot you," my designated rescuer rationalized. "Besides," he said as if trying to impress upon me that he was acting on behalf of the good guys, "we had reliable information that he was looking to make a deal with the other team."

He never mentioned Carlson. I asked him if he knew why Carlson had dropped the litigation with the FCC and decided to sell the broadcast properties, or if he'd had anything to do with it. He answered no to both. Something about how easily he said it made me think he was lying. A few years later, I heard rumors that Carlson lost DFT after being involved in some sort of illegal billing practices or overcharging on government contracts. He was forced to resign in disgrace. For all I knew, he might even have been that old white-haired guy I'd spotted sometimes on the horizon when I took the ketch out to sea. Of course, they wouldn't allow either of us to come close enough to recognize one another, so it was only conjecture on my part.

Paulson also said he didn't know anything about Weitzer or the change in the Geo Computer contract. I believed him. In retrospect, it was probably nothing more than unfortunate timing. Had the same thing occurred a few months before, I probably wouldn't have thought that much about it. Still, it was an amazing coincidence that Casey had committed suicide a few days after the proposed amendment surfaced.

But who really cares now? What was so important then …

Ahh, here's my destination, just up ahead. Nothing much seems to have changed since last year. Maybe a little colder looking, especially as the snow has begun to fall. Better remember everything because, according to Parcae, this will be the last time they'll allow me to return. Typical Parcae, so I didn't ask how she knew. She would just tell me the usual mumbo jumbo about my fulfilling my destiny, so why ask?

I found out the answer a short time later.

I was about to return to the car, my visit over; the bodyguard who was leaning against it started to signal that it was time to go.

Then I saw her standing there.

Or, should I say, she saw me. She was no more than ten feet away, which was surprising because usually my so-called protectors were very good at isolating me from the general public. It was as though she had appeared from nowhere.

Out of the corners of my eyes, I could see the chap who had just told me it was time to go; he was running in my direction, shouting something that sounded like "Hey, watch out!"

Then I heard the young woman say, her voice reminding me of someone I knew from my past, "I know who you are. I've been watching you since you first came here ten years ago. Since you first came to see my mother, every year bringing her the poinsettias for her grave."

Her green eyes stared into mine, and for a second, it was again that summer when I was on the beach with Maria.

"Here, this is yours, I believe," she said as she handed me the jade ring and turned away to disappear into the falling snow.

Somewhere on a beach on an island …

When the sun began its ascension from the sea the following morning, she was sitting on the edge of the beach, her eyes fixed upon the empty blue horizon. The waters were becalmed, with only the tease of tiny whitecaps to break the serenity of the green glass. The skies were clear, their vivid morning reds and oranges soon to give way to the intense blues and whites as the day went on.

When she knew it was to be his fatal departure, she collapsed onto the wooden dock and wept. The tears tumbling down her cheeks intermingled with the rain. When those same rains and winds grew even more fearsome, their high-pitched wailing summoning her, she rose and called his name. And although she was filled with rage, she did not damn him. No, she was careful not to, although she possessed the secrets and the power to do so.

Once before, he had been far away and adrift at sea—his mast snapped in half, the battered hull filling with salt water faster than the overworked bilge pumps could discharge it. Somehow, some off-course vessel had come upon his disabled craft and rescued him. She remembered when he'd returned.

He told her he was indestructible. She became confused when she heard the words; like so many things from his world, there was no translation into her language. She asked him what it meant.

He laughed, his eyes glowing, and explained that it meant the gods favored him and would protect him from earthly harm.

And then he used an expression that struck some ancient chord in her, for it reminded her of her people's long-forgotten tongue. "Deus ex machina," he shouted, the words echoing around his eerie laughter. "When all else fails us, the gods will save us!"

His words and ideas were most peculiar to her and not things she believed in.

"No … No, Jwah," she chided him in her simplistic wisdom. "It is not wise to tempt either the fates or the gods. No man is, as you say, indestructible, nor are the gods there for man's beckoning."

She cautioned him yet further, hoping that somehow he would understand her meaning and cease this fatal game of his. "For sometimes even the gods, as powerful as they may be, cannot control what is preordained."

But she knew he would neither listen nor change no matter what she said to him, for his very nature was the reason they'd come to find one another.

She had dreamed about this strange one who had no fear of the storms, the one who sought them out, sailing his boat with an inhuman vengeance into their very hearts. When she learned that he also had the name of the god of his people, she had to seek him out and discover for herself if he did indeed have special powers.

Maybe even powers like hers, she thought.

At first he was angry with her, surprised she had found him, and he told her to leave, as he wanted nothing to do with her. Even after she told him that she had traveled from a faraway place and many sunsets, he still insisted she go from his island and leave him to himself. But she could also see he wasn't frightened of her the way others were upon coming into her presence.

"No … No, please … I command … I beg of you; go from here,"

she remembered him saying, their eyes locking in recognition. "I no longer desire the company of humankind."

It was then that she revealed one of her secrets and confided in him about her power to see the future. His laughter rebounded maniacally throughout the jagged cliff sides when she questioned whether he was able to do the same.

"Nay," he roared, scoffing at such a notion. "I knew a magician once. A very powerful magician in my world, but he was helpless, a mere child when it came to knowing his own future."

Nevertheless, after she told him about that power, he allowed her to stay.

For more than five years, they shared each other's secrets. Her powers strengthened during that period. She knew that it was partially due to her transition from a young woman into a state of maturity, but she was wise enough to sense that something from him made those powers within her that much stronger. Perhaps, she would sometimes think when she was alone at night, walking on the pebbled beach, watching what she viewed as the heavens drift and float mystically throughout the skies, it was because he was indeed mad.

He sailed his boat many times into the storms during those five odd years. Each time, before he would depart, she would beg him not to go. Each time, he would ignore her pleas. And each time, except for the last, she knew somehow he would return.

She continued to come down to the water's edge for many more sunrises, knowing the answer but still needing to look out onto the horizon. Even after pieces of what once had been his ship washed ashore one day, she still came. Filled with anger and pain, she dragged the wreckage from the sand that day. But she felt a final truth when she saw the name across one of the splintered boards.

As the woman sat on the sand next to the few remaining relics of her man's life, her fingers tracing the outlines of the fading letters, she recalled the story that had given birth to them. It was a story that one day, now that he was gone, she would tell to the child, the one who was growing within her and whose face would carry the same black marking as her own.

And although, as with most things about him and all that he told her, she hadn't quite understood, she knew this tale by heart.

Yes, it would be soon, she realized, holding her swollen belly and rocking gently to the hypnotic rhythm of the sea, when she would give to their daughter the jade ring she wore and would tell her the fabled story of the Squirrel and the Kat.

Notes from the Author

The beautiful tale of the *Flor de la Nochebuena*, or the poinsettia, the flower of the Holy Night, is an old Mexican folk story.

The Studies and Observation Group was part of the Phoenix Program, since declassified, which existed during the 1960s and '70s in Southeast Asia.

The Parcae were the Roman Goddesses of Fate.